The Fragile Land

SIMON MUNDY

HAY PRESS

HAY PRESS

an imprint of
RENARD PRESS LTD

124 City Road
London EC1V 2NX
United Kingdom
info@renardpress.com
020 8050 2928

www.haypress.co.uk

The Fragile Land first published by Hay Press in 2023

Text © Simon Mundy, 2023
Illustration © Kate Milsom, 2023

Cover illustration by Kate Milsom
Cover design by Will Dady

Printed in Glevum by Severn

ISBN: 978-1-80447-039-8

9 8 7 6 5 4 3 2 1

Simon Mundy asserts his moral right to be identified as the author of this work in accordance with the Copyright, Designs and Patents Act 1988.

This is a work of fiction. Any resemblance to actual persons, living or dead, is purely coincidental.

Renard Press is proud to be a climate positive publisher, removing more carbon from the air than we emit and planting a small forest. For more information see renardpress.com/eco.

All rights reserved. This publication may not be reproduced, stored in a retrieval system or transmitted, in any form or by any means – electronic, mechanical, photocopying, recording or otherwise – without the prior permission of the publisher.

CONTENTS

The Fragile Land	5
A Note about Names	7
Places and Their Modern Equivalents	9
The Territories of Britannia	11
Other Territories Mentioned	11
Characters	12
BOOK ONE *The Year of Discovery* AD 473	15
BOOK TWO *The Year of Politics* AD 489	145
BOOK THREE *The Great Battle and After* Late Autumn AD 489–Summer 490	349

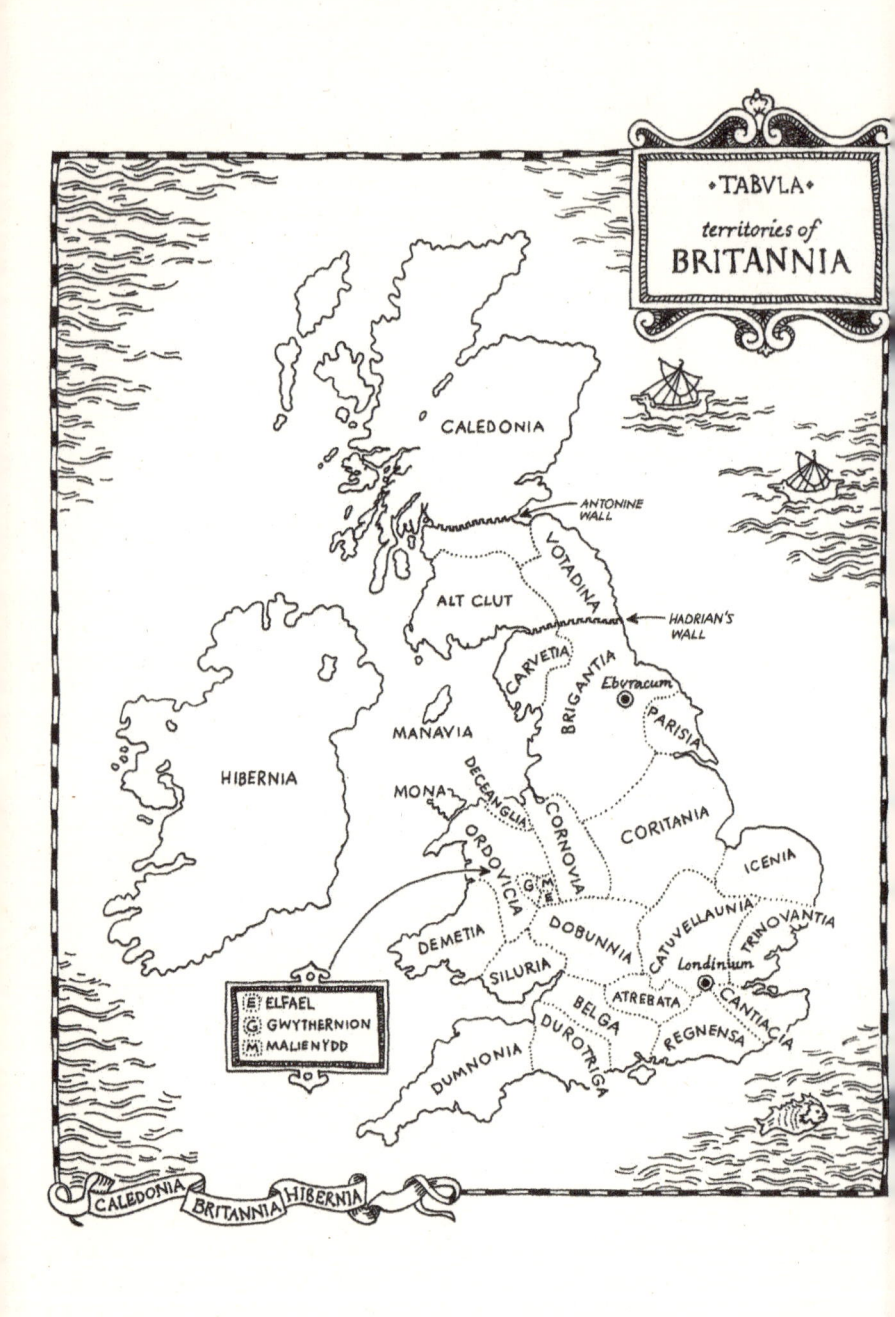

· TABVLA ·
territories of
BRITANNIA

CALEDONIA

ANTONINE WALL

VOTADINA

ALT CLUT

HADRIAN'S WALL

CARVETIA

BRIGANTIA

Ebvracum

PARISIA

MANAVIA

HIBERNIA

MONA

DECANGLIA

CORNOVIA

ORDOVICIA

CORITANIA

ICENIA

DEMETIA

DOBUNNIA

CATUVELLAUNIA

TRINOVANTIA

Londinium

SILURIA

BELGA

ATREBATA

CANTIACIA

DUROTRIGA

REGNENSA

DUMNONIA

E ELFAEL
G GWYTHERNION
M MALIENYDD

CALEDONIA · BRITANNIA · HIBERNIA

THE FRAGILE LAND

A NOTE ABOUT NAMES

This story is set in late fifth-century Britain, at a time when the Romans were still remembered, but only by people over seventy. However, the cultural battle between Roman and indigenous language and lifestyles was not yet settled, especially between the emerging Church and temporal rulers. Both felt under threat, too, from the raids by Germanic and Nordic migrants. Deciding on names of people and places therefore causes problems. Saxon and mediaeval English names had not yet been invented. The indigenous names have, for the most part, been lost, though we have clues on old memorial stones. The Romans gave territories and towns names which have survived, and I have used them for kingdoms and settlements. I suspect that, only sixty or so years after the official departure of the legions, they would still have been widely used. I have settled on the spellings I feel most comfortable with from the many variations available.

Modern Welsh I have raided at times and, to make the point that this book is not in the post-fifteenth-century English or earlier French traditions of Arthurian romances, in many cases I have used a Welsh version – so Myrddin, not Merlin. Arthur is an anachronism, and I have treated it as such. I have also used the Welsh for the three old kingdoms that were combined to form Tudor Radnorshire: Elfael, Gwythernion and Malienydd. As far as we know, they had no precise Roman allocation or loyalties to any of the named indigenous peoples, being mountain kingdoms on the borders of the Silures, Cornovii and Ordovices. They are central to the story as I tell it, though.

Welsh is a modern variety of one of the main branches of the Celtic languages labelled today Brythonic, and I have used that name to characterise the vernacular of the time. I have also used Britannia instead of Britain and Britannian instead of British, the latter being a hybrid English word coined by James VI of Scotland when he gained the English throne in 1603 and was trying to invent a joint identity, which has never quite worked. The Romans initially meant the whole island when they said Britannia, but in time they came to think of it as the territory south of the Antonine and then Hadrian's walls that they controlled. I have referred to all the peoples who were not from the old empire as Barbarians, as the Romano-Britannians would have done, with the exception of the Hibernians (Irish), who were always in a special category, along with those north of the Firth of Forth that we now label Picts.

The site of the battle of Mons Badonicus has been fought over by historians and Arthurian enthusiasts for many decades. I have placed it at the modern village of Baydon, on the Wiltshire–Berkshire border, which makes reasonable strategic as well as historical sense in terms of the story, without any pretence to archaeological accuracy. It is in a landscape so full of ancient resonance, from the Neolithic onwards, that anything is possible.

PLACES AND THEIR MODERN EQUIVALENTS

Alabum	Llandovery
Aquae Sulis	Bath
Badonicus, Baydun	Baydon
Bremetennacum	Ribchester
Burdigala	Bordeaux
Calleva	Silchester
Calcaria	Tadcaster
Camulodunum	Colchester
Canovium	Caerhun
Cataractonium	Catterick
Cicutio	Brecon
Condate Riedonum	Rennes
Corinium	Cirencester
Cunetio	Mildenhall (Wiltshire)
Deva	Chester
Dubris	Dover
Dunedin	Edinburgh
Durobrivae	Rochester
Ebvracum	York
Glevum	Gloucester
Isca	Exeter
Isca Siluris	Caerleon
Isurium	Aldborough (Yorkshire)
Lavobrinta	Forden Gaer (Shropshire)
Letocetum	Wall
Lindinis	Ilchester
Lindum	Lincoln
Londinium	London
Luentium	Dolaucothi/Pumsaint
Magnis	Kenchester

Mamucium	Manchester
Massilia	Marseille
Mediolanum	Whitchurch (Shropshire)
Moridunum	Carmarthen
Noviomagus	Chichester
Olicana	Ilkley
Pennocrucium	Penkridge
Petuaria	Brough
Ratae	Leicester
Sabrina, Savrina	River Severn
Segontium	Caernarfon
Tamara Ostia	Plymouth
Tamesis	River Thames
Treverorum	Trier
Vectis	Isle of Wight
Venta Belgarum	Winchester
Venta Siluris	Caerwent
Verlucio	Heddington Wick (Wiltshire)
Verulamium	St Albans
Viroconium	Wroxeter

THE TERRITORIES OF BRITANNIA

Alt Clut
Atrebata
Belga
Brigantia
Cantiacia
Carvetia
Catuvellaunia
Coritania
Cornovia
Deceangelia
Demetia
Dobunnia
Durotriga

Dumnonia
Elfael
Gwythernion
Icenia
Malienydd
Manavia
Novantia
Ordovicia
Parisia
Siluria
Trinovantia
Votadina

OTHER TERRITORIES MENTIONED

Angeln
Aquitania
Armorica
Caledonia
Gall
Hibernia

CHARACTERS

Aelle, a Barbarian agent
Alban, a saint of Catuvellaunia
Ambrosius Aurealianus, Overlord of Britannia
Antonius, Bishop of Viroconium
Arcarix, Prince of Deceangelia
Arthur, Overload, 'Tygern Fawr' of Britannia
Badoc, King of Siluria
Bedr, steward and student of Myrddin
Branwen, Princess of Elfael
Budig, Prince of Armorica
Caerwen, Queen of Cornovia
Caldoros, King of Dumnonia
Candidianos, King of Dobunnia
Caradoc, Prince of Elfael
Catacus, King of Atrebata
Ceretic, King of Alt Clut, father of Cynwyd
Clovis, King of the Franks
Corbalengus, King of Ordovicia
Cunegnus, King of Cornovia
Cunogeterix, ancient chieftain
Cunorix, King of Catuvellaunia
Cynwyd, King of Alt Clut
Doldavix, adviser to Cunegnus
Dubricius, Bishop of Isca Silures
Eldadus, King of Atrebata, father of Catacus
Evan, soldier of Arthur's guard
Flaminius, merchant of the Belgae
Geraint, Prince of Elfael (later, Arthur)
Glyn ap Erfil, messenger
Gorlois, King of Dumnonia
Gwain, steward and captain to Arthur
Gwenan, lover of Arthur

Gwidellius, Bishop of Londinium
Gwynafir, Princess of Burdigala
Heol, King of Armorica
Idriseg, King of Elfael
Maglicus, father of Myrddin
Mandubrac, King of Catuvellaunia
Medraut, son of Morganwy
Meg, wife of an innkeeper in Elfael
Megeterix, King of Deceangelia
Meurig, boy of Olicana
Modlen, scribe to Arthur
Morganwy, student and ward of Myrddin
Myrddin, adviser to Arthur
Olwen, Princess of Gwythernion
Padrig, Bishop of Hibernia
Peredoc, enforcer
Seona, servant and lover of Myrddin
Sioned, woman of Segontium
Slesvig, Barbarian warlord
Tegernacus, King of Coritania
Uther Pendraeg, Overlord of Britannia, Arthur's father
Vortebelos, King of Brigantia
Vortigern, Overlord of Britannia
Vorteporix, King of Demetia
Wermund, Barbarian warlord
Ygraen, Queen of Dumnonia, Arthur's mother

BOOK ONE

The Year of Discovery
AD 473

I

IT WAS ONE OF THOSE MORNINGS which is hardly a morning. The mist had rolled over the hill behind – but rolled seemed too active a word for it. Instead the moisture sat pointlessly around the trees and drenched the new wooden bridge across the brook, making it just as slippery as the stepping stones had always been. It wasn't raining, but it would be soon. The sheep, penned for lambing, looked mucky and indifferent – but then, they always did. There was no world to watch from any of the watching points. The patient cloud locked them into the head of the valley as securely as the bastion gate. Only the stream was full of noise. The boy picked his way through the mud and wrapped a cloak, quite new and thick-threaded, about him. Even though the early spring day was not particularly cold, the drizzle made it feel miserable enough. He carried nothing with him; he would need both hands for the journey back.

The road, such as it was, pitched sharply outside the last gate. It settled down after it had crossed the stream, to the side from where enough trees had been cleared to make meadows. But that was a while away, and the boy slithered on the uneven wet stones, cursing the lack of grip on the worn soles of his boots. By the time he had reached flatter ground he was below the cloud line, and the mist had concentrated into gentle rain. It dripped from the ends of the boy's hair, finding a way through the cloak and into the matted wool shirt. There was a mile or two to go before it was going to get any better. He was tempted to cut further into the shelter of the trees, but it was a longer path that way, and it didn't look much drier, anyway. He told himself and a couple of uninterested pigeons that he would rather have had the snow and crisp morning of the winter just ended than this stuff, but the truth was he would have preferred not to have had mornings at all.

After a mile the road veered away from the water and climbed a little, following now the side of a loose stone hillock that was dwarfed by the majestic slopes of the main valley but big enough to screen home from the rest of the hills. On a clear day, which this was not, you could get a good, close view of the surrounding country. There was a forward lookout near the summit, and a path to it which hid in the cover of the trees for as long as possible. This morning, though, there was nothing to see and no one to man the guard post. The boy had the road to himself. The woods thickened on one side; on the other they alternated with irregular fields – few and far between (there were only three houses to pass), but enough to make him feel that he was more out in the open and a little less safe. There had never been any trouble as long as he could remember, but nobody else seemed to think that was very long. So he kept alert as he walked, more for something to think about that wasn't wet than out of fear.

The road dipped again into the tree cover and meandered towards a ford over the big river that flowed out of the hills to the west. It was not a big river by the standards of the world, but it was as big as the boy had seen, and was too great to wade through alone at that time of year. An oak had been felled across it just upstream from the ford and a handrail of woven saplings joined along it to give some purchase on slippery days like this. The boy thought about taking the bridge at a run, but then thought better of it.

Halfway across he paused. He thought his eye had caught something in the water just below, lodged against the rocks where the current leapt and eddied at its fiercest. It had shone – strange on a morning without sun – but now that he looked closely there was nothing much to be seen: a stuck branch and a shred of cloth. A trick of the light and the water. He pressed on.

Beyond the scurrying river he had to climb again, this time higher and harder, and the road could not choose its own way, but had to work as best it could round boulders and through cliffs three times the height of a man. The noise of the river followed him for a while, sometimes close, sometimes far below and just keeping him company in the distance. Then it was lost and the road broke into the open above the trees. He was on a hill unlike the others, with their rolling slopes and long, high summits that formed a ring around him in all directions. This hill stood almost in the centre of the ring, and though it was smaller, it was impressive in its isolation. On one side it broke away nearly sheer to the valley floor; on the other it tailed back sharply until it met the closest giant in the outer ring and formed a bar, with only a narrow coll wide enough for a road to pass between them. It was a perfect defensive gate provided by nature for the valley. But the boy was already inside the defences, as he had been for as long as he could remember and, he supposed, all the time before. He lumbered up the steep bank on the southern side, just a local path now, and approached the village that perched against the top of the hill, rock at its back, ramparts surrounding the rest. They were old, he knew, though they had been rebuilt within his lifetime. Exactly why he did not know.

At the main gate he waved to the man on duty. He should have identified himself and stopped for an inspection, but there was no real need. The gatekeeper was his father's cousin, and apart from the usual annoying comment about how much he had grown, so much that it was hard to recognise him — one day he'd get an arrow in his chest if he kept on like that — the boy was let through without too much of an inquisition. Sometimes he felt that the whole world must be made up of his father's cousins, and they all thought they were funny.

The village was up and working, but only just. In the forge there was the beginnings of a good fire, and the smell of baking lingered in the air. He was suddenly hungry, his stomach reminding him that he had just trudged four miles in the drizzle. The feeling worsened as he walked the length of the one significant street to the end, where the temple church stood on its mound. The boy turned right, still climbing a little. He should have turned right again, through the final palisade fence to the hall, but his stomach was driving his legs now, and he was carried past the gate, past three more houses to the inn. Outside it a man stood on a ladder painting red a wooden harp that hung from a hook above the door.

He didn't bother to look up as the boy approached, but spoke anyway. 'Morning, Geraint. Bit early for you to be up here, isn't it? Where's the rest, then?'

'I've come on my own. Father's sent me to fetch someone and take him back with me.'

'Who would that be, then?'

'Not sure, exactly. Someone I was to ask for at the hall. They'd know who I was after.'

'Hall's back there. What are you doing over here?'

'Well, I thought…'

'You thought you'd come and cadge some breakfast off me before you went asking,' the man said, putting down his painting cloth and climbing down, wiping his hands on the skirt of his tunic. 'Well, it's an excuse for me too. Come on, lad, we might as well find out if Meg's feeling generous.' He stopped at the foot of the ladder and clapped the boy on the back. 'Good God, you've grown. Bigger than your father now, aren't you? Don't look much like him, either, come to think of it, but then that's an advantage in itself.'

He steered the boy inside and shouted through to where Meg was already preparing slabs of bread and meat and honey and pouring out mugs of weak breakfast ale. She was a young woman, and at nineteen was only five years older than the boy himself and at least ten years, probably fifteen, younger than the innkeeper. Her long straw hair was pulled back and braided, and she had her work clothes on, but she was still lovely, with mild grey-green eyes and the walk of a natural athlete. To the boy she was just older, though, and he barely noticed the perfection of her as she slapped plates and mugs down on the long trestle table that filled the centre of the room.

'Geraint, you stop him shouting like that,' she admonished, cuffing her husband as he sat. 'I saw you coming up the lane before he even stopped pretending to work on that sign. Good to see you, boy. How's Branwen?'

'All right, I suppose.'

'Full of the news, aren't you? Tell her I asked, will you. Tell her to get herself over here a bit more, too. I could do with someone sensible to talk to – not just this old fish.'

'Love you too,' grinned the older man, 'and you watch, young man. You'll get better treatment than I do, just because she misses your sister.'

The boy muttered into his mug and wolfed down the food. 'Can't be long,' he said, without enthusiasm. 'I'd better find this man for Father. He told me he wanted us back by midday if we could make it.'

Meg stood behind him and put her arms round his neck. 'You can wait long enough to dry off and finish this lot. I'll take this and get the water off it.' She unfastened the brooch that held his cloak and hung it on a peg beside the fire.

Half an hour later the boy emerged from the inn feeling that the morning was better than he had thought. The cloud was clearing and the drizzle had eased so there was barely a spot hanging on the breeze. From the front of the inn he strolled over to look at the view from the top of the rampart which ran from the grounds of the temple church round the end of the village to his right. He clambered up the wooden steps to the platform that rested on the earth barrier, a battlement in the length of the log barricade. In the distance the ring of hills barred the view to the west. On the crest straight ahead twin burial mounds broke the skyline, great barrows of kings who had ruled a thousand years before the Romans came. He could see below him the wide clearing in the forest, a perfect oval, and at its centre the pair of massive stones which stood for their dead kings facing the setting sun. Closer, but still on the valley floor, he could pick out the road and see the square remnants of the fort the Romans had made for themselves – built in a day, the story went, though he didn't believe it. There was still a decent building or two, but they held sheep now, not legionaries, and the brambles had taken over where the efficient imperial defenders had lodged hundreds of years before.

The boy was dreaming of the legions his grandfather still talked of proudly, as if he had served under the emperors. It was just possible, the boy thought, though he couldn't quite see his grandfather in one of those toga things that he had seen in paintings in the old house that faced the fort on the other side of the road. And he certainly didn't believe his grandfather when he pretended that he had reached as far as Rome itself before his emperor lost his campaign and the legion had broken up. It was unimaginable.

The boy felt a touch on his shoulder and heard a voice beside him. 'Are you the one they call Geraint?'

'Yes,' he answered. He thought of turning to see who had spoken, but somehow the hand held him still.

'Do you know those barrows?'

'I often look at them when I come here – I don't know why,' he said.

The voice that replied was soft and deep, old enough to be fatherly but young enough, the boy felt, that he could laugh with him easily and often. 'I do. You're looking at your ancestors.'

'How do you know?'

'Just one of those things.'

The boy felt the pressure leave his shoulder and he turned at last. 'Who are you?' he asked.

'I'm the man you've been sent here to fetch, and we'd better start back soon, before the weather changes its mind.'

Looking at the man was a disappointment after hearing his voice. He was middling in every way. Not short, not tall. Not dark, not fair. A bit rounder than a warrior would have been, but not enough to be like most of the farmers around. He had not shaved recently, but the beard did not look deliberate, and there seemed to be a bald patch underneath his chin which matched the small patch on the crown of his head. His cloak was hard to categorise. It wasn't made from the coarse wool used for a soldier, nor the fine weave of a woman's gown, but it was of superb material, light and full at the same time, almost plaid except that the greens and reds and browns of countless shades mingled in patterns that never quite allowed the eye to decide whether they were triangles or squares or stripes. At the shoulder a brooch was pinned, and it was unlike anything the boy had seen: a lion's head in white stone so cleverly carved that the eyes could have been alive.

'Do you like it?' the man asked. He was smiling, and his eyes were somehow different from the rest of him. They had the same feel about them as the lion's – warm and immensely strong, though they were grey-blue and had such kindness and depth that the boy felt immediately confident.

'It's extraordinary.'

'It is indeed. I had it made for me. A friend modelled for it. I'll tell you the story some time, when we know each other a bit better.'

The boy tried again, 'what should I call you?'

'We'll come to that later, when we get home. Come on.' He led off at a surprisingly brisk pace and the boy scuttled after him.

Once they were clear of the village and into the woods again, they relaxed to more of a stroll as the man asked his companion about himself – what life had been like as he grew up, what he remembered of his mother (which wasn't much), how his studies were going: especially his studies. The boy realised as they came to the river that he had been talking all about himself for well over a mile without getting anything in return except an encouraging 'well, well' or another question, yet

CHAPTER I

he had an overwhelming sense that he had known the man all his life without ever remembering having met him. That, though, was true of a lot of Father's friends. They turned up out of the distant past, Father treated them as though they had never been away, then they disappeared again as quickly as they had appeared. None had taken the keen notice him that this man did, though, and the boy wondered if he was really interested or just passing the time on a long, damp walk. He also wondered why he had never called him Geraint since that first question in the village.

At the tree bridge Geraint stepped aside to let the older man go across first.

'No, after you. I'm sure you have a trick for not slipping off this thing which I should copy, if I've got any sense. I'm one of those people who'll trip over a blade of grass if you give me half a chance.'

Geraint laughed and stepped on to the log. Halfway across he stopped, just as he had on the way out, convinced again that something in the river had flashed. This time he was sure it wasn't just a trick of light, and he realised that it was unlikely to have been before either. It had been even wetter on the outward walk and the grim grey cloud had hidden the sun completely.

'What is it? Why have you stopped?' his companion called from the riverbank.

'I thought I saw something in the river. Twice.'

'And it's not a fish?'

'I don't think so. It seemed too still for that.'

'Well, let's have a look. But for heaven's sake, boy, don't jiggle that rope as I come across. I'm quite damp enough without a swim this morning.' He started to follow Geraint on to the bridge.

They stood together on the tree trunk, peering down into the water. In the pool below them, close in to the far bank, a light seemed to shine. It was impossible to say whether the light came from within or whether it was just a trick of the morning.

'You're right,' said the man, 'there is something down there. Let's take a look, shall we?'

They crossed the final length of wood and gingerly lowered themselves down the bank to the water's edge. A small ledge of rock reached out into the fast-running stream, and it was in the lee of this that they could see the light in the water.

'You lean over, boy. You're young enough for such manoeuvres. I'll hang on to your ankles.'

The boy lay stomach down on the rock. The water of the pool was moving just enough to stop him seeing clearly what lay beneath, except for the dull blue-green light which came from deep in its centre.

'There's definitely something there,' he said. 'I can't make out what it is, though.'

'Well, don't talk about it all day. Fish it up here.'

Geraint rolled up the sleeve of his tunic and plunged his arm into the water. It was ice-cold, and his fingers began to go numb after only a few seconds. It was also far deeper than it looked, and until his arm was immersed almost to the shoulder he could find nothing. The light diffused as his hand searched, so that he had to feel round in ever-decreasing circles to make sure he wasn't missing anything. Just as he thought his fingers were going to drop off with cold and he was on the point of giving up, he touched something hard – not rock, though: too shaped and regular for that.

'I've got it, I think,' he said.

'Get it out, then, boy, get it out.'

'I'm trying. My hand's so cold I can hardly get a grip on it.'

'No giving up now. Forget the cold. Come on.'

The boy forced his fingers to close round the object and pulled. Nothing happened. Whatever it was, it was stuck fast in the riverbed.

'It won't move,' he said.

'Don't give up so soon.'

He tried again, wondering silently whether his curiosity was worth all this trouble, a freezing arm and a wet tunic.

'Oh, yes. It is. It very definitely is,' said the man, kneeling to hold his ankles.

Geraint looked round sharply. He had said nothing, only thought the question. 'Why did you say that?' he asked.

'I'm sorry. Getting ahead of myself. Now concentrate. Give it a good pull.'

He did. Still his strength was resisted, but he felt a slight shift, as though the mud was loosening its grip reluctantly. This time he could move the object sideways, but it didn't want to rise.

'It's coming, I think.'

'About time. My knees can't take much more of this.'

'What about my arm?' he asked.

'Quite so.'

Geraint pulled his arm from the water and flicked it dry before sticking his blue fingers under his tunic to try to get some warm blood back into them. Once he could feel the tips again through the pins and needles, he inched a little further forward on the rock and plunged his hand back in again. This time he felt the round top of the object straight away, and pulled firmly. It eased out smoothly but slowly, the riverbed unhappy to let it go. In a moment his hand broke the water's surface, and they were greeted by the sight of the roundel of a hilt.

'What have you got?'

'I think it's part of a sword. It feels too big for a knife. But there's not room enough in the water for a long one – it's probably broken.'

'Keep it coming, lad. Keep it coming.'

He transferred the hilt to the warm dry fingers of his right hand and lifted through the water. Suddenly, in a shower of droplets which sparkled in their own right, the sword leapt free and into the air, as if it were a live fish and Geraint no longer needed to do the work. For a moment he held it where it was, hanging it the air above the pool, then slowly drew it towards him and rolled over on to his back. As he did so the pool seemed to sigh beneath him. Glancing back, he could see that where there had been light before, there was now darkness just as intense, far blacker than the other water.

'It's amazing,' he whispered. And it was.

He was holding a short sword, of the sort worn by Roman soldiers in the time of the legions, its hilt made of a metal he had never seen before, with the lightness and brilliance of silver but with far more strength. Five rings of this bound a central core, surmounted by the roundel which he had first held when he had reached into the water. This too was made of the same sparkling metal, but set into it on one side was a medallion of amber, so clear and flawless it could almost have been orange glass, except that deep within it a delicate line of black traced the letter 'C'. The other side was flat and white, not marble but exquisite ivory. Into it, very small, was carved a relief which was hard to make out at first, but when he looked close enough the boy could see that it was a lion's head and that he had seen it before that morning.

'Is this yours?' he asked his companion with awe.

'Mine? No. It's yours now. You found it. But maybe that suggests it is right that we should be together when you did.'

'It looks Roman, but there's not a mark on it. Surely if it had been in the water for so many years there would be some rust by now, or something coming loose?'

'Perhaps on most swords, but not this,' said the man. 'It could have settled down there quite recently.'

The boy shook his head. 'How? It was lodged too firmly for that. There hasn't been a Roman legion anywhere near here for generations. And I can't see anybody just leaving it there if they dropped it.'

'Perhaps you're right,' the old man shrugged. 'Is there a clue anywhere? Look on the blade.'

They peered at the sturdy blade. For most of its short length it was plain, but high up there seemed to be some lettering inscribed.

'Can you read?' asked the man.

The boy looked at him with disgust. 'Of course I can. I don't know why, but they made me, Caradoc and Branwen learn, even though nobody else is bothering and Father can only just about read his own name in Britannian. He hasn't a clue about Latin.'

'So what does it say?'

The boy ran his finger across the fine writing, as if it would bring it to life, even though the blade was washed clean by the pure stream water. Strangely the lettering did seem to stand out more clearly for a moment and grow to a dark red, somewhere between blood and wine.

'Per Gloria Dei,' he read haltingly. He felt the inscription lead his finger round the edge of the sword and across its other face, 'Et Vita Constantinus.'

'Excellent,' announced his companion. 'Splendid. Know what it means?'

'That's easy,' said the boy with confidence. 'For the Glory of God and the Life of Constantine.'

'You'd better keep it safe, then. Or it had better keep you safe. It's hard to know which way round it will be. Let's get off this stone and back to the hall. I'm hungry, wet and cold, and there's a lot of talking to be done.' The man jumped back on to the path and strode off, leaving the astonished boy wondering what he was meant to do with the sword. After a moment he clambered back up the bank and scurried after him.

'Who do you think Constantine was?' he asked when he had caught up and fallen in alongside. 'A centurion? It's too good for a centurion, though. Maybe he was Pro-Consul in the service of one of the emperors the legions proclaimed here.'

'You mean Carausias and Allectus? It's probably not old enough for that, do you think?'

'He must have been Roman.'

'We're all Roman, thanks to Caracalla. Or we were until Magnus fell out with Theodosius and his son lost interest in us. All our own fault, as usual.'

The boy glazed over, sensing that his companion was about to lapse into a history lesson – or politics, which was even worse. Then he brightened. 'Could it even have been Emperor Constantine himself?'

'Now you're letting your imagination run away, aren't you.'

'Why not? It's fine enough.'

The man with the lion brooch shrugged. 'True.'

'Anyway, we at least know whose it was.'

'Is,' the old man corrected him.

'Sorry?' Geraint looked baffled.

The man stopped and asked to see the sword. As he held it there was a change in the quality of the wind, as though the air about the sword was singing under its breath. Geraint stood transfixed, watching the man run his hand across the blade, the colours in his cloak gently turning a golden brown to match the amber in the hilt. He talked to the sword itself, not the boy. 'Constantine is very much with us. And though you have the stamp of the empire I think we'll find that it is Britannia's Constantine who makes use of us and we have to protect again, don't you?'

With concentration he held the sword against his body, pointing to the ground so that the ivory lion of the hilt rested against the brooch at his shoulder. Above them the cloud broke and a shaft of sunlight shot through, turning the tree bridge and its pool below them suddenly gold. The sword's amber shone with it, intensely, as though responding to the sun, and Geraint watched fascinated as the pattern of the dark 'C' within it moved, dissolved and reformed as the letter 'A'.

The moment passed and the cloud covered the sun again. Geraint was given the sword back.

'Have a look at the inscription now,' he was told.

One side was the same – 'Per Gloria Dei' – but the other now read 'Et Vita Arturus', and its red tint seemed lighter and richer than before.

Geraint was now as frightened as he was intrigued. 'Who's Arturus?' he whispered.

'Is that what it says now? I thought so. Excellent news. Come on, young man. Home. There's some explaining to be done.'

II

THE MIST STILL HUNG AROUND the hilltop as the boy and the man passed through the bastion gate and made their way across the yard. On the threshold of the timber hall, water dripping from its thatched roof, a small welcoming party had gathered: a young woman of perhaps eighteen, a boy of about Geraint's own age or a little more and an older man.

'We're back, Father,' Geraint called.

'I can see that. And enough time you've taken about it.' A spare and sprightly little man in his middle years, his hair greying at the sides, stepped forward to greet them. He grinned. 'And I can see why. You're no thinner, Myrddin. It's quite a climb for a man in your condition.'

'If that's your idea of a greeting, Idriseg, then I'm turning for home now. How did you end up in such a godforsaken spot, anyway?'

The two men grasped each other by the arms as old comrades. 'Nothing godforsaken about this spot, my friend. God-protected, more like. And where's this home you're threatening to walk back to? I've heard of you living all over the country.'

'True enough, old man,' grunted Myrddin. 'I suppose I'll have to put up with your jokes for a night or two.'

'Quite right. Let's go in and get some ale into you. It's only my own stuff, but it's quite drinkable.'

Idriseg led the way over the stone step and through into the darkness of the hall. 'You and the boy found each other without difficulty, then.'

Myrddin smiled. 'I found him. And then the sword found him, so I knew I was right. You've done a good job, Idriseg. He's turned out well.'

'That he has. It's almost frightening at times. How like his father he's becoming – but a better temper, a much better temper. What do you mean, the sword found him?'

'What I said. But as to meaning, you'll have to wait until I do all the telling.'

'Do you know the most irritating thing about having a sage for a friend, Myrddin? Constantly having to wander round wondering what the hell you're talking about. Sit down there in front of the fire and Branwen will sort some food out for you.'

Myrddin and Idriseg sat themselves at the long table in front of the fire that was blazing in the centre of the room, radiating heat through the paved floor. Idriseg sat with his back to the fire; Myrddin gazed into it. Other men came into the hall to greet the new arrival, but Idriseg nodded them away and with an understanding bow they withdrew again. Geraint and the other boy hovered behind him, not knowing whether to join their elders at the table or find something else to do now that the job of delivery was done. But Geraint was intrigued and troubled too. He now knew the name of the extraordinary man he had guided from the village, but knowing his name was Myrddin didn't tell him much. He was itching to show off the new sword and tell everybody in the camp about the wonders of its discovery, but Myrddin had confiscated it from him as they approached the bastion, telling him the time was not right. Another of those irritating enigmatic remarks. And there was all that stuff from his father about looking like his father more and more. That was quite simply baffling. Geraint decided he might as well sit down and demand some answers. As his sister Branwen put bread, cold meat and fruit curd in front of their guest, Geraint started to slide on to the bench next to him. But Idriseg caught his eye.

'You've done your job for now, and done it well, Geraint. Go and help the watch or something. Both of you,' he added, looking at the other boy. 'My old friend and I have important matters to discuss.'

'Politics?' asked Geraint.

'Politics and old times.'

'And future ones,' murmured Myrddin.

Idriseg took Geraint's wrist. 'We'll call for you later. There are things for you to know, but Myrddin and I need to catch up for a while. He's come a long way and I've been out of action up here for too long.'

Geraint nodded and untangled his legs from the bench. 'Caradoc and I'll do some work in the armoury,' he said, winking at the other boy, who grinned and followed him out of the hall.

Myrddin waited silently for a moment while Branwen finished setting his place with a jug of the camp's best ale, spiced with apple and mulled over the fire. He sipped the warm drink and tore off a hunk of bread, spreading the dark-purple fruit curd on liberally. 'You do well for yourself up here,' he said.

Idriseg shrugged. 'It's not exactly Corinium, but we manage. The winter's been hard, though, and I'm hoping things stay quiet enough again this year to get some proper planting done. I need to get round the district a bit more often as well. I get the reports, of course, and there doesn't seem to be too much of an immediate problem, but you never know. To be frank, Myrddin, I'm feeling a bit cut off in these hills, and I hope you're coming to tell me I can pull my weight a bit more. If I don't I can see that some of the younger men are going to start getting restless. They expect me to be making more of a mark in the province. They're a bit sick of people asking where they come from and who their leader is and then everybody looking blank when they tell them.'

'I can see that. I'm sorry.'

'It's not your fault.'

'It is, my old friend, it very much is. But if I'm right things are going to get a lot worse before they get better, and if we're to have any hope of holding this island together in any sort of civilised way then what you have been doing all these years will be beyond price.'

'I hope you're right,' Idriseg said, staring at Myrddin as if trying to read his mind, but it was futile as usual. 'So when do we tell him?'

'And what?'

'And what and how do we break it to the others?'

'That's up to you,' Myrddin said. 'You've watched him grow up, and you can judge the reaction of both boys and the rest of your men better than I can.'

'You flatter me, Myrddin. First, though, tell me the situation. I've had no real news for nearly a year.'

* * *

The afternoon was well established by the time Idriseg and Myrddin emerged into the weak sunlight. Idriseg looked preoccupied. Myrddin kept him company as he made his way slowly to where the two boys were idling by the well, peeling willow sticks for baskets. They had been at it for an hour or more, and had stripped a good pile. They had also run out of conversation. Caradoc brightened as his father approached, sensing that they would not have to do much more.

'Finished, Father?'

'I know more about the world than I did this morning, if that's what you mean, but I'm not sure I wouldn't have rather stayed ignorant. Myrddin never was good at glad tidings, were you, man?'

Myrddin grunted. 'Hardly my fault. I only do what I have to.'

'True enough. Don't take it to heart. Geraint. Caradoc. We need to talk to you now. And it had better not be here. The camp has ears in its soil, and I don't want this spread about until Myrddin's ready to go – which won't be till tomorrow at the earliest. We'd better walk for a while.'

The boys put away their knives and threw down the last of the willow with relief. They strode after Idriseg and Myrddin through the gate and turned left, past the bastion, where Idriseg waved to the sentry and called out that they were off up the hill for an hour or two and only to look for them if they weren't back by sunset. They walked in near silence for ten minutes as the path climbed sideways along the hill, still in the woods but increasingly with glimpses out across the valley. Geraint was beginning to think that he had done quite enough walking for the day. He couldn't see why it was necessary to climb to the summit of their home hill just to talk.

'Because gossip can be dangerous when only half the story is heard, and because you need to know before others do,' said Myrddin as they paused for breath. Not for the first time that day Geraint stared at him incredulously, wondering how his thoughts had been read so easily. He glanced across at Idriseg, who was grinning, and at Caradoc, who just looked baffled – but that wasn't unusual.

Idriseg laughed. 'I don't know why we bother to talk to you, Myrddin, when you know what we're thinking anyway.'

His companion swatted a nettle. 'Not always,' he said, 'and if the only voice I heard was my own life would be even duller. Come on.'

They broke cover above the tree line and within a few minutes could pause and look out across the valley. The vast royal compound that Idriseg dismissively called his camp was hidden, but Geraint could see across to the village in the fort from where he had collected Myrddin that morning, and beyond that to the remnants of the

Roman camp and the bigger but abandoned fort on the hill beyond. The bowl of his world was laid out for him to see and feel at home with. There was another world beyond the ridges, and the road that he could make out, threading between the Roman camp and the village, led to it, but neither he nor Caradoc had travelled to see it, and he realised that they had never even climbed higher up the hill to find a better vantage point. Idriseg discouraged exploring, pointing out that anybody they could see from the top could also see them and watch them return to the camp. Why they should, or why it mattered if they did, had been questions that earned a clout more often than an explanation.

Myrddin led them on until they reached the summit itself, however, and they could see not only beyond the ridges to the north, beyond the wooded flank of their own hill where the hall now lay wreathed in the beginnings of the evening mist, but behind them to the south, the range of still greater hills that marched in barren disarray to the horizon, where two great peaks could just be made out, like a pair of dark-blue fingers poking at the gathering cloud.

'We're not quite there yet,' chivvied Myrddin, and led them along the crest of the hill. He stopped at a small mound, barely noticeable until you were close up against it. Geraint threw himself down on its mossy grass, though, and looked about him. Weirdly he realised that he could see further in all directions.

Myrddin prodded him with his foot. 'That's Cunogeterix of Cornovia you're lying on,' he mentioned mildly, 'but I don't suppose he'll mind too much since it's you. He was a nice man. Died too young, though. Totally unnecessary.'

Geraint jumped up nervously. 'Sorry.'

'Oh, I shouldn't be. He's been there for three hundred years, now and you're more polite than most of the sheep that wander over the top of him. Sit down and take a look around you. It will tell you why he was laid to rest here – or at least, it should do, if you're thinking straight.'

Geraint sat down gingerly and stared at the ground beneath him. The thought of sitting comfortably on the old warrior's bones was complicated. On the one hand he felt embarrassed and irreverent. On the other there was a feeling of contentment, as though he and Cunogeterix shared more than a spot of ground.

CHAPTER II

Caradoc flopped down beside him and closed his eyes. 'It's a long way for a talk,' he muttered. 'It had better be a good one.'

His father growled above him. 'You're lucky to be here with us three, lad. You keep quiet.'

'No, Idriseg, he has a point,' said Myrddin. 'I've been waiting for this moment for so long I'm afraid I'm enjoying the suspense more than I have any right to. Geraint, wake up and look about you. Tell me what you see.'

Geraint lifted his head and let his eyes take in the landscape, the folding hills which on three sides seemed to stand like ordered ramparts to the horizon. He could see at least five great hill forts, two abandoned, but three with thin veins of smoke rising and bending eastwards in the wind. Most of the rest was forest, but here and there irregular fields had been cleared and laid out in the valleys, where there was water and the woods could close around them again, protecting them from jealous eyes.

'I see my father's kingdom,' he said.

'Kind of you, son,' said Idriseg, 'but you see much further than that. To the north I rule nothing beyond the stream below the great fort. To the west, it is true. All the land you can see lies within my boundary, but only because the clouds are gathering in the far valley and you cannot see over them. But to the south I reach nowhere near the peaks, only to this side of the mountains that look so black in this light. And the east? Fifty, sixty years ago I could have been sure that, even if I did not exactly rule there, the people were my cousins. But not now. The plains are another country now. I hold these hills and the forest on the other side for ten miles or so, to where the main road north cuts through. After that everything's changing. And from what Myrddin told me earlier, not changing for the better – though it was never much good in my lifetime, if truth be told. That's why I try to keep us quiet in the hills. Being noticed in the wider world is not a policy for peace these days.'

'He's right, Geraint,' Myrddin added quietly.

'So what's that got to do with me?'

'Look again,' said Myrddin, 'especially towards the dangerous east. You have to save it, then you have to rule it.'

The boy peered at the land to the east. After the forest he could see occasional hills sprouting from the plain. One range was short but high; another seemed to have a huge cliff on its western end; then in the far distance a line of an escarpment could just be made out, so far away that it was hard to tell whether it was land or cloud.

'That's ridiculous. It's nothing to do with me. My place is here with my father, and with Caradoc, who'll rule after him.'

'You're right about Caradoc,' said Myrddin, 'but nothing else.'

'Well, I suppose that's something,' murmured Caradoc, still with his eyes shut, 'and it won't be the first time Geraint's got everything else wrong.'

Myrddin moved close to where the boys rested on the mound of Cunogeterix, and rested his staff on its summit. 'Maybe not,' he said, 'but that's the last time you will call your brother Geraint – at least in private.'

Caradoc sat up sharply and shouted. 'Why the hell not? That's his name.'

Myrddin stood his ground. 'No, my boy, it's not.'

Idriseg interposed. 'I think you'd better stop leading them on, my friend, and just tell them, now, don't you? We haven't got long before the sun goes down, and you've barely begun.'

'I'm sorry. You're right. I have lived with the story so long now it's hard to let it go – and even harder to know where to start.'

Myrddin grasped his staff and put his right hand on Geraint's shoulder. 'First of all – and it's a long all – you are Caradoc's foster-brother, not his blood brother. Idriseg has been a father to you and will be, destiny willing, for many years to come. He is not your real father, though, for your father is dead, and has been for nearly two years. Your mother, I'm sorry to say, has been dead for far longer than that; in fact, she lived for only a few months after you were born. How she died comes later in the story.'

Geraint stood and faced Idriseg, his face pulled between fury and tears. 'Why didn't you tell me this before? How could you? How could you let me grow up thinking you were my father when he was alive all the time?'

Idriseg reached out. 'I—'

'Don't blame him.' There was command in Myrddin's voice for the first time, and the staff in his left hand seemed to quiver against the burial mound. 'He told you nothing because he was bound on oath.'

'Whose oath, and why?'

CHAPTER II

'An oath to me, to your father and, more importantly, to the Council of Kings. And why? Because it was — and is — dangerous. Had it become known, even within this little kingdom, who you really are, you would not be here now to berate us. I'm sorry, my boy, but it had to be this way, however painful it is for you now. Believe me, this pain is better than the pain of death. The man on whom you and I are standing can tell you that. Here. Take my staff for a moment.'

Geraint reached across and slowly wound his fingers round the head of Myrddin's staff. For a moment he just felt self-conscious and looked down to the ground to avoid Caradoc. But then, as his eyes moved to the foot of the staff, he realised he could see beneath it — beneath the grass to the hidden stone chamber, and then within that too. A man lay there, still dressed in a dark cloak, green once, perhaps, and around him lay his sword, shield and the ornaments his horse would have worn. Across his chest rested a torque of beaten gold, and as the boy stood astonished, the figure below him seemed to raise his arm in greeting and relief. Geraint cried out in terror and dropped the staff, stepping back and grasping Idriseg's forearm hard in fear.

'Who am I?' he whispered.

Idriseg gently took his hand. 'What did you see?'

'I don't know,' he said.

Myrddin led the boy off the tomb. 'You saw him salute you. And he was right. Your name is Arthur, and you must get used to it, for that is how you will be known soon — not quite yet, but soon.'

The boy was still shaking. 'The sword. It changed to read Arturus.'

Myrddin smiled. 'It did indeed. You see, my boy, the world around you knows who you are, even if the people do not.'

Caradoc, the only one among them who had felt and seen nothing unusual, and who was trying to work out whether he was pleased or disappointed that Geraint was not his real brother, turned to face his father. 'What's so special about being called Arthur? It doesn't sound like a proper Brythonic name, or even Roman — more like something the Barbarians would dream up. Geraint's done up to now. If he's going to stay part of the family I don't see why I can't carry on calling him what he always been called.'

Arthur stepped forward towards him. 'You can if you want. I don't understand any of this any more than you do.' He turned to Idriseg.

'I'm cold, I'm frightened and I want to go home. I wish I'd never met this man today, Father.'

Idriseg put an arm round his shoulders. 'You met him a long way before today, lad — well before you knew me. He brought you from your mother. It was a long and difficult journey, as he'll tell you soon, and it is these hills and forests that have protected you since. In the great world Arthur is a name they have been waiting for — and it's a name many will hope is never discovered. Myrddin, he's right about it getting cold — if you haven't any more spiritual reasons for staying up here, I think we can tell the boys all they need to know for the moment on the way down.'

'You go on with the boys. You've had enough of my business for one day, and you can tell the story as well as I can. I'll have plenty of time with Arthur from now on. I'll stay here for a while. I have to gauge the weather and come to some decisions. Tell the sentry to expect me an hour after dark.'

Geraint frowned. 'But how will you see your way back?'

Myrddin smiled. 'I expect the moon will show me.'

'Come on,' urged Idriseg. 'I need mead and a fire.' He held each of his sons by the elbow and led them off the hilltop, back down towards the woods and home. For a few moments they walked in silence. Once Caradoc looked back, and in the gathering dusk he could just make out the shape of Myrddin standing rigid behind the barrow, his staff raised to the evening star.

The story Idriseg, King of Elfael, told Caradoc and Arthur as they filed down the hillside that evening — and well into the night — was both extraordinary and fascinating. It was so far out of their experience, encompassed as it was by the forests and hills of their father's kingdom, that it was near impossible for them to comprehend that they were at the centre of it.

Idriseg began ninety years before, when Magnus Maximus had marched his locally recruited legion out of Segontium to claim the Western Roman Empire for Britannia — telling how he had conquered or allied with Armorica, defeated Gratian and fought his way to and over the Alps before losing finally in Istria to Theodosius, Emperor in Constantinople. He told them (for they had forgotten from their lessons) how the death of Theodosius twelve years later had left both empires in the hands of regents and how Stilicho, Regent in the

West for the boy emperor Honorius, had lost control of Gaul to the Barbarians, leaving Britannia isolated and increasingly vulnerable. Determined that the Roman age should not disintegrate because of court politics and military inefficiency, Britannian troops had rallied round another strong usurper, as they had done successively for over a hundred years – ever since Constantine the Great himself had been proclaimed Emperor in Ebvracum and brought unity for the last time. The new Britannian general had called himself Constantine III in emulation, and had nearly wrested Gaul back from the Vandals and Sueri, but had failed ultimately. In the mean time Britannia had been left even more exposed to attack along the flat east coast. The forts, many of whose best troops had left with Constantine, were inadequate. When the civitates – the provincial authorities – of Britannia had appealed to the Emperor himself, the letter had arrived just as Rome had fallen to Alaric and his Visigoths. The ancient city had not been the capital for decades, but its fall was enough to convince Honorius that Britannia was a province he could never defend again. His reply enraged the Britannian leaders, and they had thrown out the last of the Roman officials, taking over the administration with their own magistrates. And when Constantine III was killed the next year, the sixteenth of Honorius's reign, they had finally given up hope of remaining part of the political empire. Only the Christian Church, relatively new in their lives but still imperial, seemed to link them now to the glory days of Constantine the Great's Rome. Even that was changing in Britannia, rejecting the trappings of Roman splendour as out of keeping with the age once Rome itself was Barbarian, and opting instead for the self-sufficiency and humility advocated by the monk Palagius, himself Britannian (though his followers had had to bring his doctrine back from Carthage and beyond).

You cannot simply overthrow three hundred and fifty years of imperial authority and expect the world to be the same, however. It was not only the Roman magistrates who found themselves removed from power. The people themselves rebelled – not only against Rome, but also against the comfortable elite among their own leaders, who had built their magnificent villas and temples on the back of the fields and minerals of Britannia. There was a new order, a new religion and no place for gilt statues, erotic wall paintings and gladiator shows. The great houses could not be maintained without servants or slaves and, with no Roman officials to force them to work, those who had been without freedom just melted away into the countryside, carving out their own smallholdings. Within five years the aristocracy found their coins and silver plate useless, their villas cold and impossible to maintain, their farms unmanageable.

Those still trying to keep some sense of government had turned to Vortigern of the Ordovices, husband of Magnus Maximus's infant daughter, who had remained in Segontium when her father had ridden out nearly thirty years before. At first he had united the country and had kept the coasts safe – but only at the cost of hiring thousands of mercenaries from the Barbarians themselves, giving them land and tithes in return for their service against their own overlords. This was, after all, the practice of Roman generals since before Caesar's day – back to the age when Britannian warriors had served the Ptolemys in Egypt. Those days were gone though. Vortigern's recruits were loyal enough, but their sons realised the power they held, and thirteen years later opened the coasts to their cousins from beyond the sea. Vortigern was an old man by then. While the new generation blamed him for the breakdown of his military policy, the Pope in Rome sent Germanus of Auxerre to denounce those who followed Pelagius's teachings as heretics, though it was really their politics, not their religion, which was suspect. Vortigern had seen himself as Britannian first, Roman only by civilisation. Any loyalty to Rome had been sundered by that letter from Honorius. His point had seemed to be proved when, beset by his own mercenaries, he had swallowed his pride and written to the Emperor Valentinian III's Consul asking for help once again. Even though Germanus, the 'Pope's Envoy', was still at his court in Britannia, the new emperor's answer had been the same as the old's: Look after yourself.

For the kings of the civitates, including Idriseg's uncle, who had commanded the Cornovii, this was the final straw, and they stripped Vortigern of his overlordship. His name now meant nothing. They turned to a young soldier who had been arguing recklessly against Vortigern's policy since taking up arms two years before. Ambrosius Aurelianus, though only twenty-one, seemed to have all the right qualities.

Unlike Vortigern, a man from the mountains of the west, where Roman systems had never completely taken hold, Ambrosius was from Verulamium, in the heart of the civil and military establishment. His family came from generations of public servants who saw their duty as good governance in the interests of the empire, whoever happened to be wearing the purple at the time – Idriseg's grandfather told him that within his span of memory there had been months (even seasons) when nobody knew who the Emperor was. By the time news arrived from Rome you could have missed two, they were installed and murdered so fast. But that had not affected the professionalism of the magistracy or the legions. Ambrosius promised that only a return to those ideals could save Britannia Prima and Seconda from disintegration in the face of the rebellious Barbarians. For a time – indeed, for many years – he succeeded. He did unite the civitates under his command, and he was helped by the terrible plague which swept Europe for nearly five years. While people fled the cities and feared close contact with their neighbours (after which life in the towns had never recovered), the plague also made sure that there were fewer Barbarian attacks and, when they did come, people were too dispersed to be obvious targets. Ambrosius could intercept their war bands as they camped outside the stinking ruins of the towns. And those of Barbarian birth who had rebelled against Vortigern now found themselves too preoccupied with surviving to worry about who ruled them.

Germanus was sent again by the Pope in Rome to combat the ideas of Pelagius. But he found a peaceful country, too impoverished by plague to be interested in the finer points of ecclesiastical policy. There were few temples left to be turned into churches, and no riches with which to decorate them. In truth there could not be an argument between Pelagian austerity and Papal splendour when there was nothing splendid to put on show. Germanus went home satisfied that the Church in Britannia was fully obedient to the Pope. In reality, those who had the time to worry about religion shrugged their shoulders and carried on doing the best they could with whatever they could find left over from the age of the emperors. It was not much, and in any case, while most people liked what they heard about Christianity, there were still many of the best families who clung to the ways of their ancestors, and many Barbarians who rejected anything that tasted of Rome, whether Minerva, Mithras or Christ. After fifteen years of difficult peace, Ambrosius thought that his task was done.

'That was ten years before you were born,' Idriseg said to Arthur, 'and then everything changed again. Perhaps because we had enjoyed peace, those of us who had been young when we had fought under Ambrosius found the descent into chaos once more even harder to deal with. It was more than a catastrophe. It was as though everything we had suffered and survived, everything we had built and been proud of, would be taken apart in a summer.'

It was almost dark now in the woods. Caradoc swore as he tripped over a root and sprawled at his father's feet.

'Just like that,' mused Idriseg, 'one moment we were full of confidence that we knew where we were going, the next we're flat on our faces and in pain. Are you all right?'

'I've cut my knee,' grumbled Caradoc, 'but I'll live.'

Arthur offered him his arm. 'Lean on me for a bit.'

Caradoc pushed him away. 'I can manage. You concentrate on finding out what's so amazing about who you are. It's pretty turgid stuff so far.'

Idriseg bridled. 'You need to know this as much as he does. Whatever becomes of Geraint – I mean Arthur – you will still have a kingdom to care for after I've gone, and you cannot do that unless you understand the forces against you.'

'What's the hurry? You're not going to die yet.'

'You cannot assume that. Neither can I. Why do you think we live up here at the camp instead of restoring the mansion the Romans left by the road? Why do you think I post sentries round the clock and watch the borders?'

'Because there's nothing better to do?'

'Don't be cheeky, boy,' he roared. 'I'm your king as well as your father. Because beyond the forest there is danger, and I have kept you from it to protect Arthur. Elfael may not be a big kingdom, but it is a safe one – as safe as it is possible to be in times like these. You don't understand – neither of you do – what lengths others would go to make sure that Uther had no legitimate sons. And they would kill you both just to make sure they had got rid of the right one.' Idriseg calmed down. 'Does your knee hurt?'

'I said I'll be fine.'

'We're almost home, anyway,' said Arthur.

'So we are,' said Idriseg. 'That's a pity. I wanted to tell you both the most important part of the story without anybody else overhearing us. We'll just have to find a corner later and have it guarded. Myrddin will be back by then, and it's as much his story as yours, Arthur, so it may be for the best. Once your sister's had a look at that cut, let's warm up and find something to drink.'

Idriseg paused at the gate. 'For now, at least, you're both still my sons.'

III

ALMOST AN HOUR LATER Myrddin slipped from the shadows and startled the sentry, who had heard nothing of his approach – no stick had cracked; not a branch had rustled.

'Are you going to open this gate or do I have to stand here all night, young man?' he demanded.

Too late, the sentry issued his challenge, and then blushed in the dark as Myrddin stood his ground and grinned at him. 'I was told to expect you,' the warrior mumbled apologetically.

'Just as well. I hate to think what formidable defences I would have had to face if you had not been.'

The gate swung open and Myrddin passed through, issuing the guard with a mock legionary salute as he did so. 'And ave Caesar, and good night to you,' he chuckled.

He found Idriseg, Caradoc and Arthur in a round hut towards the edge of the camp, not in the hall where they had met that morning, where he expected them to be. They sat on stools around a small table, with Idriseg strategically placed with the fire at his back. There was bread and meat and mead and – he presumed in honour of the momentous occasion – a dish of pears that had been preserved in honey syrup through the winter. The plates were wood, but the dish he recognised as from the Cornovii potteries of the previous century – fine ware which was becoming a rarity since production had been closed down at the time of Vortigern's wars.

Idriseg waved him to the spare stool. 'We were famished after all that walking,' he said, 'so I'm afraid we started without you, but there's plenty left, and plenty more if we need it. Did you converse with the moon and move the stars?'

'Don't joke about it, my friend. The stars are not for moving.'

'He loves all this stuff, Arthur, so you'd better get used to it. I fully expect to see him flying over the hills one day, starting thunderstorms.'

Myrddin sighed and helped himself to a cup of mead. 'Have you told them everything?'

'Not yet,' Idriseg admitted. 'I managed to get as far as the middle days of Ambrosius before we came in earshot of the camp, but that still leaves the most important part. That's why I brought them in here, rather than into the hall, where we would be bound to be interrupted by people coming and going. I've posted a couple of men at a discreet distance outside to prevent eavesdropping.'

'I'm glad to hear it. Any leakage now could be fatal.'

Idriseg looked gravely at his friend. 'You don't think you're making too much of the dangers?'

'No, I don't,' said Myrddin. 'There are factions in all directions, but the one thing that would bring them together in the wrong way would be the knowledge that none of them were going to control the overlordship.'

'Quite. Well, we'd better finish the story for these two before they die of boredom and too much mead. We had reached the point of the story about twenty-five years ago, when Ambrosius's peace fell apart. You were more involved than I was, so it's just as well we waited.'

Myrddin nodded, then sat quietly while he cut his meat and bread. The boys looked up expectantly, Caradoc absently rubbing his injured knee.

'There was no sudden invasion,' he began. 'That would have been easier to cope with, at least in one way – it would have been too obvious to ignore. Instead there was a gradual rise in the number of raids across the sea, and there were ships and more men. They did not come to settle in peace, making their presence felt round a few coastal villages, demanding a bit of land or joining those families who had come before and established decent Barbarian communities. They burned and slaughtered when they landed and worked their way inland for twenty miles or more before claiming all the territory they had emptied. Ambrosius was slow to react, but one can hardly blame him. There had not been a raid of any real seriousness for nearly ten years, though there were stories from Gaul that the Franks were on the move, pushed as much by the nations behind them as by their own ambition to fill the gap the Romans had left.

CHAPTER III

'It was hard for Ambrosius to know where to concentrate his defences. The raiders were as likely to strike near Hadrian's Wall (which itself was constantly being breached from the north) as along the south and east coasts. The sea-facing forts, which had had virtually no work done on them since they were damaged in Vortigern's time, were rebuilt too slowly and too cheaply. Ambrosius was a Roman bureaucrat at heart, although he had been a great warrior in his youth. But by then he was the same age your father is now and he would rather send diplomatic notes than lead an army in the field. The system had changed, too, and even he did not realise how much until he tried to co-ordinate the country once again. The administration of the civitates had been badly reduced by the plague, and there was no efficient way of getting things done quickly. The governors had become kings, disinclined to take orders from Ambrosius to move outside their area, whatever his official title. Without anybody really noticing, Britannia Prima and Seconda, Flavia Caesariensis and Maxima Caesariensis had become Britannia. Forty years after Honorius had admitted as much, the Roman age had truly ended.

'Ambrosius suffered two defeats, one among the Trinovantes, the other with the Cantiaci, before the rest of the country awoke to the danger. By then they were not facing isolated raids but a continuous stream of ships disgorging war bands along undefended coasts and as far up the rivers as the water would carry them. Too late it was realised that the men were untrained and dispersed, and those who had experience amongst the Barbarians were too old to be long in the field.

'In desperation Ambrosius sent an embassy to Armorica seeking help, even if it was just ships to counter the invaders in the south while they were still at sea. He had good reason to hope for a positive answer, for many had crossed from Britannia in Vortigern's darkest days and might feel the pull of kinship. There was a strong imperial tie, as well. When Constantine III had been checked in southern Gaul from reaching the seat of the western empire, many of his army had retreated to Armorica and reinforced the legions who still held good order there. In time they became Armorican legions in the Roman tradition, with no connection to the empire itself. And in time they turned to Constantine's grandsons, Constans and Uther, to command them.

'That's where I come into the story. I had left my home among the Demetiae and sailed for Armorica when I was a little older than you, though not much. The intention was to study the new religion, though I found myself discovering more about the old ones – not just the Roman and Persian cults, but the ancient beliefs of our own people as well. Armorica was alive with them all then, though many were in their final days, and people often believed in two or more at the same time.

'Within a year of landing I found myself in the retinue of the royal brothers. Constans was the more scholarly – indeed (though I shouldn't say so here, perhaps), he was much the cleverer of the pair; a gentle man, not afraid of war when it was inevitable but not inclined to it, either.

'They were not much older than I was, however, and Uther valued my companionship more than I did his, though I was flattered. Whereas Constans would debate and question every point, Uther would sit and listen with awe. At first I merely embroidered what little I knew, but gradually I changed from storytelling (for it was not worth much more than that when I was so young) to issuing advice. Uther took me into his service, whether I wanted it or not, and made me his closest confidant. The older courtiers didn't like it much, but I had no say in the matter.'

Caradoc was kicking Arthur under the table and mouthing a message at him. Arthur nodded and reached for the jug of mead.

'No you don't,' growled Idriseg. 'You've had quite enough. Sit still and listen. You need to know this.'

Caradoc sighed. 'What's this got to do with us, Father? It's all history.'

'So will you be unless you behave,' Idriseg bit back. 'You'll look back at this as probably the most important evening of your life.'

'That bad!' Caradoc subsided with bad grace.

Arthur grinned. He felt the same way, but knew better than to say it.

Myrddin continued as though nothing had happened. He was staring past Idriseg into the glowing embers of the fire. 'Ambrosius's embassy arrived at a perfect moment for Armorica. Uther was too big a personality to rule jointly with his brother. Constans thought him too stupid to be involved in government. I am sure that if the call from Britannia had not come when it did, they would have ended up fighting each other, and in the context of what has happened since, that would have been catastrophic.

'As it was Constans agreed that Uther should take an army of five thousand and a fleet of sixty ships to join Ambrosius. I was sent too,

CHAPTER III

of course. It was not how I had imagined I would return to Britannia. We landed on the coast of Dumnonia on a wet April morning after a crossing which was as rough as it was fast. We were all but thrown ashore, and two ships were sunk in the storm – perhaps overwhelmed by the sea, perhaps thrown against the rocks, we never knew. We regrouped quickly, though, and the Dumnonian forces under Gorlois (another two thousand) joined us on the third day ashore at Isca. This was Uther's first meeting with Gorlois, and they were immediate friends. Very different men, of course: Uther headstrong and impetuous, Gorlois strong but thoughtful – a man who, once he made a decision, was full of determination, but took his time. He was a good listener – something that Uther could never have been accused of. They made an impressive team.

'We were formidable as an army, but we had a long way to go. Ambrosius was said to be holding his own, but only just. The latest news we had was that he was safe enough at Corinium, but was moving back and forth in a loose triangle between Venta and what was left of Calleva – not much, by all accounts. In any case, he was penned. We didn't realise just how bad things had become until we reached the hills above Aqua Sulis in the Civitas of the Durotriges and found a rearguard camp of his band, who told us that they were preparing for Ambrosius to retreat there within a day. The roads were not what they had been under the legions, but most were still passable, and we caught up with Ambrosius himself within a morning, just east of Verlucio. There was a hill fort nearby with its ramparts just about serviceable – at least, after a day of hard work.

'We were now an army of fifteen thousand, Britannian and Armorican, but with the traditions of the legions and the old training to hold us together. It was a proud sight, and for the first time in years there was a feeling that Ambrosius had a realistic chance of wresting Britannia back from disintegration.'

Idriseg poured another round of drinks (half measures for the boys) and smiled. 'We did, too. Ambrosius was a good general and tactician, but he was no centurion. He had no feel for the men. That was Uther's great strength. He was a soldier first and foremost, and Ambrosius knew from the start that he could point Uther in the direction he needed to go and he would sweep all before him. I joined with Silurian troops at Glevum a week or two later. By then it was already clear the

Barbarians were in trouble. They were used to splitting the Britannians and picking off their armies in skirmishes, not facing us united — they didn't have the manpower for that. When it had just been Ambrosius trying to exert his authority he had found it hard to stop each of the civitates acting alone, which played straight into Barbarian hands, but with Uther and Gorlois together and happy to take orders, he had the arguments he needed to keep them in line.'

Myrddin continued. 'The result was spectacular. Within four months, by the end of the summer (and it was a hot one), we had taken three-quarters of the country back into Britannian hands. The Barbarians had a few enclaves in the south, where the forests could hide them. We never quite regained the marshlands of the Trinovantes beyond Camulodunum, and the far north was uncertain, but we had Ebvracum, and were able to garrison Cataractonium most of the time without too much problem.'

Arthur sipped his mead and reached across to take more bread. 'But the peace didn't last?' he asked.

Myrddin shook his head. 'Not really. Well, for five years it could hardly have been better. Uther was in charge of the military side and Ambrosius held the diplomatic reigns, which suited everybody — or at least, most of the kings who mattered. They could see that the alternative was far worse. But the longer peace lasts, the more people believe it cannot end, and the politics begin to break through. Nobody was watching what was happening in Gaul, let alone Constantinople. They thought they could forget the Barbarians and get back to fighting each other, conducting little raids and counter raids over where the old boundaries had been. As long as Ambrosius was clearly in charge this did not matter too much. They were local disputes, no more. He rotated between the main provincial capitals — Verulamium, Corinium, Viroconium and Ebvracum — and Uther paraded wherever he was needed.

'But then Ambrosius weakened — physically, not mentally. Some say he was poisoned, though I never saw any real evidence of it. He was nearly sixty, after all. But he was clearly ill. He lost weight fast — strange for such a big man — and he found it hard to concentrate. His skin began to turn yellow and his face seemed to shrink, so that his eyes stood out with a ferocity they had never had before, except that now there was not the fire behind them to impose his will on others — only just enough to keep himself alive. He was fading, but the end was a long time coming – many months – and in those months people sensed that he could no longer hold Britannia together. The kings began to defy him and each other openly. Little wars broke out – the worst of them between the Cornovii and the Deceangeli, but there were others. The far lands were all but lost, as the Barbarians leagued with the Votadini to the north of their enclave. In the far south the island of Vectis was lost to Hengist's heirs, and has not been recovered to this day.

'In all this, Uther, your father, behaved properly to the end, though it was hard for him. He wanted to march out in all directions to quell the troubles. Ambrosius had more sense, even when he was dying. He summoned all the kings to Verulamium for a High Council. I remember he even used the word senators and titled himself Pro Consul to invest the meeting with the authority of the empire, however hollow the truth of Rome's influence. But it brought together those of Uther's Armoricans who still saw themselves as Constantine's legionaries, and it made a useful point to Vortigern's old party, which still preferred Pelagian Christianity to the Papal sort. Most came, and those that did not sent an envoy senior enough to make it clear that Ambrosius still had their ear.

'Ambrosius was carried into the old basilica on a golden throne, wearing half purple. Both he and the building had been cleaned up thoroughly for the occasion. They even cleared away the weeds from the amphitheatre and found a troop who could put on competent productions of Plautus and Seneca. None of the kings were brave enough to admit that they had forgotten so much Latin that the jokes passed them by. Ambrosius told them that he believed he was dying. It was a brave admission, because he could have looked weak. In fact, he seemed more noble than he ever had in battle. A High Council was his natural arena. There always was more of the senator about him than the general.

'He told them to elect a new overlord in his place, while he was alive, and he put forward Uther as his candidate. It was a shrewd move. No one expected it. It had always been assumed that Ambrosius would find a Britannian successor or leave the matter until after his death. Uther was most surprised of all. For months he had been manoeuvring to seize power once Ambrosius was out of the way, and here he was being offered Vortigern's old position by right. Ambrosius argued that, as a grandson of Constantine III, Uther had as much of a claim to administer Britannia as anybody. Nobody mentioned that he also had the army, though that was in everyone's minds. Most of the Armoricans were landless legionaries, and had stayed with him in Britannia. He was the only one with professional soldiers on full-time alert. By backing Uther, Ambrosius guaranteed a smooth transfer of power, and maintained his own authority till the end. He was a great man. Perhaps the greatest in Britannia since Constantine the Great marched out of Ebvracum over a hundred and seventy years ago.'

Idriseg broke into Myrddin's narrative quietly. 'It was extraordinary when Ambrosius died. It was almost as though he had stage-managed it himself. After two days of argument we finally agreed to let Uther have the overlordship – with the proviso that any son of his would have to be born in Britannia if he was to be considered a future candidate. On the final evening of the Council Uther was given an old Roman staff of office by Ambrosius. Uther stood up from the round table at which we all sat, bowed to him and turned to give a speech of thanks. It was a short one. Your father (for so he was) had many good qualities, but eloquence in public was not among them. He paid tribute to all Ambrosius had achieved. He reminded us of the state we had been in under Vortigern – rather too forcefully, as far as the Ordovices were concerned, but they were in no position to argue. He said how honoured he would feel if he managed the province half as well (he was careful to keep to the fiction of the old Roman titles). Then he asked us to toast Ambrosius, and we all stood and turned to him with our goblets raised. It was only then that we noticed that he had slumped down in his throne. He was quite dead.'

Myrddin grinned. 'After the shock had worn off it was said that listening to Uther make a speech was enough to finish anybody off – which was unfair, but only slightly. Whatever the cause, Ambrosius's timing was impeccable. The kings had no moral option but to stay in Verulamium for his funeral and endorse Uther during the three days' mourning before heading home. It gave me the chance I needed to carry on Ambrosius's diplomacy where he had left off. Uther had made me his official secretary as soon as his overlordship had been approved.'

'By the time we all left for home,' remembered Idriseg, 'we were confident that Britannia was in better shape than it had been for several years. Uther was obeyed, if not always respected, and Myrddin – you won't mind me saying this, I hope – was respected, if not always liked or entirely trusted.'

'Why didn't you trust him?' asked Arthur.

'I'll answer,' said Myrddin. 'Partly because I am from the Demetiae, who are always thought to be too close to the Hibernians for comfort. Partly because I had come from Constans's court in Armorica. And partly because many doubt whether I am really a Christian. They think I am a sorcerer – or even a Priest of Neptune.'

'Are you?' Caradoc wondered.

'I am many things and nothing at the same time. It's truest to say that I don't like easy answers. I see power all about me, some of which I can harness, most of which I do not understand. Some call that sorcery. I would call it honesty. And honesty does not often fit comfortably into one convenient code. Men who like to know where they stand find that difficult to deal with. It makes them wonder whose side I am on, and the truth is I often do not know myself. I can only tell them what I see.'

'Uther believed in you,' said Idriseg, getting up and laying more logs on the fire, 'and so do I, though we do not always agree. It's getting late. You'd better tell them the rest before they fall asleep.'

'The kings rode home once Ambrosius Aurelianus was decently buried,' Myrddin continued. 'We thought that Uther was as well placed to contain the Barbarian threat as anybody had been for sixty or more years, and in truth he was. However, things began to go wrong almost immediately, and they had nothing to do with Germanic Barbarians or Franks, Romans or the Church. The problem was closer to home and far more human.'

'Be careful, Myrddin,' advised Idriseg. 'He's just a boy still, and it's already been a hard day.'

'I'm sorry. There's no easy way to tell this story, and he has to know it all or none of it will make sense.'

'Go on,' said Arthur.

Myrddin nodded. 'When Gorlois of Dumnonia came to the Council of Kings he brought with him his queen, Ygraen. Like Uther she had been born in Armorica of Britannian parents. Some said that they were even cousins of sorts. She was only sixteen – a year older than you are now, Arthur – when she was sent across the sea to marry Gorlois. It could have been a disaster, but Ygraen was a beautiful woman – so beautiful that Gorlois was in love with her from the moment she stepped from her ship early one morning on the River Fowey. From then until the night of his death Gorlois would not be parted from her, even though it meant that Dumnonia's King effectively stayed out of Ambrosius's campaigns in later years.

'Ygraen was twenty-one when the Council was called, and she was just as anxious as Gorlois to go with him and see Verulamium. Their daughter was only three and stayed at home. Dumnonia is a rich kingdom, and Gorlois and Ygraen arrived at the Council looking very much the young and confident royal pair. The effect on Uther was as predictable as it was unexpected. If we had seen Ygraen through the eyes of Gorlois and Uther perhaps we could have prevented tragedy, but we had other matters to think about. Uther saw his friend arrive with the most lovely woman he had ever seen – hair dark but with a flash of red, eyes green and a figure so slim that she seemed to float on the horse's saddle, and yet full enough to carry motherhood. This was all a sideshow to her smile, though: confidence, intelligence and a thoroughly irreverent sense of humour all in one pull of her lips. Gorlois was proud of his queen, and determined that the Council would know his pride. Uther could barely speak as long as she was in the hall. I don't think it ever occurred to Gorlois that Uther's admiration could become anything more than that. Even if he had, the damage was done. The joy of seeing her combined in Uther's mind with his new rights as overlord. Power, desire and jealousy mixed together in a way that the impulsive Uther, who at the best of times found it hard to separate reason from instinct, found impossible to resist.

'Anyway, after Ambrosius's funeral they rode back to Dumnonia, and we all thought Uther would be far too busy to worry about his infatuation with Ygraen. It was not as though there weren't other girls around who were just as determined to claim the new overlord for themselves, and fathers in many kingdoms who were keen that they should. And he did nothing to discourage them. I'm afraid, Arthur, you may find that you have several rivals up and down the country who can justly claim to be the sons of Uther Pendraeg, and it will be difficult to prove one way or the other. Thank God we do not have a system where the Council has to pick the eldest son, otherwise there's no knowing who we might end up with.

'For months we thought no more of it. Uther had to secure the north, or as much of it as he could. He quelled an uprising by Vortigern's old supporters among the Ordovices and the Deceangeli – Idriseg can tell you as much about that as I can, since he was in the thick of it.'

'On Uther Pendraeg's side?' asked Caradoc.

Idriseg cuffed him and looked properly indignant. 'Of course! I'm no rebel against the properly appointed overlord. You should know your father better than that, young man.'

'Sorry.'

Myrddin smiled. 'It's a fair enough question in these times, Idriseg. Loyalties are not as certain as they once were.'

Arthur shifted impatiently. 'So what happened?'

'The autumn after Ambrosius died, Uther announced that he was going to visit Dumnonia to consult Gorlois. It was a sensible enough decision – indeed, I advised him to do it. Gorlois was one of his most reliable allies, and one of the shrewdest kings in Britannia. It was also known that he had no interest in extending his kingdom and was preoccupied with securing his coast against raids from Hibernia or against the Franks, who were threatening Constans in Armorica. The northern Barbarians who were proving so difficult to dislodge from the east were never a concern for him.

'Uther, as you know, had made his headquarters at Londinium, and he rode out from there in the third week of October. It had been a wet and stormy month, but for the few days he rode south-west the sun shone, and it was one of those weeks when the colours of the land make you think there is no better country than this island. We stopped and paid our respects to the Durotriges at Aqua Sulis and then camped at Lindinis – quite dilapidated from its old splendour – before crossing into Dumnonia itself. Gorlois greeted us at Isca, as he had so many years before when Uther had first landed, and then suggested we ride north between the moors to see the works he had been carrying out on the coast at Tintagel, where he had decided to place his western capital, partly because it commanded the northern sea lanes and partly because he wanted to show that kings did not have to make do with the wrecks of old Roman cities. The main work on the hall and the defences were finished, but there was not as yet enough space to house both our parties properly, so most of the retinue camped a few miles away at Rhydcamel, where there was a well-sited fort.

'Gorlois told us that Ygraen was waiting for us in the new palace and would welcome us there before dark. Now, I don't think at this stage, perhaps at any stage before the event, Uther had any intention of harming Gorlois, but he could barely contain his excitement at the thought of seeing Ygraen again. Gorlois was just pleased to have his friend back in his kingdom and Ygraen – well, I think Ygraen was a young woman who enjoyed the attention of powerful men as much as any other, especially that of a kinsman and fellow Armorican. We gathered in the hall as the sun went down and we feasted and drank far more than we should have done. Gorlois was the only king in Britannia who still had the riches to buy good wine from southern Gaul and Iberia – his tin was worth just as much as it had ever been – and for all of us the sight of an amphora of first-class red was too much to resist after years of rough mead – sorry, Idriseg, no offence intended.'

'None taken. I couldn't agree more. Still, if you are going to finish this tale, you'd better have another cup, however much you hate it.'

'Perhaps I will. So, of course, after the food there was dancing. The hall was crowded, so the dancers moved closer together than they would have at a formal royal ball, and as the night wore on the torches burned lower and the fire glowed rather than blazed, and Ygraen found herself locked in step with Uther, brushing back and forth to the strumming of the harps as all the gods were toasted – the old ones of Rome, Bacchus and Minerva, the older ones of Armorica and Britannia and the angels of the new religion. All seemed to be dancing with us and in us as we swayed and spun about the floor. Ygraen and Uther were not the only ones – Gorlois was captured by a girl from the north, the daughter of a Barbarian slave, as blonde as Ygraen was sable, and I was in the arms of one from my own country, wild and western, whose family had fled some local revenge. We all came close to love.

'Ygraen was teasing Uther, there's no doubt of that, but it was no more, as I knew when I saw the look of fury in her eyes when she spotted Gorlois playing with the breasts of his fair slave. It was well after midnight when Gorlois broke away from the dancing and motioned to Ygraen that they should go to bed. She left first – Gorlois preferred to sleep in a building of his own away from the hall – and he followed a while later, after he had bid goodnight to his guests and retainers.

'He bowed to Uther Pendraeg first, and told him to enjoy the music as long as he wished. While Gorlois went round the others Uther turned

CHAPTER III

to me and asked a question I wish I never answered. "Would Ygraen make love to me tonight," he asked, "instead of Gorlois?" I thought he was joking, so I said, "Only if you smell like him and wear the same clothes. A woman will trust her nose and the touch of cloth more than her eyes in the dark." I laughed and moved off to find my Demetian girl, for I had an affair of my own to take care of. I remember Uther looking more thoughtful than usual and not laughing with me, but I didn't notice that he had slipped out until later, as the drinking finished and I was taking my girl to bed.'

Myrddin paused and looked across at Caradoc. 'You look sleepy, my boy.'

'No I'm not,' he began indignantly, but even as he said it his eyes drooped and his head dropped on to his arms, resting on the table.

Myrddin smiled at Idriseg. 'It's better for us all if he doesn't hear the next part of the story. You know it, of course, and Arthur must, but it is still a secret, and for the sake of Britannia it must remain that way for as long as possible. This is the first time in all these years I have told this story. I couldn't while Uther was alive.'

'What happened?' asked Arthur.

'It was some time before I knew myself,' continued Myrddin. 'I was too busy making love. But afterwards, once the girl beside me was asleep, I felt like clearing my head in the cool night air. Outside the hall there was a fine mist, and it was drizzling a bit, which brought me to my senses. There was not much wind, and though I could hear the waves crashing against the rocks far below, it was too murky to see the sea itself. I had only gone a few paces when I saw, or thought I saw, Gorlois step from his door. I waved, and was surprised when Gorlois almost jumped with shock and hurried across towards the edge of the cliffs. I followed, more out of curiosity than anything else. I found Gorlois kneeling beside a naked man who was lying face down on the grass against the low wall that runs to the edge. At first I thought Gorlois had killed Uther, because Uther's clothes were piled beside the body. I was about to shout for help when the man I thought was Gorlois said, "Myrddin, thank the gods it's you. Help me! It's all gone wrong."'

'I realised the man I was talking to was Uther, dressed in Gorlois's clothes. They were much the same size and only a few years apart in age, so the deception was easy. Uther was distraught. It was Gorlois who lay naked in front of us. I felt his neck, but it was cold, and no blood flowed.'

"'Help me," repeated Uther.

"'What have you done?" I demanded. Uther shook his head. "How is he?"

"'Dead," I said. "How do you think he is?"

"'I never meant that, I never meant that," he kept repeating, swaying back and forth on his knees beside the body. The explanation could wait, I decided. First I told Uther to get back into his own clothes, and then together we redressed Gorlois. We couldn't leave him where he was. It would have begged all the wrong questions. We hauled his body up to the edge of the cliff and let it drop over. It would be all too plausible that he had mistaken the path. The mist was closing in, and we could easily have fallen ourselves. I knew that by the time Gorlois was found in the morning when the tide went out, the sea would have washed him clean and there would be nothing to tell he hadn't died on the rocks.

'By this time Uther was shaking. I knew he could not return to the hall in such a state. I told him to ride to his troops at Rhydcamel and pretend he had been there since the end of the feast. He was to come back in the morning only when a messenger arrived with the news of Gorlois's death. Before he left he told me what had happened. Uther had followed Gorlois out of the hall, picking up a rock as he went. The plan was to do exactly as I had suggested – he would make love to Ygraen wearing Gorlois's clothes. He led Gorlois over to the place where we found him later, pretending to discuss plans for building a defensive fleet. When Gorlois turned his back for a moment Uther struck him on the head with the rock and stripped him. He did as he intended. In the dark of Ygraen's chamber he made love to her for almost an hour and, in the clothes of her husband, she never knew what he had done. I don't think she ever suspected. She thought Gorlois had left her to inspect the sentries and had fallen to his death. At the time I was certain there were no witnesses – neither to Uther's sex with Ygraen nor our disposal of Gorlois. Now I am not so sure, and I am less easy than I was.

'Uther swore that he had never meant to kill Gorlois, only to knock him senseless so he could borrow his clothes. How he thought he could leave him so long without Gorlois coming to and wondering why he was lying naked inside his own castle I have no idea. But Uther was drunk, and he could be an idiot – never thinking through the

CHAPTER III

consequences of his actions. It made him a great fighter, but a bad king. He never did know his own strength. The blow that felled Gorlois would have killed any man.

'The next morning Gorlois was found on the beach. The waves had indeed washed him clean, but they had gone further, laying him peacefully on his back. His right hand rested across his chest and he held a great shell, completely unbroken, and about his head a light-green weed had wound, so that he seemed to be wearing a wreath of the sea's laurel. It took until after midday to raise him up the cliff path and lay him to rest in the hall. Ygraen was beyond comfort, and Uther was white with grief when he saw his friend and host stretched out by the hearth. The grief was real – so was the guilt, which almost broke him when Ygraen fell crying into his arms.

'You were conceived that night, Arthur. You are the result of that great passion. Ygraen always talked of it as the last and best time she made love to Gorlois. Uther never talked of it at all, of course. And I? Well, I protected what I could – you, Ygraen, while I had the power, her young daughter and Uther himself. He is remembered now as a stern and solitary man, not the adventurer of his youth. It was the night our innocence ended.'

'Why are you telling me this?' asked Arthur.

'Because you must be greater than Uther and because you will not understand what happens in the coming years if you do not know where the threads begin.'

'Do you know? Can you see already?'

'I cannot say. I am not a prophet, though your father liked to call me one. But I have dreams, and the dreams are clearer than they should be, and too often they pass through when I am awake in all other senses.'

'Will you tell me?'

'No, not yet. They may just be the fantasies of an old man whose sorcery never was very good. You are young, and you may conquer my apprehensions as well as your enemies.'

'Is there more to tell?'

'Of course. You need to hear about your mother and about Uther's years as overlord. But it can wait until the morning, for the rest is common history, and I want Caradoc to hear it too. Then we must prepare you for the days ahead. We have a long way to travel.'

'Where must I go?'

'First with me, then wherever you are needed. We'll have plenty of time to talk about it on the way. Take him to bed, Idriseg. I'll carry Caradoc.'

Idriseg put his arm round Arthur's shoulder and drew him close to his side.

'You began the day the younger son of one of the smallest kingdoms; you finish it as the heir to the overlordship of Britannia. You have a right to some sleep.'

Arthur nodded and allowed himself to be led out into the night. Myrddin picked up Caradoc in his arms as though the sixteen-year-old was no more than a bag of hay and followed them back to the hall. The moon was high, now, and the ward of the fort was silvered. The shadows of the sentries stretched across the grass and a pair of owls called to each other at different ends of the woods.

'Stop,' Myrddin called softly. 'Look at that.' He pointed to the sky away from the three-quarter moon.

A great star was moving fast across the heavens – so fast it seemed to leave a trail of light behind it, and from this tail fell a shower of smaller stars. A moment later the clouds closed in front of it and they could see nothing more than the ghost of the moon.

Myrddin peered at Idriseg through the dark. 'I was right, my friend. I was right.'

IV

ARTHUR COULD SEE as soon as he woke that it was one of Idriseg's safe-weather days – the sort of day when the cloud covered the hills so far below the camp that it almost touched the valley floor and the rain pummelled the ramparts and filled the ditches. It was 'safe' weather because nobody in his right mind would go raiding on such a day. The sentries stayed as dry as they could under the meagre thatch on the bastion shelters and consoled themselves that they would hear the splashing and swearing of any assailants long before they saw them. Arthur curled up under the blankets and hoped profoundly that there would be no expeditions planned for that day. He was stiff and tired, as much in

CHAPTER IV

spirit as body after the momentous events of the previous evening, and he had the makings of a hangover. Caradoc was still asleep, but he could hear Branwen clearing up behind the curtain. It was as it had always been. This time yesterday he had never met or known about Myrddin, never dreamt that he was not in the home of his real father, never guessed that he was an impostor in Caradoc's future kingdom.

There was a gap between the curtain and the wall, and through it he could glimpse Branwen as she changed into clean clothes. Until now her body had been just his sister's body, as familiar and unremarkable as the house itself. He knew it as well as his own – well, almost – and it seemed absurd to try to think of it now as that of somebody who was not even a relation. She had slipped off her underdress and her bare buttocks pushed through the curtain for an instant. Arthur smiled. Not bad, really, if a bit on the plump side, he thought. Though he couldn't see the princes of Britannia queuing up for a sight of her, the men of the camp were not exactly spoilt for choice.

Half an hour later he was awake enough to be bored and hungry. He slipped out of bed and into his shoes, and pushed through the dividing curtains into the main body of the hall. The fire had been stoked and a few of the men lounged about with mugs of hot ale, plates of cold meat and eggs roasted in the warm ash. Arthur grabbed some for himself and looked about to see if anyone was treating him any differently than before. Had the news of his high birth leaked out during the night?

Clearly not, he decided, as he was shoved away from the ale jug and then ignored as usual. Either that or candidacy for overlord was not as impressive as he had assumed.

'No need to hurry – we're not going anywhere today,' a voice said.

Arthur looked round to find Myrddin standing next to him, warming his back at the fire. 'The world has waited a good many years for you. It can wait until this rain lifts. And if it can't, I can. There's no point in setting out on a long journey in stuff like this.'

'Good morning. Where exactly were we intending to go?'

'Yes, I suppose you might want to know that. I'll tell you a bit later. I still have to give the King all the details, and it wouldn't do to talk to you before I talk to him, if you see what I mean. Let's finish our breakfast and I'll go and find him.'

Arthur ate, and then hung around aimlessly, wondering how to prepare himself. If his life was about to change for ever there seemed to be no point in carrying on with his usual pursuits. Idriseg had not appeared, and there had been no mention of lessons. He was even driven to helping Branwen and the other girls, but they soon made it clear they would rather do without him, so he mooched back towards his bed.

Caradoc still slept. The rain still fell. There were the beginnings of a leak in the corner of the wall at the foot of his bed.

Arthur pulled out the basket of his private things and began to go through them. There was not much to show, really: his hunting knife, a box of Roman denarii (the oldest from the reign of Diocletian), a brooch with a broken pin, some wooden toys, including a chariot with both wheels missing, some glass beads that Idriseg had once told him came from Massillia and a black cup with a silver rim which had belonged to his mother – though now he had no idea whether it had been his real mother, Ygraen, or Idriseg's wife. Even his basket was suddenly full of questions and uncertainty, and he pushed it back against the wall with a frustrated shove.

Caradoc slept on. Arthur usually knew better than to rouse him, but he was bored and, he realised, angry at the changes he had to accommodate without any choice. He shook his foster-brother by the shoulder, gently at first, then with increasing force until the prone boy was rocked back and forth on his side. There was no response.

'It's no good,' said Myrddin, appearing from behind the curtain. 'My fault, I'm afraid.' Arthur was still disconcerted by his habit of breaking in as though they were halfway through a conversation. 'I commanded him to sleep last night, and only I can command him awake again. If it makes you feel better you can shake him until his head rolls off.'

'What did you do to him? I never saw you give him any herbs.'

'No, nothing like that. A suggestion, that's all. Don't ask me how I do it – I have no idea – but it works.' Myrddin edged Arthur aside and placed his hand on Caradoc's head. Immediately the boy stirred, rolled on to his back and opened his eyes.

'Is it late?' he asked.

'Not particularly,' smiled Myrddin, 'but we have work to do and we need you for it, so get ready and join us in the hall in ten minutes. Come on, Arthur, Idriseg is waiting.'

CHAPTER IV

They found Idriseg sitting at the great table in the hall, poring over a vellum scroll with the Magistrate and the Tribune, the two most senior officials of his kingdom. He barely looked up as Myrddin and Arthur came in, but waved them over to join him.

The scroll, Arthur saw, was a map showing the kingdoms of Britannia and the capitals of the civitates, on which the kingdoms since Vortigern's time had been based.

'Myrddin was in the east three months ago,' Idriseg was saying, 'and found Londinium all but deserted.' He looked up. 'Isn't that right?'

'Not deserted, but certainly very quiet,' said Myrddin. 'I would say there was less than half the amount of people there you would have seen ten years ago, and that was pretty sparse compared to the years before the plague. The temples looked mostly abandoned, and the forum only had a few stalls. I just saw two ships moored at the waterfront. The place seemed nervous, and they spoke of two raids at least during the winter.'

'From what's been coming in I think that's the pattern for most of the country,' Idriseg continued. 'We know about the new outbreak of plague at Viroconium, though it doesn't sound as if it is anything like as bad as the one they had thirty years ago. But nobody feels safe since Uther died. That's my sense. We need a new Council and a new leader as soon as possible.'

The older of the King's advisers murmured, 'But where, and who will call it?'

'Quite,' said Idriseg. 'Any ideas, Myrddin?'

'It will be called by the Dobunni, and it will be held in Corinium on the Feast of the Spirits this October,' he replied.

'How can you be certain? Has it actually been called?' asked Idriseg.

'No, but it will be. I am sure enough that I am intending to be prepared. That is why I am here now, my friend. If I'm wrong then there's no harm done – we will just bide our time. But preparation is everything. As it is we only have five months to make sure he's ready.'

'Who?' the Tribune asked.

Myrddin brushed the question aside. 'Whoever the candidate is. Bound to be one of Uther's sons, I should think, though there may be others. The Ordovices are sure to put someone forward from Vortigern's line, and I hear the Brigantes are arguing it was time the overlord was a northerner, but then they always say that.'

Idriseg rolled up the scroll decisively and clapped Myrddin on the back. 'Either way, you will have a contingent from Elfael to support you when the time comes. We can't let the big kingdoms have everything their own way, can we?'

'I think you'll find the opposite is true. The big kingdoms will never agree on a candidate that comes from one of them. The Cantiaci won't have a Brigantian, and vice versa. They'll look for a compromise – and where better to find one than Elfael?'

'But who should we support?' asked the Magistrate.

Myrddin held his gaze. 'You'll know when the time comes. If I am right in what I see, it will be obvious enough. Trust me.'

'I do, Myrddin,' said Idriseg. 'I always have. Though it can be painful at times.'

Arthur stepped forward. 'You wanted to tell Caradoc and me the rest of the story of Ygraen and Uther,' he said.

'I did indeed.' said Myrddin. 'Come, Arthur, come, Caradoc, we'll find another house with a fire and leave Idriseg to matters of state.'

When they were settled in the same small room that they had used the evening before, Myrddin turned to the elder boy.

'I seem to remember you fell asleep just as I was explaining how Gorlois of Dumnonia fell to his death one night.'

'I remember, I think,' lied Caradoc.

'Good. He mistook his way in the dark and sea mist at Tintagel and was dashed on the rocks below.'

'Father told us that before.'

'It was a terrible accident,' said Myrddin solemnly, 'and left Dumnonia in considerable difficulties. Gorlois had been an exceptional king, and Ygraen was devastated. Uther stayed on in the kingdom for nearly a month – far longer than he had planned – and then left me to see to the arrangements for a new king. I was also to help Ygraen return to Armorica if that was what she wished, though Uther made it clear that he would much prefer her to remain in Britannia, and to join his court at Londinium.

'As you know, of course, after a while I persuaded her to come with me to Uther's court, bringing her daughter with us. Uther's devotion to the widow of his friend was touching to see, and very deep. And though Ygraen never recovered from Gorlois's death fully, she was a princess of Armorica, and she realised that Uther's protection was

CHAPTER IV   61

important. When at Christmas it was announced that Uther and Ygraen would marry it was seen as the most sensible and statesmanlike course of action. Ygraen was soon declared pregnant. If they were to be together, the timing could hardly have been worse. Barbarian raids had increased along the east and south coasts. Uther could not remain inactive in Londinium; he had to lead the campaign to secure the ports and rebuild the country's defences. So he rode out in April and I led Ygraen to Isca of the Silures, a fine town where she could almost look across the water to Dumnonia and remember Gorlois.

'That was where you were born, Arthur, at the end of July, a little early by the reckoning from Ygraen and Uther Pendraeg's Christmas wedding, but you were healthy enough. Ygraen nursed you until you were four months old, then she gave you to me to find you a foster-home before the worst of the winter set in. I had already spoken to Idriseg, and we carried you as far as Magnis, where we handed you over to him in great secrecy one stormy November night. Ygraen and I returned to Uther, who had abandoned campaigning for the season and moved to Corinium. He was as passionate about her as he had always been – especially so after their half-year apart. Ygraen had accepted her position, and she was fond of Uther, genuinely believing him to have been her rescuer after the sudden death of Gorlois, but there was still part of herself that she kept at a distance and, I believe, she was not as reconciled as a princess should have been to giving you up to be fostered. In the deepest and coldest part of the winter – and it was hard that year – it was announced that Ygraen was once more carrying a child of Uther Pendraeg's.

'She was not the strong young woman she had been two years earlier, though. There was a sickness in her I could do nothing to heal. As part of her thickened with the child, the rest – the part which was Ygraen herself – seemed to change and lose heart. Uther's physicians just put it down to a hard pregnancy, and the women treated her with herbs and balms, but I was worried. I could tell by the spring that neither the baby nor Ygraen were thriving as they should have been. The colour had drained from her face, and her skin had a translucent quality, as if her soul was covered by stretched cloth.

'Ygraen died the night of the summer solstice, quietly, as the whole court celebrated in the late evening sun. She was so young. Before she died she made me promise to keep her daughter safe and to make sure you grew to fulfil your destiny in your parents' honour. In my grief I agreed, though it has been a hard promise to keep, and will soon be harder still.

'Uther Pendraeg was never the same after Ygraen's death. He blamed himself, though the world believed he had been honourable beyond the call of duty. His love for Ygraen had become far more important to him than defending Britannia. In his heart he wanted to return home to Armorica, to fight alongside his brother Constans if he needed to. But he was overlord, and the kings would not appoint another. The pull to return across the sea became almost irresistible when his brother died three years later and Armorica called him to return and take the regency for Constans's twelve-year-old son.

'Uther stayed, though. Just as he had made up his mind to accept Armorica's offer two large Barbarian war bands landed within a few days of each other, one sailing as far inland as Londinium, the other effectively cutting off his route home by using the cover of the island of Vectis to sail up the water and attack Venta. It was among the most serious challenges Pendraeg had faced, and he was professional enough to put his own will to one side. The old Uther was not the impetuous soldier I had served before his Britannian days. Now he was taciturn, slower to come to action and sadness rarely left him. He was also becoming cruel – something he had never been before. If he had inflicted pain it was because he did not fully understand the extent of what he did. With Ygraen, Ambrosius and Constans all gone, though, he understood completely. For those who had invaded and kept him from returning home there was no mercy. There was no peace agreed with the survivors of battles any more. If he was victorious only four men were allowed to live: two to attend to whatever customs they had for the dead; two to be shackled to a ship and set adrift as a message to any that contemplated the crossing. The rest were butchered and any women were given to the troops as payment. Few of them survived for more than a few days, many preferring to kill themselves rather than face rape that could continue hour after hour.

'He was no longer overlord but rather a tyrant. Any king or any king's man who resisted him – even entered into mild dispute – could expect the same treatment as the Barbarians. There was a son of the King of the Brigantes who threatened to take his men home unless Pendraeg turned north to help his father. Pendraeg had him taken

CHAPTER IV

into the fields, spreadeagled on a wooden frame and pointed home. Then, after his own serving girl was forced to bite off his balls, he was whipped with thorns and left for the crows.'

Arthur looked white. 'Why are you telling me this? First you tell me I am the son of this tyrant, and then you make me listen to his atrocities. If this was the sort of man he was, why should I acknowledge him as my father? I will stay here with Idriseg and Caradoc as I have always done. You can find one of Pendraeg's other bastards to govern in his place.'

'That is exactly why,' answered Myrddin. 'Because you are horrified, because you would not resort to such cruelty. Of all his children you are the one with your father's resolution, with the courage of the Constantine line, but with your mother's heart. This country does not need one of Pendraeg's bastards. It needs you.'

'And if I refuse?'

'Why would you?'

'Because I have no wish to be a leader. I am happy here in Elfael serving my father — he's still my father, whatever your story — and after him Caradoc, my brother.'

'Think of the world, Arthur.'

'This is my world,' he shouted back, suddenly furious. 'I know nowhere else. I have looked out from the top of our mountains and I cannot see any lands beyond that I want to live in, let alone rule. Who are you, anyway, to come here and take away my life, tell me that my parents are not my parents, that I am the son of a tyrant and a woman who died before I could remember her? You are just a royal adviser who thinks he can fool kings with magic. You are a Demetian, a half-Hibernian con man. You are not even a proper Christian. Why should I believe anything you say?' Arthur rose from the table, kicked his stool to the wall and strode towards the door. 'Whether of Elfael or Armorica, I am still a prince, and you are an unemployed servant who I had never seen before yesterday. I will not do what you demand, and I will not listen to any more of your ridiculous stories. Caradoc, come on. Let's get out before he sends us to sleep again or turns us into mice.'

'I'm trying to turn you into men, not mice,' Myrddin said quietly.

Arthur turned back to face him. 'That is none of your business. We are princes of Elfael, and we do not need the advice of foreigners.'

'And if it is your destiny to receive it?'

'Then I can still reject it. I have free will. I'm a Christian, remember. Not someone who makes bronze gods out of streams.'

'You can insult me all morning, Arthur. I have heard it all before, and worse.'

'You're right. I can insult a servant for as long as I like.'

'Maybe. But it will not make you any more right,' Myrddin pointed out. 'Even about servants – I am just as much a prince as you are, whether you like Demetia or not. You think I am doing this because of some personal desire to see my prophecies fulfilled. Nothing could interest me less. I believe that you are the only man who can save Britannia from the Barbarians and, more importantly, from itself.'

'And I believe that's nothing but fantasy,' countered Arthur.

Caradoc rose and joined his younger foster-brother. 'Are we going?'

'We are. We'll tell Father that this man is dangerous and raving.'

'You can tell Idriseg what you like,' retorted Myrddin, 'but your father is dead. He died two years ago; he was probably poisoned, as they said Ambrosius had been – but this time I believe them.'

'The father you want me to have is dead,' said Arthur. 'Mine is in the hall.' And with that he stepped out into the rain, followed by Caradoc.

Myrddin sat and looked through the open door for a moment and sighed. He had not foreseen Arthur's reaction, but he should have expected it, he realised. You could not appear one morning, destroy everything the boy thought himself to be and then be surprised if he reacted with more than mild curiosity. He had every right to be angry. He had been deceived by those he had most reason to trust. And to be asked to take charge of the embattled kingdoms of Britannia at the age of fifteen was hardly a prospect to fill a child with confidence and pleasure. Myrddin acknowledged to himself that he had been too wrapped up in his own need to tell the story after so long, to find Arthur and lead him out to heal the island. In Arthur he saw a return to the days of his own grandparents, when it was said you could travel from Moridunum to Ebvracum along stone roads, spending every night in a town inn with hot water and underfloor heating, knowing that the legions of Rome would keep the peace. He remembered being shown the magnificent mansions with mosaic pictures in the floors and paintings of birds and lovers around the walls, of using coins to buy goods from all round the empire, wine from Gaul, oil from Iberia, precious metals from Dacia, spices from beyond Palestine. He could not bring back the empire. Indeed he had heard the empire in the west had had no emperor capable of justifying the title since Valentinian III had died eighteen years before. Ambrosius could at least claim to have ruled in the name of the Emperor. Arthur, if Myrddin ever completed his mission, would have to rely on the legitimacy of ancestry, the strength of his sword and the trust of his electors – the divided and selfish tyrant kings of a new Britannia. He was right not to seek out such a life.

There was no help for it, though.

Myrddin fingered the lion brooch at his shoulder, feeling the warmth that somehow always flowed from it. A pall fell across his eyes and he saw an old man, lying alone on a dishevelled bed. The tent in which he rested leaked and around him was the muffled clatter of a dispirited camp the night before a battle. Myrddin sighed and followed the boys out into the rain.

V

THEY SET OFF FROM THE CAMP the third day after Myrddin arrived. The weather had cleared up, and there were hints that spring might have been serious enough to let the sun through for more than a few hours. Caradoc had wanted to go with them, but Idriseg had forbidden it. Branwen had given Arthur a surprisingly warm kiss as they made their farewells. It had never occurred to him that she might be very fond of her little brother. They both blushed, but knew it was important. Idriseg had tried to insist that four of his armed troops accompany them, but Myrddin had argued persuasively that they would draw far less attention to themselves if it were just a man and a boy travelling together than if they stormed across the country in a platoon. So in the end it was agreed that they would at least check in with the southern border post in the remains of the Roman fort before the great river, just so Idriseg knew they had left his own kingdom safely and on time.

The way through Elfael began as it had done when Arthur had set out to fetch Myrddin three sodden mornings earlier. After leaving the bastion of the camp they followed the stream down through the woods and up a bank. But then, where Arthur had carried straight on towards the river and the crossing where the sword had appeared for the first time, they instead turned right on a path that hugged a low hill on its southern side before dropping into a narrow gully of a road, cut deep into the land by centuries of cattle and carts. After a mile or a little less the road passed below a small stockade, one of King Idriseg's new fortified villages, set on a hillside overlooking the woods. It ran alongside the home stream, which meandered between the rampart and a simple wooden building which was able to hold most of the villagers – one of the new churches which Myrddin had noticed were springing up well outside the towns where he had been used to seeing them in converted Roman temples and basilicas. Being a fine morning there were plenty of people about, most of whom Arthur knew well and, though he was given enough respect due to a young prince, there was also plenty of banter about the size of his pack, the dull choice of travelling companion and whether he thought he was off to seek his fortune. With good reason, given the dangers of a divided country in the years since Uther's death, when there was nobody to enforce order except in the most local way, they believed that anybody leaving the kingdom by choice was either peculiar or suspect. Arthur showed Myrddin the inside of the church, then dropped down from its mound to the larger roadway which led across the stream.

Here they turned south and began to climb. The track was relatively straight, which made it shorter work than it would have been had it zigzagged up the thousand feet to the summit. They rested for a while at the top and Arthur realised he was looking at the same swathe of country he had seen from above the camp two evenings before, though this time he could only see in three directions. The mountain above home cut off the view to the west. The track crossed another on the top of the hill, then narrowed as it headed down steeply into the secluded valley below. Myrddin and Arthur trudged through the undulating country, climbing for a mile then descending equally sharply into the next valley with its inevitable shallow stream.

This was home territory for Arthur. For him all country was like this, but for Myrddin the woods and bare hilltops were full of magic. He would point out mounds and terraces many hundreds, perhaps three thousand years old, listen to the streams for their names and let the water run through his fingers in ritual libation before he drank and crossed. For him the trees by the roadside carried messages imprisoned in their bark – who had planted, who had cleared and who had passed that way on more than a farmer's errand or a social outing of boys heading for the girls in the next village.

They came across another new church – this time not on virgin ground, but held in an old round enclosure of stone and yew. Arthur found it perfectly natural, but it filled Myrddin with fury. He found everything about the church, except its existence, an affront. The followers of the new religion, he almost shouted at Arthur as he waved his staff in irritation, had every right to use the enclosure – indeed, if it were to become the dominant religion they had a duty to incorporate the old sanctuaries – but they had to respect them, too.

Myrddin ranted against the alignment of the new building, how it cut across the lines of the old graves, how it paid no heed to the placing of the ancient stones and the trees which completed the outer ring, how trees had been felled from the ring to provide the timber frame of the church itself. The spirits themselves had been torn out, Myrddin cried, and their power reduced to mere curiosities and folk tales.

That was bound to be the way when a religion only accepted one intolerant god, one point of view, regardless of place or age or circumstance. As he held his staff above him into the path of the sun, a ray of light shone from the amber at its head towards the church and the lion brooch began to glow. A wind gathered in the trees and the larger stones standing within the tree ring grew black and damp, so that they shone in the beam. Arthur couldn't tell whether the light it focused was just redirected, or whether it started in the staff. It hardly mattered. The result was the same. As the light struck the western wall of the church the wind fell away and a mark appeared, a stain as though the rendered walls had been burnt. And in the mark Arthur saw a shape gather and grow clear – though what it was he could never quite explain. It might have been the figure of a woman or the line of the mountains above them, possibly even a branch tipped with ripe fruit. But when it was set Myrddin smiled, lowered his staff, turned on his heel and set off up the track at twice his normal pace. The wind calmed and, as they left the enclosure, Arthur swore he could hear music among the stones behind him.

At every hilltop now there were glimpses of the country beyond Elfael – the crest of distant ridges, the twin peaks Arthur had seen and wondered at as he stood by the barrow on his first evening with Myrddin – but they were only glimpses, obscured by another fold in the land, another line of woods cutting in front of the road south. The sun was at its highest when Myrddin called a halt and slipped his water skin from his shoulder. They sat down within the roots of an old oak and unpacked the bread, meat and apples Branwen had prepared for them. Myrddin took off his boots, rested his feet on the cold grass and grinned across at Arthur.

'Sorry about that,' he said.

'About what?'

'I'm afraid I lost my temper back there, and I'm never quite sure what's going to happen when I do – especially in a sanctuary as ancient as that one. If you don't know the spirits of a place, it's impossible to know how they are going to react.'

'What happened? It seemed as though you were drawing the elements together.'

'I think that's exactly it,' said Myrddin. 'You're learning.'

'What about the mark on the church?'

'It was strange. I haven't seen that before. The mark could have been just that – a mark – but I don't think it was. The shapes were hard to read, but they were distinct. What did you see?'

Arthur chewed a mouthful of his lunch and peered thoughtfully at a patch of buttercups. 'Like you I thought it was clear, but when I try to pin it down and describe it, the image keeps changing in my mind, just as it seemed to on the wall of the church. I think there were three basic shapes, though.'

'So do I. Go on.'

'At first a woman appeared, without clothes, and seemed to lie down so that she became the land, and the rise and fall of her body became the hills and mountains. Then it was as though their substance disappeared and you were just left with the line along the top, the crest. That seemed like the branch of a tree – a cherry, perhaps, like you see round the old Roman houses. At the end I thought I saw fruit of some kind drooping from the end of the branch. Then when the light went from your stick—'

'Staff.'

'Sorry, staff. Anyway, when the light was drawn back in and the wind dropped, there was just a round mark on the church wall, the same shape as the round wall outside.'

'You're right. I hadn't noticed that,' Myrddin said, biting into an apple and regarding it intently. 'Now I'll tell you what I think was going on. The spirits of that place were waiting for me – not me especially, but someone with my training – and they had been waiting far longer than the short time since the church was built. I feel they have been waiting since the Romans came and brought imperial gods. When I walked in and felt the history of that ring (or rings, I should say, because there were three: the stones at the centre, the yew trees and the perimeter wall), they took me as their agent for a moment and used me to beam that mark against the new church. Do you remember where on the wall the scenes appeared?'

'This end – I mean, the end nearest the road we are on now.'

'That's right. At the opposite end from where the Christians place their altar. It was outside the spot where they place the stone bowl that they call – I suppose I should say we call – the font, for anointing children as a sign of entry to the religion. A simple custom, and I must admit a lot less painful than many of the old initiations.'

'You don't think the mark fell there by accident?'

Myrddin packed away the remains of his food and stood up stiffly. 'I'm not sure I believe in accidents,' he said. 'I think, however, if they try to rebuild that wall in future it will no longer belong to the Christians. It will always resist them. Or perhaps it is more benign than that. Whoever they mark from their font will be blessed by the old gods too. I hope so.' He finished his lunch and put his boots back on. 'Come on. We've got better things to do than worry about the future of minor deities. I want to be out of this kingdom by evening.'

They strode off along the track, following the familiar pattern of woods divided by swift streams, high bare hills and the occasional family farm carved out of the valley where the soil was good. Now and then they startled a deer or watched a hare leap for cover along the edge of the grassland. At one stream, where a fallen tree had blocked the water's path and created a wide pool behind its dam, a heron stood on one leg and eyed them quizzically before turning to more important matters among the fish about its feet.

'Did you learn your powers, or have you always had them?' asked Arthur as they came over the brow of a rise and started down into the woods again.

'I'm not sure what you mean by powers. It's the other way around. I'm aware that other people don't seem to be able to see the things I can, and that sometimes I don't know whether what I am seeing is a memory of the past, an extension of the present or a jump forward into the future. It's confusing and, I suppose, for those around me it must seem alarming – or just plain mad. I prefer the word lunatic myself, "influenced by the moon", which does have something to do with it. I can sense things better at some phases of the lunar cycle than at others – or maybe it's my own cycle and the moon has nothing to do with it. I don't know. Plenty of people have tried to make sense of it all to me, but most of the time I realise pretty quickly that they are inventing most of the explanation. Their answers are no better than my own.'

'But you helped me see into that barrow,' Arthur insisted, 'and the light did shine from your staff against the wall of the church.'

'Did I? Perhaps you saw for yourself and I merely directed you to look in the right place. I knew the old chieftain was in there, and I saw some of what you saw. And the church? The light and wind was there; so were the stones. Maybe it was just a trick of light as the sun shone through the tip of my staff when I held it up in my moment of anger. That is what a Greek philosopher or one of the Alexandrian scholars would tell you. One of the new priests would too, I expect.'

'Is that what you think?'

Myrddin stopped to admire a patch of late bluebells still blooming in the shadow of the trees. 'No, not really,' he said, 'I think I do have a gift of seeing, and once in a while the sense of how to use it effectively. That is the part I have learnt through study and observation.'

Suddenly he quickened his pace and hurried on ahead, leaving Arthur to scurry after him.

'Observation,' declared Myrddin, 'that's the key. It is far too little valued these days. People look to see what they expect to see and regard anything that surprises them as magic. I have no expectations, and so can see what is there, whether I understand it or not. I note what came before and what happened after. I look for the effect and do not try to deduce the cause until I have seen the same thing happen often enough that I can be sure I observed it accurately. I may not be able to make it happen when I want it to, but I will have a fair idea of the circumstances that might lead to it again.'

Most of this Myrddin had seemed to address to the mud in the road as Arthur ran alongside. As a result, when Myrddin stopped suddenly Arthur found himself several yards ahead before he realised he was out on his own. He turned to find Myrddin staring at him intently.

'That is what I have to teach you,' he said. 'Not how to use a sword or wield an axe, not how to ride a horse into battle or command men. You'll learn that from others, but mostly from yourself. I have to teach you to trust your eyes more than your mind and your mind more than your heart – and when to do the opposite.'

Arthur looked away, embarrassed at the strength of Myrddin's attention, and walked on.

Myrddin watched him for a moment before moving off again. 'And it won't be easy,' he muttered.

They had now walked further through Elfael than Arthur had ever been before. Idriseg had always made sure that he remained secure in the interior of the kingdom, where knowledge of this supposed second son of the King could be confined and controlled as essentially a family matter. Elfael liked secrets, and while everybody knew everybody else's business they were careful to keep it from outsiders. Conversation with someone 'from off' would never go beyond the general pleasantries, and nothing of any detail would be revealed, however liberal the wine or intimate the evening. Though the structure of the landscape was familiar, it was new territory now for Arthur, and he slowed as he followed the track, taking in the contours of the land and the lie of the farms they passed, with a nod and a word from Myrddin to those labouring in the yards and a calming pat for the excited dogs that greeted them a hundred yards from every house.

After another mile they came out from the cover of the trees. Arthur stopped and marvelled at the country that unfolded below him. They were on the edge of everything, it seemed. In front, the land dropped away sharply to the floor of a great valley, and through it a river many times as wide as any Arthur had crossed ambled towards the plains. To their left the country opened out and the river was lost in the haze as it entered a vast forest from which isolated hills poked their summits like distant islands. On the far side of the valley the land rose again in a scarp even more precipitous than the one on the edge of which they stood, and at least twice as high. Behind it a low range of mountains, with nothing of the enclosing softness of Elfael's jumbled hills, glowered black in the shadow of the clouds which gathered from the west. Much of the valley floor was cleared for pasture, and cows grazed in open paddocks along the river.

'The water marks the border of Idriseg's kingdom,' remarked Myrddin, as he caught up. 'Beyond that to the left is Dobunni country, and those mountains belong to the Silures – both in theory. In practice it is land so much in the corner of their territory that nobody is really sure who, if anybody, controls it. My own feeling is that neither have much of a say, and that it will evolve into its own separate kingdom, like Elfael, before long. We have to cross that river tonight, but not here. We'd have to pay for a ferry, and I'd rather not be that public about our comings and goings, if you don't mind. There's a passable ford about six miles upstream where we won't get too wet.'

Arthur was not to be hurried, though. He rejoiced at the variety of the land, its wide expanses and long horizons. He had seen the panorama from the top of his home hill, but that was different, almost a dream, with peaks and forests too far away to be real or reachable.

Here he had his first sense that Britannia was not all like his own country, that it was a wide and varied land, around which other people moved about their business. For the first time he understood what being overlord, the heir to Uther Pendraeg, involved. It meant that he would not only have to travel this land, he would have to know it, feel familiar with all its kingdoms, understand the news that messengers brought him, not as an observer from afar but as an intimate, seeing the towns and fortifications in his mind's eye, riding the roads from memory, not from guesswork after an evening's study of a chart left behind by the legions.

'Are you coming or not?' Myrddin called over his shoulder.

Reluctantly Arthur adjusted his pack and followed Myrddin down the track, which now cut straight across grassland to the valley floor. At the foot of the hillside a long silver line ran straight and uniform – a military road. Arthur knew the one which led to the fort below the village from where he had collected Myrddin those few days earlier. But this was a road of a different order. Still well maintained and now, in the late afternoon, well used. From above Arthur could see carts and groups of riders, traders with their packhorses and the inevitable herd of cattle.

CHAPTER V

Myrddin saw him watching. 'That used to be illegal, you know.'

'What did?'

'Driving cattle along a legionary highway. Could be fined a month's supplies for that.'

'Why?'

'Think, boy. You've got five thousand well-turned-out troops marching fast in perfect columns only a man's width narrower than the road itself. Everybody's wearing sandals. Then two things happen. First the columns break up as all the soldiers try to avoid the cowpats. Second, the whole thing grinds to a halt as the front of the army comes up against the cows. Not only could it be very funny, it could be a disaster if you were in enemy territory and expecting an ambush. No centurion would want to be caught in the open like that, would he?'

'I suppose not.' Arthur conceded.

'But you won't find too many orderly columns of any sort these days, let alone the Twenty-Third Legion in full array, so it hardly matters, except that the roads will have disappeared under the grass in a few more years if they keep being manured so well.'

'Do we take that road?'

'We do, though we have to cross it first and tell that sentry of your father's — I mean Idriseg — that we have arrived without mishap and will be in Elfael for a few miles yet.'

Although the road seemed just below them, reaching it was not quite so simple, and nearly another hour had passed before the track plummeted the last stretch to join the neat flagstones. By then Arthur's knees were aching from bracing himself against the descent with the heavy pack on his back, and he was relieved to feel the flat and level surface of the pavement beneath his feet. Myrddin was all for pushing on as fast as they could, but as they crossed he agreed that they could break for a few minutes and sit on the trunk of an elm conveniently felled by the side of the road.

After they had stretched their legs and wiped the worst of the mud from their feet, Myrddin led the way along a side road that branched off to the left. This was no track, but an equally well-paved military way, leading to the old legionary camp above the river — the furthest west that the Romans had had a permanent presence in this part of the country, Myrddin told Arthur.

'I'm afraid you'll find it a bit disappointing now, my boy. It's a hundred and fifty years since they bothered to garrison it properly. There's a few of the old barracks still standing, and the Commander's house is in reasonable shape, but the stockade's falling to pieces and your father's troops are growing vegetables where the parade ground used to be.'

'Have you known it any different?'

'No. But I have travelled and I know how it should look. I'm sorry, Arthur, but I don't see why we should abandon the standards of an age that is past just because we cannot be bothered – or because there is nobody around to make us do better. I believe in the Britannians as strongly as anyone, but we have come a long way in the last four hundred years, and I am not going to stand by helplessly while we slip into the primitive ways of the Barbarians. There were plenty of things that I won't miss about the Romans. They could be harsh masters. But they knew how to build, and they knew how to keep things running. We may not have the knack.'

With that Arthur could see they had arrived at the gates of the camp. They gave their names to the guards, who saluted and swung open the timber gates, despite Myrddin's announcement that they would not be staying, they were just checking in as the King had asked them to do. But the guards were bored, and it was unusual to have two such distinguished guests passing through. They insisted that the travellers should share some broth and cheese, at least, before going further. It was a welcome gesture, and though part of Arthur was anxious to move on, another part of him was nervous about leaving Elfael for the first time in memory, and he was pleased to have an excuse to stay for a little longer in the kingdom that was home.

Myrddin was right about the state of the Roman base. Most of the buildings that remained were covered in brambles and dog rose, and it was hard to make out where the orderly grid of streets had run under the tangle of grass and nettles that now enjoyed control. The guard tower over the gateway was still intact, in a ramshackle sort of way, and one of the buildings overlooking the river and the border village beyond had been cleared and repaired enough to provide living quarters for the half-dozen men who patrolled the Elfael bank of the ferry crossing in the name of King Idriseg. The two guests sat outside on a log chatting to one of the guards (who inevitably had a cousin at headquarters) while the food was prepared.

'It's been quiet enough here,' the guard admitted in answer to Myrddin, 'but then, I can't remember a time when it was anything else on this stretch of the river. There's nobody much to have a fight with, and little enough to fight over. We have to supervise returning cattle if they stray across, and some Saturdays boys take the ferry over when they shouldn't, but they're usually too drunk to row, let alone give us any serious trouble. That's about the extent of it.'

He paused as his companion emerged with wooden bowls of broth and hunks of goat's cheese.

'Mind you,' he continued, 'I've heard it's not so funny down the other end of the river,' he pointed to the south.

'Why?' Myrddin asked.

'Three ships of raiders last week.'

'This far west?'

'That's what worried us. It's not certain who they were. Some say they were Franks; others say thew were Barbarians who had sailed round from Vectis island; yet others say they were Hibernians. Apparently they slipped past Venta in the night and were heading upriver to Glevum before they were stopped. Quite a battle, I hear.'

'But they were stopped?'

'Oh, they were stopped, all right. But it's worrying.'

Myrddin agreed, finished his food and stood up with determination in his face. 'Time I got you to work, my boy.'

Arthur nodded and shouldered his pack. 'You'll tell my father we passed through?'

'He'll know by morning,' promised the guard. 'I'd go with you as far as the ford, but we're a bit short of men just now, and I doubt if you'll see any trouble on the main road.'

Myrddin and Arthur thanked the men for their hospitality and headed back up the slope to the junction, then turned left where the road ran straight along the foot of the hills. Sometimes the river was within a few yards of them, sometimes several fields away, but the road itself did not deviate. They made short work of the few miles to the ford, and the sun was still warm as they halted at the crossing.

Arthur looked at the stones which led across the river, first to a shallow island in the middle where the water was divided by a bank of rough shingle, then across the deeper channel to the other side – another kingdom. He turned and gazed back at the Elfael hills rising a short way behind him, drawing him back from the border. Myrddin was leading impatiently across the stones. He reached the island and called over.

'What are you waiting for?'

'Nothing much.'

That was only partly true. Arthur was waiting for the courage to cross, for the voices telling him there was still time to turn back for home, to reject the lunatic plan of the old man in front of him, whatever his sorcery, to quieten. He could return, they whispered, explain that Myrddin had changed his mind and journeyed on to find a different victim to turn into Uther Pendraeg's successor. Arthur could go home to Branwen, be Caradoc's loyal brother and serve the kingdom of Elfael as best he could.

In his heart Arthur knew Idriseg would never have him back on those terms, though. If Myrddin's story was true, then Idriseg had kept his side of the bargain, shouldering the trouble and expense of bringing him up as a prince of his own household. There could be no going back before he had seen Myrddin's course through and been put up for the succession. Then there was a chance that the Council of Kings would baulk at the idea of so young an overlord and appoint someone else. Only then could Arthur return to his hills with dignity and be sure of a welcome.

He sighed and followed Myrddin across the river. As they reached the far bank, Myrddin clasped an arm round his shoulder.

'Well done, boy. That's the first test. It may not seem it, but in fact it was one of the most difficult you will ever face.'

'I didn't want to cross.'

'I don't blame you.'

'But there seemed no way back – or at least, none that I could take without shame.'

'You will find that you expect more of yourself than others do. That's the burden. but it makes moments like this easier,' he said, peering down the road in front of them. It was Roman, and was still well kept. 'We'll make ourselves known at the border post along there and then find somewhere for the night. If I remember there's an inn about three miles further on – a good one, too, if it hasn't changed. We'll be there in under an hour.'

Arthur nodded and started on ahead.

CHAPTER V

'Wait,' called Myrddin. Arthur stopped.

'Now we're across the river you must carry this,' Myrddin reached under his cloak and detached from his belt the short Roman sword they had found in the stream on the first morning. Arthur was almost ashamed. He had nearly forgotten the sword, so much had happened since – or not forgotten, exactly, but certainly that first extraordinary moment in his time with Myrddin had slipped into the background, as though it was already part of legend rather than an event which had astonished him so profoundly only three days before.

'Take it,' encouraged Myrddin. 'Carry it with honour. Care for the sword and the sword will care for you.'

Arthur slipped the scabbard on to his own belt and furled his cloak against it. For a moment he glanced at the river. It was hard to know what had changed. Maybe the water had calmed and cleared so that the riverbed showed its stones to the afternoon sun. Maybe the wind had crept up a fraction, so that the woods of Elfael became talkative in the breeze. The air was full of greetings and farewells together, and Arthur felt a new spirit of resolution, a freshening of his mind so that the journey he had embarked upon was no longer daunting and incomprehensible but inevitable and right. He found his pack lighter and his stride lengthening. The sword of the line of Constantine had passed to him, and so too had the authority.

Myrddin smiled as he watched his charge grow taller and broader, the swagger in his walk and the upright determination of his head. There had been times when Myrddin wondered if he had found the right boy, whether Idriseg, in seeking to placate the old overlord's adviser, had passed off his Geraint as Pendraeg's son so as not to admit that the child had died in infancy. With the sword so plainly in its rightful place Myrddin was certain that his quest had been justified, as would be the months of teaching ahead. Arthur might not be the man to save Britannia for ever, but one could only do the best in one's own generation. Myrddin also had renewed belief in the course he had set upon from the moment he had decided to help Uther salvage his position after the murder of Gorlois nearly seventeen years before. Gorlois had paid dearly for that night. So too had Ygraen, the unwitting victim, and though retribution had been slow in coming Uther had surely paid as hard as the crime deserved. It was time to rescue the innocent country from the appetites of its rulers.

That night they reached the inn as the dusk began to settle. As they rested at the table and waited for the meal of mutton stew and barley, Arthur watched the sun setting on his living father's kingdom, and wondered when he would see it again. Just in front of them the great river swung north to its source and for a few miles yet it marked the boundary of Idriseg's power. There was still sorrow in Arthur's mind, but already it was slipping into nostalgia, and for the first time the excitement of the task he had undertaken began to take over.

* * *

The following morning was crisp and bright, and the road shone white in the May sun. They left early and made quick time in the placid country of the valley – such good time that they had reached the night's destination, the village nestling in the abandoned fort of Cicutio, by the middle of the afternoon. Myrddin stuck to his plan, however, and stayed where they were rather than pushing on and sleeping in the open. Had he been on his own, he explained, he would have been happy to do so, but Arthur was his charge and he was disinclined to take unnecessary risks by venturing into the hills as night fell. They were following a legionary route, and there was sense in following the timing that went with it. The commanders had placed their forts where they matched man's stamina for the day's march.

Although the road onwards from Cicutio was Roman, the country was more mountainous, and the way could not be laid out with the precision the engineers would normally have employed. Instead it clung to the sides of steep slopes and obstinate valleys, pushed through invading forest and stumbled over unforgiving passes.

It must have been hard for the original soldiers, often under attack from above, sometimes trapped in indefensible ravines. At the second midday out from Elfael Myrddin pointed out the overgrown remains of a camp they had used as a staging post between the major forts. Only the bank and fragments of the stockade remained to show what had once been a place that would have meant life or death to the harassed legionary in hostile country and, as Myrddin reminded Arthur, victory or defeat for the Britannians trying to prevent the legions subjugating them to the empire. After this difficult terrain, though, they passed over a watershed and dropped from the spring at the head to a valley that looked more promising than anything they had encountered all day, as it opened gradually towards the south-west. The marshy reeds gave way to woods of beech and oak. Rowan and hazel gathered beside the eager rivulet, then they strolled down to sheep pasture and finally to strips of calf-high oats and barley as the river expanded and slowed its frantic uplands pace.

They reached Alabum at nightfall. For Myrddin this was truly home territory, and he was instantly recognised and welcomed. They had hardly passed the watch-post three miles from the town when they began to meet acquaintances.

'For the moment you had better stay as Geraint of Elfael, son of King Idriseg,' Myrddin told Arthur as they dropped out of the mountain country. 'It's safer that way, and it also saves long explanations. There's nothing strange about me taking on an apprentice from a good family. In fact people will be pleased that you are from a nearby kingdom, rather than from somewhere in the east. There's not much regard for anybody from beyond Corinium among the Demetiae – or the other way round, for that matter.'

'I wouldn't know how to be anyone else,' Arthur admitted. 'That is who I am.'

'Yes, I suppose you are. I have lived with the other side of the story, so I find it difficult to think of you as you have actually been growing up. I think of Ygraen and Uther and the child I handed over in Magnis.'

Alabum was a town, like so many others, that had seen better days. Only a few of the buildings seemed to be occupied, and the travellers passed overgrown yards and tumbledown warehouses on either side of the road, as though great industry had been and gone, or masses of produce had been gathered from the interior and stored ready for shipping from the ports to the south. But Myrddin explained that these sheds and loading areas were not about moving goods out. They were for supplies going in the other direction.

'There's nothing much left now,' he said sadly as they headed for the fortified remains of the town, 'and I cannot remember back long enough to have seen it much different, though it looks even shabbier than a couple of years ago. All this was about taking away very little.'

Alabum had only minor strategic importance, in that it provided a camp a pleasant day's march from Moridunum, but for the Romans and the Demetiae it had far greater importance as the last easily accessible place before setting out into the hills for the gold mines at Luentium.

'Gold came out, and in amounts that would have needed only a mule or two to carry to the merchants, but slaves went in by the thousand – and slaves need feeding in the mines. They might not have lived very long doing that work – and the overseers didn't care whether they lived or died. Once they became useless for work they were sent to the games at Venta, and were fed to whatever animal killed them. If they died on the job they were just mixed with the ore rubble and thrown into whatever spent shaft needed filling up. While they were working, though, they needed to work well. So in Alabum they were fed and allowed to recover their strength before being moved to the mining camp. When they were strong and fit they were loaded with sacks of food and anything else the camp commanders wanted and sent off, whatever the weather. These huts were probably the last half-decent accommodation most of them ever saw.'

'We still need gold. Why don't we mine it any more?'

Myrddin shook his head. 'Can't be done. We, the Demetiae, don't have the slaves or, frankly, the mining knowledge. There are not the furnaces to take the gold from the rock or the labour to deal with the waste. Most of all, nobody is minting new coins in Britannia, and Ambrosius was the last man grand enough to have a court that could afford gold for decoration. We mined gold here for a hundred years before the Romans came. In part it was to control the gold that they bothered to come at all. And now look at the place. You would think we were primitives with no history and not much of a future. And all because nobody can get this country organised enough to stop the kingdoms arguing and send the Barbarians home. It makes me so angry sometimes. At others I just feel despair at living in such an inadequate generation.'

They walked on despondently. Soon, though, they were leading a straggle of curious children and hawkers trying to sell them everything from apples to crudely wrought nuggets of gold set into leather necklaces or amulets. Myrddin waved them away and led Arthur to a house at the side of what was left of the forum. Their host had known Myrddin since they were boys, and he spared nothing in making sure they were properly looked after. They found comfortable beds and a fire and a foot bath.

CHAPTER V

The next morning of their journey found Myrddin up early and in excellent spirits, whistling while he combed his beard and straightened out his cloak. They breakfasted as well as they had dined, and though Arthur had crept to bed long before Myrddin had finished reminiscing about his childhood, he had to be hauled up to the table.

Arthur listened to Myrddin suspiciously. He was used to the calm and thoughtful sage, not this energetic and capricious loudmouth.

'Is something going on I should know about?' he asked.

Myrddin stopped humming and grinned at him. 'Nothing alarming, unless you mean me. I'm nearly home, that's all. I shall sleep tonight in my own bed and close to my own library.'

'Much further?'

'No, we'll be there by mid-afternoon at the latest. The road's good from here. The King of Demetia has his pride, and this is the second-largest town in his kingdom, so he likes to make sure we can all go about our business without walking through the long grass.'

The farewells were protracted and the pair found themselves travelling in a party of ten, complete with pack mules, as others decided that they needed a trip to Moridunum's excellent market. Arthur was glad of the company. Myrddin was an extraordinary man, but two complete days with nobody else to talk to had been quite enough. There were two or three lads of his own age in the group that set, each equipped with a list by their mothers for needles and oil, glass and pottery, and an array of stores which seemed to be as much wishful thinking as firm orders with any prospect of success.

It was not much after midday when Myrddin tapped Arthur on the shoulder and pointed to the left of the road.

'That's where we're going.'

'I thought we were going to Moridunum?'

'They are. But we're stopping short. My home. To the left of the river. On that rise before you come to the hills again.'

Half a mile later they left their companions and turned off the road, forded the river and followed a track through the small wood which guarded what Myrddin described as his palace.

VI

THE RAVEN-HAIRED GIRL who ran to meet them at the gate and threw her arms around Myrddin with a wail of delight was much the same age as Branwen, thought Arthur, as he stopped at Myrddin's side, smiling vacuously at the reunion.

Myrddin was not trying very hard to disentangle himself. 'Morganwy, Morganwy, it has not been that long – barely half a month...'

The girl looked up. 'I never know,' she said. 'You leave and—'

'Enough of that,' Myrddin said, stroking her hair affectionately. 'I want you to meet our guest. He will be with us for a while and part of our lives for much longer. This is Geraint of Elfael. Geraint, Morganwy. She could be my daughter, though she is not, and I love her as though she were.'

Arthur stepped forward and bowed.

Morganwy, her head still resting on Myrddin's chest, stared at him with eyes so dark brown they were almost black, and the hint of a smile puckered the corner of her mouth. Then she looked back up at Myrddin. 'He's only a boy,' she said.

'And you're only a girl. These things change, and faster than you think. But you can welcome him better than that. You can start by letting go of me and getting us something to drink – and then I'll show Geraint round the palace.'

'So you are a king too,' Arthur observed.

'No. I only call it my palace as a conceit. My uncle was indeed King (or Chief, as he would have expected to be called) of Demetia. But I'm royal enough to enjoy the pretence.'

Geraint found soon that Myrddin's description of his home as a palace was fully justified. It was unlike anything at the court of King Idriseg. There were no round houses of wood, wicker and thatch. There was no great hall, curtained and with a hearth at its centre. The only

CHAPTER VI

concession to their own century was the site: on a rocky spur above the valley – Myrddin explained that he was Briton enough to want to see the country around him, not hide about in the trees – and the stout stockade with its earth rampart, corner bastions and wooden drawbridge. But even those had touches that Arthur felt were not of their own time.

Myrddin led the way across a square, framed by the stockade on one side with stables, storehouses and quarters for the staff to the left and right. In front of them rose a slim two-storey building of stone and plaster. The walls were rendered white, and only the door, high and imposing like the door to one of the old temples they had seen in the towns along the way, let light into the space beyond. A classical pediment surmounted the columns of the portico and within its triangle sat a marble relief. In the middle a lion and a dragon held the moon between their paws, the lunar disc circled by stars. The beasts' heads faced outward and down, towards the humans passing beneath, as if to remind them of the majesty of the dwelling into which they came. And in the diminishing angles of the pediment, resting naked backs against the tails of the lion and dragon, reclined two helmeted goddesses, spears resting in hand with the points towards their feet.

Arthur gazed up at the magnificent sculpture and Myrddin paused, turned back and looked with him.

'Like it?'

'I've never seen anything like it. It's...'

'Rather splendid. I agree. Found it in a tip outside Verulamium a couple of years ago. I remember it in Ambrosius's time above the entrance to one of the temples – can't remember which one. I call her (or them) Luna Britannia, which is as accurate as I can be. Anyway, I had it brought here in pieces. Come on in – but look up as you do.'

Arthur followed his companion under the portico and glanced above him. At first he thought he saw a forest of lights, but soon he realised they were stones or jewels, each reflecting back towards him with a different and subtle colour.

'Shells, actually,' murmured Myrddin with pride, 'and of course you notice that they are arranged to show the constellations at midwinter.'

'Of course.'

'Very un-Roman, I know, but I liked the idea. The shells are genuine enough. They came from a collapsed grotto at a villa destroyed by Barbarians outside Noviomagus. I salvaged what I could.'

'Is it all like this?'

'Like what?'

'Taken from old buildings? Nothing new.'

Myrddin looked pained. 'You make it sound as though you would rather live in a mud hut with a leaking roof, smoked out at night, boiling in summer like the meat in the cooking pot and freezing all winter in damp clothes and constant mud.'

'It's not that bad.'

'Yes it is. You just don't know anything better.'

They stood in a hallway three times the width of the entrance with doors on either side. Old javelins and shields were arranged around the walls in patterns. Myrddin waved at them.

'They may look decorative, but you can have them off the walls and in your hands in seconds if you need too. Unobtrusive defence. Civilised but effective. I've got an old ballista out the back that I keep in perfect working order.'

'I've never seen one working.'

'Terrifying thing. I hope you won't have too. Sends a bolt straight through three men on the other side of the river.'

'Where now?' Arthur asked.

Myrddin ushered him on with a bow. 'Straight through. Let you get the feel of the shape before I confuse you with the rooms.'

Arthur bowed back and walked on. They passed through a heavy oak door and out into the daylight once again. Arthur stopped and marvelled. He found himself in a covered walkway, laid with flagstones. He could see for the first time that this was no ordinary building. It was a hollow rectangle, on the inside of which the walkway ran, one side open with beautiful carved columns supporting the roof. Within that a quiet garden lay, with a fountain playing gently at its centre. Beds of herbs were arranged in squares, separated by stone paths and carved benches. Flowers were just beginning to open in the late spring sun, and the sound of the fountain gave an immediate sense of peace.

'Well?'

Arthur moved slowly towards the low wall that divided the walkway from the garden and sat. 'I know people used to live like this a hundred, a hundred and fifty years ago. But I had no idea anybody still did.'

'You're right. Very few do. I think I know of only four original villas in this sort of repair. And the art of gardening has almost died. This is a cheat, really. It's my own perfect villa. I built it up from a ruin with the bits and pieces I found lying unwanted by the new order. Whenever I go to one of the old towns or find myself in the buildings that are being turned into these new Christian dormitories, I look for the things that people disapprove of or have no idea what to do with and have them carted home.'

'That's a fountain, isn't it?'

'From Londinium, no less. It used to sit in the private courtyard of the Pro-Consul. I especially like the combination of sea beasts and nymphs around the base. You'll see them later.'

'How do you keep it all safe? I thought most of the Roman places were open to plunder.'

'Very few know it's here. That is what the stockade and rampart is for. Just another fort. But there's no reason why people could not live like this if they wanted to. It's all silly prejudice. It started when they threw out the last of the imperial officials. Once you start a revolt it's hard to stop. People turned on the rich, and especially those who rejected the new religion. Vortigern wouldn't have been able to stop it, even if he had wanted to – which he didn't. He was a man of the hills, and felt more comfortable in Barbarian surroundings than the trappings of Rome. Ambrosius tried to restore a few things, but he had neither the resources nor the political backing; and Uther had many fine qualities, but artistic appreciation was not one of them.'

'Is that why you have this – to preserve the art of the past?'

'In part. Why destroy beautiful things through neglect? Mostly because it's more comfortable, as you'll find out. But there is a deeper reason, I suppose. I am not convinced that our new ways will save us, nor that the new God has any more answers than the old ones. I see too much that I can use but not understand. I cannot believe that all our troubles are the result of our sins, nor that we have to tear down everything to reach salvation.' Myrddin grinned. 'And I'm a collector. None of this may survive me, but while I can I want to enjoy whatever this island lets me have, whether Britannian or Roman. I'll show you inside.'

He guided Arthur by the shoulder. 'Let's start with the baths.'

'The baths!'

'Why not? There's no virtue in being unclean, young man.'

'But the water will be perishing.'

'Not here.' Myrddin led him to the far corner of the garden court and through a door far smaller than the one at the entrance. Arthur found himself in an anteroom, with pegs for clothes and marble benches covered with neatly folded linen towels.

'Shoes off,' instructed Myrddin, unlacing his, 'then the rest.'

Arthur did as he was told and followed Myrddin into a shallow basin of water that separated them from the next room.

'Aagh!'

'What's wrong?'

'I thought you said the water wouldn't be cold!'

'It's not. This is just to get the dirt off your feet.'

Arthur soon recovered. He stepped out of the footbath on to stone floors that were gloriously warm to the touch. In the middle of the inner chamber a flight of steps led down into a pool of clean water, steaming gently. A shaft of late afternoon sunlight filtered in from an opening high in the wall, and Arthur was sure he heard music as he allowed himself to be led into the enveloping warmth of the water.

Myrddin read his thoughts. 'My own harpist,' he announced, 'in the gallery up there behind the screen.'

'Is this how it used to be?'

'Not quite. I don't have male slaves from Dacia to tend the fires or to oil and comb my back clean. I don't have the oil at all – or at least, it's too precious for this. I sometimes manage to get a flask or two sent over the sea with the wine; though I have found that if you boil sheep fat and scent it with herbs you can make a substance which cleans just as well.'

'The heat seems to come from the ground itself.'

'In a sense it does. This room – indeed, most of the rooms of the house – rest on brick piles. In between there is space for hot air to circulate from the fires lit in all the corners. My servants saw us coming up the valley and had the place warmed by the time we arrived. Very thoughtful of them. But you see, I pay in gold coin. Imagine that.'

Arthur tried and failed. His mind was dealing with too many revolutionary ideas at once. Instead he lay in the warm water, luxuriating in a way he had never known before, and drifted. For the first time the enormity of what had happened to him in the last week began to sink in. He was not sure whether he had stepped backward or forward in time. Perhaps neither, but he had stepped out of the world he had known and had thought to be the natural order.

CHAPTER VI

Myrddin washed himself aggressively, dipping his head completely under the water, scrubbing with a tablet of sweet-smelling grease, it seemed to Arthur, until he tried it in turn and was surprised to find the dirt of the journey and the days before lifting off his skin more completely than usual. And all the while the harp played in the hidden gallery above him, sometimes tunes he had sung around the fire in the hall of King Idriseg, sometimes music far more complicated that cascaded about the walls and had melodies that were barely begun before they moved into another mood, restless music leaving the simple songs of the warrior far behind.

Eventually Myrddin hauled himself back up the steps of the bath and, standing naked on the edge, clapped his hands sharply. The music stopped. Myrddin gestured Arthur to follow and made his way back into the anteroom. The water in the sunken footbath was still cold, Arthur noticed, but it seemed to have been cleaned and replenished since they had passed through first. Myrddin was standing with his back to the door. He was not alone. Two girls dressed in corn-coloured tunics, so loose at the sides that their bodies could be glimpsed as they moved, offered towels. Arthur stopped, wondering how to cover himself or whether to retreat back into the bath. He blushed furiously and Myrddin did nothing to help his state of confusion by laughing loudly.

'Find a towel for him before he turns an even worse colour, for heaven's sake.'

One of the girls, black haired and no older than Arthur, giggled and brought a towel laid across both her arms, her eyes sparkling and her head cocked mischievously.

'Geraint, meet Sioned,' commanded Myrddin, and she gave a little ironic curtsey as Arthur grabbed the towel and wrapped it about his middle. 'Sioned has served me ever since she was captured during a disagreement between the Ordovices and Cornovii when she was ten. She was not treated very well by the warriors. I met them near Viroconium and she was a poor thing – weren't you?'

Sioned nodded and began to dry Arthur's back.

'I bought her for much more than she was worth to them as a slave, but at least she is not one here, and is safe. And this is Seona. Their names are close, but that's all – they come not only from different kingdoms, but different islands.'

The other girl, a little older, Arthur thought, than Branwen, smiled at him before turning her full attention back to Myrddin.

'Hibernian red hair, eyes so green — and I would trust her with my life and more. The Ordovices caught her three years ago on a return raid against the High King. The rest of her story is the same as Sioned's, though she was even closer to death and madness when I brought her here. Now they are not slaves. They are free to go at any time. But they stay to serve me, which is kind of them.' Myrddin lowered his voice and rang his hand through Seona's hair as she rubbed the towel across his chest. 'And we have a kind of affection for one another that suits us.' His hand traced her cheek and then slipped through the side of the tunic to her slight high breast. Seona kissed his shoulder and let her towelling hand drop to his groin.

Sioned made to follow suit for Arthur, but he pushed her hand away roughly and glared in embarrassment. She looked surprised and a little hurt, but drew back and inclined her head in a curt formal bow.

Myrddin laughed even louder. 'I'm sorry, my boy. It was thoughtless of me. I was forgetting you are not a warrior yet. This is my homecoming routine, and I have to say it is one I look forward to. It keeps me smiling on the road — dreaming of Seona and Sioned waiting for me as I step clean and sweet from the bath and into their hands.' He kissed Seona's red hair and put a kindly hand on Sioned's shoulder. 'Thank you, my dears. I think it better that we talk later.'

Arthur visibly relaxed as the serving girls withdrew, and he looked around for his clothes. He could only see his belt, but hanging from a peg was a new linen undertunic and a robe of deep blue fringed with gold thread.

'Is this for me?'

'It is. We had to guess the size, but it should fit pretty well. You will find others in your room when we get there, in case you prefer a different colour.'

'Others? You mean I have more than two?'

'In my house you do. I'm afraid you will have to put up with one of my eccentricities while you are here — that is my unreasonable dislike of muck. We are princes of Britannia, not peasants or brigands of the roads and ditches. I want clothes that are clean and fresh, and I want those around me to have the same. The servants think it very peculiar, and almost inhuman. I think it is just pleasant and healthy.'

They finished dressing and walked back into the courtyard garden. Arthur had recovered his composure, but was not certain his temper or his respect for his elders would survive too many more surprises. It was not that he didn't like Sioned, he thought. Quite the opposite. But what was he meant to do in a situation like that? She had seen more of him than Branwen had ever been allowed to do – at least, since he was a boy – and he had seen enough of her to realise he might find it difficult to control himself if they were alone.

Myrddin turned right outside the door to the baths. 'I think we'll have a look at the study next,' he announced, 'since you will be spending most mornings in it with me over the next few months.'

Arthur groaned inwardly, but politely looked as interested as he could.

'There will be mathematics,' Myrddin went on, 'not to mention geometry, cosmology, astrology and botany, comparative religion, law – Britannian and Roman – the line of emperors, a little Greek, the theory of kingship, Aristotle and Plato and how to versify in public.' Myrddin stopped and looked down at his charge. 'Don't look so pale,' he said. 'It won't all be on the same morning.' He reached over to grasp a door handle set into the corner, then changed his mind.

'Maybe that's better left till tomorrow. Come into somewhere more comfortable,' he said, and led the way past the study door, turned left and entered a large chamber that seemed to occupy most of one side of the building.

It was not a hall as Arthur understood a hall should look. The walls were painted in reds and yellows, with scenes of idealised life – banquets and hunts, feasts laid out by peaceful springs, handmaidens dancing. A fire burned at either end and torches flared from ornate braziers against the walls. Between them were divans covered in red damask – a little threadbare, but grander than anything in Elfael – and in the centre of the room a fabulous mosaic was set into the floor. In each corner a different wild beast stood in pomp, while in the middle a woman, robed in the old Roman way, smiled up, her head wreathed in flowers. It was the finest room Arthur had ever entered, and he stood in the entrance humble and in awe.

Myrddin turned. 'What do you think?'

'What can I say?' he said.

'Well you could start by saying you like it.'

Arthur shook his head. 'That would just be stupid.'

'You mean you don't?'

'I mean it doesn't come close.' In truth, when he thought about it later, what most impressed him was not the richness of the decoration, nor the ingenuity of the great mosaic floor, but the fact that it was complete. He had known old buildings from the Roman times all his life, but they had always been ruined, or at best dilapidated, and used without any regard for how they should have been — walls dividing rooms into two, paint flaking from the walls, damp streaks bubbling behind the plaster. Here was a room as its artist had meant it to be, furnished and lit to give delight and comfort in equal measure. And equal measure was its key. Everything had proportion and complemented everything else. It was a room in balance, with only the shadows of the torch flames haphazard in the breeze from the windows and the sound of the fountain playing outside.

Myrddin led him further into the room and sat back on one of the divans, crossing his legs in contentment at Arthur's appreciation. 'Now we can eat well and properly, as it should be done — not out of wooden bowls in the filth of the farmyard.'

Arthur took his place on a divan by the opposite wall and relaxed as he studied the detail of the wall paintings. He saw Myrddin had closed his eyes for a moment, and Arthur too savoured the quiet. Even the wind seemed to creep about the palace corridors with well-trained respect for the ordered tranquillity Myrddin had constructed. They sat in comfortable silence, enjoying the rest at the end of their travels.

There was a rustle in the doorway and Arthur looked round to see a small procession enter. The dark-haired girl whom Myrddin had introduced as his ward Morganwy was in front, a step or two in front of Sioned and Seona, one carrying a silver dish of preserved fruits, the other a flagon and silver goblets. Behind them three men in purple tunics held out the main dishes of the welcome meal — a large bird trussed and browned on a dish of sliced apples held the central place of honour. To its left a fish, larger than any Arthur knew, lay as on the riverbed, but with roots and leaves, glazed and steaming, in the places of stones; to the right, a loin of beef, boneless and cleaned of fat, resting in a nest of late spring flowers.

To Arthur's surprise Myrddin stood and bowed to Morganwy with great ceremony. Not knowing what was expected of him, Arthur flushed pink and scrambled to his feet and copied Myrddin in a gawky imitation of his bow. Morganwy extended a languid arm and bade him sit as the food was placed on a low marble table at the foot of the couch which was placed like a throne against the furthest wall.

The men retreated and returned with smaller tables, which they put before Arthur and Myrddin, and deep finger bowls of minted water. A moment later Seona and Sioned were back with plates, knives and piles of flat bread. The plates were not the chipped and polished wooden ones of the Elfael hall, nor even the heavy pottery, riveted with repairs, which King Idriseg brought out on special occasions. Myrddin's feast would be on platters of eggshell white, with painted maidens in blue and pink floating around their rims trailing vines and roses. The girls and menservants bowed to Morganwy and Myrddin and withdrew.

Myrddin remained standing, waiting for a sign from Morganwy. Arthur looked confused, not only about what to do next, but also as to why Morganwy, not Myrddin, occupied the place at the head of the room.

At last Morganwy nodded, and Myrddin clasped his hands together, raising them in front and above his forehead. Arthur thought he would pray in the manner of the priests who occasionally passed through Elfael, sometimes looking to set up as hermits, sometimes travelling on a mission from Hibernia or Armorica, but increasingly fleeing from Barbarian atrocities in the east and north of Britannia. Myrddin had a different ritual in mind, however.

'An invocation,' he began. 'May we enjoy this food on behalf of our ancestors so that they may share it with us. May the spirits of this country lie quiet about this house. May our own gods protect and foster us. May our own spirits breathe in harmony. On this first night may our destiny be set. And may that destiny be kind, fruitful and mindful of our people's needs.'

With that he dropped his hands to his side and stood, eyes closed in concentration, for a moment. Then he placed a cup of wine on the floor in front of the tables of food, poured a little oil into it, unhooked one of the torches from its bracket, and set the torch to the cup. Flame flared green and orange from the fuelled wine. Myrddin waited until the fire had died, then lifted the cup and poured the remains of the mixture into an urn at the side of Morganwy's couch, then refilled it with wine. This time he raised his glass to Arthur.

'My friends, my children, my future,' he toasted. 'Let us eat better tonight than we shall in the months ahead, for there is work to be done. You may be the student now, Geraint, but Morganwy has gone ahead of you. Think of her as your predecessor graduating to be a queen.'

He took a long draught of wine. Morganwy stepped forward, kissed him on the forehead and pressed him back to his seat.

'You are sweet when you are being majestic,' she said, 'but we are famished, and the cooks have been preparing this for three days, so the least we can do is eat it hot. The lectures can wait for the morning.'

The food was as impressive as it looked. Morganwy served them with slivers of meat and boneless fish. Dishes of jelly and creams, sweetmeats and anchovies were presented and dispatched. Arthur was taken to bed that night by Sioned, filled with wine and salmon, goose, beef and honeyed fruits. He was too unsteady to mind when she undressed him and eased him into a carved bed of extraordinary softness. He was asleep before noticing that she had slipped naked in beside him. Nor did he wake when she slipped out again half an hour later, wondering whether she was disappointed or relieved.

VII

THROUGH THE WEEKS that followed Arthur remained Geraint, son of Idriseg of Elfael, and student of Myrddin of Moridunum. He soon found that the palace was almost a village in itself, despite the seclusion of the inner courtyard and the wonderful privacy of the rooms which surrounded it. Two outer courts flanked the main building, and within the stockade there were storehouses and byres, armouries and a smithy and a long, low shed Myrddin called his factory, and which seemed to be dedicated to making 'nothing in particular', as he put it — or more accurately the manufacturing of whatever idea of his which was felt to have passed the experimental and moved on to the prototype stage. A smaller shed behind it, Arthur discovered, housed the lingering remains of the failures – or, in Myrddin's words again, 'those ideas which need a little more work'. They lay in piles like a midden of great timber and metal beasts, a wheel here, a jagged edge there, inviting the speculation of some future scholar as to whether the Demetiae had astonishingly invented flying machines in the century that the Roman empire fell.

The outer courts had quarters for those who worked in the palace, some arranged like dormitories (one for men, one for women) and others two-roomed apartments for those that were married or who had children. Then there was the kitchen, the dairy, the cellar, the meat larder, the laundry and the wardrobe (which Arthur found not only made and mended clothes, but also restored the tapestries and furnishings Myrddin had salvaged on his travels). There were workshops for painting and gilding, a jeweller and, most fascinating, a pottery with its great kiln. There were days when the palace yards seemed to be a wall of heat as the kiln and the smithy, the kitchen and the jeweller, the factory, the laundry and the bath house all stoked their fires at once. By July Arthur could not wait to escape the dust and noise and either linger by the fountain or get out into the open countryside. There he would droop in the river, lazy and shallow after weeks without rain, or clamber on to the bare hilltops in search of wimberries with Sioned and Morganwy.

But that was for the afternoons, and the weekly day of rest which Myrddin always held on a Monday, partly to annoy the new priests, partly because it suited his mood and the day was the moon's. In the mornings there was study.

Arthur found he was not the only one under Myrddin's tutelage, and that Myrddin was not the only teacher. He insisted that all the children from the palace should be able to read and write, an unheard-of stipulation. He also invited any of the children – or anyone else who wished – from the surrounding area to attend, and a school room had been set up close to the outer wall. Here Bedr, one of Myrddin's old students, gave lessons in Latin and Brythonic (new as a written discipline, since the adoption of official Christianity had ended the prohibition on setting it down in literary form), logic, religion and history. Myrddin, apologetic that he could not be on hand more often, appeared occasionally to demonstrate whatever point seemed essential at the time; the art of combining substances, perhaps, or the rules of proportion, architecture, the stars, painting, poetry and music. When he taught, nobody was a servant or master, nobody young or old. He told them the world was only divided between the curious and those who thought they knew everything and were therefore no use at all.

Morganwy too, would take a few classes, though her arts were different. She taught a few of the older pupils the reading of signs in the air, the portents of the rain and wind, how to watch animals for the coming of storms or drought, how to scan the sky for birds that told of coming danger. She could pierce the veil of cloud before the moon and tell from its colour the progress of a child's birth. She had outstripped Myrddin as an apothecary, and knew not only how to find and prepare the extracts from plants and rocks to relieve pain and stem fever, but how to induce sickness and visions, increase the enjoyment of lovemaking or heal the wounds of war. For Myrddin much of this remained a mystery, and he often wondered whether she had learnt it in the years before she had come to him, whether she had discovered the knowledge herself through study and experiment, or whether (as she protested with an impish smile and a light in her eyes which Myrddin found disturbing and almost cruel) she had the gift of intuition and the power of her ancestors.

Morganwy seemed to have taken a special interest in Geraint. Although, in theory, he was only meant to join classes occasionally (since his education in Elfael had given him more than the basics of literacy, and he had learnt from his elders his fair share of weather forecasting), he quickly realised that Bedr and Morganwy were teaching at a different level. Outside class she would take him into the hills, sometimes at night. Once she blindfolded him and made him interpret the place, its past and its future, from the smells and sounds alone – what animals lived close by, which plants were strongest, what the wind would bring and what all those things said about who had cleared the land and the life of those who would settle there in years to come. For, she pointed out, people did not decide how and where to live by accident. Water and the soil, the shelter and the grazing, the slope and the strength of the rocks, the hunting and the fuel – all were elements which, if you could read them properly, could explain the pattern of life. Some sorcery, she explained, was a gift, like being able to sing. But most of it was about patience and humility, not guessing until the elements had revealed themselves and their properties had been cross-checked against the

CHAPTER VII

existing knowledge. When she told him this in the dust of the palace yard after class, it had seemed dull, dispassionate stuff, not the wizardry Arthur was beginning to think she possessed. But when she whispered it in a fold of the dark hills, his eyes covered, and her hands stroking his ears and lips, her soft voice urging him to scent the land and then pulling him to the ground so that it was not the earth that he was aware of but her as she guided every movement, then he could feel a strange new force invade his senses. She would laugh and break away then, tear off the blindfold and race him home.

One late summer evening, when they had eaten and were sitting in the garden, while Morganwy was describing how to use borage against melancholy, tansy for the digestion and feverfew for headaches, Arthur interrupted the flow of useful tips. He put an arm round her shoulder and she nestled against him.

'Who are you?' he asked. 'I mean, how did you come to be Myrddin's ward? Were you born round here?'

Morganwy looked up at him and frowned silently for a moment. 'If you don't know, then I can't tell you,' she said at last. 'All I can say is that my parents are dead, I was born a long way from here and I have been with Myrddin for a few years now, ever since it became too dangerous to stay at home. But at least I know who you are.'

Arthur was surprised, and for a moment unaccountably afraid. 'Do you?'

Morganwy frowned again. 'Yes, of course. You are Geraint of Elfael, and for some strange reason Myrddin has decided to groom you for great things. Though why he should pick a boy of your age from absolutely nowhere when he could have had any prince in Britannia or Armorica makes no sense to me. He's quiet barmy, I think, sometimes.'

'Me too,' Arthur grinned, 'in both things – I think he's a bit mad and I can't tell you more than you know. We shall have to be a mystery to each other.'

Morganwy reached for his hand and idly counted his fingers. 'It's fair that way,' she admitted, 'and I think mystery is better than knowledge, don't you?'

'You're the teacher.'

'So I am.' Morganwy broke away and stood up. 'So I am,' she repeated, strolling away. 'Maybe I should remember that and the four years between us.'

'Morganwy, I didn't mean…'

She was leaving. 'No, I know you didn't. But you were right, even if you didn't know what you were saying.' And she left Arthur staring at his feet, wondering if and how he had spoilt the evening.

* * *

Most mornings after the first month, when Bedr and Morganwy had reported on his state of knowledge and progress, Arthur spent with Myrddin in his study. This was the heart of the palace, with a great oak door, bolted at all times (even when they were working inside) opening on to the middle of the far side of the garden court. Alone of the rooms, it rose to a second storey, with shuttered windows on the upper floor that looked out across the country in all four directions. There were times, Myrddin explained, when he did not wish to rely on messengers to tell him who was arriving and where they were going when they had left.

Unlike the rest of the palace (in which proportion, cleanliness and unobtrusive order ruled), in the study spiders seemed to make their homes at will, and when the sun streamed through the windows, it did so through a thick filter of ancient dust. The rushes on the floor had not been moved for so long, they appeared to have merged with the terracotta tiles – fine in their age, and no doubt stripped from a grand abandoned villa in the rich south, but now brown with accumulated grime. On a great table downstairs scrolls and tablets, parchment and styluses were piled in cheery confusion, the perfect evidence of the way Myrddin's mind jumped from one idea and one reference to another. He was not a still thinker, pondering each step in the argument, placing each fragment of knowledge in its allotted place. He would rarely sit at the smaller table upstairs, studying a piece of writing and now and then making a tidy note. He would instead grab a document from here, a map from there, and scrawl an inspired memo to himself in a Latin or Greek shorthand, replete with connecting arrows, circles and underlinings, which would appear to future generations closer to runic cipher than the sketches of a learned classical scholar.

At the back of the ground floor a great case with evenly divided compartments, each labelled in gold with a Latin alphabet letter, stood between two fine bronzes. In them scrolls going back three centuries were stacked – copies of Cicero and Aristotle, Ovid and Tacitus, Pliny

CHAPTER VII   97

(a particular favourite of Myrddin's because of his Celtic origins) and Plautus. Arthur came to know them well, though he could not claim, to his slight embarrassment, ever to have read a scroll from one end to the other, except some of Plautus's plays, because he needed to know how they finished.

Dotted about the room were the smaller pickings from Myrddin's scavenging: glass jugs and amber cameos, votive figures from at least two dozen different cults, fragments of plates decorated with Dionysus and Hercules, a bronze tablet commemorating the recall of the Twenty-Third legion from Deva in the time of Hadrian, and pieces of ancient altar, one inscribed to the memory of an Ephesian merchant who, having braved the pillars of Hercules and the pirates off Armorica, had foundered with his cargo of olive oil off the coast of Dumnonia a hundred and eighty years before. Such was the irony of history that, although the story of his birthplace, voyage and demise was clearly legible, his name had been chipped away, except for the final 'cus'.

In pride of place, on a table of their own and held upright by two stone tigers, were five volumes bound in leather and tooled with precious metals. Such things were new to Arthur. He had seen scrolls, though in nothing like Myrddin's quantity, and had learnt to use a tablet – either a set of wooden ones, held together with leather thongs and waxed to giving a writing surface, or a slate, on which he could use either a sharp iron stylus or a piece of soft chalk. The five texts on Myrddin's shelf were totally different, though.

On the second morning Myrddin had explained. 'This is a relatively new invention, and as far as I know there are only a few – perhaps less than a hundred – in Britannia. It was just coming into fashion at the time of the overthrow of the magistrates, when my father was young. It's called a codex, and I must say it's far easier to use than one of the old scrolls, though it's heavy to carry around when you are travelling. It's expensive to make, too, and more difficult to copy into accurately. Here – be careful, but have a look.'

Arthur picked a volume from the middle of the row and ran his finger over the leather, inlaid with a filigree of silver. The two ends were held together with a delicate bronze clasp, and he unhooked it gently. Inside, the closely written Latin text began on each page with an extravagantly decorated letter, so florid that many were difficult to read.

Myrddin smiled. 'A good choice. You are going to have to read it over the summer, in any case.'

Arthur looked more closely at the opening lines: Gaius Suetonius Tranquillus, De vita Caesarum. 'You want me to read all of it?' he asked, trying not to sound too horrified.

'Every word,' said Myrddin. 'He's a good writer. You'll enjoy it once you get going. There's another reason, though. By the time you leave here you will have to have some understanding of what you are going to face if you do indeed find yourself elected. The best way I can help you is to teach you how others have gone about the task of uniting a factious and unruly nation. Yours is not an empire, but the distances involved are not small, and the problems will be much the same. You have to know how the great advances were achieved, but, perhaps more importantly, where the failures could have been avoided. Besides that, your Latin is awful. I don't want you to be one of those leaders who has to rely on priests and advisers in order to communicate with any other leader. You must be able to read the dispatches which come to you and draft your own replies. Even if the scribe fair copies it, you need to be able to check that he has written what you intended. Many wars have been fought because of bad secretaries. And if you are going to do all that, your Latin should be as polished as those that serve you.'

Arthur stared at the codex glumly. It might be good advice, but it was not his idea of a perfect morning. He soon discovered, though, that lessons with Myrddin were not all about ploughing through ancient Latin texts. For all that he venerated the civilisation of the empire, Myrddin was a Britannian man of learning, first and foremost. Looking back years later, Arthur realised that he had absorbed most of his learning not among the scrolls and charts, but on the upper floor of the study, where two comfortable chairs were placed, a jug of fruit cordial sat on a small table between them and the summer's heat was tempered by the breezes that coursed up the valley and through the tower windows. The ceiling was painted as a tribute to the heavens and the world itself, with the head of men, one in each corner, representing winter and spring and of women portraying summer and autumn. Above their heads at the centre Apollo rode in his golden chariot to the west, and on the eastern side, as though creeping over the horizon in the early evening, rose two stars and half the moon.

Myrddin would talk, but when he talked of history and the theory of power he did not talk in the dry way of Thucyidides or Plato, but as a bard, weaving the stories into a great narrative epic, part remembered from his own teachers, part impromptu, part composed and shaped before he went to sleep at night – he found that, if he recited his lines back to himself as his last conscious thoughts, they remained embedded the next morning and he could insert them into the day's work without difficulty.

First thing after breakfast, when Arthur had come in from his swordsmanship lesson and washed, he would climb to the eyrie and, without a word, settle himself at Myrddin's side. Myrddin would not seem to notice him – indeed, he barely seemed awake, his eyes hooded in concentration, his hands clasped across his ample stomach, and the stream of words would begin. Exactly an hour later, often in the middle of a couplet, he would stop, open his eyes, smile and reach over to pour himself a draught from the cordial jug. This first hearing would fascinate Arthur, but he retained very little of it, so from four to five in the afternoon Myrddin would repeat the episode and Arthur would be called after the evening meal to summarise as much as he could to those Myrddin assembled round the fountain or gathered under the colonnade if it was raining. At first Arthur found that he could retell only snippets of what he had heard, but as the weeks wore on, his powers of retention began to develop and he grew in confidence until the evening session would not be much shorter than the original and Myrddin's poetic cadences started to come naturally to his pupil. So it was not only the information that Myrddin taught Arthur, but the ebb and flow of metre, the architecture of rhetoric and the way to stitch the story together with rhyme.

The story itself was that of settlement and retreat, conquest and decline. He told how the peoples of Britannia had once not only been part of the empire, but had been part of an empire of their own which owed nothing to Rome. How 750 years before you would have been able to ride from the far north of Caledonia to the borders of Cappadocia, from the Pillars of Hercules to the shores of the northern sea, and still make yourself understood in one variant or another of the language of Gaul, whether it was Brythonic, Gaelic, Galician or Galatian. He explained how the horsemanship of their ancestors, newly equipped with iron swords, had swept all before them to the east. How the people of the ocean coast had traded and developed the language – the language of the sea – over three thousand years or more.

There was the story of the sack of Delphi, when the Celtic armies had threaded through the mountains from Macedonia, braved the thunder and the falling rocks as they escaped with the astonishing treasure left at the shrine of Apollo (and here he looked up at the figure on the ceiling in mute apology) and transported it across the continent from people to people until it finally came to southern Gaul, was looted by Roman rebel soldiers and sunk deep without trace in a sacred lake. There were the names of the great, Cunobelinos – Overlord in the reign of Augustus, when Britannia was still independent and whose great capital became the city of Camulodunum – and Boudicca of the Iceni, the butcher of Londinium. There was Molmutius and Brennos, Dumnorix of the Aedui and Orgetorix of the Helvetii and Leir, son of Bladud. So many of them had the same story in common: a story of valiant resistance against the overwhelming forces of Rome or the Barbarians from the east. And in the middle of each attempt to hold the territory in Celtic hands arose the almost inevitable divisions and treachery that allowed the outsiders to prevail.

Anybody becoming Overlord of Britannia would face very much the same quest, to secure the freedom and prosperity of the country without allowing it to disintegrate into civil war once the external threat appeared to have been removed. The threat, Myrddin assured him, would always be there, even if all seemed quiet.

'Britannia is a rich island,' he said, 'and there will always be those who are prepared to fight their way on to its land.'

Arthur would at least have the advantage that there were no longer Roman legions to face, with their relentless tactics, their utter ruthlessness to those who did not surrender and their siege machines and artillery which had destroyed every great hilltop defence in Europe. Those defences which had awed generations of undisciplined warriors had never held out for more than a few weeks against the ballista and the tortoise – and the deliberate spread of fire and disease which the legions had employed just as much as the sword. How ironic it was, Myrddin said, that after those extraordinary centuries when no forces could resist the naked warrior of the Celts, and the equal number of centuries when Latin had become the language of government,

CHAPTER VII 101

both Rome and the Celts were now back where they started. Only in Gallicia and Armorica, Hibernia and Britannia could you be sure of hearing the old tongues, and only in the countryside of Latium itself and the houses of the new religion could Latin be said to be secure.

The greatest mistake, he argued time and time again, was to defend a position when only attack could bring a victory. That, above all, was the lesson far too few of the chiefs and kings remembered, and it had always cost them dear. When they were on the move, advancing and attacking as they went, they had had the ascendancy. When they settled down in their fortified compounds and waited for new, hungry aggressors to come to them the result was inevitable: comprehensive and brutal defeat. Too often, at the moment when it seemed the defences had held out, petty squabbles within their own ranks, little dynastic disputes about limited power, had brought treachery, and with it destruction. Those not killed were enslaved or subjugated. A general had to kill at least five thousand to merit a triumph through the streets of Rome. They made sure their numbers were indisputable.

Attack before you are attacked. Remove the chance of treachery by acting firmly but without causing resentment to build up. Avoid revenge. Make sure you know more about your enemies than they know about you. Remember that if you have power it is a burden and a duty, not a right.

Be aware that it will be incomprehensible to those without power that someone who has it might not want it. If you are without power you have nothing, but if you have it there is little to enjoy. These were the themes that emerged from the poetry that Myrddin recited morning after morning until Arthur found himself wondering why he was being prepared for such a miserable existence – one of blood and betrayal, the meaningless possession of territory and the seizure of lives. He had been happy in the misty hills of Elfael. He was happy this summer in Myrddin's exotic palace with too much to do and the company of Sioned and Morganwy and the men and women of the Demetiae. He found their accent as quaint as they found his, but the teasing didn't hurt. He had come to love the luxury of the baths after a day of study and exercise; to marvel at the skill of the harpist as he improvised; to wonder at the details of the painted rooms, the mosaics and the statuary that stood with such disguise about the garden and, with the whimsical brilliance which seemed to come so naturally to

Myrddin, in the bushes and thickets of the hillside where it could be glimpsed suddenly as your gaze wandered through the upper study window.

There had never been a summer like it. Though he knew he was learning at a pace he would never have thought possible, there seemed to be no work that his father, Idriseg, would have called work. He listened to Myrddin's narration, experimented with Morganwy, fell in love with Sioned (though Myrddin instructed her to return to her own quarters at night, an injunction he did not observe with his red-haired Seona), followed the practical sense of Bedr's lessons, improved his Latin, began on Greek and came to understand as much of the geography of the world, he felt, as if he had marched to Nubia and back.

There were days when he rose at dawn to go hunting, learning to ride over the roughest terrain with confidence that, with the pressure of his knees and the twitch of his fingers on the rein, he could master his horse. He had already become a good tracker in the forests of Elfael, but he was taught to track humans with the accuracy he had previously reserved for hares and boar. In the clear meadows by the river half a mile from the ramparts he mastered bowmanship, and could hit the centre of the cabbage set up as a target either from his station at forty yards or on horseback from twenty.

Some nights Myrddin would wake him after only two or three hours' sleep and lead him to the roof of the northern bastion, where even the dwindling lights from the evening's fires could not pierce the dark. They would map the heavens in their minds, reading off the constellations, discussing what the rising of one or the ebbing of another might mean for a child born in Moridunum in the morning, and whether the star that fell through Leo to Arthur's gasps of excitement portended great success or tragedy, or nothing at all. Myrddin argued for tragedy; Arthur declared that something so spectacularly beautiful could not bring other fortune than the best.

On one point, though, Myrddin was insistent. When, towards the end of August, a new comet began to climb from the southern horizon, a shiver went through him as he picked out its new form, the unknown body in a constellation too small for there to be any mistake, and he forecast that nothing good could come from such an invader. The more he scoured the stars for corroborative evidence, the more agitated he became, and when Arthur asked him quietly what all the fuss was about, instead of explaining gently, as he did throughout their vigils together, he stomped down from the walls with an oath and stalked back to the main building. Arthur shrugged his shoulders and turned his attention back to the comet. He could just make out the streaming tail, though he could barely see any movement. He admitted to himself that he was thrilled, but a little disappointed as well. When Myrddin had told him of the phenomenon he had expected something much bigger and faster – a giant of a star traversing the night sky as fast as a bird, trailing great white feathers and eclipsing anything it passed. Instead all he could make out was a slightly misshapen star among all the others – hardly a glorious addition to the firmament, and certainly not one which could signal doom on the scale Myrddin was proclaiming. He would have been surprised to see Morganwy turn white with terror when Myrddin strode into her room, shook her awake and told her what he had seen and where. A moment later she was crying in his arms as he tried to comfort her and retreat from the forecasts he had shouted. Myrddin loved Morganwy, but he tended to think of her as his partner in learning, and there were times when he forgot that she was his orphan ward and a troubled girl not yet twenty.

After that night nothing settled as it had before. The three months since Arthur had arrived began to take on the air of a perfect interlude before reality barged in again; a golden time recalled through a haze of regret. Myrddin was irritable and inclined to complain about the pace of everything, especially Arthur's mastery of politics and theories of war.

Morganwy changed, too, though it was hard to say how. She would cling to each of them in turn, some days closeting herself with Myrddin for hours, after which she emerged calmer but with a frown and hardly a civil word; on others she would latch on to Arthur as he emerged from fighting practice and pretend to be teaching any obscure point that came into her head, while actually talking about nothing very much, skipping from one digression to another and absently tearing the petals from unlucky flowers she had wandered past. More irritatingly, as far as he was concerned, she would often appear when he was deep with Sioned. Loafing, Myrddin called it, and Morganwy would butt in and start talking as though Sioned didn't exist, which might have reflected their difference in rank, but did nothing to endear Morganwy to Arthur. It was as though she was trying to drive them apart. Sioned and Arthur would look at each other with mutual desperation while Morganwy carried on her irrelevant monologue. Eventually Sioned would touch Arthur's arm, he would shrug and she would disappear.

Through all this Arthur himself was changing. His body was expanding as fast as his mind. He was not only growing upwards – at least a finger's length, Sioned estimated – but outward, as his shoulders broadened and his legs thickened. A combination of Myrddin's excellent kitchen and the daily weapons training was building him fast. The last vestiges of treble voice vanished, and with them his boyish rituals before sleep. He rarely thought of Caradoc, except in a vague way, wondering how they compared now. But his new veneer of sophistication, his angular strength, made him seem a different lad from the one who had followed Myrddin out of the hills little more than a few dozen weeks before. It was hard to imagine a life outside the palace, with its industrious routine and unparalleled comfort. Then, late one morning at the end of September, a messenger rode in, spent two hours delivering his intelligence to Myrddin and, receiving the reply, rode off, heading north.

VIII

'You will need your sword back soon,' Myrddin observed, as they talked after the meal that evening. 'We leave for Corinium next week.'

'Already?' Arthur asked. He had thought that the prospect of completing his studies and finding out if all Myrddin's forecasts were more than dreams would be a relief. In the event he found that leaving the security of the palace, its luxuries and antiquated splendour, held no attraction at all.

'The election is still called for All Hallows (as they've started calling the Feast of Spirits), but it seems the various camps are already assembling, hoping to manoeuvre their faction into position. I think that's a mistake. I think we should not declare until the last possible moment, and then appear as the obvious compromise. But we need to know what we're up against. That messenger came direct to me from Dobunnia. They wanted me to let them know whether I would be attending, and in what capacity. I sent him back with the news that I would be there, and that I would not be the elector for Demetia; I would be an impartial observer. Nevertheless, I sent the messenger via the borders of Elfael with instructions for Idriseg to join us, either at the ford or at Magnis in ten days' time.'

Arthur nodded. There was not much he could say. Myrddin made the decisions. He would follow along as he was told. 'What do I have to do till then?' he asked.

'Carry on as normal – except I think we'll stop the formal lessons from tomorrow, unless you particularly want to carry on. You've made as much progress as I had hoped – rather more, in fact. I think I can safely present you in Corinium as the most literate of the candidates, if not the most senior, and certainly the least expected. In the mean time you might as well enjoy yourself while you can – though I want you in good shape. You must carry on the battle training. Things may get a bit gladiatorial before they are decided.'

Arthur was not sure what was meant by that, but he was certain he did not like the sound of it. 'You mean I may have to fight my way through the election?' he asked.

'I hope not, but we'll see. There are plenty of people besides you for whom this is a once-in-a-lifetime opportunity, and they are not going to pack up their tents and go home without a fight. Whether it is actual or just political will depend on the mood, I suspect. So, as I said, you'll need your sword back.'

The sword Arthur had pulled from the stream had been confiscated by Myrddin as they had first approached the palace. It was too conspicuous a trophy, he had said, and would immediately raise suspicions about his identity, especially if the enigmatic inscription was spotted. Instead he had hidden it among his own belongings and hung it on the wall of his study – another piece in his collection of empire memorabilia.

Now Arthur was allowed to take it down and handle it again – not just for inspection (or to play with, Myrddin goaded), as he had at home. After several months training in swordsmanship, with the long sword of the cavalry man, the knee-length weapon of the Britannian warrior and the Roman legionary's short stabber, he was a competent wielder of a blade, though the most he had ever cut with one was a haunch of beef and a sack of straw. His sword, he now realised, was somewhere in between; an all-battle blade long enough for using on a horse, short enough for close combat. It was strange to feel the hilt again and to draw it from its new scabbard. Something had changed, though Arthur was not sure whether it was in the sword itself or him. It seemed lighter, almost delicate, compared to the heavy iron practice weapons in the yard. He had forgotten the elaborate tracery along the blade, the intricacy of the lines that wove in and out of each other yet formed a united pattern – a metaphor, Myrddin said, for the forces that made a successful army or the elements that held together the state. The inscription was still there – of course, thought Arthur, and then realised how easily it had changed its message when it had first come into his hands; it could just as easily have changed its loyalties again.

Arthur fingered the edge. It would have to go to the armourer for sharpening before it was ready to take into battle, he thought, and shivered as the idea of battle rose before him. He had spent all his life so far avoiding a real fight. That he would inevitably have to join one soon – indeed, that his principal role for years to come would be to force and survive the slaughter – was repugnant, and he was surprised that it was repugnance rather than fear that came over him. He let the sword fall in his relaxed hand so that the grip and thrusting angle came naturally to him, as he had been taught. Whatever his misgivings, it was at least beginning to feel like his sword, rather than one he was borrowing from Myrddin's stock. Though he had worn it on the trek from the borders of his own country to Demetia – except for a mile or so either side of the towns – he had not flaunted it openly, and he wondered when he would be allowed to buckle it on for the first time in public. Patiently he replaced it in the scabbard and hung it back in its place on the wall.

With no lessons and no preparation to be done for Bedr, Arthur had time on his hands in that last week before they set out for Corinium. He hung around the workshops and the storerooms, looking at nothing in particular, but absorbing the techniques of making and mending, creating and restoring that harboured under Myrddin's roof. When it wasn't raining (which was not often) he read in the garden. When it was, he lounged on one of the couches by the fire or mooched about under the covered quad, watching the water soak the remains of the summer's herbs. He helped with the apple gathering on fine days – not just apples, but quinces and pears, rowan berries, wild damsons and medlars. The dog roses were raided for their hips and the crab apples and hazelnuts harvested. Every edible and medicinal fruit and leaf was carefully sorted and allotted its place, the bruised fruit for cheeses, jellies and wines, others for pickles and drying, the best for storage under straw, the herbs for infusions. There were expeditions into the woods to drag back, cut and split logs for the winter, expeditions when all the men went to fell and hoist, strip branches from the copses to weave for wicker, shape into spears and arrow shafts or put aside to season. There were dedications and libations, prayers of thanks when a new crop was found, disappointed explanations when a favoured bush turned barren. There were the first bonfires of the year and the first tastings and the filching of fruit that had to be sampled fresh from the tree amid all the pious industry.

He helped not just to be helpful – though it was true that this had always been his favourite time of year, when everyone was busy and the plenty dispelled the terrors of the coming winter – but mainly he was helpful because it kept him close to Sioned.

Myrddin seemed to encourage them, which was embarrassing; and Arthur thought that he had shown no sign of great interest. Sioned had averted her eyes, but not far or often enough. When they were in the same place there was no great demonstration of affection, and they barely spoke, but there were other signs: the way the horseplay would stop, the way they took twice as long to do the things they had been rushing through five minutes before, the way they never answered a question the first time unless it was from each other.

One afternoon Myrddin watched them from the gate as they carried baskets of apples towards him up the hill from the orchard. He smiled, clasped Seona about the shoulders more tightly and kissed her auburn head. Then he watched them again, more intently this time, suddenly aware that he was about to end whatever it was that they were discovering, that this would be the first and last carefree harvest of Arthur's life, if everything went according to plan. Perhaps, though, there would be no great triumph in Corinium. Perhaps the Council would pour scorn on his arguments for electing a boy only just turning sixteen to the highest responsibility in the land – whoever his parents had been (and there were plenty in the Council who had no great love for Pendraeg or any of his sons). Then they could just come home, and Sioned would have her obscure Geraint, Prince of Elfael. They could even stay where they were while Myrddin took his place at the Council, helping Morganwy run the palace, with Arthur continuing his studies through the winter. He was able enough to profit from it, and Myrddin would have been happy to adopt him as he had adopted Morganwy.

Seona nuzzled closer. He looked down at her, distracted from Arthur for a moment, then felt a breath of wind and a drop of rain on his cheek and glanced up at the clouds gathering in the sky to the northwest. The first of the season's storms was brewing. He was about to turn away when a movement on the stockade bastion at the far corner to his right, the north, caught his eye. It was Morganwy, he saw, wrapped tight in a black cloak, despite the mildness of the autumn dusk, her dark hair blowing free across her face in the gathering evening breeze. She too was gazing at Arthur and Sioned, he saw, her hands gripping the balustrade tighter, as though fighting not to fall. Below them all Arthur too looked up, laughed to Sioned and waved. Myrddin raised his arm in greeting, frowned, let his other arm drop from Seona's shoulders and turned inside. Morganwy was soon following, as though something in the wind, the sudden change, had thrown the tranquil scene in the valley into a disarray which only they could see.

* * *

The last two days were spent in preparation for the journey. Myrddin had hardly appeared during the week except when a meal had been imminent, and even then only when summoned. For the rest he kept to his study and would answer no questions, except from those coming from Morganwy, and she was as tight with information as he was.

Arthur had been given two new tunics and a cloak fit for the gathering of the great in Corinium. New leather was measured and stitched for his feet, a new sword belt and buckle cut and fitted. Sioned even trimmed his hair, despite his protests, and he savoured his visits to the bath chamber, knowing that it was a luxury he would be lucky to find in such perfect order anywhere else in Britannia. He ate furiously, suddenly aware of the superb cooking in Myrddin's house, and realising that the rough forage of the road was going to be hard to get used to again.

Myrddin decided to hold a feast the night before they were due to set out, partly as a gesture to the neighbourhood in celebration of the fact that at last a Great Council was to be held, and with it the

CHAPTER VIII

prospect of a return to something like decent government, partly because he would be away from home for the new and old Feast of the Spirits, and so felt it would be proper to honour the household with festivities a few days early. Arthur wondered whether Myrddin would choose the evening as the moment to abandon the fiction of Geraint, but in the event nothing was said, except that Myrddin, in his rather longer than necessary speech towards the end, asked them all to raise their cups of wine to his future, and assured him that they had all enjoyed having such a distinguished Prince of Elfael among them for the summer. There were plenty of other excuses given for the raising of cups – twin sons born at a homestead further down the valley, a reasonable if not outstanding harvest, no sign of raiders in the area for over a year (though there had been reports of a short but bloody battle on the coast – so there was a raising of glasses to the courage of the victims), the memory of Dumnonian and Hibernian visitors after Easter, the acquisition of some excellently undamaged sculpture from an abandoned house in Viroconium and, most of all, the safe delivery of the wine itself, a fine shipment of the best the Bituriges could supply from Burdigala in Aquitania. This required toasts to the sailors, the country and the fraternal links with the Bituriges themselves.

By the time Arthur stood at the inner door of the palace in his unaccustomed role as visiting dignitary bidding goodnight to the guests, he was not completely sure how to keep his feet and body still at the same time. He mumbled pleasantries and was a little too effusive in his farewells to the friends he had made in Bedr's class – but then, they were in no better condition than he was.

When Myrddin had seen the last of all but the immediate household safely on their way, and the outer and inner doors securely fastened, he clapped his hands together in relief that the feast had gone well and he could now relax and, to disapproving looks from the abstemious Bedr, hauled Arthur, Morganwy and two or three stragglers back to the fireside for, as he put it, 'a last look at the amphora'.

It was well into the night by the time Morganwy and Sioned pulled Arthur up between them and guided him like a pair of shepherds to his room. Sioned was dismissed and Morganwy undressed him tenderly as he mumbled apologies; she helped him to his bed, blew out the lamp and went back to Myrddin. She thought she might have to perform the same service for him, but he was as much master of his mind when drunk as when sober, and besides, Seona made it clear by unmistakable flashes of her green eyes that, whatever sentimental endearments Myrddin offered his ward, Seona would be in charge for the rest of the night. Finally the last libations were made, the torches were doused and only the sound of the fountain was left to disturb the quiet of the palace courtyard.

It was another hour before Sioned had the courage to steal out of the room she shared with Seona (who spent more nights with Myrddin than not) and two other high-born captives. She moved stealthily round the colonnade and into the door that led on the right to Morganwy's and on the left to Arthur's rooms. She turned to the left and, as quietly as she knew how, eased the iron latch up and pushed. Nothing happened. She pushed harder. There could be no doubt. The door was bolted on the inside. She laid the latch back down again and, crying with disappointment, crept back to her own room.

The door was bolted because she had not been the first to make the journey that night. Arthur was asleep almost as soon as Morganwy had left him and heard nothing of the opening and bolting of the door forty minutes or so later. He didn't wake either when the hanging corner of his woollen blankets were lifted and a body slipped in beside him. He woke gently, as gently as the kisses on the side of his neck and the stroking between his legs, a feeling he had never had before. He wondered for a moment how drunk he must be to be dreaming this, the caress of Sioned's lips, the tug of her fingers. He half-turned on to his back and passed his hand into the long hair that cascaded over him. He felt the response as she moved up to find his lips and slide the tongue tip between them. It was all new, and he wanted to grab and seize charge fast and furiously, but he had too much alcohol in him for anything to happen with speed, just as the girl knew, and she took her time and pleasure. Only when she was ready and he could do nothing consciously any more did she move on top of him, forcing him to go at her pace. Eventually she cried out and rolled over on to her back, pulling Arthur round with her so that they kept joined and she let him move and push with all the vigour he wanted to until the drink, the satisfaction and exhaustion brought him to a stop. The girl drew him down to her and held him for a while until he slept again. Still she stayed, holding him tight against her breasts, listening to his breathing as he went beyond dreams into the deepest part of sleep.

CHAPTER VIII

There was the first hint of the night's black turning to grey outside the shutters when Morganwy at last released him, let him slip off on to the bed, unbolted the door and skipped naked back to her own room with a mingled sense of achievement, loss and unease. The dawn was fully broken by the time she had relived the night, worried and exulted alternately, and was ready to sleep.

Arthur woke soon after, feeling ill and strangely elated at the same time. The illness he could account for; his head ached and his mouth was dry. Where the elation came from was harder to understand. Then he remembered his dream and smiled. He threw off his bed coverings and headed for the bath. Later, as Sioned massaged away the hangover, he told her about his dream, though not in as much detail as he remembered it. He was amazed when, turning to her as her fingers finished their work on his back, he found the tears streaming down her cheeks. He thought he must have gone too far, suggesting lovemaking she found horrible, and when he apologised was even more confused as she ran distraught from the room. Even this was outdone by his bafflement when, meeting Morganwy as he headed for the hall, she kissed him a fond good morning and patted his behind.

* * *

The morning was still young when Myrddin assembled the travellers in the yard and declared them ready to leave. Sioned and Morganwy both gave Arthur lengthy and sorrowful farewells, and Myrddin was seen off dutifully. He was no longer the shabby wanderer who had appeared in Elfael, nor the palace aristocrat with exquisite antiquarian tastes. He was dressed as a warrior of his people, and he rode the best horse he could find in some of the best horse country of Demetia. They were not retracing their furtive steps on foot. Myrddin wanted to let people know he was passing through on matters of state. So, as well as Arthur, they rode with ten others: a half-brother of Myrddin's from the country south of Moridunum (who was deputising for their aged and infirm uncle as the formal representative of the Demetiae) and his two sons, five men of the valley and two of Myrddin's household to manage the supplies. The baggage contained skins of wine (though not the best, Myrddin assured Arthur, with a hint of grandeur), new knives, swords and shields from the armoury carried spare as barter goods for food along the way.

The aim was to reach Corinium on the morning of the fourth day. They could reach it sooner, but Myrddin did not want to show undue haste, and he wanted to give himself time to gather information on the road. He had every intention, too, of arriving in Corinium as part of a larger contingent representing the middle peoples of Britannia Prima.

By evening on the first day they had reached Cicutio, which they found even more miserable than it had been when they passed through in early summer. The weeds had remained uncut, and there were only a few people about – hardly enough to justify its status as an important junction of the main two roads traversing the far west of the country and the border between Demetia and Siluria. The storm, which had been threatening for two days, caught up with them as they arrived, and it was with gratitude that they found a building with its roof intact and enough wood lying around for a good fire.

The wind had died down in the morning, but the rain was still driving down out of the mountains by the time they set out again. Though the route was easier, it was also more open, and they wished they had the tree cover away from the riverbanks. There was no sign of Idriseg and his company as they crossed the river by the ford at the Elfael border, though damp and disheartened guards told them he had sent word that he had decided to escape as much of the weather as he could by leaving later, and that they would meet at Magnis. Myrddin nodded and rode on. It suited him just as well not to delay. The rain had eased to half-hearted drizzle, but it managed to wet them thoroughly enough.

In the event there was a shout behind them on the road just before they left the last of the hills behind them and reached the plains which marked the beginning of the country of the Dobunni. Arthur looked back, let out a yelp of joy and urged his horse to a gallop back along the road. 'Caradoc!' he cried.

'Geraint!' Caradoc replied.

The boys drew up their horses together and sat grinning at each other until the rest of Caradoc's party arrived at a steadier pace.

Idriseg looked his foster-son up and down and then turned solemnly to Caradoc. 'No, boy. This isn't Geraint. This is some giant Myrddin has summoned out of the forests. And look at the clothes on him. Geraint never travelled in such good stuff.'

'But Father…' Arthur protested, and the old man smiled.

'How are you, boy? It looks as though the Demetians have been feeding you, which is more than I thought they would have the sense to do.'

'It's been amazing,' he replied.

'I should hope so too. If Myrddin doesn't amaze you, no one will.'

Idriseg had brought twice the number of Myrddin's men, and it was a good-sized party that made its way to Magnis that night. They found better lodgings than they had at Cicutio, and the rain had given way to a warm and perfect autumn day when they remounted on the third morning. With thirty men in the group it was deemed a matter of courtesy for officials of the Dobunni to escort them to the next halt, Glevum. There, they were told, they would be joined by the embassy of the Silures, numbering a further sixty men, with representatives from Venta and Isca.

With Caradoc and Myrddin, Arthur rode behind the emissary of the Demetiae, the King of the Silures and King Idriseg, the three senior men in their western force.

So it was that Arthur arrived in Corinium in the early afternoon at the end of October 473.

IX

THE FORUM AT CORINIUM was not the spectacular centre of commerce and government it had been in its glory days, but for this great election the Council of Dobunnia had done its best to clear up the worst of the rubble and the weeds from the piazza. The roof of the old basilica had too many holes in for comfort, and only one or two of the shops along the inside of the colonnade still functioned, and these mainly with shoddy goods on trestle tables. But Myrddin was as much amused as pleased to see that the inn on the eastern side of the forum, which had served the capital of Britannia Prima since Hadrian's time, still flourished, though the beer was watery and the thin, acid wine expensive. It must have been, he reflected, one of the last places in the country to take coins, however clipped and of whatever age. 'Proud but quaint' was the best that could be said for the bar, though it had had to move with the times and accept any barter which customers were prepared to offer.

To Arthur, the disappointment was crushing. After the manicured splendour of Myrddin's palace, the dilapidated tragedy of once-great Corinium was a painful shock. He had expected a bustling city, almost Rome itself. Instead he found a largely deserted shell, inhabited only by those families too stubborn to leave and one or two officials pretending to keep the offices of the kingdom working as they had done since the time of Corio himself, more than four hundred years before. Away from the forum the old market was abandoned, and the workshops, the mint, the sculptor and mason's yards, the boarding houses and town residences of provincial grandees were left open to the sky and the limestone mud which washed in from the untended streets. Only Caradoc was impressed, never having seen stone buildings of such size in any state of repair.

'Have we become so hopeless?' Arthur asked Myrddin in despair.

The older man shrugged. 'It has been going downhill for a long time, but the real damage was done thirty years ago – nothing to do with Barbarians. Ambrosius was always fully in charge here. It was disease which achieved this. People moved out of the town for safety and never came back. By the time they could have done, things had changed. There was neither the trade nor the will. The great families had nothing to come into Corinium for, except to pay their taxes, and it was easier to make the collectors come to them once the tax was counted in goods rather than money.'

'The boy's right, though,' said Idriseg, as they rode through the quagmire that pretended to be the Via Fossa. 'It's worse than it was even in Uther Pendraeg's time. I was here ten years ago, and you could still get a room in a proper house then, even if the town was quieter than it should have been. Bloody shame.'

The various delegations had made their own arrangements to accommodate them for the week leading up to the Great Council. Some camped outside the old walls, suspicious of the city, feeling that they were too much under the control of their hosts there. Others garrisoned themselves further away still, finding farms along the main roads or hiding in secluded valleys. At Myrddin's command, the western contingent of Silures, Demetiae and the southern Cornovii decided to stay together, to accept the goodwill of the Dobunni and base themselves in the best of the remaining houses within the city gates. Their hosts had made a considerable effort to make the old buildings habitable, but it took two days of strenuous housework before Myrddin was prepared to agree that the rooms were fit for leaders of their nation. It was not just a passion for tidiness, he explained. The Ordovices, Brigantes, Dumnonii, Cantiaci and Catuvellauni were all known to be preparing candidates. He wanted three conditions at least from his headquarters: he wanted to be close enough to the forum to hear the rumours before they spread out to the country; he wanted any of the opposing leaders, arriving cold, wet and muddy from their outlying camps, to be intimidated by the sophistication of the westerners' arrangements; and he wanted to be able to count on his forces being able to move in fast if the Council broke up in turmoil.

As the week went on and life became established in the makeshift apartments they had cleared for themselves, Arthur noticed a change in Myrddin's behaviour. In Elfael Arthur had known him as the stranger with the forces of nature at his command, a man of lights and winds, changing colours and impossible stories. On the road he had been the leader, the guide and mentor. Outside Moridunum he had been the great Prince of Demetia, the comfort-loving connoisseur and scholar. But in Corinium he changed again, back to the role, Arthur decided, that he must have played at the Armorican court of Constans and Uther in his youth, with the exception that he was now a man of the Council in his own right. At one level he was the perfect courtier, acknowledging the superior rank of those who could claim the title of king; on another level he became the pole around which everyone moved, a man with a word for all, advice and information for the great, gossip for his equals, crisp and decisive orders for those in the combined entourage of the kings of the west. Arthur was seeing, he realised, one of the great practitioners of the political arts at work, a man who had studied the rhetoric of Cicero and practised the old senatorial skills of Rome in an age when the sword and poison usually spoke louder than debate. He would take one man by the shoulder, another by the hand. He would bow in homage or incline his head in curt acknowledgement. He would whisper confidentially as though his listener was the most important fixer in the future of the island. He would rally a throng around him and mesmerise them with the flow and temper of his argument.

Arthur wondered which Myrddin would serve him if the election was won. For the time being he might have been invisible. Idriseg and

Myrddin moved among the magnates, exploring candidates, discussing the increase of Barbarian raids, deploring the incursion of foreign settlers following their war bands into the lands of the south coast. There was the question of whether the Votadini from beyond Hadrian's Wall would attend or whether they would be pre-occupied with their perennial struggle against the peoples north of their fortress at Dunedin. So Caradoc and Arthur explored what was left of the city, joining up with a few lads of their own age who had managed to tag along with the main party from various Dobunnian settlements on the road.

Occasionally they ventured out of the city walls into the rich open country. A little way back along the Via Fossa to the west they found the old amphitheatre, far better preserved than the silted-up houses and damaged temples of Corinium within the walls. Weeds and grass covered most of the seats, though, their wooden planks rotting. In the arena there were no gladiators or players and no space for the boys to play out their fantasies of confronting great beasts or facing death with a trident in their hands. Instead they found the embassy of the Brigantes camped, tearing up the seats for firewood, complaining loudly about the hospitality of the southerners, comparing their meagre billet with how an important delegation such as theirs would have been welcomed in the north. Despite the taunts, though, the amphitheatre was as sensible a camp as anywhere, close to the old town but not inside it, and with the high turf banks and narrow entrances making useful and ready-made defences if fighting broke out. There were plenty who predicted that it would.

The Council had been called to start on the Friday, with the election itself to take place on the Saturday, the eve of the spirits in the old religion – much the same in the new, it seemed to most of those uncommitted, one way or the other. That would allow the new overlord to be presented to the assembled forces on the Sunday, appropriately the Feast of Fire, so that the celebrations could take place in an auspicious climate before the business of establishing the regime began.

By Thursday it transpired that Myrddin's strategy of lodging himself at the centre of town and speaking confidentially to everybody of note had paid off. He took Arthur to one side and murmured with pride that he, as former counsellor to Uther Pendraeg and a confidant of Constans of Armorica, as well as a Prince of Demetia (Arthur quickly felt Myrddin hardly needed to remind him of all this), had been nominated by at least five kings to act as Presiding Consul to the discussions and the election. Still he had told nobody, of course, that he had a surprise candidate himself ready to emerge at the appropriate moment.

Arthur knew he should have been flattered to receive these confidences, but they left him uneasy. He began to doubt something in Myrddin's motives. Was he genuinely intending to present Arthur as the only person, the true son of Uther Pendraeg and Ygraen, who could unite fractious Britain against a ruthless enemy, or was he enjoying himself too much in a game of political finesse which would install him back in the inner chambers of power he had become accustomed to? Arthur, for the first time since the night on the hill above the camp at Elfael, when he had seen the hand of the dead chieftain raised to greet him, felt alone and without control of his own fate.

He congratulated Myrddin without much enthusiasm, but it hardly mattered. Myrddin had already moved off, his eyes catching sight of someone over Arthur's left shoulder to whom he could bring the news with the same air of a great secret of state being imparted. Arthur frowned and ambled off, wandering the streets. He went through one of the open porticoes into an abandoned building. A thick layer of earth covered the floor and grass was flourishing, despite the meagre light that filtered through into the further recesses. A statue of Demeter lay in two pieces where it had fallen from an apse in the wall. Absently Arthur picked it up and tried to balance the portions back in their rightful place. They wouldn't stand up, so Arthur laid the bottom half back where he had found it and left the head and torso in its niche. Better half a goddess in working order than none at all.

His eyes were growing accustomed to the gloom, and he peered through a doorway, its stone lintel cracked and sagging alarmingly, into the room beyond. He was not the first to have been this way, he noticed. There were footmarks in the dirt that covered the fine pavement. The room was bare except for a pair of rusting torch braziers hanging forlornly from the walls beside the door. But as his eyes adjusted to the half light, Arthur could make out the remains of fine paintings on a red background, nymphs still dancing with their garlands about them under a coat of mould.

There was another door in front of him, and the gloom seemed even more dense beyond it. The footsteps led on through and, for want of anything better to do, he followed. He found himself in a much smaller room but higher, its walls bare of decoration except for a Christian symbol, a chi-rho, painted neatly on the back wall, as though its very plainness gave it solemnity. Two thirds of the way into the room, in line with the door, there stood an altar of white stone, its surfaces polished to the sheen of marble. It was plain on the side facing the entrance, but Arthur found a cryptic inscription carved on the back. Strange, he thought, to go to all the trouble of carving a message and then to align it with the back wall. then he saw the scuff marks on the floor and realised the altar had been turned round deliberately, and recently, so that it was its plain façade that was presented to anybody entering. He examined it closely, intrigued as to why someone should bother to manhandle such an unwieldy relic in the chapel of an abandoned house – and not a particularly important one either, compared to the grand mansions he had seen elsewhere in Corinium.

In the top of the stone a deep cut had been made, so deep and yet so thin that it must have been drilled steadily and laboriously with a fine iron bit. No normal stone-splitting tool would have been able to make such a fine incision. It was about the width of a woman's hand. Examining it more closely Arthur found there were in fact two cuts, the second crossing the first at a very slight angle, only a degree or two out of line. Fine dust and fragments of stone still lay across the surface, nearly obscuring the second cut, which also seemed to have had some waxy substance poured into it, as though it was a mistake by the mason he had been anxious to cover up. It was an intriguing (but not that intriguing) puzzle, and Arthur suddenly found the closeness of the damp air in the gloomy house claustrophobic, and made his way back into the daylight.

Corinium had been growing in population all through the week. As well as those delegations who had decided to set up inside the town itself, however makeshift the accommodation, there was a stream of carts and packhorses from the surrounding countryside laden with goods ready to supply them. The summer had seen good pasture and harvest, and while the fear of raiders was never far from anybody's minds, there was enough in the farm storehouses to make a journey to Corinium for the small luxuries of life (which had been hard to come by for many years) a worthwhile piece of enterprise. With money no longer readily available or welcome, except in the nostalgic surroundings of the forum

CHAPTER IX

Tavern, most delegations had come equipped with everything from spare clothes and bales of cloth to gold trinkets, silver and bronze cloak brooches, amulets and torques and, in the case of the Trinovantes, a cache of fine amber traded with Barbarian settlers in one of the more peaceful interludes of the year. By the time Friday, the day of the first Council sitting, dawned, Corinium was almost the bustling capital it had been in its glory days, nearly a hundred and fifty years before. Horses and men crowded the streets leading to the forum. Old shops had been cleared out and goods for buy or barter spread out on mats or swiftly constructed tables. By and large the ruins of the old city were holding up well under the pressure of the sudden influx. The officials of the Dobunni had had the foresight to have the wells checked and cleaned; they had established water collection posts along the river that ran past the eastern wall, and designated midden points in the furthest and most forlorn areas of the ruins. Nonetheless the streets were soon filthy with the detritus of men and horses, and it was a relief to walk beyond the walls or into the clean space of the forum and under the wonderful vaulting of the basilica.

Inside that great building, far bigger than Dobunnia had ever been able to really justify, carpenters had erected a screen carved with patterns of interweaving leaves and the symbols of power. Beyond it a semicircle of seats had been placed with three on a raised dais facing them at the centre.

On Friday morning the delegations of the nations of Britannia began to assemble in the forum. Among them the kings, flanked by their guards, greeted each other as old friends, managing thus far to pretend that there was no enmity between them, that they had not spent much of the previous five years stealing land, cattle and slaves from each other as much as uniting to drive out the Barbarians. Several, indeed, had had to make what accommodation they could with the war bands and their followers who had sailed out of the east or from those parts of Gaul overrun with Franks, and in truth controlled far less territory than the grand titles suggested. Those in the south had the extra burden of finding a home for the many cousins from across the sea who had been forced to flee as the Franks threw them from their land.

Arthur and Caradoc led Idriseg's retinue as he jostled his way into the forum and meandered his way to the front. Despite the small size and obscurity of his kingdom – perhaps, in fact, because of it – he was a popular figure, respected for his valour in the early successful days of Uther Pendraeg's campaigns, liked now for his lack of identification with any of the powerful factions manoeuvring for position in the race for supremacy. He was greeted by old comrades and young warlords alike, and had a bow, a warm hand and a smile of welcome for each of them.

Arthur caught sight of Myrddin across the throng and found himself disconcerted by the difference between Idriseg's open and genuine greeting – a kind word, the sharing of a memory and then a cheery 'see you later' – and Myrddin's political arts, seeking out the most powerful, drawing them aside and adopting an expression of serious importance as the chosen faction's position was explained. All this when Arthur knew that Myrddin had his own plans which could hardly be more different from the carefully prepared strategy of the assembled kings. Arthur felt slightly disgusted as he watched his mentor agreeing fulsomely with Vortebelos of Brigantia and promising that, should it fall to him to decide, his candidate would have Myrddin's full support in the first vote.

After an hour or so the forum was crowded with kings and their retainers and a good number of the simply curious. Most of the main players had worked their way to the front when Myrddin caught the eye of a man on the basilica steps. He raised a great bronze horn to his lips and blew a fanfare. The forum went quiet and the leaders of the nations came to the front of the crowd, turned on the steps, bowed to their people and filed inside, with Myrddin the last to enter. Their advisers, sons and warriors followed, Arthur and Caradoc among them.

The basilica, so dark and dank the day before, was now a blaze of light. Braziers stood against the walls and tallow lamps burned brightly beyond the screen beside the chairs of the assembly. Only the kings themselves or their representatives, together with one other aide to relay messages, were allowed beyond the screen, and once they were installed the way through was barred by two men at arms, each wearing ceremonial golden torques and carrying spears and shields with finely wrought silver bosses. The privileged retainers within the basilica grew quiet as they pushed forward, straining to hear the events in the debating chamber. This was a fruitless exercise, as each king in turn stood up and made a suitable, lengthy and essentially similar speech of welcome. Since each nation and tributary nation upheld their right to the full, it was clear this preliminary stage was going to last most of the morning.

Arthur soon grew bored and he and Caradoc slipped away, agreeing to return later in the day when something more interesting was happening. They joined up with three companions from the Silures they had become friendly with on the ride from Glevum and wandered through the streets, which suddenly seemed almost deserted again with so many crowding into the forum. They took the road out of the eastern gate and across the small river which ran alongside the walls.

The fresh air of the country in the autumn was welcome relief after the foetid crowds of the city, and the boys threw themselves gratefully on a grass mound at the side of the road and talked of home. It seemed a world away. Yet so did the high politics and the fate of nations being decided amid the ruins of the old city. And to Arthur the secret he held, and which he had carried with him unspoken since he and Myrddin had walked out through the gates of the camp in the cleft of Elfael's hills – the secret that he was to be produced as the ultimate leader – seemed the most unlikely part of it all. He could see neither how his name (either name) would come up, nor how once raised it would bring anything other than, at best, rank laughter, and at worst outright hostility towards anybody who raised it. Idriseg was not such a fool, and Myrddin was too canny – he would see the chance of serving the Cornovian or Dumnonian candidate and quietly shelve his outlandish plans. Then Myrddin would either resume his life at the court of whoever emerged victorious or slink back to Moridunum and his beloved Seona and Morganwy, stopping here and there at abandoned mansions to acquire a statue or two. Which brought Arthur to Sioned and the sudden furious wish that he had never left the glorious dream of the last night in the palace and the summer at her side.

'Geraint?' asked Caradoc.

'Mm.'

'What are you thinking?'

Arthur hauled himself back to reality. 'This and that.'

'Which and what?' Caradoc persisted gently.

'I don't know. I suppose I was thinking about what a strange few months I've been through and wondering what we'll all be doing this time next year, or even five years after that.'

'Dead, I should think,' one of the other boys muttered morosely.

'In someone's army fighting Barbarians,' announced Caradoc, with confidence.

'Yes, but whose?' asked Arthur. 'And will we be fighting each other as much as the foreigners? I can't see the Ordovices agreeing with whoever Myrddin comes up with – unless it's their man, of course – and if it is then I can't see the easterners like the Catuvellauni taking orders from him for more than a few months. It'll be chaos.'

Caradoc shrugged. 'Who cares, anyway? It's nothing to do with us. They'll never bother with us in any case. They'll be too busy defeating the Silures,' he said, and he hurled a handful of grass seed good naturedly at the other boys, who returned the compliment.

'I don't know,' said Arthur distractedly. He stood up and brushed himself off. 'I'm going back to hear what's going on. Coming?'

They shook their heads and with a brusque wave Arthur started off towards the town.

The Council had taken a break after the opening pleasantries and were just returning to their seats for the afternoon session when Arthur ambled back into the basilica. It was emptier now, most of the onlookers having become as bored as Caradoc and his friends and made their way back to their quarters or to the bar, which was doing excellent trade in the far corner of the forum.

Idriseg spotted Arthur as he came through the doors and beckoned him over.

'Anything happening?' Arthur asked neutrally.

Idriseg shook his head. 'Not much yet. We're through the worst part, though, and nobody succeeded in starting a war. The interesting stage will be now, when we see who is being put forward as candidates. Myrddin's been installed to preside, and he's given us a simple enough procedure. Each candidate will be proposed. Then his proposer will sing his praises for a while. Only when all the candidates are announced will Myrddin take a preliminary count, just to weed out the ones with no support. Then the real fun will start. I'd better go.'

Arthur nodded as Idriseg bustled back to his place. Arthur strolled to the side of the building and sat down on the paved floor with his back against the cold stone. He felt left out, not only from the great debate inside the screen, but also by his own age group, who were mucking around the town or wasting time by the side of the road.

CHAPTER IX

Already he seemed to have the cares of responsibility, but only the power, or rather the powerlessness, of an observer.

The voices quietened until the only sound was the calm authority of Myrddin reminding the Council of the procedure for the afternoon. He heard a name called and the first of the speakers – from the far north, he thought, by the strangeness of the accent; perhaps even the legendary Votadini, who had indeed shown up (though only at emissary level). There was a murmur of dissent as the name of the candidate was revealed, quelled by Myrddin, and the Ordovician spokesman rose to his feet.

Some time later Arthur was woken by a friendly kick to the base of his tunic. He scrambled to his feet to face a grim Idriseg.

'Sorry, I was just—'

'I'm sure you were fascinated.'

'I couldn't really hear what they were saying. There's an echo, and I must have dozed off.'

'Indeed you did.' Idriseg forced a smile and clasped his shoulder. 'You may have missed the most interesting part of the day.'

'What happened?' Arthur tried to put some enthusiasm into his voice. Now that he was here all Myrddin's stories and all the training seemed ridiculous. None of this had anything to do with him. These were powerful men debating to whom from their own number they were going to entrust the leadership. Any romantic notion Myrddin might have had about sweeping Arthur to power in a blaze of grateful applause from his peers was plainly fantasy.

Idriseg was replying. 'We've had candidacies from three purported sons of Uther from all ends of the country, one grandson of Ambrosius himself, the Vortigern descendants (of course) and inevitably fanciful claims from someone who says he can trace his lineage simultaneously to Cunobelos of the Trinovantes four hundred years ago and the Emperor Caracalla. He was asked pointedly whether he'd met any of Boudicca's daughters recently. Then there are the serious ones, of which those from the Cornovii – Cunegnus himself, of course – Dumnonians and Dobunni are the most likely to get somewhere. There's a long way to go yet, though, and frankly there are a few of the more irresponsible nations who will be prepared to push their candidate, by force of arms if necessary, if they lose the vote. I keep telling Myrddin that this isn't Athens a thousand years ago, but he can be a hopeless idealist at times.'

'Rot,' said a firm voice behind Arthur. 'I'm no such thing. But this is all going far better than I'd hoped.' Myrddin looked solemn for the benefit of anyone watching, and spoke quietly, but his eyes were sparkling.

'What do you mean?' asked Arthur.

'It's excellent. Quite excellent. None of the minor candidates will back down, and the major ones would be foolish to withdraw and risk the chance of spending the next few years fighting under the generalship of an illegitimate idiot with a power complex and an ancestry to prove. I'll have to make something happen to bring them to their senses. We reconvene in a few minutes. Just watch.' And he loped off into the fresh air of the forum for a drink before the final session of the day began.

By early evening the electors were tired, sick of circular debate and claims of greatness. Most of them were kings themselves, so prepared for the usual currency of rhetoric, but they were not likely to believe the absolute validity of others' pompous assertions, even if they felt duty-bound to make them themselves. Tempers were beginning to fray, and when one putative son of Uther threatened another with his sword, Myrddin was forced to restore order. It was the moment he had been waiting for.

Caradoc and his friends had rejoined Arthur behind the screen, together with a crowd of those who had wanted to see how the day's debate would end and had drifted back into the basilica.

'What's up?' Caradoc asked.

'I think Myrddin's about to perform,' Arthur whispered. Part of him felt weary cynicism, but another part felt the excitement from knowing that he had never yet seen Myrddin fail.

Myrddin rose from his presiding chair and spoke with the firmness of a natural orator. His voice carried easily through the space of the basilica, so that the murmur of voices from the back was quelled as effectively as the shouts at the front.

'I, Myrddin, Prince of Demetia, son of Maglicus, son of Vorteporix, granted the title of Protictoris by Magnus Maximus himself, speak to you now and, with the authority you yourselves have vested in me, command you to order.'

'Good, isn't he,' chuckled Caradoc.

'Shh!' grinned Arthur.

Myrddin raised his staff in front of him at arm's length. The angry candidates put down their weapons and stood shamefacedly.

'Here we go,' said Arthur.

The amber ball at the head of Myrddin's staff began to glow. It was impossible to say whether it did so of its own accord or whether it was just a trick of the late afternoon sun slanting through an opening high in the basilica wall, whether the chill that came over the building was invoked or whether it was just the wind of the last day of October rising across the plateau, whether the crashing of the door against the wall was the inadvertent push of an incoming warrior or the slam as the spirits, released for their feast night, sealing the basilica for their own purposes. The glow grew brighter and the kings gazed at it, transfixed. Myrddin's voice was quiet now, almost soothing, so that it was hard to remember later exactly what he had said, easy only to recall the meaning.

'There is another son of Uther Pendraeg, a son of his true queen, Ygraen of Armorica, and through them both the line of Constantius and the protectors of Britannia, Prima and Seconda, Flavius and Caesarensis, to Caradoc and Cunobelos. He is not among you, but he is with us in Corinium. Only one man can lead us now. In the years to come, before our final victory, we shall face the fires of the Barbarians, the plunderers from across the sea, our land shall be parcelled among heathens, our daughters carried off for rough pleasure, the white dragon and the red shall tear each other until they lie bloody and burnt at the foot of a foreign warrior. Unless you find the man who can draw the sword from the stone with his right hand, the sword of the emperors, the true emperors who marched out from Britannia to claim back Rome and never returned, defeated by the treachery of sybarites and eunuchs in the east. Find the sword. Caledfwlch, it is called. The sword Constantine left for this man and him alone. Find the man who can draw it and you have your leader.'

The glow faded from the head of the staff. The chill seemed to rise from the walls and Myrddin slumped back into his seat as though exhausted. The assembly sat thunderstruck for a moment, then a murmur of awe began as the people regained their senses.

Of all unlikely people it was Corbalengus of Ordovicia who composed himself first and took the floor.

'I have heard this prophecy before,' he began. 'Shortly before leaving for this gathering a woman of good family was suddenly returned to us. Sioned had been captured as a child and thrown into slavery, though we thought she had died with her father. She returned as a free woman.'

Arthur started and frowned. Suddenly a wave of irritation, mingled with fear, rushed through him: fear for Sioned now that she was no longer in Moridunum; irritation at Myrddin for using her so blatantly in his scheming.

Corbalengus continued. 'The night before I rode out she was brought to me and said, "Look for the boy with the sword which grows from the rock itself. He will be your lord." I believe Myrddin speaks the truth, and the prophecy will save us.'

After a few minutes more of debate, during which it was decided that nothing more could be achieved that night until Myrddin's prophecy had been proved one way or the other, the kings formally processed out of the basilica and returned to their camps. Among those who were candidates or sponsors of candidates there was an air of desperation – to find and possess the sword before their rivals did. They knew that however just their claim or convincing their arguments, there could be no public legitimacy now unless they held the sword as well. Agents were dispatched about Dobunnia, searching for anything which could reasonably pass for a sword embedded in rock. The trouble was that any trickery was likely to be easy to unmask, for if a false sword was found, then any fool with a strong right arm would be able to withdraw it, not only the next true overlord.

Myrddin was delighted with himself, and showed none of the confusion of his colleagues as he joined Idriseg, Caradoc and Arthur in the forum.

'Somebody should find it within an hour or two. If not I'll have to help them out in the morning.'

'You mean, tell them where it is?' asked Arthur, incredulous.

'Not exactly. But close enough to get an election by the end of tomorrow, as planned.'

'Is this some trick of yours?' Arthur asked, although appalled at himself for thinking Myrddin capable of such a thing.

Idriseg looked shocked. 'What do you mean by that, young man? Are you suggesting that Myrddin – who has served this country for over thirty years and who has held the kings together today when we could have been at war – would seek power by false prophecy?'

'No, of course not,' Arthur retreated swiftly. 'I was joking, that's all.'

'A joke in very poor taste, boy,' thundered Idriseg.

'I'm sorry, I...'

Myrddin waved the apology away. 'Think nothing of it. I would have wondered exactly the same thing if I had been you. Only I might have been a little more subtle in the way I put it.'

X

SOME TIME LATER Arthur was strolling along the old walls alone as the dusk closed in across the rolling country to the west. He was thinking of home, but wondering which home that was: the home of Branwen and Caradoc, secure and hidden in the hills; or the home of Morganwy and once, so recently, of Sioned. Which was the better life? That of mosaic floors and bath houses, or of the freedom of the woods and the smell of winter fires in smoky halls? It was hard to choose. Either, he knew, was better than camping in these ancient ruins, so depressing in their dereliction – not because of how destroyed they were, but because of what they said about how the country had changed for the worse in a hundred years or less. How could people have let that happen just because a foreign empire had broken up? He had heard Idriseg say all his life that freedom was better than slavery to a distant power. But was it, really, when the choice seemed to be between civilisation and a return to primitive living that their ancestors would have been ashamed of even before Rome's conquest? Surely they could do better and still fight off the war bands from across the sea? Surely these cities could be rebuilt under a strong overlord and people could live in comfort once again?

His train of thought was broken as Caradoc and his three friends came running down the street from the direction of the Via Fossa gate.

'They found it,' yelled Caradoc, breathlessly.

'Found what?'

'The sword Myrddin prophesied. Geraint, it's here. It must have been standing in one of these old temples or something for years waiting for us.'

Caradoc was wide-eyed with superstitious enthusiasm. Arthur started to feel the same elation, then a flicker of suspicion crossed his face.

'Where did you say?'

'One of the back streets on the other side of the forum. It's amazing. Come on.' And Caradoc led him across the town at a run.

They found a crowd gathering at a dilapidated house, which Arthur recognised as the one he had explored earlier in the day. A wry smile crossed his lips as he watched the men around him jostling to pass through the doorway and into the dim chamber beyond. There was a call for lights and a man was dispatched to find torches. By the time he came back there was a rumble of wonder among the crowd. A sword, a wonderfully hilted sword, had been found pushed into a great white altar – surely an impossible feat in itself. Nobody could draw it from the stone. Everybody was pushing forward to be the next to try.

Myrddin came striding up from the forum, looking solemn and a little anxious; though as he passed Arthur (by now pressed against the wall on the far side of the street by the crowd) he winked and mouthed, 'Not yet.' Arthur nodded and prepared to watch events unfold.

A path was half-cleared for Myrddin, accompanied by five kings, each of whom had either nominated a candidate or been nominated themselves. They fought their way through, trying to maintain their dignity and authority in the crush, trying to look as though their own victory was assured and inevitable. As Myrddin reached the altar in the far reaches of the house the torches were brought forward and the rooms fell quiet. Myrddin held up his hands and repeated the prophecy that he had made in the Council of the drawing of the sword from the stone. Then he called 'all true and worthy men' to try to recover the sword of kings, for only that way would the new leader emerge.

And they came. First the members of the Council grasped the hilt and pulled. The sword moved slightly, enough to give them hope, but stuck stubbornly in its housing. They withdrew, disconsolate and baffled, their hopes of legitimate election disappearing with their strength.

The attention turned to the men in the crowd. Could it be that the new leader was hidden among them, a member of a nation which had no candidate, a warrior with no political allies? As it became clear that any man could test his skill and strength in the quest for ultimate power, the crowd grew impatient, pushing to see but also to be next in line, in case by some terrible stroke of fate the man in front should draw the sword before their turn came.

Myrddin comforted every man as his dejection at failure hit home, reminded the next that it was a great and ancient sword and that, however desperate they were to claim it, the magnificent hilt with its lion head and amber badge must not be damaged, nor the altar overturned. They complied, but the result was identical: the sword gave a fraction, then stayed firm.

It was after dark when Myrddin declared that there would be no more attempts that day. He called for guards to keep watch overnight and announced that the contest would resume the following morning, after the Council had convened to discuss the matter. The crowd was loath to disperse, and milled around the building and the nearby streets. The list of those who had failed Myrddin's sword test was impressive. Unless a candidate was agreed upon, many of the most powerful nations in Britannia would leave the Council with their leaders humiliated. The word was that Myrddin was playing a very dangerous game. If that humiliation turned into a refusal to accept the new overlord, the chance of united action against the outside would evaporate. Worse still, when there was no one else better to fight, they could always fight one another.

Arthur tagged on to Myrddin's party as it made its way back to the Demetian quarters. Since it was his own sword, as he saw it, that Myrddin had expropriated for his demonstration, Arthur was at a loss as to what was expected of him the next day. He had taken the instruction of 'not yet' to mean that he should not join the ranks of those attempting to pull the sword from the white stone, but where that left him, he had no real idea.

Idriseg marched into the house some time later, wet from the rain that had begun to fall steadily, his shoes caked in the thick white mud that the streets turned to so quickly in Corinium. Many a citizen over the past two hundred years had cursed the system of making the surface from crushed limestone, a technique which worked perfectly well in southern Latium most of the year round, but was hopeless in damp Britannia, with its worsening weather.

'There's trouble,' he announced curtly.

'Where?' asked Myrddin.

Idriseg jabbed a finger at his old friend. 'You'd better be right about the sword business, because otherwise we're going to have more than a brawl round the fire.'

'Calm down and tell me what's happening.'

'The Brigantes are saying there's a coalition of the western nations to make sure the overlord doesn't come from the north. The Trinovantes are saying the same about the east, pointing out that they understand the threat best since they are the first ones to suffer from any invasion. There's a battle developing just outside the western gate. Two Dumnonians started throwing stones at the Brigantian meeting. Drunk, of course, but that hardly mattered by then. You'd better get down there and do more than deliver a prophecy.'

Myrddin turned on his heel grimly and disappeared into the inner room he had requisitioned for himself. A few minutes later he reappeared, decked out in his cloak of shifting colours, carrying his staff and wearing a long sword at his side. Arthur rose, ready to follow him.

'No,' Myrddin commanded. 'You stay here. I don't want any accidents before tomorrow.'

Caradoc appeared beside him. 'I'll come, though.'

'No you won't,' Myrddin confirmed. 'You don't even have a sword. Your father is going to need you in different ways from now on, and the last thing I want is for unarmed lads to get caught up in senseless skirmishes before we've even had the election. Come on, Idriseg. We'd better get this cleared up.'

The older men left, their entourage grinning sarcastically at Arthur and Caradoc. One even had the nerve to pat them on the head.

Caradoc swore. He was red in the face with fury. He was a prince. He was humiliated.

Arthur bowed his head. Tears welled up in his eyes: not for himself – he had no wish to fight if he did not need to, and he could see the sense of Myrddin's prohibition – but for his brother. He knew that all the attention had shifted over the last few months, and for Caradoc this was just another public demonstration of his demotion.

'You can have my sword,' said Arthur.

'Don't be stupid. You haven't got one, either.'

CHAPTER X

'Yes I have – I've had it since Myrddin arrived at home. He's been hanging on to it, for safekeeping – at least, that's his story. It seems it's got some special powers.'

'What special powers?' Caradoc asked.

'I don't know yet. But I've seen it transform itself at least once.'

'So where is it?'

'Come on. I'll get it for you.'

* * *

The street where the sword rested in its altar was lit by braziers, but there was nobody hanging around outside. They had all rushed out to the scene of the fighting, either to join in out of loyalty or boredom, or to watch the event develop. Caradoc and Arthur made their way nonchalantly to the door and peered in. Two guards stood at the entrance to the inner chamber. They looked barely awake, but Arthur didn't want to risk trying to get past them. There was no explanation for what he was about to do – and if there had been, now was not the moment to try it out.

'You distract them,' said Arthur. 'See if you can get them out into the street.'

'What are you going to do?'

'Get the sword. Like I said.'

'Don't be stupid. That sword's embedded in stone. You're not getting it. Unless you really are going to be the overlord.'

'You don't believe it, then?' Arthur asked.

'That story? Of course not.'

'Thanks for the vote. Just try it, will you?'

'All right, but don't blame me if it makes us look even sillier than we do already,' Caradoc said, and stepped back a few paces so that he could take a convincing run at the door. Arthur pressed himself against the outer wall, ready to dart in when the moment came. They both paused, and glanced up and down the street to make sure it was still empty.

'Now,' commanded Arthur.

Caradoc spurted forward into the building, shouting to the guards that there was trouble at the end of the street and they were needed. He rushed out again, yelling for them to follow.

The startled soldiers glanced at each other and ran after him.

Arthur knew he only had a moment before they gave up chasing Caradoc and returned to their posts. He slipped through the entrance and scuttled into the room where the sword sat peacefully in its place. As he grasped the hilt he felt the familiar heat from the amber surge into his fingers. Instead of pulling hard, then struggling, as all the previous contestants had done, he gently twisted the sword a touch and eased it gently upwards. He felt the stone yield and the blade rise in his hands. Arthur smiled to himself. Whether it was the result of fate, Myrddin's stratagem, or just his own luck in having seen the stone during the afternoon before the sword had been placed there, he could not say with any certainty. But his theory had worked, and the sword was back in his hands. Perhaps his true destiny was to rescue it, not the other way round.

He didn't stop to dwell on the thought. He darted out into the street and turned left, back towards the forum and away from the direction in which Caradoc had led the guards. He paused by the remains of the old market and waited, as arranged, for his foster-brother to join him. Caradoc ran up breathless a few minutes later.

'Get it?' Caradoc asked.

'Of course.'

'Great. Can I have it?'

'Don't you want to know how I did it?' Arthur asked.

'Who cares?'

Arthur held the hilt to him, the blade pointing to the ground. The lion head glowed faintly in the moonlight. The sword was light and warm in his hands, as though resisting being given up again.

'I think you'll find quite a lot of people do when you turn up with it. Myrddin, for one. Father too.'

'We'll see. Come on, give it over. I'll have missed everything otherwise.'

Arthur, more reluctantly than he had expected, transferred the blade to his right hand and gave it, hilt first, to Caradoc.

'Thanks. I'll pay you back.'

'I'm sure you will,' muttered Arthur, and he watched as Caradoc ran off, brandishing his new weapon, towards the noise beyond the walls.

Arthur wandered back slowly through the unlit and deserted city to their quarters. There he nodded to the few men who had remained behind to watch over their belongings and slipped through to his space in one of the further rooms. He rolled out the mat he slept on and eased himself to the floor, propping his head on a bundle of his other clothes. He tried to sleep, pleased with himself. Perhaps it would be Caradoc now who would be recognised as overlord. After all, he wanted the title far more than Arthur did. And Caradoc, as the true son of Idriseg, would be a worthy commander, given time. Myrddin would eventually be reconciled. And Arthur could return to the hills, perhaps even take charge of Myrddin's land while he was away, and join Sioned as a scholar and man of peace.

* * *

Outside the walls of Corinium arms clashed and men shouted in the night. By the light of fires and torches the arguments raged. Myrddin tried to make himself heard above the clamour, but without much success. Idriseg and his men, together with those of Demetia, tried to force a wedge between the northerners and the men of Dumnonia to prevent bloodshed. So far one man lay dead and there were a few others with minor wounds, and Idriseg knew that it wouldn't take many more casualties on either side for the skirmish to erupt into wholesale fighting. And fighting by night was always a disaster.

It was into this scene of confusion that Caradoc rushed from the western gate, brandishing the sword above his head – a futile gesture, for it was a less than full-length sword, perfect for the close combat of disciplined ranks, but all but useless in the open fighting of Britannian conflicts. But the sword was his protector, as it would have been any man who carried it, and the warmth of its hilt suffused Caradoc's arm and gave him the strength and courage of a warrior beyond his seventeen years – or perhaps it was the foolhardiness of a boy who had never seen the blood of battle and in his heart could not imagine that he could come to any harm.

He threw himself to the front of the Demetian column, ignoring the steady order Idriseg and Myrddin were trying to hold among their own men and to impose on the factions to either side of them. To Myrddin's horror, Caradoc charged forward, beyond the protective line of spears, towards the heart of the skirmish.

Wise or not – and Idriseg's later words on the subject of his son's action were caustic – the appearance of the young man in full-throated battle cry, unarmed except for a Roman sword of exquisite workmanship and without so much as a shield, was astonishing. The feuding groups paused and drew back, dropping away from Caradoc's fury. Gradually they quietened, until the only sound was the boy's frenzied challenge.

Myrddin raised his staff. When he cried 'Caradoc!' his voice seemed to fill the valley with the deep crack of thunder. It was a cry of command which could make even the berserk falter and fall silent. Caradoc stopped as if held by a rope, his sword arm still raised above his head, its silver blade catching the light of the torches. There was a whisper in the knot of men.

'The sword. That's the sword.'

Myrddin stepped forward from the phalanx of his men. 'Come here, boy,' he said.

Caradoc at last came to his senses. He seemed to shiver as he let his arm drop to his side, and turned.

'Where did you get that sword? No – I know where you got it. How did you get that sword?'

Caradoc waited for a moment before answering. When he did, his voice was clear and strong. 'From the stone. From the white stone.'

There was a rumble of voices. Was this to be their new leader? He was brave enough. Or a fool. Only one or the other would have careered into the line of battle as he had. It would be a useful skill against the Barbarians, though he might not live long to enjoy the triumph.

Myrddin was not satisfied. 'You pulled that sword from the altar yourself?'

Caradoc again paused before replying. 'Yes. Myself.'

'You're sure?'

'Quite sure.'

Idriseg strode forward. He looked anxious, his fear for his son's future overcoming his anger at his idiotic behaviour in defiance of strict instructions to stay behind.

'Where's Geraint?' Idriseg demanded.

'Where I left him. Asleep,' Caradoc said.

'Show me that sword.'

'No. I drew it. It does not leave my hand now. And I shall be the only candidate tomorrow.' And breathing heavily, red with the light of the fires and the righteous flush of victory, Caradoc marched back towards the western gate in the walls of Corinium.

CHAPTER X

'Wait!' Myrddin commanded, his staff raised high once more. Caradoc felt his legs obey, even though he wanted to walk on, ignoring the orders of the man the sword gave him courage to despise.

'If you drew the sword in the private of the night on your own – what did you do with the guards, by the way? – and if you are telling the truth, you will not mind drawing the sword from the stone again in front of all of us.'

'Of course,' Caradoc said with confidence, though for the first time since he had run through the streets to join the battle there was a sense of doubt in his heart and nervousness in his stomach.

'Then,' continued Myrddin reasonably as he approached Caradoc and put a masterly hand on his shoulder, 'you will give me the sword back now so I can replace it.' Gently he prised the hilt from the young man's fingers. 'Shall we go?'

He urged Caradoc forward. Behind them Idriseg raised his arm and the throng, who had been prepared to fight to the death moments before, fell into line and followed. They made their way in rough procession through the town gate and into the deserted streets, the blaze from their torches throwing confused shadows on the crumbling stucco walls of the empty houses and the windows, the eyes of the abandoned stores. They pressed on past the forum and the walls of the basilica until they came to the building which held the white altar, in front of which sat two shamefaced and dejected soldiers of the Dobunni, the guards who had so singularly failed to prevent the removal of the sword.

They leapt to their feet as Myrddin and the throng behind him filled the street. One guard pointed accusingly at Caradoc, but Myrddin pushed him away, called for torches to be brought forward and stalked inside. He held Caradoc firmly by the elbow as he marched to the altar.

'Stay here until I tell you to move,' he instructed the boy quietly as they reached it.

Myrddin moved round behind the stone. He held the sword high in front of his face, the lion medallion to the front. There was a hush from the jostling men that pressed into the chamber as he lowered the blade into the slot in the white polished stone. He seemed to press it down and adjust it somehow, as though to test it was set securely. He beckoned to Caradoc to join him.

'Now,' he began, 'if you can draw this sword you will be presented to the Council tomorrow as the true heir of Uther Pendraeg, the

Overlord of all Britannia. The kings of the island will serve you. They will expect wisdom as well as courage. They will call for the uniting of the forces against the Barbarians, the restoration of peace between nations, the strength of a new order to replace the chaos which has never been far away for more than a hundred years. All this is in your hands if you can draw this sword. If not, we will know you have lied and you must swear to follow whoever does possess this sword without question and wherever he commands. Is that clear?'

Caradoc nodded and bowed his head. His hands were sweating, and despite the cool of the night outside, the stench and heat from the men and their torches suddenly made his head swim. Nevertheless, Caradoc was no coward. He stepped forward in front of Myrddin, grasped the hilt of the sword in both hands, planted his feet apart to give him maximum purchase and pulled. As it had done so many times that day, the sword seemed to give, to rise a little way, then refused to move any further. Caradoc strained. The beads of sweat trickled down his brow into his eyes. But the sword stayed where it was. He roared in shame and frustration, then collapsed behind the stone, fighting the urge to let the tears come.

Surprisingly Myrddin's voice was gentle when he spoke, his very quietness quelling the laughter and argument that buzzed in the crowded room. 'Caradoc, stand up.' Myrddin lifted the boy until he stood, hiding his face from the accusing eyes. 'You have done us a great service tonight. But for your bravery, your realisation that only this sword could prevent war and bring men to their senses, we would have had a massacre tonight. You are not to be our leader, but you deserve our thanks.'

Caradoc raised his eyes in amazement. He expected ridicule and reprisals, not thanks.

Myrddin continued. 'You also proved two things more which perhaps needed to be proved: that the sword will unite us; and that whoever draws it from its place in the morning will truly be the man to take the title of Ambrosius. Now. That's enough. We will leave new guards, and more of them. The rest of us will sleep.'

It turned out not to be one of Myrddin's more accurate predictions. Arthur woke to the sound of Caradoc being flung to the bed roll on the floor next to him by Idriseg, shouting that he had brought notoriety and disgrace on the house of Elfael and that he would not listen to any

CHAPTER X

excuses. And, while he was at it, Idriseg fumed, kicking Arthur where he lay, where was this amazing brother while Caradoc was making such a fool of himself? Asleep? Typical! Idriseg paced up and down for a few minutes more before hurling a final curse at both of them and stomping back out into the street.

'What happened?' Arthur asked after watching Caradoc lie face down for a while.

'Nothing,' the elder boy mumbled into the bedding.

Arthur let it be for a few moments. He knew well enough that when he was in this mood Caradoc would only tell him when he was ready.

'Did we win? I mean, was there a battle? Did we stop the fighting?'

Caradoc stirred reluctantly. 'Yes.'

'Anybody hurt?'

'Don't know. Ask Myrddin – if he's speaking to you.'

Arthur sighed. 'Oh, he'll speak to me. He hasn't much choice.'

They fell silent again. Around them they could hear the rumble of voices as the men went over the events of the day: the gathering in the forum, the Council, the near breakdown, Myrddin's prophecy, the attempts to draw the sword, the outbreak of fighting, Caradoc's absurd charge and the final anticlimax as the sword ended up back where it had started.

Arthur wanted to sleep as he had while the events of the night had unfolded on the other side of the city. But now his mind was too turbulent, and the thoughts rushed through without logic or direction. There was the apprehension of the morning and his role in the drama of the Council and the sword. He would start the day obscure and without enemies and end it marked out and with plenty. Maybe his trick with the sword would not work again. Myrddin would usher him into the altar room and nothing would happen. Maybe, and he realised he profoundly hoped it would happen like this, one of the competing kings would prove not to be as dense as he looked and would examine the altar before he tried to pull the sword and so come to the same conclusion Arthur had done. It was, after all, not a matter of magic, but of deduction. Maybe (this too was attractive) the Council would throw out Myrddin's whole scheme and the politics would have been resolved during the night. A candidate from among them would be elected and Myrddin would be sent home with thanks for his efforts and apologies for ignoring him. Arthur would go with him, chastened but still part of the old man's retinue, and Sioned would be waiting on the road to Moridunum.

Sleep came eventually to Arthur as the light began to seep over the gentle country to the east. By then it was only Myrddin who paced the old streets and chased his visions from the walls.

* * *

The Council of Kings was late assembling the next morning, and it soon became clear that the night had not produced any miracles of diplomacy. Positions had, if anything, hardened after the close brush with open civil war, so unconsciously averted by Caradoc. The debate was bad tempered from the start. The kings had plotted and manoeuvred in conclaves and caucuses throughout the night, and the result was a series of alliances and counter alliances that soon cancelled each other out and revealed the total absence of any consensus. Myrddin was glad several times that he had ruled at the start of the day that weapons and bodyguards must be left outside the basilica. As it was, the discussion descended into shouting and shoving within the first hour. Genealogies were mocked, legitimacy questioned and the evaluation of each other's performance against the Barbarian incursions was frank to the point of insult. Myrddin wryly observed that at least the kings of Britannia had no illusions about their capabilities, even if each attributed the frailties to everybody but themselves.

It was a process he understood was necessary, though, if they were to arrive at the moment when he could impose a solution. The timing had to be right. He could not leave it so long that important factions started walking out, vowing to deal with Barbarians and their neighbours as they saw fit. Already there had been one impassioned challenge to settle the contest by single combat, with the last king standing – in this case a Brigantian little admired for his subtlety – taking full power. Because the challenge had come from the north it had been laughed out of Council, but Myrddin knew that he might not be so lucky if one of the other major nations, the Catuvellauni or the Cornovii, took matters into their own hands.

He waited for an exhausted lull in the arguments before rising and announcing a series of complicated votes aimed, he said, at leaving nobody in any doubt about who had been appointed and why. In

CHAPTER X

reality, as he had intended, within no time at all the Council was so confused as to which vote they were on and what its outcome meant that the proceedings were in danger of collapsing altogether. Myrddin caught Idriseg's eye and nodded.

He stood, raised his staff and, in his most imposing voice, called for silence. He was not granted it immediately. His usual authority was not enough to quell the Council. Indeed a shout of 'Go to hell, you old bugger!' was given the biggest cheer of the morning. Myrddin stood his ground, the tip of his staff starting to glow. Gradually the noise eased and he gained their attention. When he spoke it was quietly, smoothly, as though he was the voice of reason after the clamour of force.

'Where is the boy who dared to wield the sword from the altar last night?' he asked. 'Caradoc, son of Idriseg, where is he?'

Idriseg stepped forward. 'Outside,' he said, 'and doing as he's told for once.'

There was laughter. A voice with a Cantiacan accent was heard. 'He's no good. We saw him. He couldn't take the sword from the stone.'

Myrddin smiled. 'Precisely. But somebody did, and it was not me. I was with you outside the walls. There is somebody here who can fulfil the prophecy. We are not going to resolve this matter any other way.'

There was a rumble. Myrddin took that as assent. 'Bring the boy here.' A lieutenant of the King of Ordovicia was sent to fetch Caradoc, who looked scared and shaky as he was led in front of the Council. He stood facing Myrddin, his eyes fixed on the floor.

'Look at me,' commanded Myrddin.

Reluctantly Caradoc lifted his face.

'You had the sword of the prophecy last night. We know it was not yours to wield.'

Caradoc shook his head. 'No. But I...'

'No matter,' Myrddin interrupted. 'We all – or at least enough of us – saw it replaced it in the altar, and saw you fail to draw it from there again. It was not yours to hold.'

'No,' whispered Caradoc.

'Somebody else took the sword for you?'

'Yes.'

'Did you wrest it from him?'

'No. He gave it to me as a favour.'

'A favour. He had the sword of the overlord and he gave it to you as a favour? Why?'

'Because I wanted to join you and my father on the front line and I had no sword of my own. Father had made sure of that.'

'Who was this benefactor, this generous man? Is he among us here?'

Caradoc looked about him briefly. 'No.'

'Where is he, then?'

'Outside.'

'His name?'

'I don't know. I call him Geraint. I always have done. But you call him Arthur.'

'Do I?' Myrddin paused, and stared at Caradoc for a moment, then let his eyes take in the whole assembly. 'Let him be brought forward so we can see this hero – one who would draw the sword of his fortune and hand it to a friend. How many of us would have done that? How many of us would have had the nobility to give up our ambition and relinquish the chance to lead this island?' Myrddin gestured, and the man who had fetched Caradoc went out again in search of Arthur. When they returned there was a whisper of disbelief. He was so young, so junior. There was nothing special about his dress. He was just a youth from the hills. Myrddin called for quiet once again. 'Who are you?' he asked.

Now that the moment had come Arthur was surprised to find that he felt no fear. He realised he did not care if he was overlord or not. If he was elected he would try to do what was expected of him; if not, he would return home and take his place where he could. So he answered Myrddin firmly, standing straight and looking Uther Pendraeg's old adviser in the eye.

'I have always been Geraint, son of Idriseg of Elfael. But you have told me I am Arthur, son of Uther Pendraeg. Perhaps, therefore, I am both.'

'Have you drawn the sword from the stone?'

'Yes, and from the river long before that.'

'Did you give the sword to Caradoc here?'

'Yes.'

'Why?'

Arthur looked at his foster-brother with affection. Caradoc seemed downcast and broken, still, as though his pride had evaporated with his claims the night before.

CHAPTER X

'Because he is my brother. And he is the elder. He needed a sword. I knew where one was to be found.'

Myrddin grew sterner. 'Yet you knew that whoever was able to draw the sword would be named overlord. Didn't you care?'

Arthur turned away from Myrddin. He was suddenly tired of his master's game. The election was in the hands of the kings, not Myrddin. It was therefore to them that he spoke.

'I am too young to lead you,' he began, 'even if the story Myrddin of Demetia will tell you is true. Uther Pendraeg had served Ambrosius Aurelianus for many years before you made him overlord. And there is nothing to say that you must pick me. You have great men among you. And other sons of Pendraeg. Choose from them and leave me in peace. When I am of age I will serve the cause you set me as best I can. I drew the sword for my brother. If I draw it again, you must choose who will wear it into battle. For an overlord is the servant of the kings and their people, not their emperor. And I have done nothing yet to deserve that trust.' Arthur looked around him, waiting for the hoots of derision and the snarls of contempt. None came.

Instead their host in Corinium, Candidianos (whose great grandson was to become the last Britannian king to hold the city) came forward and grasped his arm. 'We accepted the prophecy. We have failed to agree on any of those who have put themselves forward. They have all spoken of their armies, the lineage and their power. Yet if these were so extraordinary we would not need to have this debate at all. The man to lead us would be the obvious choice. There is no such man, Arthur. Yet you have spoken with humility and honour. That is rare enough in these days of little emperors and strutting tyrants. Come. Show us that you can indeed draw the sword. Then we will know this is not some trick of Myrddin's. Then we will decide.'

The Council murmured its agreement and Candidianos led Arthur out of the crowded basilica into the forum and down the lane leading to the altar chamber. Arthur felt the same confidence and familiarity as the evening before, when he and Caradoc had first collected the sword. He realised with a smile that he had now trodden the street more often than any street in Corinium, other than that which led from their quarters to the forum.

The kings and their followers crowded into the small room where the sword rested in its carved white stone, the lion head so lifelike it seemed to grin at them in the dim light of the torches that the guards had set up on either side. Myrddin and Idriseg stayed at the back of the throng, aware that if they were too close when Arthur made his move they would be accused of helping him in some way. Candidianos guided the boy forward, then stood back as Arthur moved behind the altar and grasped the hilt with both hands, as he had the night before. He twisted the blade slightly until he felt it click clear of the locking filament of stone, then drew it slowly but inexorably upwards. There was a gasp as the blade cleared the stone. The beauty of the blade and its delicate writing seemed more pronounced than ever in the glow of the torches, and when Arthur reversed it to raise it above his head, the amber that backed the lion's head mirrored the firelight.

Candidianos spoke quietly. 'You have been as good as your word. Now put it back.'

Arthur looked at him in puzzlement. 'Back?'

The King nodded. He was still a young man himself, perhaps ten years older than Arthur, but he had the natural authority of a man who was used to ruling from one of the great cities of Britannia, decayed though it was. 'We need to know that you are indeed the only one who has the skill.'

Arthur shrugged and lowered the blade into place once more, then stepped aside.

Candidianos turned to the company. 'Each leader of a nation and all those who claim they are of the lines of Uther Pendraeg, Ambrosius Aurelianus or Magnus Maximus will take their turn, whether they made the attempt yesterday or not. This will be done in front of us all or not at all. If more than Arthur can pass this test we will begin our discussions again. If not, unless he refuses, I will declare Arthur our new overlord, our "Tygern Fawr". Does anyone dissent?'

Nobody answered.

'Very well. Let us begin.'

The kings and their candidates filed forward, each trying to wrest the blade from its housing, each in turn failing as he pulled and strained to haul the blade straight up. The line was long and despondent. Nobody could match the boy. Candidianos watched and greeted each failure with a sympathetic 'Well tried', until all who wanted to had made their attempt. Then he turned to Myrddin.

'We wait for you, Myrddin. You have neither tried nor told us who the boy is and how he came to be here.'

CHAPTER X   143

Myrddin stepped forward. 'I have no desire to rule you, so I will not draw the sword. But what about you, Candidianos? You have not attempted it, and this is your kingdom.'

'I have held back. It would not have been right for the host to have gone before his guests. But perhaps now I should take my turn.'

The warrior stepped behind the altar. Alone of all those who had taken part he examined the hilt and the stone carefully before taking grip. For the first time Myrddin was nervous. If he used his head, not his muscle, there was every chance he would discover the simple secret. Candidianos frowned and ran his finger over the surface of the altar. Then he looked over to where Arthur stood, watching intently. Arthur's feelings were now divided. He half-wanted the Dobunnian to succeed and relieve him of the burden, especially since he knew that he would never have known how to take the sword himself if he had not stumbled on Myrddin's preparations two days before. But the other half of him was growing to like the thought of power, the sensation of being respected and followed by all the high-ranking men of Britain. For a moment Candidianos and Arthur caught each other's eye. The older man smiled and nodded fractionally, too slightly for anybody but Arthur and Myrddin to notice. He tugged at the hilt. Nothing happened. He pulled again, then let go and threw his hands in the air in defeat.

'Arthur, if you can take it once again, the sword and the island are both yours,' he said, and walked away.

Arthur bowed and returned to his now-accustomed stance, his hands around the hilt, his feet a little apart. He twisted it a fraction and lifted. The sword rose in his hand. This time he did not put it back but, holding it by the blade, came into the centre of the room, offered it first to Myrddin, then, when he shook his head, to Idriseg, who also declined it.

Candidianos placed both his hands on Arthur's shoulders. 'We will follow you. For you have the skill and the courage. But first Myrddin must tell us your history and how you came to be here. We knew the stories that Uther Pendraeg and Ygraen had had a child, but nothing had been heard for so long many of us believed it was just a story.'

Myrddin raised his staff for attention. 'My friends,' he began, 'I believe we have found the man to lead us. He is young, but with the blessing of God, and of the spirits that will reign tonight, he will be with us for many years, even beyond the span of most us assembled here. And he is trained in the arts of peace as well as the theory of war. I have seen to that, though the test of battle is yet to come. Let us return to the Council and follow the procedure we set ourselves at the start. Then we will feast. Tonight the spirits walk free. So shall ours. And tomorrow the new overlord will hold his first Council of Kings. He will choose his advisers and companions, his allies and his foes.'

So Arthur came to lead the province of Britannia, with all its nations south of Hadrian's Wall and, for many years, well beyond it. He was never a king, for he was the ruler of kings, yet also their general and their servant. He ruled by their consent but – in theory, at least – also with their obedience. His parents were Armorican, but he was raised in country that never quite belonged to any of the great kingdoms. Perhaps it was this that made him difficult to pin down, even for the people of his own time. But if he was not a king, neither was he an emperor, for emperors were a thing of the past, even though they struggled to hold on to the illusion of what Rome had been. In the year that Arthur came to prominence the Western Empire was contested between Glycerius and Julius Nepos, neither of whom could hold the loyalty of the senate for more than a few months. It was not much better in Byzantium, where Leo I and his seven-year-old grandson, Leo II, tried to contain the currents of politics. In Gaul, Childeric, son of Merwich, the Frankish King of the Salians, was conquering all of the north except for the heartland of Armorica. Britannia had lost faith in great men. It could no longer count on helping or being helped from beyond the sea. A way had to be found, finally, to do as Honorius, Emperor of the Western Empire, had instructed more than sixty years before: look to its own defences. Maybe, in Arthur, there was a man who had the mind and the courage to bring the country to life once again, to do more than defend, to create an age of triumph from the ruins.

BOOK TWO

The Year of Politics

AD *489*

XI

THE MARCH GALES had shifted direction, and now came driving directly in from the sea. In their vanguard the rain shot against the land and into the backs of the men gathered disconsolately on the cliff path. Sixty feet below the waves made sand from boulders. It was not a day to expect invasion. Any boats caught in the open would be fighting to keep clear of the anvil that the shore had become. It was the sort of day Arthur had come to treasure in the last few years, a day when the rain kept enemies and allies alike too wet to argue. The wind was the Overlord's friend.

He leant against the doorpost and watched the rain scudding westwards. There was no sign of the still centre of the storm. He could do with another three days of this before the state of the camp and the horses became any real worry. By then the boats that he knew had been a day into their voyage when the weather broke would have been either sunk or scattered harmlessly on random coasts, their desperate warriors too exhausted to be a threat. With luck there would be few enough survivors to accommodate them as they wished on terms of his choosing. God knows there were parts of the country that needed their farming, if not their habits. Any more than fifty, though, and there would have to be executions and a skeleton crew sent back to the far side of the sea to tell the tale. At moments like this, when politics at home were worse than the risks from the sea, Arthur felt a pang of sympathy for the men who took to their boats. He knew from interrogations what they had left behind: unworkable land, villages gradually becoming inundated as water levels rose, and plenty of new people from the east, cutting off any retreat. To sail for three days and be certain of a hostile country on the other side, even one rich in untilled land, took courage and determination. If they weren't such pagan murderous bastards he might feel sorry for them. As it was...

Arthur sighed and turned back into his temporary palace, as he referred to it with sarcasm wasted on most of his entourage. He moved across a long narrow hall, timbered and smoke-filled. The wind blew back any smoke that tried to escape, though the warmth made the fire worth the smarting eyes on a morning like this. He stood and watched the flame, resting his hand on the shoulder of the boy who stirred a pot simmering over the logs. The boy looked up with hero worship and pride, but Arthur was caught up in more complex thoughts and his paternal smile was automatic.

There was a rustle of clothes and the clink of a sword behind him. 'Either you're in love or you're a bear with a sore head. Neither is much bloody use.'

Arthur kept his eyes to the fire. 'We have a choice, Candidianos, and as usual both decisions are probably wrong.'

'If there are only two you're a lucky man.'

'We can assume that the wind will have dispersed the Barbarian ships, or at least spoilt the appetite for a fight for a few days. If they've been separated it'll take us a while to find them, in any case. So we can either stay where we are and secure this coast properly or we can move south again. I'm not happy with the Cantiaci. I think they're preparing to make a treaty. We might forestall that just by coming towards them.'

'Or force them into it even faster. There is a third possibility.' Candidianos was a short but good-looking man in his early forties, and he spoke quietly, never feeling the need to let the whole hall hear. 'We could just pull back to Ebvracum and see what happens. It's only thirty miles. We could quarter the army better and keep the horses fed for longer than we can out here. We'll need to resupply the men within a week, whatever we do.'

Arthur shook his head. 'We haven't gone to all this trouble just to garrison up in Ebvracum for a month, pleasant as it would be. Quite apart from the signal it would send that we've nothing better to do, your rabble of kings would soon start getting restless. There are too many troops who will be thinking of their planting.'

'So you're back to two choices.'

'Unless you have others?'

Candidianos smiled. 'Not for the moment.'

Arthur turned the pot-stirring boy towards him and squeezed his shoulder gently. 'Give me a spoonful of that,' he said. 'What is it – the usual hog and mutton?'

'Yes sir. And barley.'

'Oh, well, that's something to cheer me. And it's hot.'

The boy stirred furiously for a few seconds and reached across the hearth for a ladle, reverently filling it to the brim and handing it to his master. Arthur offered it to his counsellor.

'Not yet, thank you.'

'You know me – no decisions without food,' he said, sipping from the ladle. 'The more I think about it I can't see the point of going south again. The men will be tired. The Votadini and the Parisi will be furious that we are not interested in their problems. It will look as if we didn't know why we came north in the first place. And we may make things worse, not better, by uniting the southern Barbarian settlements against us, especially if the Cantiaci are on the turn.'

'Does that matter?'

'Well, we'll have to deal with it sooner or later. I'd rather know that I have fresh troops and a solid group of northern kingdoms behind me when I do, though.'

Arthur drained the ladle and handed it back to the scullion. The lad could not have been more than ten. 'What do you think?'

'Me?' The boy stared in astonishment.

'You'll have to come with us. You might as well tell me while you can.'

It was the child's turn to stare into the fire, copying the solemnity he had seen on Arthur's face a few minutes before. 'I think we should find a battle and show the Barbarians there's no place for them here.'

'And I think you're the first person who's said something helpful all day,' grinned Arthur. He clapped the boy firmly on the back and strode out into the rain.

* * *

The army was camped at the base of a low hill, forest rising behind and a river in front, tumbling with the exuberance of the early spring. The men had woven hurdles of willow and hazel to provide makeshift shelters and shield their campfires from the full force of the wind.

Arthur moved along the line purposefully, looking to the men like a leader who had no doubts and no heed for the elements as they huddled in their drenched cloaks and tunics, each a colour or weave that denoted the kingdom and region from which they came. It had been one of Arthur's earliest measures as overlord to make sure he could identify each of the forces in battle. In theory it gave the men pride and identity and a sense of comradeship, but Arthur had another reason: he wanted to know exactly where each of the kings was leading his troops at any moment – not as a matter of generalship but as part of the roll call. Too often in the early battles one force or another had hung back, allowing another kingdom to take the brunt of an attack or waiting to see which way the battle would go before deciding whether or not to follow Arthur's strategy. Sometimes they had tried to dupe him by allowing the standard-bearer into the heart of the battle alone, carrying the kingdom's symbol, based on the old Roman badge, and carried like a legionary staff. Now, with the colours of all their soldiers in full view, he knew in minutes if there were waverers or turncoats among his Council.

There were troops with him on the campaign from five different nations, called in response to urgent appeals from the Parisi, beset by raiders on the north-east coast; appeals backed by insistent demands from the Votadini north of the wall that he take the situation under control. The Votadini had sent demands but no help, which was typical. Instead he had the Parisi themselves, who were not exactly a force to be reckoned with, and a rather larger and more disciplined regiment from their southern neighbours, the Coritani. The main force came from the two largest and richest magisterial areas, at least in terms of people – that of the central kingdom of the Catuvellauni and the nation to whom in theory his father Idriseg owed allegiance, the Cornovii in the country around the fast-crumbling city of Viroconium in the middle lands of the west. Finally (apart from a small bodyguard from his own kinsmen, upon which his father had always insisted), Arthur had the Dobunnian soldiers under Candidianos. They were not the most numerous group – there were perhaps only two hundred of them in his army of two thousand – but they were the only ones that Arthur trusted completely, for it was Candidianos who had voluntarily ceded the overlordship to him sixteen years before in their own capital of Corinium. Arthur had not known at first whether the action was one of generosity or calculation, but Candidianos had proved to be a true friend, whatever his original reasons for declining to draw Myrddin's sword from the stone, even though he had understood the knack, and a few years later Arthur had rewarded him with the title Consul for Life.

He had arrived in front of a bedraggled detachment of the Cornovii when he stopped suddenly and turned to peer to the north-east, from where the wind had raged all day. The soldiers themselves quietened and watched their general. To them he was, at thirty-two, already a legendary figure, said to have supernatural powers that gave him second sight and the strength of ten men. Arthur turned his face to the rain, felt the whip of it against his eyes and smiled. He was right. It had changed. The drops were falling with less anger. More importantly, the wind was veering round to the south.

'Perfect,' Arthur announced to the bemused soldiers, turned and summoned one from the ranks to walk with him as he headed back to his timber hall.

The man ran after him, overcome with a mixture of terror at being singled out and excitement at meeting his leader in person. He was shorter by a head and a few years older than Arthur, wizened by the outdoor life, his skin burned almost olive even though winter was barely over. 'Sir?'

'Where are you from, soldier?' Arthur barked.

'Country round Lavobrinta, sir.'

Arthur stopped and clasped his soldier. 'Wonderful – close to my own country. Picking you cannot have been an accident. I need a hand. As you see, I am on my own.'

'It's an honour, sir.'

'Not much of one, I'm afraid. Do you feel the wind – it's changing, agreed?'

The soldier licked his finger and held it in the air. 'Clearing soon, I think – at least, it would be on my farm.'

'As I thought. Thank you. I need all the Council in my headquarters within half an hour – I want you to fetch them. Can you do it?'

'Of course, sir,' the Cornovian said, looking uncomfortable and lowering his eyes from Arthur's. 'But I am not a herald, sir. How will they know I'm bringing the order from you?'

'Quite right. You had better take this.' Arthur unpinned one of the two brooches that fixed his cloak at the shoulder. It carried a lion carved from amber and set in silver. He smiled. 'I'll want it back, though – it's one of Myrddin's.'

The soldier looked shocked. 'Of course, sir. I would never…'

'No, you wouldn't. I know. Bring it to the hall once you have delivered the message, will you?'

'Yes, sir,' he said, and held the brooch reverently for a moment before running back along the lines, unable to resist giving a triumphant wave to his comrades as he passed them to an ironic cheer.

Arthur was in a hurry now. The depressed general who had leant against his doorway and hoped for the storm to last another three days had given way to one with an idea and a plan to go with it – not the careful sort of plan worked out by his officers and backed by the formulae of Caesar's practice that Myrddin had made him study until he could no longer bear the thought of another self-congratulatory page, but the sort of plan that came on the wind and could not be thrown back.

He burst into the hall and shouted to Candidianos, who was lounging, stretched out, on a bench with a mug of ale resting on his stomach.

'We're on the move. Council in twenty minutes.'

'Bloody hell, Arthur, in this weather?'

'Especially in this weather.'

'This had better be brilliant. Otherwise the Council will be about as cooperative as wild geese.'

'It is,' Arthur assured him.

* * *

One by one the members of the Council of Britannia or their representatives on the campaign bustled in, surprised at the urgency of Arthur's summons. Each of the nations with soldiers in the field had two men; then there were three more sent as permanent envoys from the Atrebates, the Dumnonii and the Votadini. It meant that there were still almost half the nations absent, but it was small enough to be manageable. Arthur secretly disliked having to address the full membership. On the few occasions over the last sixteen years when it had proved unavoidable he had found the meetings as fractious as they were interminable. Far better to have to deal with the real battle leaders and let the envoys spread the news, good or bad, after the event, when nobody could interfere.

CHAPTER XI

It was a field war council that met a few miles from the north-east coast that March morning. After a night in the windswept and sodden camp the protectors of Britannia were initially more interested in the Overlord's blazing fire than in the details of his tactics. Arthur was politician enough to let them warm up, sample the broth from the cauldron and watch the steam disperse from their cloaks before launching his plan. They were not given too long, though, and once they were settled and the impromptu herald from the hills above Lavobrinta had delivered back his lion clasp and been rewarded for his labours with a horn brooch carved with the Overlord's symbol, Arthur was brisk.

He had been watching the wind, he told them. The reports they had had of a large force of Barbarian ships heading out to sea from the eastern continent had filled him with foreboding. If they landed much further south, in the lands of the Iceni or Trinovantes, the chances of stopping them early were minimal, given the lack of taste for a fight among those nations. However Arthur was convinced that they were heading further north, since it had been learnt from captured Barbarians that land was considered more plentiful. There was word too that these were a different people from the settlers in the south, so that they were just as likely to be resisted by the established newcomers as by the Britannians.

The storm had been a godsend – literally, he believed. Had it continued for another day the ships would have been destroyed or scattered irrelevantly along the coast, so few men on board fit enough that they could be dealt with by the local militias.

Setting up the militias under civic control had been one of Arthur's first strategies as overlord. Under Myrddin's advice he had given each magistrate within reach of the coast the job of repairing a Roman fort and maintaining a force of one hundred men on permanent alert. The jokes about the Ploughman's Army had subsided after a while as they proved surprisingly effective at stopping the smaller raids and acting as an early warning system for the larger ones. Most of all they had made people more confident that something was being done, though Arthur was under no illusions about dealing with a more serious assault.

Now the storm was easing at exactly the right time for another, more decisive outcome, Arthur told the Council. The wind had been coming in as a north-westerly gale. That would naturally have driven the Barbarian ships away from the army assembled to meet them, and their sails and oarsmen would not have been strong enough to let them do anything but run before the wind. They would find themselves landing on the northern flank of the Iceni coast, if they landed at all. Once the gale had veered to the south-east and abated, though, the Barbarians would be able to regroup and take back control of their direction. Arthur calculated that the main force would be heading straight for them, within a few miles. If he was right, there should be sightings at first light the next day. He hoped the intelligence as to when the fleet had put to sea and his guess of the time it would take to make the crossing was accurate. If not, they were in trouble. The Barbarians would land in darkness, have the night to establish themselves on dry land and move on before he had a chance to counter them.

Arthur paused and glanced round the faces gathered by the fire. Nobody seemed anxious to disagree. Outside the wind was quieter than it had been for two days. It no longer howled through the wicker walls and pushed the wool hangings billowing into the hall. There was just a gentle moan from the trees and the drip of steady rain.

Arthur continued. There was no telling exactly where the ships would land. He hoped the scouts in the coastal forts and in the headland watch-posts would pick them up and send dispatches. But the sea was running faster than a horse at the moment. There would be a strong element of luck. However, they should be prepared. He wanted all his forces moved up to the coast itself. He believed the Barbarians would make for the mouth of the River Abus, some ten miles to the south of the army's present position. He wanted to persuade them that this was not an option and force them around Oceli Head and along the wide-open coast that ran northwards from it. That way he could move the troops swiftly along the shore to deal with incursions without the fear that the Barbarians would slip through on to the south bank of the river. If they did then he would have no time to work back to a crossing point beyond Petuaria, and even if he succeeded, the Barbarians would be able to split his forces in half.

He ordered two detachments of troops, numbering no more than fifty men in each band, to be posted on either side of the river. They were to build a series of beacons to be lit as soon as the first ships were sighted, making it clear not only that the Britannians knew they were coming but that both banks of the river were equally well defended, without showing that there were defences of any strength beyond the river itself. The beacons would give Arthur time to arrange his main force to the north. Were there any questions so far?

The Council remained silent. Arthur turned to his centurion and clarified the order for the river guard to be mustered and moved out.

'For the rest of us,' he went on, 'the next two days will either prove that we have been wasting our time, or that we have achieved an important breakthrough.'

* * *

The early spring light had almost faded and the evening was well advanced by the time the army had struck camp and marched to its new positions, or as close to them as Arthur was prepared to venture before the morning. A line of dunes protected them from the sea itself, and the last remnants of the foul weather. There was a cold night in prospect, and the air had a touch of frost in it as the storm clouds dispersed, but Arthur had forbidden the lighting of any large fires. The men were to be allowed nothing stronger than watered ale. Only the bards were to sing. Arthur did not want any early Barbarian arrivals alerted that this was anything other than empty country. So the men huddled in small groups around the few sticks they had been allowed to gather and light, doing their best to do as their commanders had told them and put up with suffering tonight in return for imagining the feasting after the coming victory. There were plenty, though, for whom the equally compelling thought was that this might be their last night alive, and that it was a pretty miserable way to spend it.

The army was stretched along a five-mile line and divided into its national regiments. The smallest contingent, the Dobunni, had taken the central position, the assumption being that they could be reinforced from either side if necessary. The Catuvellauni were concentrated on the southern flank, the Parisi and a few of their Brigantian neighbours taking the northern. Arthur stationed himself between the Catuvellauni and the next group, the Cornovii, where he felt confident the first landings were likely to be made. In between the main camps the cavalry scouts were posted, three men to a unit, ready to ride and alert the nearest command point at the first sign of a ship.

By midnight the three-quarter moon was out and the sea beyond the dunes had quietened. The waves could still be heard thudding into the beach, but only with the resentful last mutterings of the anger they had let out all day. The watches could see clearly across the moonlit water for a mile or two. It would have been hard, but not too hard, to spot any Barbarian vessel heading for the sand or, more likely, for captains with no port to go to or pilots to guide them through the shallows laying up for the night with prows turned into the wind, waiting for the dawn.

Arthur did not sleep. He never could before a battle. There was too much resting on his shoulders, even if there was nothing very useful to be done. Instead he rode alone from one camp to another, having a word with the sentries and the officers of the watch, checking the lookouts. He had often been told that it was dangerous, that there were plenty who could not accept the Pendraeg succession or who wanted their own leader as overlord. There were spies, too, they told him, from the nations who had made accommodations with the Barbarians and saw the way forward as the adoption of their gods and customs, even the guttural snarl of their language. For many of the leaders of these southern nations (the richest and the most vulnerable to continual attack) the political reality that Arthur represented – the maintenance of Christianity as it had been adopted in the previous century, tolerance for the old gods of Britannia and government based on the traditions of Romano-Britannian administration as far as they could be upheld in these very changed times – was a romantic dead end.

None of these warnings had been heeded by Arthur since he had been elected overlord. Myrddin's advice had been simple, if fatalistic: 'Treat every man you meet as your equal and your friend, even if you know him not to be. Those that wish to hurt you will do it anyway, but you do not have to give them an excuse.'

For Arthur, though, talking to the men (not just the officers) was nothing to do with politics. They were the fighters who had to put his strategy into action. As he made his way between the campfires he would stop and ask about a tactic, a trick of the trade, listen to the stories of the seasoned campaigners who had been on expeditions he had not. He listened to the jokes about other nations, about the merits of their women, the splendour of their children. He examined the mementoes they carried and bestowed blessings on their lucky tokens – a buckle or an amulet, sometimes an old gold coin strung as a medallion from the neck. He had learnt to decline politely the request to test his strength as 'the bear of Britannia' against the muscled

CHAPTER XI

show-offs, telling them to preserve his and their own strengths for the Barbarians. The moments he valued most, however, were those when he spotted a face behind the fire he recognised or the voice of a soldier who had followed him from battle to battle over the years. Then he would often dismount, tether his horse and beckon his comrade away from the others for a few minutes' private discussion in the close hours of the night.

By the time the moon had set and the darkness began to edge to grey, Arthur had ridden the full length of his lines and back. Taking two mounted Cornovian men with him, he made his way across the matted grass and early spring flowers up to one of the lookout points perched on top of the dunes. They dismounted below the ridge, secured the horses and crept to the summit, careful not to show themselves breaking the line of the land as it would be seen from offshore. At the watch-post one sentry sat huddled by the dying remnants of his fire, his two comrades sleeping close by, wrapped in their dark-green cloaks.

'Anything out there?' Arthur asked quietly.

The sentry jumped. 'Who...? My lord!' He began to scramble to his feet.

'Stay down,' Arthur ordered. 'Stay just as you were. I don't need a fanfare. Just answer my question.'

'Nothing yet, I don't think, my lord.'

'What about the river beacons?'

'Not lit – that I am sure of.'

Arthur crouched on the damp turf and peered along the coast to the south. Out to sea white horses still reared upwards from the waves, though the waves themselves were no longer the furious monsters of the day before. They were enough to deter a landsman like him, though. Arthur had never ventured on to the water, except for the crossing of a river mouth. Despite the ambush he was planning, he had boundless respect for the men who were prepared to brave the seas to reach Britannia in search of the perfect country.

He could just make out the shape of the land in the pre-dawn gloom. Had fires been lit on the headlands above the River Abus, they would have shone clearly. The wind had dropped to not much more than a strong breeze and the rain had stopped. The clouds still ran fast from the east, but they were high, now, and broken. It would be a fine day for fighting.

'Keep at it,' he grunted to the sentry. 'How long have they been asleep?'

'I only took the watch when the moon went down, my lord.'

'And they saw nothing? No shapes flying north under the moon?'

'Nothing that they said.'

'Very well. Let them sleep, then, but only till you can see the sun.'

'Yes, my lord.'

Arthur slipped back down to his waiting companions and remounted. He was less certain of his tactics. He had expected a ship by now if there were to be any – at least heading towards the mouth of the river. Maybe the storm had been more effective than he had thought and the Barbarians had either drowned or been forced back on to their own coasts. That would be the best outcome, he thought at first, but then realised it would leave him with more problems than it would solve. He would have no reports from his spies of when the next attempt would be or where it would come from. He would have to disband at least half his forces to return home for the spring planting, and then could find himself needing to muster them again. If that happened the Council were likely to be sullen and uncooperative, pointing out that this expedition, about which he was so definite, had proved futile. In such circumstances he could easily find himself outnumbered and defeated only a few weeks later. Better, far better, to have something to show for the day, even if it was only a skirmish with two or three shiploads of men straggling ashore to tell of the heroes lost behind them.

Arthur led his companions along to the next lookout a few minutes' ride away to the south. It sat a little higher off the beach, and by the time he had repeated his surprised sentry routine there was just the hint of red in the sky to the east. The sun would soon push against the horizon. This was the perfect moment to spot any vessels that were afloat. The report was the same, though. Nothing moving except the turbulent water and a handful of fishing boats putting out from a village further up the coast for a quick hour or two after the storm but before the sun dulled the catch. Arthur paced impatiently back to his horse, clambered up and turned towards his headquarters on the landward side of the sands. He had no wish to slaughter anybody, Barbarian or not, but he needed a victory, and he did not like finding himself chasing shadows.

They had been riding for only a few minutes and were passing the first of the lookouts he had visited when there was a shout from the head of the dunes. He reined in his horse and wheeled round to see the figure of a soldier, one of those who had been sleeping obliviously half an hour before, come tumbling towards him down the turf.

'Ships?' Arthur yelled back.

'No, my lord,' the soldier, a short figure, tripping over the hem of his cloak and in too much of a hurry to have picked up his spear, was breathing heavily as he drew up beside Arthur. 'The fires. Smoke above the river.'

Arthur smiled. 'Excellent.' He turned to one of his mounted lieutenants. 'Get down to the Catuvellauni. I want twenty men on horse, no more, sent down to the river mouth. They are to show themselves in as many different positions as possible to the enemy. I want those in the ships to think that they are all there is to worry about, just deterrent enough to make them head for a quieter place to land. Tell Cunorix not to attack immediately if a ship appears and lands. If there are others behind I don't want them sailing away out of trouble. If there are no others then we can easily deal with the rabble when it suits us. Understood? No attack until I say.'

'Yes, my lord.'

'And if you meet the herald from the river forces on your way, he is to report back immediately – straight to me.'

'Understood, my lord.'

The horseman urged his mount to a canter. Arthur turned for base, shouting back to the sentry, 'And make sure you and everybody else keep out of sight.'

* * *

The sun had been up for over an hour when Arthur's increasingly nervous waiting was ended by the arrival of the herald from his decoy troops at the mouth of the River Abus.

'We did as you ordered, my lord, and lit the beacons as soon as a ship came into view.'

'I'm sure you did. How many ships? That's the point, man.'

'One definite, sir. Another possible. When I left it was too far away to confirm as a Barbarian sighting.'

'It's hardly likely to be one of ours in this weather, is it?' he said.

'Don't know, sir.' The herald shuffled uncomfortably. He never felt quite comfortable reporting to the Overlord. Maybe it was Arthur's accent, which was from so far west there were words that didn't sound like proper Brythonic at all. Maybe it was that he could never quite decide whether he was being treated as a fool or not. Arthur had a way of treating all his men as if they were fellow commanders. If you didn't know the answer it made you feel worse than if he just shouted an order and treated you like an idiot.

'Well, I do know,' he said. 'It's not one of ours. We haven't got any reconnaissance ships patrolling anywhere north of Londinium, which is stupid, but there it is.'

'I see, sir.'

'So that's two. How did the first react?'

'She was heading upriver, like you said, sir. So we lit the fires on both banks and made as much noise as we could. We worked it so that lines of a score of men would appear on the high ground and then disappear. We hoped it would mean that they wouldn't know the proper numbers, my lord.'

'Did it work?'

'Think so, sir. Least, they had the oars on her and turned. Then they put the sail back up and she headed out to sea again.'

'Direction?'

'North, sir.'

'And the second?'

'I left too soon to say, my lord. I thought you would want to know first thing.'

'You thought right. Get yourself some food and then get back down to your unit. I want you heralds working in relays until ordered to withdraw.'

'Sir.'

Arthur gathered his staff around him. This was going to be an unusual battle. There was no point in leading his forces on a co-ordinated charge as he would have done in a conventional arrangement. The units were too far spread out along the coast for that to have any success. Instead he would use wherever he stuck his standard as the command post, relying on a stream of heralds to distribute the orders to each of the regiments. It might mean that he would never have to draw his sword at all, though that would not look good. There was nothing the men hated more than the Overlord living up to the title without lifting a finger. There would have to be a moment when he joined in.

Two ships would not constitute the battle he was hoping for, though. Cunorix of the Catuvellauni could mop them up without much difficulty once the trap was laid. That trap was simple enough. Let the first ship land and its exhausted cargo disembark. Allow them to rest on the sand and drag the ship up on to the beach. By then the second ship should have beached as well. Once they had shipped their oars and half the men were over the side, then appear over the summit of the dunes and fall upon them with as much speed and ferocity as possible.

That was the fall-back plan, though. Arthur wanted something rather more glorious. For that he would need time and luck.

His assembled staff numbered no more than ten plus the troop of heralds, four for each nation riding continually. Arthur had learnt during his studies of Greek and Roman strategy to make sure that messengers were always at hand and always moving, so that there would never be a moment when he was out of contact with his units. He pitched his makeshift command post – no more than his standard and a rough map of his troop positions and the enemy marked out in stones and sticks on the grass – as close to the head of the dunes as possible without breaking into view. Two men lay on their stomachs, waiting for the first direct sighting. The morning was clear and sunny now and the warmth was easing back into the air, drying the turf around them. Arthur felt his spirits rise with the temperature.

Twenty minutes later there was a yell from above him and Arthur ran to the summit. He fell to the grass and gazed out across the water.

'Two ships, my lord.'

'I can see that.'

The prows of the Barbarian vessels were low in the waves as they edged along parallel to the shore. They were perhaps a mile apart, the second just rounding the long spit of sand bar that marked the estuary of the Abus. Even from that distance, though, Arthur could see that these were no ordinary fishing boats. They had large square-rigged sails, unfurled now that the wind had dropped from its storm speed. Arthur guessed that they would be relying on the sails and only one or two oarsmen now while the men recovered their strength from the nights of exposure and armed themselves to take the shore. There was plenty of beach for them to choose. Arthur hoped they would patrol the coast for a while, trying to pick a spot a little more sheltered than most of the open dunes afforded.

'Let me know when they make a move for the land,' he said.

The soldier nodded and Arthur slipped back to his group of heralds. He beckoned to one.

'Message to Cunorix: no attack until the second ship beaches. Then full assault using all speed. No standing around looking important.'

'Understood, my lord.' The herald mounted and rode off to the south.

For half an hour the coastline of Britannia could not have seemed more still or idyllic to the men in the ships. Nothing moved on the skyline of the sand dunes. The sun dried the sodden planking of their benches and salt became crust in their clothes as the wool stiffened. The lead ship slackened sail and eased its progress while its companion closed the gap. By the time the captain gave the order to turn towards the shore there was no more than ten ship's lengths between them.

Arthur was smiling with satisfaction as he heard the news. A moment later, though, and he was urging the herald desperately to ride full speed to Cunorix and tell him to hold back from the beach at all costs. Urged by the lookouts, he hurried back to his vantage point.

'Out there, my lord.'

The sentry was not pointing south to the mouth of the river, from where the ships had emerged out of the dawn, but north-eastwards – well out to sea beyond the next headland. Arthur followed his pointing arm and swore. They were little more than dots, but he could count at least six of them lined up on the morning horizon. Instantly he realised that his simple and immaculate tactics would have to change. His wish had been all too generously granted. He had wanted a battle to demonstrate the unity of his forces. Now he was going to have one.

If the Barbarians were to stay within reach of his men, they had to steer to join the first two ships. If they continued north Arthur would have to march hard to meet them. He needed time to decide. There were two possibilities. Either the northern ships had no intention of joining those already close to landing, and would continue to sail away – in which case he might as well attack the southern ships, overwhelm them and give chase as fast as possible. Or the Barbarians would tack south again, and he needed to give them as much of a sense of security as possible before launching his attack. But how long would it take him to find out which course to follow? And if there were more ships out to sea – even more than the eight he knew about now – there was another tactical nightmare. There could be up to a thousand men in those vessels already. While he was confident that, with double the number, he could more than rout them in a surprise attack on the beach, if they were reinforced from the sea during the middle of the battle and he had already committed all his men, then the outcome would be far from certain. Arthur had always hated decisions.

As he paced about the grass, heralds arrived from the other national detachments to find out whether he had spotted the northern fleet. He ordered them all to watch and wait. There was time yet. He called for a cup of ale and some bread. Maybe food would clear the brain. The sea made the enemy so unpredictable. On land he could have chosen his ground and provoked an attack or, knowing where their forces were, moved about their flanks. As it was the best part of the day could pass without Arthur being any nearer to knowing how to deploy his army. Myrddin would have told him that there was no point worrying about the things he could not control – that waiting made things clear, not taking action for the sake of it. Arthur took his beer and lay on the turf in the warm spring sun. He need be in no hurry to kill.

After another twenty minutes he could procrastinate no longer. The first of the southern pair of ships beached half a mile away, between his post and the main body of Catuvellauni troops. The second ship was close behind. The northern fleet was swinging round and heading towards shore as well. They would be at most half an hour behind. Arthur knew it was not in the nature of the Barbarians to hold off shore to watch the fate of their companions. They were an honourable and courageous people – at least among their own kin – and would not shirk a fight unless the odds were overwhelming. In fact, showing there was some fighting to be done might hasten their arrival.

Down the coast the men of the first ship were disembarking, leaping into the shallows where the prow had grounded. As soon as their feet touched sand they grabbed hold of ropes running along the shallow gunwales of the ship and began to haul it up and on to the beach.

Slowly the ship rose from the water as more and more men leapt over the sides and added their strength, however depleted after three nights at sea in calamitous weather. The sight and smell of the land had reinvigorated them, and they shouted encouragement to each other in the guttural, clipped tongue that Arthur often wished had remained a mystery. Variants of it were beginning to be spoken in pockets all over Britannia, however, and Myrddin had insisted that he knew enough to makes his enemies believe he understood.

To the north the ships were clearly visible now, no longer shadows on the rise of the waves. Arthur counted nine of them, even more than at the first sighting, but he was relieved to see that there were no more appearing over the horizon. It already constituted a full invasion. Eleven ships in all made this the largest movement of Barbarians against the coast for nearly thirty years. The intelligence had been right. Either they were becoming greedy or conditions at home were far worse than anybody realised. He would worry about their reasons once they were safely defeated and under his control, though.

Arthur returned to the makeshift map he had traced on the ground. To deal with the number of warriors the ships would soon disgorge he would need most of his army closer together.

The ships were making passage south-west fast, clearly using the oars as well as the sail. That made up Arthur's mind. He did not want to have the full weight of the Barbarian army on the beach at the same time. He summoned a messenger and sent the order down to Cunorix. Attack the moment the second ship grounded, as he had first told him. Then he sent the herald to the furthest flung of his troops, the detachment from the Parisi, ordering them to close up to the south. By the time they had joined up with the Cornovian units, the main body of the fleet would be nearing the beach. With luck they would be concentrating on coming to the aid of their comrades under the hammer of the Catuvellauni. They would not suspect that the Britannians were still holding back the majority of their soldiers in reserve.

This was the moment before a battle Arthur always dreaded, the endless minutes when his orders had been issued but battle was not yet joined. It was worse that day because he himself was not in the vanguard, his troops lined up behind him, his sword of office raised ready to urge them forward. He was the spectator now, observing the moment when Cunorix would unleash his men on the bedraggled warriors unloading their possessions on to the sand.

Arthur moved up to the edge of the ridge and watched the scene unfold below him. The first ship was wholly out of the water, its prow carving of a sea beast's head looking ridiculous and impotent as it stood on the sand, tilted to a jaunty angle. A circle of soldiers had been posted a few yards up the beach, scouring the dunes for signs of ambush. Behind them a thin chain of men ran from the ship's side, unloading the cargo – not much; the Barbarians brought little with them. They had come because of the tales of riches that waited in Britannia. They expected to take whatever they wanted when they arrived. Those men weakened by the voyage lay in the sand, relishing the sun on their faces and the feel of dry land beneath them.

The second ship was lowering its sail and steering to come ashore alongside the first. It would beach gently, the peaceful and unchallenged landing of its companion taking away the urgency. There was only the relief of rest after a long voyage to be looked forward to. Arthur wondered if Cunorix had received his message, if the men were arranged properly around the head of the dunes to cut off any escape. It was so quiet. Maybe they were not there at all, and had slipped away on their own business. From his vantage point Arthur was too far away to hear the shouts of welcome from the men of the vanguard as the prow of the ship met the shore and the first warriors fell over the side into the waist-high water.

He heard clearly enough, though, the roar from above them as the Catuvellauni under Cunorix swarmed into sight and careered down the slope of sand and shingle, swords and lances flashing in the mid-morning sun.

For a moment the ninety Barbarians from the first ship stood or sat in bewildered shock, caught between the noise of greeting and of imminent death. Then the discipline of experienced fighting men took charge. Those furthest up the beach closed ranks and retreated until they were level with men who, seconds before, had been lying drowsily on the sand. There was confusion as they rushed to arm themselves from the pile of stores they had unloaded or climbed back into the ship to retrieve them.

They were in a disastrous position. The Britannians outnumbered them many times. Some could barely stand after the pounding they had suffered in the nights at sea. The ship was already beached and offered no safety. They had the disadvantage of facing upslope. To

Cunorix, charging in front of his men, and to Arthur, watching from his vantage point in the distance, there seemed only one possible outcome – ignominious slaughter.

The situation was equally obvious to the men trapped by their stranded ship, however. This could not be a glorious battle taking them straight to the home of the gods. It would be a quick and miserable defeat. They had only a few seconds before the fury of the Catuvellauni descended on them. There was only one way of escape – back into the sea from which they had just emerged so gratefully.

First a handful, then the whole mass of men strode back into the surf, their woollen clothes slowing them to a painful trudge, their weapons too heavy to allow them to let their feet go and swim. Their hope was the second ship, still afloat except for the forward few feet of the hull.

XII

FURTHER UP THE COAST the scene could only just be made out by the helmsman of the leading ship in the main fleet. He could see figures attacking from the high ground and the shape of one of the ships slipping back into the water. The course he had been steering would have brought him ashore a mile or two to the north, just as Arthur had predicted when planning to repeat the pattern of attack. But now he veered towards the ship floundering in the water under twice its usual complement of men. Already the vessel that lay on the beach had been fired, its slender stores of cloth and arms passed back behind the Catuvellaunian lines.

The sudden retreat into the water brought the Britannian charge to a sputtering halt. A few lances were thrown at the men retreating through the water, and a few men rushed into the waves to kill if they could, but Cunorix soon ordered them to withdraw. Fighting in water was a fool's game, and throwing in spears a waste of good arms. Once the ship was fired, a gesture he knew was full of terrible religious symbolism to the Barbarians, he ordered his men back up the sand to regain the height advantage and form up in orderly fashion behind the shingle, where the footing was firmer. The seas were still running with a strong swell after the days of storm, and waves broke over the sides of the ship as it tried to hold position close enough into the land to let the ambushed men be helped to clamber aboard. A few were cut down, and one man was too exhausted and heavy in his sodden clothes to reach safety and drowned in little more than his own depth of water. Once all that could be saved had been hauled out, the ship eased away from the surf into deeper and calmer water. It was too heavily laden to make much headway along the coast. The best that could be managed was to hold position until either help arrived or darkness came. Cunorix was confident it would drift ashore eventually, and when it did, his army would carry on where it had left off.

Arthur was not so confident. There was more than an hour of stalemate while everybody waited to see what would happen. He had lost the initiative. Everything depended now on the actions of the main fleet. Either it could abandon the stricken men to their fate at sea or in the hands of Cunorix and sail away to an undefended shore; or it could come straight to their aid.

Noon had come and gone by the time a new phase of the action began to unfold. The remains of the beached ship were now smouldering embers over which Cunorix's men warmed themselves, roasted rabbits and occasionally shouted abuse at the Barbarians trying to keep themselves afloat and out of range. The leading ships of the fleet had been hauled over, a mile out to sea, waiting for the rest to catch up. When all nine ships were within hailing distance of one another orders and strategy were passed from ship to ship while the sails were furled and the oarsman held steady in the swell. Arthur, watching with increasing impatience, grinned to himself. He was glad he was not being bobbed about after half a week at sea with a battle to fight. Those men that were not sick would have their sea legs, and would spend most of the first hour on land trying to stand upright. They would hardly be fit to rush ashore, scything their way through the Britannians who were warm, rested and bored with waiting for battle. Everything now would depend on timing. The weather was changing again. The gentle southerlies of the morning had given way to a more purposeful breeze from the north-west and clouds were thickening. Arthur summoned his horse and left his command post, riding north to inspect the detachments that had been consolidating behind the protective ridge of the dunes.

Soon it was clear a decision had been made out to sea as well. The fleet had raised sail to take advantage of the wind. The ships were speeding towards the Britannian shore now, and Cunorix's men roused themselves from the sand and reformed in battle order.

Cunorix knew that the seaborne warriors would be ready and eager for battle, despite their ordeal and sea fatigue. There would have been no songs to compose about a gentle landing and a stroll into the country behind. He dispatched a rider to find out where Arthur had placed the rest of the army and how long the reinforcements would take to arrive, for Cunorix could either let the Barbarians think he was their only obstacle and fight them as they disembarked, or he could retreat on to the higher ground and wait until the full complement of Britannian nations was lined up with him.

In the event there was no time for the luxury of an answer. The ships swept towards the beach in a line, far enough apart to make Cunorix have to decide where to attack first, close enough together to be able to come to each other's aid once they had reached dry land and seen where the fighting would concentrate. The landing was different from the morning's relaxed leap into the shallow surf. This time the hulls were sailed and rowed hard against the shore. Half the men in each ship were at the aft oars; the others stood or knelt in the bows, ready with their shields to jump the moment there was ground underneath. As the first Barbarians' feet splashed on to land, the front rank of the Catuvellauni charged forward, ready to meet them before their swords were steady in their hands.

It was a risk to move so fast, before he knew the odds. But Cunorix knew his men well, too. They were not the sort to wait for the enemy to come to them, whatever Arthur's old Roman textbooks said. They were at their best when they charged and cut and killed at close quarters, taking the initiative and living on the heat of the battle until it was over. So, as each group landed, Cunorix met them with a hundred men, running down the shore to slice into them and stop them joining up with the previous detachment. Soon the noise of the waves breaking was drowned out by the clamour of the fight, the thud of swords on wooden shields, the cries of men in fury and catastrophic pain, the agony of each wound magnified by saltwater.

Cunorix led a quarter of the army, over five hundred men. This was more than enough of a force to take on the first few loads of

Barbarians. Each of the ships could carry well over a hundred, sometimes nearer two hundred or more. But some had not set out full, others had lost men to the storm and not everyone who had survived the nights at sea was in any state to win against a ferocious enemy before they had reached the first grass of the dunes. It took time, as well, for the men who had been rowing to detach themselves from the oars, lay their hands to arms and join the fighting.

For the first half-hour the Catuvellaunian force more than held the beach. A few Barbarians managed to slip away behind the ships and paddle away out of danger. They did not seem worth worrying about. The main force were pinned on the edge of the waves, pushed up against Cunorix's men as the tide came in. Soon, though, it was the tide of battle, not the sea, that was turning. More and more Barbarians reached the shore, despite the men sent to repel them, and Cunorix could see that unless help arrived with Arthur fast, his men would be outnumbered, outflanked and stretched too thin along the beach. Ship after ship disgorged its troops, only a skeleton crew of sailors staying on board each to hold them steady and refloat them on the rising tide, easing them out into deeper water so that the stores would be safe and the ships themselves kept from harm. If there was to be any more burning of ships to be done, it would be their ritual burning the night after victory.

On the right flank the battle was going well for Cunorix. Very few Barbarians had managed to reach the safety of firm ground. But further along the story was less happy. Bands from the later ships to beach were coalescing into a formidable force and wheeling his men round so that it was they who were in danger of finding their backs to the sea. The Catuvellauni needed more men and more time to regroup. Neither of these was happening, it seemed: just the slash of the long swords of the Barbarians, so finely made that the leather jerkins of the Britannians were no better than the skin on sausages at fending off the cutting strokes. Only those with old chain mail inherited from great-grandparents who had served Roman units had a measure of protection. But mostly the Barbarians slashed at the legs and arms. A man disabled was as good as dead.

Cunorix's five hundred were soon beleaguered. The Barbarians scented victory, a glorious end to their travels. The gods had been with them after all. The storms at sea, the defended shore, the orders from home to leave or be killed as the new savages from the east took their lands and women, the rising sea waters that were drowning their villages, the cold and the rain for summer after summer that destroyed the corn and left no fodder for the winter – all of these were tests, they were sure, just as those that spoke to the gods had told them. Here on a warm spring afternoon they would take new land and find new women. They roared as they pushed up the sands into which blood was soaking and mingling with the incoming tide. The last of the ships, the overladen survivor of the first attack, joined the action. Thirty of its men were too ill or wounded to fight and another dozen tended them and the ship itself – but that left a hundred and seventy to add to the turmoil in front of them. Above the battle crows and gulls were fighting their own war, working out who would have the scavenging rights to the fallen.

Then over the ridge poured horses. And on their backs rode Britannians in cloaks of red, screams of outrage in their voices, with lances ready to impale and swords hanging for the first slash against Barbarian limbs. Behind them men stood with different instruments, making the music of war. There were the Gaulish pipes screeching out their challenge, trumpets that the Barbarians had thought had died with the last legions forty years before, even the great horn that wound round the soldier's body and sounded a deep, booming note of challenge.

The first fifty horsemen caught the enemy on the wet sand, speared and galloped back up the beach. The second fifty drove men back into the water. The rising tide had cut the beach to half the width it had been in the morning. The ships were rising off the sand. A third troop of cavalry reared over the horizon and delivered its ferocious message. The harsh music thundered on, and with it rose the hearts and confidence of the Catuvellauni. They retreated, reformed, stood their ground and, as the wave of horsemen drove a third and fourth time into the northern flank of the Barbarians, they charged again. There were no more horsemen to come, but nobody on the invading side knew that. Behind the horses men without swords or shields were running on to the shingle. They stopped, well out of range of the throwing arms of the Barbarians. They scooped handfuls of pebbles into pouches. From their belts they drew leather slings and waited for the horsemen to ride off for the next charge. The moment there was clear sight of the enemy they loaded the stones into the slings and loosed a volley towards the Barbarian men, still reeling from the terror of the horses. A shower of rocks clattered among them. Many of the pebbles hit shields or skipped across the shallow water. But more smashed into heads and bodies, drawing blood, bruising chests and backs already bruised by the hammering of the storm-ridden nights of the voyage.

Again the horsemen charged. This time another rider appeared – on his own except for a standard-bearer – for a moment above the battle. The Britannians saw him and cheered. His standard, not a flag, but a golden disc stamped with two dragons and supported by laurel and snakes entwined, was raised to the right.

Cunorix looked up to his left from his position behind his men, where he had turned and turned his horse, cajoling the tired, encouraging the frightened back into the action. He looked up at Arthur.

'Show-off,' he muttered, 'but about fucking time.'

Behind the exhausted Catuvellauni the green-cloaked men of the Dobunni, urged on by Candidianos, swept into sight and down the slope. The numbers on the southern flank were more than even now, and though the Dobunni numbered only half the Catuvellauni, they were fresh. The Barbarians would have fallen back, but there was nowhere to fall back to except the sea. The best they could do was meet the onslaught with the fury of those who know that the only choice left is triumph or immediate death.

Arthur's standard was raised to the left. Now it was the turn of the northern peoples, led by the Parisi, to defend their own shore. Below them was the force from the final three ships to land. They were too far away from the cavalry to have engaged in battle, and had had time to form up and recover before racing towards the hottest part of the fighting. As the Barbarians started along the beach to join against the Cornovii, the Parisi and the Coritani charged down at their backs, catching them before they could reach the others. The Barbarian forces were now split into three, and were outnumbered two to one or more. From an invasion they had been confident of winning, it was turning into a massacre as the tide forced them on to the swords of the Britannians and the incoming water washed the blood from thousands of wounds into the sand at their feet.

Arthur had given the order that there were to be no prisoners of any rank, and it was carried out with ruthless enthusiasm. He did not want anyone left to negotiate a truce with, because there was to be no truce to negotiate. Those that could flee could take their chances in a land where the Barbarians would find no shelter. They had destroyed the Western Empire, but they would not destroy Britannia. They could sail north, but not west. With all his infantry engaged Arthur withdrew the cavalry and sent them back over the dunes to cut down any of the enemy who had slipped behind the battle lines.

By late afternoon the battle was won and the slaughter almost complete. Though the ships still floated out of harm's way none of them had enough oarsmen on board to make a voyage of any length. The noise of war had subsided and the only cries were those of the carrion birds and the wounded. Burial parties moved among the bodies, carrying the Britannian dead and wounded away from the water's edge. Those that did not survive would be given Christian honours in simple graves without their swords. No longer did they follow the pagan traditions of lavish grave possessions. A man's clothes and perhaps his cloak clasp and belt buckle were enough to introduce him to heaven.

The Barbarian wounded were killed where they lay. The bodies were looted of their arms and finely worked metal. Their swords, forged with steel finer than anything found in the west for two hundred years, were especially prized. Then the carcasses were left to the sea from which they had emerged confidently so soon before. Away from the shore, the redundant ships edged alongside each other. The two least damaged by the storm were selected, and slowly the men and stores from the others were transferred across the water, so calm now, the storm might never have been.

From almost a thousand men who had reached the shore, fewer than sixty had survived on the ships. Perhaps forty more had slipped through the Britannian cordon. The rest were corpses without names or memorials. The two half-strength Barbarian ships turned south and headed away in sadness from this truly barbaric land, taking with them the message that only savagery of a kind their gods had never sanctioned could be expected, and must therefore be used in turn against the Britannians by all those who wished to settle there in future. They could not sail for home, but there were lands nearby where their tongue would be understood and their kinship recognised.

Arthur stayed away from the beach. He had no wish to inspect the horror he had unleashed. Instead he sent his messengers to spread news of the victory, then rode to where the Britannian wounded had been mustered. The physicians and healers moved among them, administering the rough medicine of the battlefield. On fires of gorse and driftwood cauldrons boiled with herbs to clean and cauterise. Fighting in the sea had its advantages. The salt, though agony, might have saved some from infection. Most of the conscious injured had slashes to legs and arms; several had lost hands. They were the lucky ones. They could be stitched and bound. Those with wounds to the head or the body had little hope.

It had been a victory, but a costly one. No Barbarian gave up his life without a fight. The injured lay in rows around the fires, waiting to be tended or to die. The Catuvellauni, who had borne the brunt of the early part of the battle, had suffered most, and Arthur felt a pang of guilt that he had not brought the rest of his troops on to the scene earlier. He knew he could not have acted any differently, for he had not known where the ships would beach and in what formation, but still he wished he had had more men in reserve at the right place and the right time. He dismounted and moved among the casualties. He had a word with everyone, even those too dulled by pain and loss of blood to know him. For Arthur, though, it was a penalty of generalship. He had been able, indeed, had a duty, to stay behind the lines and keep control. Without that there could have been no victory. But he had not had to draw his sword or risk his life all day. The least he could do was to comfort the men who had, telling them what they had won and what it would mean to their children and neighbours. Over each he made the sign of the cross and gave a blessing.

XIII

ARTHUR LAY ON A SHEEPSKIN BED watching a kite circle in the early morning air, high above the old spring-line road that divided his camp mound from the sudden scarp of hills. The sky was clear and the day would be warm for May. He could – perhaps should – have risen an hour before. But Gwenan was cradled by his left arm, and the gentle caress of her breath on his chest as she slept was too peaceful to disturb. Occasionally his thoughts slipped away from politics and war to her and the accidents that had brought her to him. He did not want to dwell on the certainties that would take her away. He kissed her light-brown hair, so much lighter than that of the girls he had known when he was young in the greater hills at home. It was hard to know how old she was: perhaps twelve or fourteen years younger than him, at a guess. Probably she had no idea herself, and Arthur had never asked in the months since Christmas that she had come to his bed. Eldadus of the Atrebates had announced to much laughter that he was tired of the Overlord riding around the country without a woman, so that the whole Council had to lock up their daughters. So she was his Christmas gift, his Gwenan, his little Venus. She was the daughter of one of the Atrebatan women taken and raped by a band of Barbarians who had been driven away. As a half-Barbarian she could expect no family favours, but Eldadus thought Arthur might enjoy her for a while. And he had. She had seemed to accept her status as an offering with equanimity, if her quietness could be interpreted as that.

After a few weeks, though, as she accompanied Arthur from camp to camp over winter roads, he had heard that she was letting it be known that if favours were wanted from the Overlord, people would be wise to approach him though her. He had smiled and denied it, but secretly it suited him very well. She filtered out the intrigue and kept him informed in a way which not even Myrddin managed (on the rare occasions now that they were ever in the same place).

The kite swooped out of view. Gwenan stirred and nuzzled closer under the cloak, which was all they needed to keep warm that morning. Arthur slid his fingers under the untwined mass of hair and stroked the small of her back. There were two moles there and another just under her breast that he could never leave alone. She groaned awake and Arthur kissed her hair again. Gwenan opened her eyes and reached up her lips to be kissed properly, and Arthur knew he could not start the day without making love to her, however late into the night they had stopped before. He gathered her into his arms and rolled her beneath him.

'Good morning, my lord,' Gwenan giggled, 'or is that too much to ask?'

'Much too much,' Arthur whispered into her hair, 'and this the best way of saying it.'

Another hour passed. Eventually they lay contentedly and talked. Gwenan ran her fingers through his hair and looked studiously at his face.

'Arthur,' she mouthed.

'Yes?'

'Nothing. I was just saying your name. It's a strange name.'

'It is. I was happy to be known as Geraint all my boyhood, but apparently Arthur I must be.'

'Why?'

'Something to do with a prophecy, apparently. It's Arturus in Latin.'

'So why don't you use that?'

'Fashion – only the churchmen are given Latin names these days. Us leaders of men are meant to be more homely and more patriotic.'

'But how does that become Arthur?'

He raised himself on an elbow and stroked his lover. 'According to Myrddin, and this is probably the best explanation either of us is going to get, it's a legendary name, something about being like a bear,' Arthur grimaced. 'But he also thinks it's meant to mean Ap Uther, which was too hard for the bards to say, so it became shortened to Arthur.'

'Oh,' Gwenan said, sounding disappointed.

'Yes, well, I think it's a silly name too, but I'm stuck with it now – and so are you. If you start calling me Geraint again there'll be trouble.'

She giggled. 'I'll just call you My Lord all the time in case I forget.'

Arthur thumped her gently. 'So you will.'

The camp was noisy with business by the time a washed and robed Arthur left the small house he was using and ambled over to the bakery. He asked for something fresh, and with much unnecessary bustle was offered his pick of a tray of warm oatmeal buns. He lifted a pair with thanks and began to munch them as he made his way across to the timber hall that stood at the centre of the compound. He was not sure what he was going to do when he got there, but he was the Overlord, so it would hardly look good if he was known to be spending all morning in bed with his lover – though maybe that was just what his rather severe reputation needed, Arthur advised himself.

The camp was small but secure and relatively comfortable. It was also quiet, as it had been for nearly a month. Arthur had picked it as his spring quarters because it was close enough to be within two days' ride of any of the kingdoms likely to give or be in trouble. It also saved him the time and effort of cleaning out the crumbling public buildings in one of the old provincial centres like Londinium or Viroconium – and the diplomatic difficulties of being the guest of any one of his Council. It was a welcome chance to work out his tactics for the rest of the campaigning year after the euphoria of his triumph a month before at the Battle of the Landings, as it became known within days of the event.

Arthur had spent the obligatory two days feasting with his men before the army had been disbanded and each man sent back to his farm to take care of the planting and the lambing. He had wasted a few more days relaxing in Ebvracum, then made his way south.

Although the sunlight outside was strong, little of it penetrated into the gloom of the hall, and Arthur's eyes took a moment to adjust as he pushed past the curtain screening the doorway.

'I wondered if I'd catch you awake before lunch,' a voice said, 'but it seems I've misjudged you, as usual.'

Arthur stopped, a bun held in his mouth, and peered towards the back of the hall. He chewed for a second. 'Myrddin?'

'Do you need to ask? I've been away too long, haven't I?'

'No, no. I didn't know you were coming, that's all,' Arthur said, and ran forward and grasped him firmly by the arm. 'You look well.'

'Don't be stupid, my boy – you can't see me. Tell me that when you can count the white hairs in my beard outside. Is young Gwenan looking after you? If these are the hours you keep I suspect the answer is "yes" – no wonder the country's falling apart around your ears.'

'It's not.'

'That's as may be. I didn't come all this way to argue. Morganwy sends her love, by the way.'

'Thanks. How is she?'

'All right, in her way. The boy's a splendid tall fellow. Amazing to think he's almost the same age that you were when you first came to us.'

'I suppose he must be. I haven't seen him for nearly five years. I always wondered who the father was, though.'

Myrddin gazed at him quietly. 'We all do, Arthur. She still won't say. Keeps to her line that these things can only be told at the right time – whatever that may mean.'

CHAPTER XIII

'Sounds just like you, in other words.'

'That is hardly a comfort.'

Arthur looked about him for somebody to serve them. 'Myrddin, I'm sorry – have you eaten, been given somewhere to rest?'

The older man grinned. 'I was here just after dawn – quite long enough to make myself comfortable.' There was a pause while Arthur finished eating the last of his bread and found a stool. Myrddin watched him until he was settled. 'Don't you want to know why I'm here?'

Arthur shrugged. 'Do you need a reason?'

'Yes I do. Good lord, you can be arrogant sometimes, Arthur. Do you think I would willingly leave Moridunum and Seona and Morganwy, travel for two weeks across your crumbling excuse for roads, search you out in some godforsaken old hill fort just for the pleasure of hearing your gossip?'

'Seems reasonable to me,' said Arthur.

'Well it doesn't to me,' Myrddin laughed.

Arthur became more serious. 'Is there trouble in the west?'

'No more than usual. You know what it's like. The Demetiae and the Ordovices only love each other when there is someone else to attack. Hibernia is too busy dealing with settlers from Gaul to be interested in either. They say there are boatloads heading from the north of Hibernia towards the country north of the Antonine Wall – though I think that has more to do with two wet summers and no crops than any objection to their Gallic cousins.'

'So you came to congratulate me on my triumph at the Battle of the Landings?'

'I want to hear about it, certainly.'

'And to make sure Gwenan isn't usurping your influence with me?'

Myrddin glared at him sharply. 'I have more faith in you, boy. You're not going to let a half-Barbarian girl run your policy, however pretty she is.'

Arthur smiled. 'I'm not so sure. She talks more sense than most of the tiresome little tyrants around the Council – and there's a humanity about her that you would appreciate – I haven't really found anything like it since…'

'Since what – or whom?'

'I was going to say since I left Moridunum. But I think I mean Branwen in Elfael.'

'And I think you mean someone else entirely, but it doesn't matter.'

'Well, if you haven't come to check up on me, is this just my annual visit?'

'Arthur, you have been overlord for a long time now – half your life. You have grown into it, as I knew you would – and with much more grace than your father.'

'Should I say thank you?'

'No. I did not give you the overlordship. I made your decision and that of the Council possible, that's all. At any moment you could have walked away.'

Arthur stood and strode to the doorway. Pulling aside the curtain he looked out at the sharp ridge to the east, with its white gashes where chalk had been quarried for the road. 'I feel the word "but" in your voice.'

'But... there are things that worry me, yes.'

'Things that I am doing?'

'Some that you are and at least two that you are not.'

'I see.'

'Your father was a brave man, but he was also stupid, and he became cruel.'

'And I am the same? Then why were you so keen for me to take his place?'

'No, Arthur. You are not – except for the brave part. At least, you are not stupid.'

'That's a start, then.'

'I'm concerned about the way you behaved at that battle by the sea. You must have slaughtered a whole nation of men. Could you not have taken them prisoner, used your ships or even some of theirs to escort them to somewhere in Gaul?'

'And set them free? They would have been back, laughing, with twice the ships, in a few weeks. And this time I would not have known they were coming. And they were Barbarians. Don't start preaching the virtues of Christian mercy at me. There was no room for it, and you know it.'

'How can you be sure – and even if you can, doesn't that make you a barbarian yourself?'

'We are all barbarians, Myrddin. There is nothing between us except our land, the sea and whether we worship gods or saints.'

CHAPTER XIII

Myrddin stood and came over to Arthur. He stood behind him and clasped his shoulder. 'You can do better than that.'

Arthur let the curtain fall across the doorway again and moved back into the hall. 'Maybe.'

'The question is what you should do now. You have to prepare.'

'For what?'

'I don't know any more than you do. But you cannot let things drift.'

'Is that what you came to tell me?'

'Among other things, yes.'

'Things like, lying in the spring sun with Gwenan is not a luxury the Overlord can afford?' Arthur poured out a couple of mugs of weak beer and handed one to Myrddin.

'I didn't know you were, but I guessed something of that sort might have to be said.'

'Thank you for your concern, but I can look after my own affairs.'

'It's not your affairs I'm worried about,' Myrddin said. 'It's Britannia's.'

'Are they not the same thing?'

'Clearly not.'

The two men fell silent. Arthur resented Myrddin's assumption that he still controlled his fate, that he could engineer any situation so that it fell the way he wanted it to. As far as Arthur was concerned he was a trusted adviser, a mentor, who had a right to come and go without ceremony, but not to instruct unless asked. Myrddin, though, still saw Arthur as a young man (half his own age) feeling his way in the brutish world of territorial politics; a man who could not be allowed to fail if Britannia was not to fall to the Barbarians like every other part of Europe. When Arthur had taken the overlordship, reunion with the Roman empire – in Ravenna, admittedly – had still seemed a distant possibility. Now there was no Roman empire to rejoin, only the empire in the east, where the values could hardly be more different from those Constantine had espoused when he set out from Ebvracum two centuries before. Otherwise Britannia, fractured as it was, stood alone. Myrddin had little faith that Armorica could hold out much longer. Arthur's success was not a personal matter of fulfilling the destiny he and Pendraeg had set in motion. Arthur was the keeper of Constantine's sword, Caledfwlch, and the only means of ensuring that something, however diminished, of the civilisation of half a millennium survived.

Arthur refilled his mug. 'Do you want to talk about it in here, or shall we do it in the sunshine? I've had enough of dark halls. This morning I'd like to be sitting in your courtyard listening to the fountain and drinking some of your excellent Massilian wine.'

'So would I. But even the wine is not what it was when you were a boy. Whether it's the weather or just that the merchants are having trouble getting the proper amphorae, I don't know. The stuff I had out of Gallicia last year was better by far. Now that would be a worry if it carried on. The world really would be ending.'

Arthur laughed. 'We must keep your cellar safe – whatever happens.'

'That, my lord, is not a joke.'

They left the hall and made their way through the main gate, Arthur waving away the two escorts who usually came with him whenever he left the compound.

'We won't go far,' he said. 'Just to that hump, where we can look over the road. You can see us from here, and we can see any trouble long before it gets to us.'

They sat among the spring wild flowers and watched the still countryside. Immediately below them a network of fields had been cleared, and one or two had been cut into terraces close to the springs on the range of hills, but further off the landscape was heavily wooded, except for the clear path of the old road.

Arthur waited until the old man had made himself comfortable on the tummock. 'So what's on your mind?'

'I don't think that battle of yours was a final victory, or anything like.'

'Neither do I.'

'Good. But too many in the Council do. Most of the nations of Britannia think that they can get back to business as usual, wresting a village or two from each other and pretending it's in an ancient cause, all validated by traditions that predate Claudius.'

'If I could stop it I would.'

'You'll never stop that, so I wouldn't be too concerned unless it breaks into real warfare. I do think you should have a permanent force of your own that means you can intervene if you need to, though.'

Arthur shook his head. 'No, it would never work. It would only unite both warring factions against me. I can only operate with the consent of all the kings on the Council, and I can only raise an army that has a hope of being effective if they all – or most of them – contribute.

And they won't if they think it'll be used against them when they have a dispute.'

'But you are Overlord of Britannia. You must assert your authority.'

'I am overlord, not emperor. My job is to deal with outside threats, across whichever sea or wall they come, not to referee internal squabbles. I can mediate when I'm asked and I do. Why do you think I move around so much and don't establish a permanent base, other than Ebvracum? If I wanted to I could rebuild Londinium or Viroconium. I could break away from the old Roman symbols entirely and make myself a capital in one of the great hill towns that everybody's so busy building up again. But it would fall into exactly the trap some of the kings want me to. They would say I was centralising power, setting myself up not as overlord but as tyrant, threatening their independence to rule their territories as they have done since they established their authority over the cives eighty years ago.'

'Maybe that's exactly what Britannia needs.'

'Maybe – but it is not what it wants or will tolerate without civil war. And that would just open the door to the Barbarians. Look what's happened in Gaul and Iberia, Myrddin – and in Roman lands themselves. It's exactly because everybody started to try to become mini-Roman prefects after the legions left that they have lost everything. I'm not going to let that happen here.'

Myrddin sat staring at the sky for a few moments. The kite that Arthur had watched from his bed whirled above the chalk scarp. As it dived Myrddin said, 'Fine, I'll accept that. But what is your strategy? You've been overlord for over sixteen years. That's a dangerous amount of time. You are no longer new, even if you are still relatively young. There are fresh leaders of the Brigantes, the Votadini and the Cantiaci who see you as the old guard and me as thoroughly antique.'

'It would be just as bad if I spent my whole time on the back of a horse going from one regal hall to another. They'd all think I was panicking – or worse, that I couldn't trust any of them to manage their kingdoms for more than six weeks at a time. I'd always be in exactly the wrong place.' Arthur stood up and began to pace around the grassy mound. 'Here I can keep in touch – my messengers know where I am. I'm not a threat to anybody, and I'm not sitting in the hall of some discontented king waiting for a knife between the shoulder blades or a jug of poisoned mead.'

'And you have Gwenan to keep you amused.'

'She does, which is more than can be said for anybody else around here.'

Myrddin grunted. 'Sit down, Arthur, you're making my neck ache.'

'If you insist,' he said, and, out of old habits more than anything else, did as he was told.

'You have to prepare for another invasion. I'm sure of that. I'm equally sure that it will not come from along the east coast.'

'Why? Instinct?'

'Not this time. I heard word through Hibernia – a cousin of Vorteporix. It's a roundabout way, but probably still accurate. The story is that the Votadini and their allies to the west are responding to the Hibernian settlers by trying the Vortigern route. They've sent for Barbarian mercenaries to drive the Hibernians back across the sea.'

Arthur exploded. 'Idiots! Bloody blind idiots! They must know what that will mean!'

Myrddin sighed. 'Nobody ever learns from the old mistakes of others. They just think it will never happen to them.'

'Well, it will. There'll be shiploads heading for Dunedin before they've left their beds.'

'Which is why you need to be ready. The Barbarians will not be content to sit behind what's left of Hadrian's Wall. They'll want revenge for what you did to them at the landings.'

'And you think the Votadini will side with them?' Arthur asked.

'Not willingly. But by then they won't have much choice.'

'What shall I do? I can't just raise an army and wait for something to happen. People have too much to do in their fields at this time of year. And I'm not dealing with it by hiring mercenaries myself – wherever they're from.'

'Quite right. We – you – need a different tactic.'

'Which is?'

'I don't think you can rely on the full Council. They'll be busy looking after their own interests. And just involving the northern nations will not be enough. You need a tighter group – big enough to rally an army in the field at the right moment, but small enough to sit around a table and plan things properly.'

'Sounds like a gathering of the Apostles,' snorted Arthur.

'Pick carefully – or it could be the Last Supper.'

CHAPTER XIII

Arthur growled. 'That really helps, Myrddin. Thank you.'

'It's still a workable idea.'

'Who do you suggest? And anyway, why would the Council agree, unless they pick them themselves? In which case we might as well not bother, because you know as well as I do that they'll pick the most obstructive and loudest to keep me under control.'

'This should have nothing to do with the Council, although you might coincidentally have a few Council members on board – those kings whom you feel you can really trust and who will turn out for you whatever happens. No – these men would be your confidants. They would also be your commanders, most trusted messengers and political allies. They would be with you most of the time – at least, some of them would be. And they would give you a core troop strong enough to be effective,' he said, and raised a hand before Arthur could interrupt. 'Not an army – you've already ruled that out – but with you at least for enough of the time so that you only have to call up a full Council army for the severest of threats. It's important you never leave yourself in this position again.'

Arthur looked puzzled. 'In what position?' Just at that moment he could not imagine himself to be in one that was any better. He was lounging in the sunshine in one of the most peaceful spots in his domain after more than two weeks when, apart from the occasional delegation from kings' envoys congratulating him on his recent victory, the only distraction had been making love to Gwenan.

'Don't be obtuse, Arthur,' said Myrddin. 'This position can't last – being adrift on a hilltop with no definite purpose or plan of action, looking to all the world as if you think the job has been done with the slaughter of a few Barbarians and you can have a holiday without a care in the world.'

'Can't I?'

'You can – but you will not last much longer as overlord if you do.'

Arthur looked at him sharply. 'What are you hiding, Myrddin?'

The old man paused and idly traced a complex pattern of spirals in the grass with his finger. 'There are kings who never liked you, and others, younger, who think they can do better.'

'That was always true,' shrugged Arthur. 'Has something changed to make it a specific threat?'

'I'm not sure. Just a feeling in my bones.'

Arthur jumped up and confronted Myrddin. 'Oh, come on. Don't give me that old rubbish about winds and spirits changing. Either you know that there's a plot hatching or you don't.'

Myrddin sighed. 'Very well, have it your way. But I don't want you rushing in and removing people. At least, not yet.'

'I'm not a fool. Though if it's serious enough it will have to be stamped out before the message is given that I'm too weak either to know or do anything about it once I do. Who is it?'

'I've heard – and it is only hearsay – that the Catuvellauni want you out.'

Arthur looked genuinely shocked. 'Cunorix! Surely not.'

'You had no idea?'

'But why? He fought superbly at the landings. He could not have been more loyal.'

'That's all true, and I don't think it actually has much do with you – at least, not directly. Cunorix wants to expand his power base in middle Britannia, especially at the expense of the Cornovii. He'd like to squeeze them between his lands and the Ordovices, move into old Viroconium. First he has to conquer the sliver of Coritanian territory that keeps him apart from Cornovia. If he can do that and keep the Iceni under his control, using them to keep Barbarian coastal incursions to a minimum, his becomes the territory through which every bit of business on the island has to pass. He sees that as the way to make him the strongest player in the land, and therefore the natural overlord. You he sees as part of a past age. Worse: you are from the west. He has no love of men from the hills. He would take his kingdom up to Elfael and beyond if he could.'

'And how do Brigantia and Dobunnia feel about this?'

'They don't know yet,' said Myrddin, 'but when they do you can expect war – unless Cunorix attacks first. The Cornovii are worried, but they are just as frightened of the Brigantes as they are of Cunorix – more so, thanks to history. We would help from Demetia if we could, but the distances make anything swift unrealistic, and any longer-planned reinforcement would probably just provoke Cunorix into an early strike.'

'I'll do something. I must. Give me time to think.' Arthur began to stride back to the gates of his encampment. Myrddin followed slowly.

'Luckily for you, my lad, I have already done the thinking,' he said, and watched Arthur march into the compound, then turned and looked up at the circling birds of prey and smiled. 'Now, let's meet this lovely little Venus who's been enchanting you so conveniently.'

XIV

DESPITE MYRDDIN'S PESTERING it was nearly another month before Arthur moved off from his compound above the ancient Ridgeway. The warm sun of early May had tapered off into a week of gales and a damp early June. It promised a good growing season, though, and Arthur knew that he would have an easier year ahead if people had enough food to feed themselves and his armies as they passed by. There were few worse things for an overlord than having to feed his troops off stores that were already too thin for the villagers. Reducing people to winter malnutrition in their best interests might sometimes be necessary, but it did nothing for anybody's sense of security or his popularity.

There had been much debate about where he should go. If Cunorix really was planning a coup, then to ride with a handful of men to Verulamium would be just foolhardy. On the other hand, to bypass him and head for Brigantia and all points further north could leave Arthur cut off permanently from southern Britannia if Cunorix was so minded. In the end Arthur decided to go to meet Cunorix, but with a larger detachment than his usual modest guard, and away from Cunorix's home base.

He headed north, as was his original plan, knowing that Cunorix had done the same in order to inspect his borderland with Coritania to the west of Ratae. Meeting on the road would be both natural and safer. Arthur's scouts had established that Cunorix was moving with a force of twice the Overlord's. He was also playing the numbers game, it seemed, travelling with enough men to establish his capabilities, not enough to frighten the Cornovii into an attack of their own.

Arthur knew his strategy for their encounter. He was less sure what he would do if it resulted in an outright challenge. Cunorix was a man who impressed him, even if he was not sure he liked him:

strong, determined and a quick decision-maker. He was not an easy man to change from a settled course, though, and if Arthur was a serious obstacle to his ambition, there might be no avoiding a more decisive battle than Arthur was prepared to contemplate. Arthur had theoretical authority from the Council to act in the general interest if any one of its kings moved seriously out of line, but it was an authority that had never been tested in practice. Arthur had a feeling that his nominal masters would watch and see how he fared before committing themselves against such a pivotal figure as Cunorix. It was not a summer to be relished any more.

The ride to Cunorix's encampment was a two-day canter along the crumbling remains of the great legionary routes – north until he could join the north-west road, following that to the junction with the Via Fossa on which Ratae stood three hours further on, then turned west again on muddy lanes. Though the Roman stones were rutted and slippery in the driving rain, Arthur and his men rode fast. Gwenan and the camp followers had been excluded from this part of the journey, in case it went wrong. They had been told to wait a week and then, if there was no bad news, strike camp and move on western roads up to Brigantia on its Hibernian seaboard. Myrddin had been dispatched to tour the south, partly to gauge the mood, but mostly to demonstrate that Arthur was out of sight but not out of mind.

Arthur did not expect a rapturous reception from Cunorix – wary but civil was the best he thought likely. In the event he could not have been wider of the mark. Cunorix greeted him with as much pomp and ceremony as a wet evening on a hillside allowed. An escort rode out to greet him while he was still a mile away. A trumpet sounded as they trotted up the final stretch of roads to the camp gates, hastily erected on the top of earth ramparts that the Romans had rendered useless but were now serving a purpose again after four hundred years.

Cunorix stood outside a hall surrounded by his kinsmen and advisers as Arthur dismounted. With exaggerated formality he stepped forward, unsheathed his sword and bowed his head over it before handing the hilt to Arthur.

'Now that the Overlord is with us,' Cunorix declaimed, 'I have no need of this tonight.'

Arthur bowed back and returned the sword to its owner. 'Now that I am under the protection of Cunorix I have no need to carry two swords. I have come here for your counsel, not your weapons.'

'The honour is mine,' Cunorix said, bowing again as he accepted his sword back. When it was sheathed he embraced Arthur – rather more warmly, thought Arthur, than he usually did. It was that gesture alone than made him certain that Myrddin was right. Cunorix wanted him out of the way.

'I'll wash, if you don't mind, Cunorix, then I need to talk. I won't be with you for more than a day. I know you have other things to take care of.'

'Strictly business is it – no time to feast with your old friends?'

'I wouldn't put you to that trouble beyond tonight. Besides, I've a centurion's troop with me. Can you billet them all here, or do you want them to make other arrangements?'

'There's plenty of space within the ramparts, and good water,' Cunorix replied. 'We were expecting you.'

'Good.'

'Follow me, Arthur, and make yourself comfortable. I'm afraid it won't be up to Verulamium standards, but the King of the Catuvellauni does not live in a pigsty, even when travelling.'

Arthur nodded and followed his host into the hall. There was a fire blazing on a hearth in the middle of the room. Arthur stood warming himself after the wet ride for a while, saying nothing, while Cunorix bustled about with officers, fixing the accommodation arrangements for the visiting men. Arthur slung his cloak between two beams to dry and sat on a bench with his feet outstretched towards the logs. Soon his clothes were steaming and he felt the warmth spread through the soles of his shoes and up his legs. He called a servant girl over and asked to be shown where he was to sleep that night. She led him behind a curtain to a bed at the far end of the hall, where there was a smaller hearth and a fire ready for him, a kettle of water simmering over it and a washing bowl by the side. Arthur thanked and dismissed her, but then changed his mind and called her back to undo the bindings round his stockings, take off the damp shoes and dry his feet. She was a small, thin thing, he thought, only just old enough – perhaps fifteen – to be thought a woman, with brown hair tied back severely and a pinched mouth. He was too tired to try to charm her, and lay back on the bed as she rubbed and fussed over his feet.

He must have fallen asleep, for the next thing he saw was the heavy woollen blanket covering him and the girl patiently collecting his dried clothes from in front of the fire. He lay watching her for a moment, then swung himself upright.

'Have I slept too long?'

She jumped, then turned to him, careful not to catch his eye, and shook her head.

'Is Cunorix waiting?'

She nodded.

'On his own, or with his advisers?'

The girl looked round desperately. Eventually she held up nine fingers.

Arthur looked puzzled. 'What's the matter? You can speak to me, you know. I'm only overlord, not one of the old gods.'

She shook her head again.

'Why not?' Arthur asked.

She opened her moth and pointed. Arthur peered at her, then put a consoling hand on her shoulder. She had only half a tongue – a stump just big enough to let her eat and swallow.

'I'm sorry, my dear. Did the Barbarians do this to you?'

Again the shake of her head.

'Who then?'

She was still for a moment, dropping her gaze to the floor. Then she looked straight at Arthur for the first time, her eyes blazing with a mixture of pent-up anger and constant fear. She tilted her head towards the curtain and the hall beyond.

'I see.' Arthur gave her shoulder a gentle squeeze. Cunorix was well within his rights to rule his people and captives how he pleased, but it gave Arthur no pleasure to see the result. It made the political game he was about to play even more distasteful. But he had learnt at Myrddin's side, and he knew that dislike and state business were not good company. He smiled at the girl. 'I'm leaving tomorrow,' he said, 'but I'll see what I can do.'

She held his gaze. There was no smile there, only the despairing certainty that anything Arthur might achieve on her behalf was as pointless as it was too late. Then she knelt and replaced his stockings, rewound the bindings and put on his shoes once more, before bowing and slipping out through the curtain while Arthur had a piss into the bucket on the other side of the hearth.

CHAPTER XIV

* * *

Cunorix looked up from a table when Arthur appeared and roared a welcome. 'I trust you are refreshed, my lord? It has given us time to prepare our discussions.' At the table with Cunorix sat his cabinet of nine and three of Arthur's own officers. He caught the look of wary concern on the faces of his men, then stepped forward.

'Your hospitality is generous to a fault, Cunorix. I'm sorry if I've kept you. Your staff looked after me almost too well, and I'm afraid the long ride caught up with me. But I'm at your service now.'

'No, my lord, I am at yours.'

'I do hope so, I really do. We have hard times ahead, my friend.'

There was a pause as Cunorix signalled for a mug of ale to be poured for his guest and Arthur took his place at the table.

'So, if it is not too blunt a question, my lord, why are you here? It's rare for you to visit one of us mere kings when we're on the road ourselves – rarer still to do so with so many men and so few women.'

Cunorix's contingent laughed on cue. Arthur shrugged.

'The men are not for your benefit. I don't need a show of strength, if you can call a hundred men that. I have a long journey ahead this summer, and I need a force large enough to deal with any trouble along the way, but small enough not to try the patience of kind hosts such as yourself. As usual, being called overlord is an inaccurate description. I am the Grand Balancer. I can't lord it over anyone on the Council, least of all you.'

'And where's the balance today?'

'Between victory and chaos.'

'Very dramatic. Surely we are at peace? Give yourself some credit, Arthur. There's not a Barbarian in sight – at least, not one that is not legal or in captivity. There's no fighting worthy of the name. Farmyard disputes, that's all.'

Arthur looked Cunorix intently in the eye. 'Long may it last.'

His host returned the gaze, holding it for a moment, as though wrestling with him to break the silence.

Then Cunorix laughed and called for more ale. The tongueless girl obliged, careful to only look at the table, not the men she was serving. 'Have you any reason to think it won't? Or have you just been listening to the tittle-tattle of women like the Cornovii?'

Arthur smiled. 'You know as well as I do where I've been for the last few weeks – in bed the whole time, according to the gossip.'

'Well, it's a fine life without a kingdom of your own to run, isn't it? What a luxury is time!'

Arthur let the gibe pass, holding the smile as he idly brushed a few crumbs from the table. 'It has its moments.'

'I'm sure it does. So who will you be on your way to now – or have you made arrangements of your own?'

'That depends on you, I think.'

'In what way?' Cunorix asked.

'I need your advice – and an answer.'

Cunorix waved his hand over the table in a gesture of mock obedience. 'In any way I can help.'

Arthur launched into the speech he had prepared with Myrddin. The strategy was a diplomatic gamble, but it gave Cunorix a way out, while making him seem stronger. If he refused Arthur knew he was in trouble.

'Let's start with the Barbarians. I don't think we did more at the landings than make them pause and regather their forces. Next time the victory will not be so easy.'

One of Cunorix's men, a cousin, thumped his fist on the table. 'Easy!' he shouted. 'You call that easy? The Catuvellauni who gave their lives did not find it easy, whatever it looked like from behind a sand dune.'

Arthur ignored the outburst. 'You know what I mean. We will not outnumber them so comfortably when they try again. Neither can we be sure to catch them on the beach. I also think that they will have learnt their lesson and will not try to land in the centre of the coastline – it's just too convenient for us to unite and converge on them from all directions. I think they will either try further north, taking advantage of the division of the wall, or in the far south, where our defences are weaker and there is already a large Barbarian minority.'

Cunorix tapped the table top with his finger. 'So far I agree with you,' he said, 'but if we are right I don't see that it matters much to me. My forces can turn in either direction as they are needed.'

'Precisely. You are the key figure, the pivot, Cunorix. But if you are going to be able to move fast and reinforce me, you must be secure at home. It's no use if you have to leave half your men and all your sons at home to make sure your lands are safe while you are away.'

'Fair point,' Cunorix conceded. 'But what can I do about it?'

CHAPTER XIV

'I want to strengthen this whole middle region of Britannia,' Arthur went on, 'from the Iceni right across to the Ordovices. I want guarantees that the land will be secure – a barrier through which any outflanking Barbarian force cannot pass.'

'Fine theory. But we are that already,' Cunorix said.

'I don't believe you are. I believe that there is a measure of mistrust that could weaken the centre.'

'Nonsense. But go on.'

'It's not you that is wary, Cunorix,' said Arthur. 'You are too powerful to need to be.'

'Thank you,' Cunorix smiled. He was in a mood to be indulgent.

Arthur paused. This was the crucial moment in Myrddin's plan. Confront the threat head on. Force Cunorix to demonstrate his loyalty. 'And that is the problem. You've already dismissed the Cornovii as women. Never mind that it was a joke. The Coritani and Parisi are concerned you have much the same view of them. Brigantia is not so bothered. However, any sign that you and the Ordovices were becoming too comfortable with each other and eating into Cornovian lands from either side would be another matter.'

'Speculation, Arthur, and you know it.'

'Possibly. I'd call it realistic politics.'

'I've no intention of eating into anybody's land, except through alliance and marriage. And I find it very strange that an accusation like that should come from the Overlord. Haven't I proved time and time again that I regard your authority as our protection against just such absurd adventures?'

'In battle you and your nation have been lions, and I could not have defended Britannia without you at my side,' Arthur agreed.

'That was not quite what I said, but the tribute is welcome to my men nonetheless.' Cunorix stretched out his arms in a gesture that indicated his men. Arthur thought they looked like rather more predatory lions than he wanted.

'I will take you at your word, Cunorix, because it is the word I need to hear. I fear, though, that we will need to be a little more formal than that if we are to make others share my confidence.'

'What did you have in mind?' Cunorix turned to his men. 'What could satisfy the Overlord? Hostages after the feast? Forests on all our borders? Or just so much sex and beer that we've no time for anything else?'

Arthur waited until the staged laughter died away. 'Do you think that would work?' he asked, in all seriousness.

Cunorix saw the glint in Arthur's eye and knew that this time it was he who was being mocked. He grinned. 'Not entirely, but I'd have no rebellions.'

'No, I bet you wouldn't,' said Arthur. 'I'm not in the business of turning Britannia into a great brothel, however, even for strategic purposes. There is a better, though duller, way forward that will cost you much less and bring you far more respect.'

'I'm glad to hear it.'

Arthur raised his cup and the girl with half a tongue stepped forward to fill it. He kept his eyes firmly on Cunorix as he sipped. 'I want you to seal a series of treaties with all your neighbours,' he said carefully. 'You can negotiate the terms, but it will be done under my auspices, as treaties of friendship and mutual aid in the event of attack. They will be witnessed by the Silures, Atrebates and Brigantes – in other words, those with no borders with you, but the greatest stake in making sure you do not overreach your power.'

'Don't we have that security already in the Council?'

'You know as well as I do that even when I was elected the Council was in its last throes of post-Roman authority. I was appointed out of an unhealthy combination of desperation and nostalgia – not to mention common interest. Nobody was ready to make a move for the overlordship, and everyone needed a bit of time. Why else appoint a fifteen-year-old boy, the unrecognised bastard of a tyrant many of you could barely remember? The only good reason was that I would not live long enough to become a nuisance.'

'But you did.'

Arthur sat still. 'But I did. And I intend to do so for a while longer.'

'That still doesn't answer the question – why insist on a process that is meant to exist already through the Council? Why not just ask us to reaffirm our commitment to it?' Cunorix asked.

'Some sort of celebratory meeting, you mean, with a signing ceremony – a declaration, preferably in Latin?'

'Why not? It would carry more weight.'

'No, it wouldn't,' Arthur said firmly, 'and you know it. It would be hard to organise, half the Council would make excuses and nobody would think it was worth the vellum it was written on – a document

CHAPTER XIV

that only three of us on the Council can read, in any case, assuming you have not forgotten what the monks taught you in Verulamium.'

Cunorix shrugged. 'If you say so.'

'I do. Bilateral treaties, properly sworn to and witnessed by others of equal status, would be far more likely to resist any strains put on them. News of them would spread through the villages. It would be clear that enemies would be Barbarian, not the neighbours. Armies and taxes would be easier to raise, laws to enforce. You'd be a great and noble king, Cunorix, not just a—'

'I think it better you do not finish that remark, with all due respect.'

'You're right. I'm sorry.'

There was an awkward silence for a moment as the men behind each chief eyed each other for signs of trouble.

Cunorix smiled, and the moment of danger passed, though they all knew the tension was now firmly in the open. 'It is a sensible idea – from your point of view, Arthur. If I was in your place I might attempt to do the same. But—'

'But?'

'But why should I do any such thing? The Catuvellauni are the strongest nation in central Britannia. We have the best land, the fittest and most versatile forces, and we have weaker neighbours who are – how shall I put this tactfully? – who can be persuaded to cede territory in the interests of stability, as you would say.'

'You mean they can be raided at will.'

'I might, but I don't think that is always necessary. Give me credit, Arthur – I'm meant to be one of your best friends among the kings. It would be more pleasant if we could behave as such.'

'Long may you remain so,' Arthur said. Across the table Cunorix gave a little bow. Arthur almost believed him, but pressed on. 'I have a reason for you, though. In fact, two, and they don't depend on threats from Barbarians or your generosity of spirit.'

'And they are…?'

'You are very easy to surround, Cunorix. If I cannot get support from you I can go north or south. There are plenty who would ally against you. As you yourself pointed out, you have rich pickings.'

'But that would split the country in two. One half or the other would be abandoned either to those beyond the wall or beyond the sea. And that is precisely what you want to avoid.'

Arthur went on. 'You cannot be in two places at once. That's true at all times. But don't delude yourself. If limiting or removing you is the prize, the Brigantes would be happy to act as my deputies in the north while I consolidate the southern kingdoms. You'd be caught in the middle.'

'I could kill you tonight.'

'You could. But who would the Council appoint? Not you. They would unite against you – that's the only certainty. And old Myrddin would be dispatched to perform another of his convenient miracles.'

Cunorix glared at him coldly. 'And the second reason?'

Arthur smiled and took a mouthful of ale. 'I think you'll like it better.'

'I hope so. For your sake – overlord or not.'

'There's a prize. I would not expect you to agree for anything less. I will settle all the disputes about borders, iron out the anomalies from the last eighty years. You would have secure, defensible boundaries. It would mean new territory, potential gifts to your clansmen – free from retaliatory raids.'

Cunorix shrugged. He needed more.

'You will be consul, the deputy overlord. In my absence or infirmity you will have all my authority. And unlike me, you will have a power base. Your kingdom will be your bastion. As long as I live and have the title you will not be challenged from any Britannian kingdom south of the wall, and something tells me the Cornovii's cousins in the far north beyond Alt Clut – north even by the Votadini's reckoning – will not care to contest it.'

Cunorix looked less impressed than Arthur had hoped. 'Candidianos is already Consul for Life,' he said. 'Is that what you're offering me?'

'No, not for life. But there have always been two consuls in Rome, and this would not be an annual matter. Candidianos's title is an honorary one; you would have real authority.'

'I doubt if that is quite how the noble King of the Dobunni sees himself, or how pleased he will be to find that I am to carry more military weight than him, but it's your title to give.'

Arthur waited for an answer. Cunorix, he knew, would not be able to show too much enthusiasm in front of his men.

'Well?' he asked.

'It's a good offer,' Cunorix admitted. 'One that might bring many dividends, if you could deliver it.'

'What do you mean "if"? Of course I can.'

'Oh, you have the right, Arthur. Nobody would deny that. But why should the others let you do it? You would just be shifting the advantage for getting rid of you from me to Brigantia, or, if they had the balls, the Trinovantes.'

'They'll agree.'

'Is that just faith, or do you know?'

'They'll agree, for one good reason only. This way there are limits on you. Just as I will have to share power with you, Cunorix, you will have to maintain the peace and stay within your borders. And we will have a new Council – a Council with fewer members – constituted to oversee the peace.'

'Abolish the old Council?'

'No, keep it for its present very occasional purpose: electing the overlord and agreeing a common position to the outside threats. There will be a prize for them, too. It will meet regularly every three years for one week to reaffirm us in position, authorise us to protect the nation on their behalf.'

'And what will you call this new body that everybody is meant to subscribe to but cannot join?'

'It will be called the Table, and it will have eleven members plus me.'

Cunorix looked taken aback. 'Very biblical, Arthur, but it's a very ordinary word for such an august group.'

Arthur smiled slightly. 'Apostolic was the word Myrddin used, I think.'

'I might have known he'd be involved,' muttered Cunorix with distaste.

'This is not about expensive show and titles. The members will earn any respect to which they are entitled.'

'And who will these humble giants be?'

Arthur held his gaze for a moment before replying. 'That's for you and I to discuss. Once you accept my terms.'

* * *

It was well after midnight when Arthur felt confident enough to call a halt to the negotiations, and that only happened after an hour or more spent without formal witnesses. There was an initial list of those invited to sit at Arthur's Table, and Cunorix accepted his consular role with relish once his men had headed for their billets. Cunorix was easier and less abrasive alone, Arthur found – maybe it was the wine and the fire casting their ebullient glow, but the Catuvellaunian leader seemed able to put aside his national bragging and talk seriously about the ways the country could be held together. At one point he even apologised for his previous show of strength that evening.

'You should know, Arthur,' he muttered confidentially, 'that there are those around me who feel I am too modest in my ambitions, who feel that I do not make enough of our power and our part in the Barbarian victories. They point to the glorious past of Verulamium and eye the rich lands to the north-west as though they are ours to take at will and by right.'

'Is that how you think too?'

Cunorix shook his head. 'No, Arthur, I don't. To acquire control of them by agreement would be useful, undoubtedly. I need more land for my people, and the Cornovii seem to be retreating back to the hills.'

'It's true the plague hit them hard, but they are recovering.'

'I'm glad to hear it. There are still many miles of forest ripe for clearing and fields that are growing sour with neglect. But I will not authorise their seizure, Arthur. That I promise, though I cannot stop occasional incidents.'

'Then that will be the basis of your treaty with them. Any land adjoining your borders that has been disused for more than two planting seasons or has not been grazed for the same time will be transferred to you to grant as you wish. Though the same condition must apply to your borders in the east, where I hear you are not making the most of what you hold either.'

Cunorix sipped more ale then put it aside, brushing the servant girl away when she tried to refill it. 'I can agree to that. Only, though, because now that I have fair warning I will make sure my lands are managed better where they are under such threat. I'll not be giving any up by the time I make my treaties.'

'Fine. Borders stay the same. That way we all benefit. More food, more troops, more security.'

Cunorix smiled. 'An odd concept in these times, Arthur. Security. Something we can barely feel between friends, let alone with Barbarians snapping at our shores. Was it like this hundreds of years ago? Did the Romans bring security, or merely the trappings of comfort?'

CHAPTER XIV

'Myrddin would say it was better then.'

'And you?'

'I would say more people could read, the wine was better, we had the use of money and the best stone houses were heated without smoke suffocating everyone inside. So yes, it was better.'

Cunorix laughed and flicked his thumb towards the slave girl sitting patiently by the fire. 'Reading!' he said. 'She can read – or so she pretends. Since she can't tell what she reads there's no way of knowing how much she understands. I've only got a scroll or two here, in any case, though the archive in Verulamium is full of the things from the days of the emperors. I still get letters from the Bishop telling me what the Pope thinks. Not that I care or understand half the words.'

Arthur looked across at the girl, her eyes drooping with exhaustion. 'Why do you keep her,' he asked. 'Apart from the obvious uses of any pretty servant?'

'I'm not sure. I thought I wanted her, but then I thought I wanted a slave who couldn't pass on what she heard, so I had her tongue cut.'

'A harsh move, Cunorix.'

'I realise that now. Wish I hadn't, really.'

Arthur could see Cunorix was becoming sentimental with drink and tiredness. It was a state he could use, knowing that he himself had been refreshed by his unintended sleep that afternoon. 'Would you like an exchange?' he asked. 'I could take her with me and send you a girl given to me as a prize – if you don't beat or maltreat her. Or I could buy this girl from you. I have no sheep, but she's worth some silver and a gold brooch.'

'A noble offer, Arthur. But then from you it would be.'

'Nothing of the sort, my friend. It's no issue either way to me, but if it eases your conscience, why not?'

Cunorix was starting to let his head drop to the table, his long brown moustaches dipping into the remains of the food.

Arthur clasped him by the shoulder. 'I'll take that as a yes – to all we've said. We'll draw up the proclamation about the other matters in the morning when we can have a priest with us to write it. For now, your overlord is sending you to your bed and going to his own.'

He summoned the girl, watched as she took Cunorix's arm and guided him across the hall to his curtained section. There the King's private man of the chamber took over, waving her back to where Arthur sat finishing the last of the ale.

'I hear you can read?' he asked.

She nodded.

Arthur leant on her shoulder to lever himself to his feet. 'A rare talent in a woman. Can you write as well?'

She didn't need to nod again. The glare she gave Arthur told him it was a stupid question.

'Of course you can, though I doubt you get much chance here. Do you remember accurately what you hear?'

For a second time she nodded, though less certainly this time. It could be a dangerous admission to the wrong man.

Arthur smiled and took her arm as he shuffled towards his bed. 'Well, tomorrow you are coming with me, if you are willing. I can use a girl who can keep a record for me without talking about it. Your misery may yet be your fortune, my dear, however unhappy a prospect that seems.'

She stood staring at him, her hands rubbing each other as though she was trying to convey answers too complicated for gesture. Eventually the frustration became too much. She made a gurgling noise, the stump of her tongue struggling to create the words she knew had to be said.

Arthur watched in dismay, lost for a moment for a way to help. Then he grinned, put his finger to his lips and gathered a pile of small sticks from beside the fire. He laid them out carefully on the ground. 'Now you can tell me,' he said, 'and it will always be our signal. Give me two sticks if you agree, one if you do not and want to remain here.'

For a second or two she looked at the sticks, then dropped to her knees. She selected two sticks with care, looked up at Arthur and held them out. He took them and briefly stroked her hair.

For the first time she smiled, picked up two more sticks, then all of them and tossed them to him.

'I think I get the idea. Good. One more thing before I let you sleep. Your name. Use the sticks.'

She looked puzzled for a moment and then gathered the sticks back into a pile and began forming letters on the floor. After a while she sat back on her ankles and touch Arthur's knee.

He peered down at the neat shapes. 'Modlen, right?'

She held up two leftover pieces.

'A good Christian name. Is that what they call you here?'

One stick.

'What do they say?'

With fury she brushed all the sticks away, leaving the rush floor bare to the earth.

'They call you nothing at all? That doesn't surprise me. Modlen, things will be different now,' he said. 'I hope.' He looked around for a cot or a pile of clothes. 'Where do you sleep?'

She pointed to the floor by the fire. Arthur raised an eyebrow. 'Well, you can if you want. Or if you think there's room for two over here under the covers you could join me.'

Modlen hung her head, weighing whether this was an invitation or an order.

Arthur said gently, 'Well, at least you can take my boots off while you think about it.'

* * *

Light was only beginning to seep underneath the doors and allow shapes to take form again when Arthur shifted his weight in bed and eased awake. He moved his left arm and felt it lodge against a soft body. Surprised, he reached over with his other hand and touched rough cloth. He opened his eyes. Modlen slept fully clothed beside him, warm and untroubled. Arthur gently traced her shape and thought about finding a way under the coarse wool, but instead smiled to himself and rested his hand on her side. She might expect him to play with her body, but it would almost certainly not be what she wanted. It would be impossible to move without waking her, and in Cunorix's service the chances were it would have been a long time since she had slept on a bed under warm hides. Arthur's plan to wander the camp before dawn would have to be forgotten.

XV

ONCE ARTHUR'S TROOP found the Roman road north again, some twenty miles after leaving Cunorix's camp, they made quick time towards Brigantia. It had taken two more days of hard negotiation before Cunorix could be brought back to the reasonable position he had been lulled into on the first night. Then two more days passed as priests drew up the text of a proclamation that both parties were willing to have translated into Latin and copied for distribution throughout the Council, despite the practical necessity to keep the text short because of the barely adequate stock of vellum carried by the monks when travelling away from their libraries.

The most direct route north-west by road would take them first along the main thoroughfares through the territory of the Coritani and then the Cornovii. They could avoid the Cornovian capital of Viroconium, though Arthur knew it would be a diplomatic snub if he did so. He therefore sent a messenger ahead to give appropriate notice of his arrival and the assurance that he would stay long enough to hear whatever grievances Cunegnus of the Cornovii wanted to beef about.

The sliver of land that separated the territory of the three peoples – Catuvellauni, Coritani and Cornovii – had been a flashpoint for centuries. There had never been agreement over where the borders should be, though the Romans had forced an uneasy truce. To the south, where two rivers came together to form the southern stretch of the Sabrina (or Hafren, as it was called locally) the issue was simple. At that point the Coritani gave way to the Dobunni. But there were few such convenient landmarks further north, and with no outside legions to make sure the peace was kept, the best that had been managed in nearly a hundred years was a state of sullen and armed unease.

Arthur and his retinue were aware all too well that even a middling-sized force of men moving along the roads would cause more than comment. They were confronted early in Coritanian lands by a group a third the size of their own, and were left in no doubt that, although this was a courtesy guard to ensure safe passage for the Overlord, they would be escorted firmly all day and invited to camp for the night at a site pre-chosen and made ready for them. Arthur had no objection to the arrangement. After all, it meant that his men could be guaranteed a warm and well-supplied billet for the night. He was more surprised, and irritated, to find Gwenan and the other women and servants he had asked to follow him corralled in the camp to meet him. They should have been at least a day's ride further on by now.

There was no explanation for the polite but firm obstruction. Either the presence of Cunorix so close to the disputed border, or the Overlord's unheralded progress across their lands, was making the Coritani unusually jumpy. Arthur was not going to challenge the situation, however, unless he was delayed beyond the morning.

CHAPTER XV

Instead he pretended to be delighted to find his dependants safe and well looked after and thanked his escort and, in absentia, their king, Tegernacus, for the thoughtfulness of their hospitality. In truth the diplomatic pleasantries were at least half meant. He was relieved to have Gwenan back in his care. He had been less than certain of the wisdom of sending a group of nearly sixty civilians so far with only a dozen or so men to protect them. He greeted Gwenan lovingly and accepted the arrangements made by the Coritani for him and his men with good grace.

They were camped in a large farmstead fashioned from a hundred-and-fifty-year-old villa overlooking a scarp of the hills that dropped away suddenly into a narrow valley. The farmer and villagers seemed to have been unceremoniously cleared out of their lodgings by the troops. Arthur and his immediate staff were quartered in the main building, its Roman tiled roof long since replaced with thatch, but still boasting a fine mosaic floor inside the entrance. Arthur was glad Myrddin was not with them – the old collector's instinct would have had the floor unearthed and transported back to Moridunum before the owner had a chance to haggle.

He found the best bed in the villa and flopped on to the rough blankets. He realised he was more tired than he expected. The wrangling with Cunorix and the tension that went with it had left him longing for his makeshift fort by the Ridgeway where he had spent the spring in Gwenan's care.

Arthur was so preoccupied with thoughts of the safety of his dependants and the nervousness of the kingdoms that it never occurred to him that the sight of Modlen, the only woman and the only addition to his troop, as he rode into camp would have been noticed. He was left in no doubt when Gwenan stormed into the room as he lay with his eyes closed, relishing the quiet of a proper house. It needed more than Arthur's word to convince her that Modlen was not a rival, but that her rescue was an act of charity and political revenge, that Modlen's uses were going to be purely secretarial and that her silence to Gwenan was a result of disfigurement, not insolence. In fact, it needed two hours of bad-tempered lovemaking before Gwenan relented and agreed to allow Modlen anywhere near. Not for the first time in his dealings with women, Arthur wondered why he felt so powerless to take a strong line. All the decisiveness that he could count on in a physical battle and the sure-footedness of the able negotiator deserted him when faced with a beautiful young woman in a mood. Having pacified Gwenan, he then found he had the task of reassuring an equally put-out Modlen that she was still not only welcome but essential.

Their acceptance was almost worse than their fury, he found. He could barely move a foot about his room before one or the other rushed to attend him. Soon the domestic tension made the lovely old villa more unbearable than the road. Arthur announced to his disgruntled entourage that there would be no time to enjoy the delights of sleeping inside the ancient manor for long. They would leave for Viroconium an hour after dawn.

* * *

Despite the preparedness of the escort, loading up and moving Arthur's combined men and followers, with their carts and ponies as well as horses, was a slow business. Together the procession now numbered over two hundred men, women and children. Whatever Arthur's orders, it was several hours into the morning by the time they lumbered out of the old precincts and headed down the steep slope into the valley to the west. With just his troop and their battle horses Arthur could have expected to reach Viroconium by the next midday. With this baggage train he'd be lucky to make it within the week. He watched in despair as they rumbled along the riverbank towards a bridge that had seen safer days. It marked the crossing point between Coritanian and Cornovian lands, and on the other side, waiting patiently, sat a large detachment of men equal to those of Coritania.

Arthur was greeted formally by the Cornovian captain, bearing greetings from his king, Cunegnus. His orders were to escort the Overlord and his followers to Viroconium, which was being prepared for his arrival. Arthur kept his impatience in check, relieved the Coritanian detachment of their duties with thanks and, once everybody was safely over the bridge and watered, followed his new escorts into the forests on the western side of the river.

By late morning the reluctant sunshine had turned to steady summer rain. They made a sorry spectacle, Arthur thought – more the remnants of a defeated tribe than the escort of the Overlord on a progress through his own provinces. Presumably this was precisely what Cunegnus wanted it to look like to the villagers and homesteaders

CHAPTER XV

of his nation as Arthur lumbered through. The Overlord, diminished in his power, his inadequate armed forces and his domestic rabble escorted by smart Cornovian riders on the road to the capital.

It would not do. He had swallowed his pride for long enough to ensure Conorix's agreement. Arthur was not about to lie at Cunegnus's feet as well.

The road, a new track cleared but not underpinned by stone, curled into the wide forest beyond them. Eventually it would rejoin the main thoroughfare, but until then it would offer them nothing more than a slow trudge. Arthur rode in the middle of the column, flanked by one of his own men on either side with the Cornovian guards in front and behind. After a handful of tortuous miles Arthur swore in frustration and summoned his equerry forward. Gwain was a tall Dumnonian, ten years younger than Arthur.

'Gwain, we must move on. The world will not wait while we dawdle.'

'Yes, my lord, but how? The Viroconium men are under orders to keep us together, just like the last lot. We could overpower them, but not without blood, and to what end?'

'You're right, of course. It would just confirm all the fears that Cunegnus has about my time in the east. Too close to Cunorix by half. Nevertheless, this is intolerable. It's deliberately insulting to the position of the overlord. I've put up with it for one night of Coritanian hospitality, but that's enough. If I can't ride freely in Britannia, then I have no business riding at all. I might as well slip back to Moridunum or Elfael.'

Gwain smiled. 'Shall we turn south-west, then?'

'Don't tempt me, soldier. This morning it's too easy.'

'Yes, my lord.'

'Tell their captain I wish to stop at the next clearing. Then we'll see how peaceful and constructive they really are.'

Gwain nodded, listened to the rest of his orders and rode forward to the head of the escort. Twenty minutes later the track dropped out of the forest into cleared farmland, the grass half-grown for mowing, the oats just beginning to show their heads. The Captain ordered the troops in a circle, allowing the horses to drop their heads and forage in the fresh wet grass of the meadow.

The civilians piled out of their carts to stretch their legs. The rain had eased to mild drizzle and the sun was poking through the thinning cloud. Arthur ordered his men away so that the rest could see him and summoned his standard-bearer to stand by him, the badge of office held high. He gestured to the herald, who shouted for silence among the two hundred travellers. Eventually they achieved it and Arthur spoke out, firmly but without shouting.

'I am Arthur, Tygern Fawr. I have business on this road, but this road is not my business. That is the safety and good order of the land, and it will be served better when I am with Cunegnus than when I traverse his kingdom. Therefore I will go on ahead.'

The captain of the Cornovian troop edged forward to interrupt before Arthur raised his hand to stop him and Gwain moved a step towards him.

'I know your orders, but I am Overlord of Britannia, and these are mine. And you cannot do other than obey. You are right to want to escort such a large force at arms moving through your country. Therefore you shall. And I am glad that my followers and those I love shall be well protected in these uncertain forests. However, I cannot enjoy the luxury of your company. Captain, move to my side, if you will.'

The Cornovian looked puzzled, but obeyed.

Arthur continued. 'I have complete faith in the loyalty of the Cornovii. To prove it, I leave you in command of my men as well as yours, even though many outrank you. I shall take no more than two with me, and two of your troop who know the way. Otherwise only Gwain and my silent scribe, Modlen, shall ride ahead. The others do not need to attend me in Viroconium. Indeed, they were never meant to. You will take them straight to Deva. I will join you all there, after my summit with Cunegnus. Is that clear?'

The Captain looked aghast. He was torn between two sets of orders – those of Cunegnus to round up Arthur's band, to escort the Overlord to Viroconium with courtesy, but slow enough to emphasise the authority in the territory, and the direct orders of Arthur himself. At the same time the prospect of command of such a large and distinguished force was not one he would willingly forgo. For once the constitution seemed to be on his side, though he knew Cunegnus would not be best pleased.

For a moment he struggled with the issue, then straightened on the horse's back, and in a voice that could be heard clearly by all his men called out, 'Yes my lord. It will be an honour.'

CHAPTER XV

Arthur smiled, anxious not to show his relief. 'Good. Captain, these people are dear to me. My consort Gwenan will command the civilians. You will at all times consult her and my senior officers on any matter that concerns them. They are in your charge.' He told Gwain to find Modlen a horse and dismounted, striding over to where Gwenan stood, leaning against a cart, with a look of sullen fury on her face. The arrangements were not designed to please her, but they were necessary.

Arthur kissed her gently. 'So you are my steward now, as well as my love.'

Gwenan glared back. 'But you need Modlen more than me between here and Deva.'

'I do. For you cannot write, and she cannot speak.'

'And therefore she cannot tell me what you do with her.'

'True.'

'And I have to accept that?'

'Yes, you do.'

'Is that an order from Arthur or Tygern Fawr?'

'From both. It is a burden only you have to bear. I will be with you soon, and I promise we will travel together in Brigantia, whatever happens.'

'By then I expect you will have found a second scribe in Viroconium to add to your collection,' fumed Gwenan.

Arthur did not wait for either further argument or her agreement. He kissed her long enough to cause comment around him and strode back to his horse. Five minutes later Gwain, Modlen and the four soldiers – two of Arthur's, two from Cunegnus – had gathered their packs and were ready to move on.

Arthur grinned at Modlen. 'I hope you can ride fast,' he said.

She inclined her head, snapped the reins of her horse and shot forward towards the road.

Arthur laughed. 'We'd better not let her leave us completely. Come on!' And with a wave back to Gwenan and the men, he urged his small band after her.

* * *

In Viroconium Cunegnus was standing looking at the day's building work of his new hall when a boy of his household came running through the piles of timber and Roman rubble – timber for the carpenters, rubble from the parts of the old basilica that had been pulled down for safety over a century before but still provided the obvious place (and a few conveniently complete walls) for a residence fit for the King of Cornovia. It was early evening and the sun was beginning to throw a red glow over the hills. The sound of children cavorting in the baths, now open to the air and unheated, but warmer than the river in summer, drifted up over the walls and through the partially blocked doorways.

The boy stood shifting from foot to foot, uncertain when to speak to his king. Cunegnus glanced at him, then, irritated by the interruption, began inspecting the joinery around him. The boy cleared his throat.

'Well? What is it?' Cunegnus asked.

'My lord, there's…' he trailed off.

'Spit it out, boy.'

'Yes, my lord. There's a man at the east gate who wants to see you.'

'So what? He can wait.'

'His officer says his name is Arthur. He has two of your men with him, too, and a girl.'

Cunegnus turned to the boy and gave him his full attention.

'Arthur?'

'Yes, my lord. That's what I was told to tell you.'

'Don't be ridiculous, boy. Arthur is at least two days away, and travelling with two centuries of troops and everything from his mistress to his chickens.'

'Yes, my lord. But that was what the man said I was to tell you.' The boy stood his ground.

'You say there were two of our men with him – who?'

'I don't know their names, my lord, but I've seen them here before. I think one of them is a cousin of Derwent of Pennocrucium.'

'What does this Arthur look like?'

'Quite old, like you. Tall, I think, though he's on a horse, so I can't be sure – taller than you, anyway, my lord, and his hair is much lighter. His man said his name was Gwain of Dumnonia.'

'I'm not sure I like your description, young man, but it sounds like him. What does he think he's doing? Very well. Go back and tell him that I will meet him at my river house as soon as he is able. Give me enough time to get back there and prepare, though, lad.'

'Yes, my lord.'

'Off you go then.'

'My lord, who is he – Arthur, I mean?'

'Don't you get taught anything these days boy? He is son of Pendraeg – or at least, Myrddin of the Demetiae says so.'

'Is that important?'

Cunegnus laughed. 'Now, that is a very good question – and one I have been trying to answer ever since I became king. By tomorrow I may know, and then, since you asked, you shall hear it from me in person. Now, bring him into the city. It could be an interesting evening.'

He watched the boy scurry away, looked up at the frame of his new hall, sighed and wandered out of the ruins. He turned left, passed the rickety but still complete colonnade of the forum, then took the next street on the right, following the forum's wall towards the river. He acknowledged the salutes of his subjects as they went about the business of closing up their stalls for the evening, and turned into a doorway in the block beyond the Hall of Consilium Viroconium – once the centre of power for the fourth-largest city in Britannia, now not much more, its critics felt, than the talking shop of bickering village gossips. All real authority rested with Cunegnus's household.

While his modern quarters were being built Cunegnus was living in his father's old residence, a much-faded town house built two centuries earlier, in the city's heyday. Now, though, there was no warm air flowing through the collapsing hypocaust (not that it mattered in the balmy evening of early summer that had arrived after the days of rain), and the fountains in the courtyard never ran. No ornamental fish swam in the rather murky water in the bowl, and the colonnades were chipped and in some cases propped up with timber beams. Inside, rough tables and benches had replaced the sumptuous couches and carved chairs of Roman times, and local ale was served from barrels, instead of wine from terracotta amphorae. Nonetheless the house was still comfortable enough. Rush mats covered the cracks in the tiled floors, baskets of flowers hung above the doorways and the smell of roasting drifted from the distant kitchen.

Cunegnus clapped his hands and two servants appeared. He ordered one to summon his steward and the Bishop, the other to fetch ale and tell the kitchens that there would be a small formal party of at least six eating privately that evening. One of the painted rooms was to be cleaned out and prepared. Arthur, Cunegnus knew, had a taste for such things, though he himself would have preferred to eat in a modern hall where he could see his men and be seen with them. If the Overlord was going to visit Viroconium, then people needed to see that Cunegnus was a man of substance. As it was, with Arthur sneaking in like this, the word would have to be put about that this was a secret visit of such importance to the Commonwealth of Britannia that no public engagements were to be held for the moment. A private bedroom would have to be found, too, Cunegnus guessed, with fresh water, and space for Arthur's men, though if he had a girl with him he might want to enjoy her on his own. On the other hand, if the girl was not there for fun, one from the town might have to be found and cleaned up. Altogether none of this was what Cunegnus had had in mind when he sent his thirty men to escort the Overlord and his household along the road from Letocetum.

Cunegnus had hardly finished giving the orders when a road-stained Arthur and his party were led into the yard by the boy, who was grinning triumphantly, as though he had accomplished a mission of enormous difficulty.

Cunegnus strode forward, arms outstretched to embrace his guest. As the boy had noticed, Arthur was a good head or more taller than the King, and towered above him, so that the clasp of welcome looked almost like the hug of a father and son. It was a mistake Cunegnus decided he would not make twice.

'Arthur, welcome. I hadn't expected you so soon – or,' he said, glancing at the meagre party of Gwain, two soldiers and Modlen, 'so alone.'

Arthur extricated himself from the embrace. 'It was necessary, Cunegnus, and I am sorry to visit you in such a way. But I could neither leave my household behind nor travel at their pace, and your men guaranteed their safe passage to Deva, for which I am truly grateful, even if I had to reverse their orders from you. I hope you will excuse them.'

'I see I must.'

'Thank you. There is too much to do, and, if the peace is to be kept, not enough time to allow events to take their course. And for reasons I shall explain, I need my people more at Deva than here in Viroconium. It is still in your kingdom, so I hope you will not mind if they seek the hospitality of your marshal there.'

'If you think it's how things have to be.'

CHAPTER XV

'I do. In the mean time, though, there are matters we need to discuss that cannot be the baggage of messengers. I thought it better to come straight to you in person than to demand some public conference on the road.'

'I am flattered that you need me so much, Arthur. Cornovia is not what it once was. We have strong rivals on all sides. Deva is suffering increasingly from Hibernian aggression, and we have no help from the west. But you know all this.'

'And it is precisely why I must talk to you now.'

'Very well.'

'But first we will wash, if you don't mind. It was a long and dirty ride.'

'Naturally.' Cunegnus waved his servants forward to take their cloaks and take them to their quarters. 'I remember that you like to do such things in the old style,' he grinned, 'and I'm pleased to say that here in Viroconium it is still possible, if not the fashion among most people, and therefore we have to be a little inventive at times to recreate it.'

'You're very kind.'

'The – ah – lady? Is she…?' Cunegnus tried and failed to ask delicately whether she was to go with Arthur, Gwain or his house girl. It was a more complicated question than he realised. Arthur did not want to suggest to Gwain that Modlen had supplanted Gwenan as his mistress; on the other hand he did not yet want to have to explain that she couldn't speak and subject her to the jibes of the servants. He decided that dealing with Gwain would be the kinder and eventually easier option.

'Modlen will come with me.'

'If that is what you wish,' Cunegnus said, looking her up and down, eyebrow raised. She was a scrawny little thing for an overlord's concubine, he thought. Maybe she looked better out of her rough travelling clothes.

Arthur seemed to read his thoughts, and put a protective arm around her shoulders as he followed the steward to a chamber at the far end of the yard. The man carefully placed Arthur's saddlebags by the door, smirked at Modlen and retreated. There was one large bed facing the door, and a wooden box packed with wool and straw, covered with a hide. In the corner a basin of water stood on a table, and next to it a wooden box with two smoothed pieces for a seat offered the rarity of a private lavatrina. Arthur unselfconsciously stripped off, peed and sluiced himself from the basin while Modlen found fresh clothes for him in the bags, then sat on the bed gazing steadfastly in the other direction. When he had finished he wandered over, pulled on the dry tunic and gestured to her to follow on with washing. She shook her head and hung it in embarrassment.

Arthur laughed and stroked her hair gently. 'Of course. I understand. I'll go and tell them I want the water replaced. And that I want a bed for you put in the corner, and all these damp clothes washed and dried by the morning. They'll think I'm mad, but that's no bad thing. Sometimes it pays to be regarded as not quite normal – it adds to my mystique, and they can tell stories about how strangely I behave and what unreasonable demands I make. I'm going to lie here while they do it. Then I'll find Gwain and explore Viroconium while you do whatever you need. Tonight Gwain will sleep outside my door as usual, so you'll be safe in all directions. Happy?'

Modlen looked at him with a mixture of gratitude and amazement at his understanding. Then she threw her arms round his neck and kissed him.

He laughed again. 'Well, that's probably a yes.' He went to the door, stepped out and clapped his hands until he saw a servant girl scurrying from the kitchens. He gave his orders and went back inside to flop on to the bed. He reached over and let his fingers brush Modlen's.

'You're my scribe; Gwenan's my lover,' he said. 'I wonder how long things will remain that clear and simple.'

* * *

'The threat,' said Arthur as the servants cleared away the remains of the meats and cheeses and replaced them with bowls of fresh cherries and early gooseberries, 'comes from every direction except the south. Am I right?'

There were seven of them at the table, and they had eaten from fine old red Roman plates found a few weeks before in one of the buildings being demolished to make way for the new royal house. To Arthur's right sat Cunegnus; to his left the Queen. Gwain flanked the Queen; Antonius, the Bishop, sat between the King and his principal counsellor, Doldavix. Modlen sat at the end, next to Gwain, with a pair of salvaged writing slates, on which she etched occasional notes.

CHAPTER XV

Arthur had surprised even the Bishop by announcing at the beginning of the meal that a document detailing their decisions would be drawn up from Modlen's notes in the morning. Cunegnus, like most of the kings on the Council, had become used to recording matters of state by swearing oaths in front of as many followers as possible and commanding their bards to commemorate the details in epic song. It was a custom followed by the Barbarians and by the Hibernians and the nations north of the wall, and – among those who could not read Latin or Brythonic – it was as useful a system as any. Arthur, though, believed that disputes could only be avoided for the future if the record was permanent and attested by the authority of the Bishop, and thus, if necessary, the Pope. It also gave him control of what was recorded and what was not, and gave his reports to the Council the force of law. Cunegnus regarded the whole procedure as pedantic and somehow a persistent comment on the inadequacy of royal literacy. Occasionally he harked back uneasily to the old pre-Christian edicts forbidding the writing of the Celtic languages; edicts that Arthur, echoing Myrddin, believed had made sure that the only record of their history that remained was that in the libraries of Greece, Egypt and Rome – now by all accounts being set alight by Barbarians.

Cunegnus picked the husk from a gooseberry. 'Thankfully we have only friends to the south. For the rest I cannot guess where the next assault will come from. I do not trust Brigantia – never have, never will. Never trust a neighbour whom you have defeated decisively. Tribute is accompanied by flattery, not love, and they'll take their opportunity to add Deva to the kingdom when they have a chance.'

'I can't disagree,' said Arthur, 'though I can discourage it.'

'It will take more than your disapproving words, with all respect, Tygern Fawr.' Cunegnus passed the fruit along the line and poured himself some wine. It was rough stuff, made locally from vines that had been planted in the days before even Constantine, but it had been breached in Arthur's honour, and indeed, he did prefer it to the thin ale that was the only alternative in Viroconium. 'You believe that our greatest threat comes from the continental Barbarians, am I right?'

Arthur nodded.

'Well, that may be true for all the eastern kingdoms and those facing Gaul, but frankly we've never seen one of them over here, except a few farmers fleeing from the revenge of the Coritani. My problem is the Hibernians, and believe me, they can be just as bad.'

'I still need your help. Whoever threatens any of us threatens us all.'

'Tell that to Brigantia,' Cunegnus snorted. 'There are far too many Hibernians finding hospitality in Mamucium altogether. We thought the problem had been dealt with years ago, when Cunedda came from the Votadini to bring order to the Ordovices and throw out the Hibernian settlers – not that most of them went home, of course. They just ran through the mountains until their cousins, the Demetiae – your friends Myrddin and Vorteporix – found them land. But Cunedda's sons have shown that the cure can be worse than the disease, especially Corbalengus. I could always rely on the Deceangeli to keep my western borders safe. They have been reliable in all things. Our treaty sharing the port at Deva, with Canovium responsible for its defence while leaving the administration to me, was working all but perfectly for ten years. Now, though, I'm having to reinforce it more and more. Since the Ordovices took Segontium they've made it clear that they regard Deceangelia itself as a kingdom without a future. It suits them very well to let Hibernians attack the coast while they encroach from the south and west. Mountain by mountain they are crushing the kingdom to its heart.'

'And are they right? Has the kingdom a future?' Bishop Antonius asked.

'Probably not,' admitted Cunegnus, 'But it's convenient for me to wish it well. Luckily arranging for its future is the Overlord's responsibility, not mine.' He rested an appreciative hand on Arthur's shoulder.

'It's nice to know I have such wholehearted support,' said Arthur ruefully. 'What about Cunorix?'

'I shouldn't need to worry about the Catuvellauni at all. Cunorix's borders are many miles away from mine, in theory.'

'In theory?'

'I think he wants to move well to the west. I don't think the Coritani will stop him, either. There's not so much difference between their peoples, and with the Barbarian worry at their eastern door I think they'd gladly offer Cunorix authority over some of their lands between the Dobunni in Corinium and my boundary, in return for guarantees of help securing the rest. I don't blame either Cunorix or the Coritani. That border never did make much sense, and had more to do with the military convenience of Agricola than with the sentiments of the Britannian nations. If I thought the Catuvellauni would stop there I'd be all for it. And I respect Cunorix – but I don't like him. He can be vicious bastard, and not just to outsiders. But I do respect him. He knows what he's doing. And what I think he's doing is trying to create one big kingdom in the middle of Britannia on the pretext of needing the land and dealing efficiently with the invaders. He may not want to overrun Cornovia, but he would like it to be a very different shape and with a very different king.' Cunorix paused while he drank some wine, then grimaced. 'This really is horrible stuff, Arthur. I'm sorry. I had planned to send for something better from Deva by the time you arrived.'

Arthur laughed and raised his cup. 'It's not from Gaul, that's for sure, and we'll probably feel foul in the morning. But it's all right after the second. You'd better fill me up.'

'Very noble of you,' he said, and did as he was ordered. 'How long is it since we sat like this and talked, Arthur? Must have been a long time.'

'It is. There have been times at the Council, of course. But it's been five years since I marched through Deva – and you weren't there at the time. Must have been just after your accession. I remember I came for the official feast. That's what – seven, eight years ago?'

'It was the autumn, so nearly eight. It's not good enough, is it, my lord? No wonder we can't keep together.'

Arthur sipped the sour wine. 'I'm glad you said that. It's very much why I wanted to see you so urgently, and why I couldn't countenance travelling at the pace of the women.' He grinned as Modlen glared at him from the end of the table, and quickly added, 'except one who can ride like the cavalry.'

'Lucky you,' muttered Cunegnus lewdly, and Modlen blushed. For once Arthur had more important things on his mind than gallantry.

'I need the kings of Britannia together, and I cannot wait for it to be until each has everything he wants from all the others. If we are to send the Barbarians a message they will not forget – make it clear that we are not as easy to walk over as Gaul – we'll have to do more than burn a few ships on the seashore. Our victory in the spring will be seen as just good luck, being in the right place at the right time – or, more likely, given the storm they had just sailed through, as proof that the leader of that fleet had angered their gods before setting sail.'

'We can see it indeed as a victory for the one true God,' purred the Bishop.

'I'm sure Your Grace is right,' muttered Arthur into his wine glass, with just enough enthusiasm not to sound impious. He tended to believe more in good tactics and the discipline of his men than less predictable divine help. However, he was equally happy to avoid giving the impression that the Church was unnecessary. In fact, it was an essential part of his calculations.

'All very true, Arthur, but it doesn't help me with the Hibernians, even if Vortebelos in Brigantia and Corbalengus in Ordovicia behave themselves.'

'You're wrong. It will.'

'How?'

'The Hibernians will raid as long as they think nobody will be there to stop them. They've no organisation. Even Bishop Padrig is finding he can't achieve that.'

'With Brigantia giving in to every demand they make, who can blame them?'

'I'm on my way there to discuss precisely that. Have some understanding, though, Cunegnus. Brigantia is in a position not much better than you are. If the Parisi become too easy a target for the Barbarians, they are vulnerable from the east. To the north the Carvetii are small, and will be trying to hold the line of the wall, and you are doing nothing to make the Brigantians feel more confident in their northern security. Like Alt Clut on the northern side of the wall, they may see their best interest as making opportunist alliances, or at least keeping amicable with the Hibernians.'

'You said opportunist. That is exactly what it is,' Cunengus said. 'They'll live to regret it.'

'Maybe, maybe not. At least the Hibernians have Gallic roots. Thanks to Bishop Padrig there may soon even be enough of them convinced Christians for Hibernia to be a truer part of the Roman Church than it ever was of the empire.'

'I always said you were too generous, Arthur. You see everyone's side.'

'That's my job. It's not generosity, it's having the view I need to. Remember, I have no kingdom to keep secure, Cunegnus. I have the whole Commonwealth of Britannia. However much the family hates each other, I have to act in the interest of the family, even if there are cousins who would rather I concentrate on them and ignore the rest.'

'Uncle Arthur?'

'It could be worse.'

'You may be right, but it doesn't have the ring of warrior to it.'

'Don't underestimate my ferocity just because I have the patience to think.'

Cunegnus sighed, poured himself some more wine and passed the jug along the table.

'You are right, of course, Tygern Fawr. I hope you will forgive me for saying, though, that those of us who are kings would prefer to be treated as your electors, rather than your children – or as the playthings of Myrddin's stratagems. You have been a fine overlord for sixteen years. But sixteen years is a dangerous moment. It leaves you young enough to be no better than the rest, but old enough for people to have forgotten what it was like before.'

'I take your warning seriously – and as the good advice of an old friend.'

'So it was meant. Let's drink to it.'

They drank, and Cunegnus banged on the table for two more jugs of wine.

'So, do you have a solution to our problems, or is this just an exercise in understanding?'

'Surely not,' intoned the Bishop, 'for only God has solutions.' He was a thin weasel of a man, and Arthur thought he had the humourless air of the Pelagian about him, all asceticism and false purity. Arthur made a mental note to review the reputations and appointments of all the bishops when he next went south to the Cantiaci, who seemed to be building an especially close relationship to the ecclesiastical authorities in Rome since their hospitality to St Germanus fifty years before. It was a special relationship hotly disputed by Gwidellius, Bishop of Londinium, and by the Atrebates, Parisi, Iceni and Catuvellauni, all of whom had bishops keen to be regarded as leader of the Church in Britannia, but Arthur needed an excuse to lure the Cantiaci away from the course of Barbarian appeasement, and investigating the bishops would occupy them nicely.

For the moment Arthur merely grunted assent to Bishop Antonius and the too-enthusiastic Amen of Doldavix, then launched into the explanation of his idea for an inner Council, bound by a web of treaties; of maintaining a permanent mobile force under his command specifically trained in dealing with Barbarian tactics; of calling a full Council of all the kings of Britannia once every three years. The four Cornovians listened politely, as though they were attending a seminar rather than deciding the future of nations. Eventually Arthur stopped and looked around him for the expected approval. It was there in the loyal eyes of Gwain and the shining admiration of Modlen; but Cunegnus merely cleared this throat and toyed with his wine cup while the Queen smiled weakly at nobody in particular.

It was Doldavix who broke the awkward silence. 'Forgive me, my lord, but those fascinating points sound a little far from us here in Viroconium.' The Bishop nodded in encouragement. 'I mean, they appear to be interesting solutions to your problems – perhaps not so much to ours.'

Gwain spoke up for his master. 'And what are those, and how are they different from those of the other kingdoms?'

Doldavix went on, 'Collapsing population, illness in the cities – though the plague has gone we have more sickness every year, especially among children – not enough people to sow and harvest, too many fields returning to the forest, disintegrating roads, too few boys surviving into manhood, and then the fears about our borders that the King has already told you about. We have our faith and what is left of the great cities of Deva and Viroconium here, but that continually reminds us more of what we cannot make any more than of what we have.'

'You expect me to tell you that is your concern, not mine,' Arthur said, turning to the Counsellor, 'but that would not be true. None of those things will be helped by strife between nations or the constant fear of attack. How can I help you to mend your roads and find fresh water if we need all the men to defend your borders? How can it be worth clearing the fields and planting if each season they are taken by armies or invaders? It hardly matters to the farmer which. Or if I am always demanding that Cunegnus send half his kingdom to fight on the other side of Britannia while they fear what the Ordovices or the Brigantes will do while their backs are turned? Answer me that.'

Doldavix looked abashed by the onslaught. 'But—'

'But nothing!' Cunegnus exploded. 'The Overlord is quite right. And furthermore, he has had the good manners to come and discuss these matters with us alone – something no man in his position has done since the days of legend. Thank you, Arthur. We did not name you Tygern Fawr for nothing.'

'So you agree?'

'Ah, well, we'll see about that. I wouldn't go quite so far.'

'There's something I've forgotten?'

'I doubt it. No, it's more a question of how I can be part of helping you achieve this new Jerusalem, given the precarious nature of my kingdom which Doldavix, despite his lack of subtlety, is quite right to mention.'

'I have thought of that.'

'I'm glad to hear it.'

'I will tell you the details. Then, if you agree, Modlen will note it down and Bishop Antonius can draw up a decree for us both to seal in the morning.'

Cunegnus nodded. 'Very well.'

'You're right about the Deceangeli,' Arthur began. 'They cannot survive much longer on their own. And I don't think they can hold all their western lands against Corbalengus either. He would break any treaty of limitation I made him sign.'

'No doubt about it.'

'The only way is to let logic take its course. Whom do the Deceangeli regard as their kin? Not the Ordovices, certainly. Though they are people of the mountains they have always looked to Cornovia for safety and for the good things in life. Their language is almost the same as yours, free of the archaisms and Hibernian words that creep across the sea to Segontium.'

'What are you suggesting, Arthur?'

'I think you ought to create a new kingdom, with equal parts of highland and lowland which you will rule for me. It would mean losing both names and finding a new one. Perhaps the two bishops and Myrddin can find one that is acceptable to all. Your son will marry the daughter of the mountains, and their king will be assigned King of Manavia, charged with retrieving it intact from the Hibernian invaders. It would be just reward for him – a new and better kingdom and the enjoyment of the displeasure of Brigantia.'

There was a stunned silence round the table.

Eventually Cunegnus whistled quietly through his teeth. 'Well, it's certainly bold enough, I'll give you that.'

'I think it is achievable.'

'Without starting a war?'

'By negotiation, appealing to common interest and showing that it will be better for everyone, even the Ordovices.'

'And how do you start this negotiation?'

Arthur smiled. 'I don't. You do. You make the offer of protection under my authority. I send the offer of Manavia on condition of the plan's acceptance. Myrddin works on Corbalengus. We meet for a great ceremony to launch the marriage and the birth of the new kingdom in three months' time.'

'So soon?'

'Any later and the chance will be gone. The winter will come, and with it hardship. We must make this the best winter the people of both countries have had in years. Can I count on you?'

Cunegnus thought for a moment, then stood with his wine cup raised. 'To the new kingdom,' he declared, 'and the wisdom of the Overlord, for if he turns out not to be wise we are all lost.'

* * *

Arthur lay in the dark. The thick walls meant that only high in the back wall, where a small, barred window for ventilation gave out on to the street, did the flicker from a vagrant's fire break the blackness. In the corner by the door Modlen's even breathing suggested she was in the deepest reaches of sleep. Arthur pulled the cover closer to his chin and turned over, forcing his eyes shut. His head ached from the sour wine. For the first time since he had abandoned his camp and Gwenan's bed he felt a sense of the enormity of the mission he had started. He was trying to reshape Britannia through peace and loyalty, something nobody had really tried before, and certainly not something anyone had succeeded in managing for more than a month or two in the last hundred years – not Pendraeg, not his father, not Ambrosius Aurelianus, not Vortigern. He was trying it, moreover, without armies or even a kingdom to call his own. Just his record as a leader, the authority of the Council and the mystery of Myrddin's test that had brought him to all this. He had always known it was a trick, and wondered who else did, whether they were just biding their time to expose him, and he wondered too how many of the Council would have allowed him to become overlord if Candidianos had told them the truth in the early days. He rolled back on to his back again, trying to concentrate on the steady rhythm of Modlen's breathing to dispel the oppressive silence of the night. But her trusting peace itself was enough to bring the burden of responsibility crushing down again from the decaying roof tiles. It brought back all his annoyance that he did not seem to be able to behave with the mindless self-certainty of so many of the kings he knew, men who were absurdly proud of their minor glories and unconcerned about the views of their subjects, who could be true tyrants and enjoy it. Perhaps it was because he had not been born a king, but had spent the first fourteen years as an ordinary boy in a hill camp, where the only time the Roman past intervened was when there was a summer expedition into the valley and they played among the bramble-covered ruins of the fort. Arthur smiled at the memory. Those stones had seemed so grand at the time.

Why could he not settle on anything – his rightful place, where he should live, who he should love? What was Sioned like now? Had she married? He hoped she was now the wife of a great man at Corbalengus's court in Segontium, with at least three sons. But if she was, Myrddin would have told him by now. And what was he to do with Gwenan? There had been many girls in between, often reluctant, but supplied by his hosts as he travelled the island. There had never been anybody in his bed he felt so completely at home with and able to make him slough off the costume of office, never a woman who had made him lose touch with time like her, whom he could trust as well to take over the reins of his household and even his men with natural competence. Maybe he should make her his queen. She was good enough. But would Myrddin, let alone the kings, ever let the Overlord marry a half-Barbarian orphan given to him as a present, a slave for his lust? That she had become more was not something anybody but Arthur would ever recognise. They might allow it for his sake, but they would never accept it. If he married for love, not power, then that was what would have to sustain them. Yet however much he loved her, Arthur knew well that he could not live the life of an itinerant warrior and resist the calls of other girls, of other perfect bodies. If he had believed that he could when he set off after Cunorix, he knew now as he listened to Modlen. So far he had acted like a protector, almost a loving father, to her. He was her rescuer. But for how long, and at what cost to both of them?

In the corner Modlen broke the rhythm of her sleep. The breathing became shorter, less regular. Arthur heard her turn over suddenly and toss back the cover and begin to murmur, talking without words. At first she seemed to be asking for something, then calling like a child. There was a pause. For a few minutes the silence and her calm returned and Arthur, grateful for the interruption to his own futile thoughts, started to feel drowsy in response. Then there was a sudden sharp intake of air, a gulp, and Modlen began to sing, high soft and clear, a tune that Arthur had known since boyhood. He sat up in bed and looked over to her, astonished. But in mid phrase, as suddenly as she had started, she killed the song, and the music was replaced by sobs, almost growls of fury. Arthur threw off his blanket and, almost blind in the dark night, crept over to where she lay. He knelt down beside her, touched her hair, then rested his hand on her bare shoulder in reassurance. She stayed asleep. The crying did not stop for many minutes, and Arthur felt his knees stiffen and his feet grow cold. Still he held her, and eventually she calmed and slept peacefully again. He leant over and kissed her head before hauling the cover over and making his way back to his own regal bed.

XVI

THEY MIGHT HAVE ARRIVED like a group of wandering merchants, but Arthur and his four followers were to leave Viroconium with full pomp and ceremony. Cunegnus had no intention of travelling through his country in the company of the Overlord apologetically. It was an important opportunity to show he was at the centre of international affairs, and he wanted his people to note it. The reasons were not all self-aggrandising. The progress to Deva would lift the spirits of people and make them feel that they were important enough for Arthur to visit them in person, not just summon their king when men were needed to fight on the other side of Britannia.

CHAPTER XVI

Heralds were sent ahead to inform the authorities in Deva, to warn those along the route to turn out and show proper respect, and to prepare the one major town along the road, Mediolanum, to expect them for the night for a full state visit. Modlen spent her morning with the Bishop's scribe, writing her notes out on rough hide in Britannian so that he could translate the agreement into Latin on vellum – one copy for Cunegnus's royal archive, one for herself. She was becoming Arthur's travelling library, and even in the week she had been with her new master, she could feel herself growing and changing from the angry and servile girl into somebody who knew that her place was one nobody else could take.

The document authorised Cunegnus to begin negotiations with the Deceangeli, noted that there would be a settlement on exact borders with the Coritani and, if necessary, the Catuvellauni, made a few unflattering remarks about the Hibernians and invited Cunegnus to become one of the new inner Council of Twelve.

While Cunegnus fussed over the preparations for the journey, Doldavix was detailed to show Arthur and Gwain the wonders of Viroconium. The forum, Council chamber and basilica had all seen better days, but the magnificent baths, celebrated in their time as the finest in Britannia outside Aqua Sulis, were crowded on the warm summer morning, when the fact that they were no longer heated was a definite advantage. Arthur made appreciative noises – not only about the baths themselves, but at the energetic work being done to repair or reuse many of the buildings that had deteriorated over the years, and to put up news ones in the modern timber style, where it was clear that returning to the Roman ways was not to contemporary taste.

Midday had come and gone by the time the company of more than thirty rode out of the north gate. They rode in a fast formation, without baggage carts.

Trumpets sounded at the gate as they filed through, and there was just enough of a curious crowd to show that the citizens of Viroconium regarded Arthur as worth breaking from the morning's work to see in person. Ten men at arms formed the vanguard, while Doldavix and Gwain, side by side, led the dignitaries, followed by the steward and two standard-bearers proclaiming Cunegnus and Arthur. The Queen was flanked by two women attendants, with Modlen taking her position at the rear in front of the second detachment of soldiers.

She realised she almost resented already the protocol that forced her to ride so separately from Arthur. She consoled herself that it was a lot better than being a slave in the baggage train, waiting for any of Cunorix's men who felt like it to take advantage of her inability to tell by fondling beneath her skirts as she was carried along.

Once clear of the city the company accelerated to a gentle canter. If they had started early they could have made Deva in a day, but there was no particular hurry. They would have to wait there for the rest of Arthur's party – in fact, they were quite likely to overtake them on the road. In an ideal world, Arthur thought, there was a good chance that they would all be reunited at Mediolanum that evening, and he would move on to Deva with a retinue rather more equal to Cunegnus's.

The road crossed a tributary of the Sabrina just to the north of Viroconium, then kept its straight line to the right of the meandering river for ten miles or so before crossing a ford. They rode hard for it, covering the distance in little more than an hour, and waded through the water that ran shallow even after the rain the day before. On the far bank they wheeled round and stopped to let the horses drink. The heralds had done their job earlier in the morning, and three peasant women emerged from the handful of cottages clustered by the road. They carried jugs of thin ale and wooden trays of whatever beakers they had been able to muster from the village. There were enough for the royal guests and their staff. The men had to share the jugs around. The four women in the riding party dismounted and were taken into the nearest and largest of the cottages so they could relieve themselves in private.

An hour later found them at the junction just south of Mediolanum, where their road was joined by the great north-west highway that ran from Deva all the way down Britannia to Verulamium, Londinium and eventually to the main Cantiacan port for Gaul at Dubris. Arthur half expected to find Gwenan and her small army appearing from the right as they approached, but nothing so perfectly destined happened, and there was no word from those they met along the road of such a large convoy passing through that day. He would have to resign himself to waiting.

Mediolanum was used to travellers. It existed to serve the road, and the innkeepers were licking their lips at the thought of two large royal parties stopping for the night. Cunegnus kept no hall there. Like most

CHAPTER XVI

other people he was always passing through, so the inns had all the business they could handle. To her open and Arthur's secret sadness, Modlen was quartered with the Queen and her ladies for the night, while the King and the Overlord, with Gwain and Doldavix, were given rooms in a smarter establishment three doors down.

The following morning was fine and clear. For once no clouds from the west intruded into the blue sky, and there was the certainty that it would be hot – the sort of day for lolling by a river, not for riding hard in cloaks and woollen tunics. They were up and out of the inns early, anxious to reach Deva by early afternoon so that they could feel the fresher breezes from the sea when the heat was at its worst.

Arthur had been in Deva for two days by the time Gwenan and the rest finally arrived. The horses and the people were exhausted by the journey, and as Arthur surveyed them he realised it would be a least a week before they were fully recouped and ready to move on. They could hardly have been in a better place to recover, though – Deva was still a fine and proud city, nominally Cornovian but in reality seeing itself as the centre around which the life of north-west Britannia revolved.

The respite was used to rest and replenish supplies, clean and mend travelling clothes and dispatch riders into Brigantia. Arthur had learnt the lesson of the trek up from Cunorix's camp, and intended to split his party into two. Everybody would set out together as far as Mamucium, which was only two days away, even at walking pace. Mamucium had been designated as the main Brigantian administrative centre west of the mountains. It was close enough to Cornovia to remind Cunegnus that the kingdom to the north was no natural friend, but far enough inland to be safe from unexpected Hibernian raids.

At Mamucium the group would divide. Arthur would travel with a hundred men, without baggage carts or dependants, by the northern and more exposed road to King Vortebelos at Isurium on the other side of the mountains. The less essential equipment and officials would travel along the main road that ran parallel with an armed escort of thirty, straight to Ebvracum, only a few miles south from the Brigantian capital, which served as the Overlord's northern base, as it had done for the emperors (legitimate and pretenders) since Constantine. Whatever the outcome of his Brigantian talks, therefore, Arthur knew he would be able to consolidate his forces within half a day's fast ride.

Cunegnus insisted on accompanying Arthur for the first day, which took them as far as the border between Cornovia and Brigantia, a place marked by not much more than a dilapidated fort. However, Cunegnus maintained a detachment of men there at all times, and it would allow the company to camp for the night in the knowledge that they were still under his full protection. Politically it suited Cunegnus to be able to keep his word to his officers that the Overlord's entourage would be escorted from the moment it entered Cornovia to the moment it left. It also allowed him to bid farewell to Arthur early the following morning with full ceremony in front of the resident garrison and half the men of Deva, who had been encouraged to swell the ranks for the occasion. Grateful as he was for the show of security and fond alliance, Arthur was glad to ride out of the suffocating and increasingly self-important hospitality of Cunegnus and to feel himself fully in command of his own men once again. While in theory he had the authority to override the decisions of any of the kings, he could not be seen to do so without an excellent reason. And at that moment he needed their full support. If it meant joining in a parade that was more about showing Cunegnus's status than about his own security or mission, so be it.

At Mamucium, reduced to little more than a village on a muddy little river, they found the advance heralds had done their job well. Although there was not enough room in the houses to find beds for such a large retinue, a capacious hall had been prepared for Arthur and his staff, and the cooking fires laid and lit on cleared dry ground for the men. The Brigantian Tribune offered his sword to Arthur when he arrived at the outskirts of the town, and made the usual platitudes about how honoured he was to receive him, how his men would do everything they could to make him comfortable, few as they were. That, Arthur decided, was the key point. His own troop of a hundred and thirty outnumbered the Brigantian garrison by two to one. There would be no trouble.

Why, he wondered as he allowed Gwenan to bathe his feet in the privacy of a section of the hall cordoned off by wicker partitions, did he think there would be trouble? Was he just catching Cunegnus's distrust of Brigantia? After all, he had already spent at least eight weeks that year at Ebvracum with no hint of anything but supportive noises coming down the road from Isurium. He wasn't sure, but his instinct told him something had changed, that Brigantia now had ambitions of its own that were nothing to do with the justified insecurity of Cornovia, but which were a mirror image of Catuvellaunia.

If Brigantia felt it could hold off Barbarians and Hibernians without difficulty, using its size and relative wealth to use Carvetia to the north and Parisia to the south-east as mere buffer states, useful for soaking up waves of invaders, then it would have very different political goals in mind to Arthur. Vortebelos would be intent on making Brigantia a free-standing nation, quite big enough to maintain its own defences and more worried about the similar ambitions of Cunorix than about the greater good of a united Council. Arthur's greatest fear was that enough of the major kingdoms would conclude that Britannia's usefulness had passed, and the age of smaller, independent nations had arrived.

Refreshed after eating, Arthur and Gwain left the hall while it was still light, and made their way to the camp. Along the way Arthur made a point of calling in at as many of the houses and huts as he could, greeting surprised villagers and spending a few moments listening to their fears, admiring their children and once in a while being surprised himself to hear ideas that went much further than complaints about the price of hogs and the quality of iron for working. Where many of the kings regarded such conversations as letting people dangerously close, Arthur knew the time was never wasted. With every family he visited he had allies for life who would resent less his call for them to make sacrifices, too often of their lives. Many were already giving up what space they could in the homes to let the women, children and older members of the party have a bed inside for the night, and a few words of thanks were appreciated even if, given the disparity in their accents, they were not always fully understood.

Round the camp he called each of the tribunes to him, and allocated duties for the muster and division of troops the following morning – who would ride with him to Isurium, who to Ebvracum. With each officer he would return to the campfire and talk to the soldiers. It was the first evening since they had set out for Cunorix's camp that Arthur had had all his men together without the interference of units from one king or another listening in. Arthur wanted to know what they had heard along the way, how they had been treated when he was out of sight, what rumours were doing the rounds. The most persistent ones, he found, were two stories that were unrelated but were becoming linked in the telling – that he intended to make Gwenan his queen when they reached Ebvracum, and that he had been plotting with Cunegnus and Cunorix to overthrow Vortebelos – that his journey to Isurium was just a feint to lull him into a sense of security until an army could be gathered in Ebvracum ready to take him on. Arthur did his best to dismiss both stories, but he was not sure by the end of his walk that he had succeeded. Three weeks earlier he would have been ready to marry Gwenan, almost because he knew it would cause a scandal and reduce Myrddin to apoplexy, but now he was not only less tempted, but duty had reasserted its hold on his feelings. As to Vortebelos, there the temptation lay in the other direction. He half-wished he had been planning to do exactly what the men said. He would rather be the power in Brigantia than its supplicant.

Arthur returned to the hall in the late evening dusk and completed his orders for the night. Finally he dismissed Gwain and the others, rose from the table and summoned Gwenan to follow him through the partition wall to bed. It had been a hard day's ride, and they were both stiff. Gwenan helped Arthur out of his boots and tunic, letting him savour the pleasure of lying flat and stretching before she let her light-brown hair fall free from its combs, slipped off her dress and slid on to the bed beside him. She laid her head on his chest. He stroked her hair and let his fingers drift down and along the soft skin of her back. Within minutes he fell asleep, snoring gently. Gwenan lifted her hazel eyes, gazed at his face, calm at last in the flickering firelight and kissed his chest. Then she too drifted off happily to sleep.

* * *

Four hours later Arthur woke from a dream of terror. He knelt in the mud after falling from his horse. His right arm had been cut off, and all around him the corpses of his men lay piled. The sight of death stretched in all directions. Yet there seemed to be no enemy, no Barbarian soldiers stamping through the gore, looting the torques and brooches of his warriors. In the sky carrion birds were swarming, and on top of a heap of faceless bodies next to him Gwenan's lay, with a gash in her neck that still pumped out her blood. Arthur eyes started open, and he felt the sweat on his chest. In a second the silence and the dull glow of an ember from the fire calmed him. He tried to move his right arm, and realised it was numb from the weight of Gwenan's head pressed into the shoulder. Trying not to wake her, he shifted in bed, rolling over to detach himself and letting her head settle down beside him. He felt the blood return to his fingers and the strength to his petrified muscles. Even though he had been so careful Gwenan stirred, began to turn over away from him, then reached her fingers up to his face to trace his eyes, play along his moustache and rest between his lips.

Arthur kissed the exploring fingertips and slipped his own hand on to her side, caressing the curve of her waist.

'Sorry,' he said, 'bad dream.'

She smiled without opening her eyes. 'No more?'

'No more.'

Gwenan kissed his lips and pushed against him, moving so that he could not help but ease between her legs. She whispered, 'let's dream of something else,' and pulled his head down so that his lips brushed her left breast.

They had not made love so completely since the travelling began and they'd left their secluded hill camp. For more than an hour, as silently and secretly as if they had stayed asleep, they explored each other. In the end Gwenan could take and give no more, and fell exhausted on to Arthur's chest as he released himself at last. They lay still, joined and immobile until the first birds began to sing and the summer night ebbed into dawn. Then Gwenan nestled at his side and they drifted back to sleep.

* * *

As the morning broke fully, enough of the dream remained in Arthur's mind for him to consider changing orders for the long march across the mountains. If there was to be danger on the road — either road — then there was sense in keeping his entourage together, protected by his full complement of troops until they had crossed the worst of the terrain and were close to Ebvracum. Then he could either branch off north just west of Calcaria or make sure everybody reached Ebvracum safely before setting off himself to see Vortebelos in Isurium. However, that would be a slow and anxious journey, for hauling the carts up the mountain road could not be anything else. Besides, if there was to be trouble on the road it would be more likely to be aimed at any force in which Arthur was known to be travelling than against his retinue of followers. That was the military logic. Against it was the more personal question of where Gwenan should go. Now that rumours were spreading that she was a potential bride for the Overlord, she was as much a target as he was. If she travelled with the reserve staff (as she had through Cornovia) Arthur would not know whether she was safe or not until a message came from Ebvracum. And taking her with him would reassure her that Modlen was indeed his diplomatic scribe, not Gwenan's replacement. The fact that he was arriving in Isurium with a woman companion might also persuade Vortebelos that Arthur was intent on talking, not fighting.

So that was his decision. Gwenan and Modlen flanked Arthur as he rode north out of Mamucium towards the desolation of the moors, leaving Gwain to lead the remainder of his household by the more frequented (though not much less desolate) southern road that took the shortest route across the high country before rolling its way among gentler hills to Ebvracum. With both parties rode a platoon of Brigantian scouts, ostensibly to show the way in places where the old roads had fallen into decay under the peat and to suggest hospitable places to camp. As far as Arthur was concerned, though, they were there as spies for Vortebelos. That suited him. Nothing like a trusted spy to confirm his good intentions once he reached the Brigantian court.

The way was not one Arthur had ever taken before. There were few hamlets that amounted to more than a cottage or two along the path. Occasionally a child would shoot out of a doorway and stand transfixed by the mass of men hurrying past before being pulled inside sharply by its mother, unsure whether the soldiers went bent on safe passage or destruction. For much of the morning they rode through farming country, where the forest had been cleared away either side of the road and strips of cultivation were tilled parallel to the causeway. The sun was hot on their backs, and Arthur urged his men on as fast as they could while the horses were fresh and the paving of the road under a thin layer of turf was firm and true.

By midday they had begun to climb out of the lowlands, and they paused by a spring to refresh themselves and the horses. Arthur noticed that the cistern into which the water tumbled was still watched over by a little stone relief of Minerva, albeit half-buried in the wispy grass. He smiled. Myrddin would have been torn between protecting it from

CHAPTER XVI

harm where it lay or salvaging it for his collection. The Brigantian men, though, were more reverend, unashamedly pouring a little of the fresh water around the ancient figure before drinking and filling their leather bottles. Arthur followed their lead, and earned new admiration for doing so. The Bishop of Ebvracum would not have approved, but then – Arthur reflected – that went for a great deal of how ordinary people showed their respect for the land around them. The Bishop preferred them to forget and save their prayers for the inside of his new churches, where he could control them.

After the spring line the road climbed steeply, and for a while the woods crowded in on either side where the land was too sloped for unnecessary tilling. The horses slowed to a laborious walk. While they trudged and protested, though, the easy pace gave Arthur time to talk.

He called over the leader of the Brigantian scouts, a taciturn man in his late thirties with a round face and flat nose, his skin red from sun and ale. He was not a man for the finer points of political discussion, Arthur sensed, but his rank gave him the right to be spoken to.

'Have you a camp in mind for us, or will we reach Olicana?' Arthur knew the answer but he wanted to test the man's attitude.

The scout shook his head and the ghost of a patronising smile crossed his face. He was not going to say 'my lord' too often, it was plain.

'Olicana? No, not tonight. Tomorrow, possibly – if the weather's kind and not too many go lame.'

'Bad road, then?'

'Been better up on the top.'

'And a camp?'

'Not much to choose from.'

'Any shelter?' Arthur was realising he had picked a man who was not about to volunteer information, especially to a southerner.

'There's a valley. Eventually runs east. We cross it further up. Should find a hut or two by dark.'

'How long since you travelled this way?'

'Five years, maybe more.'

'But you remember the route?'

The scout looked offended. 'Only decent one there is in these parts – over the top, I mean. But there's some among my men who are local. They'll see us right.'

'I'm sure they will,' Arthur muttered without conviction, and waved the hapless scout back to his men at the head of the column.

Arthur had not found out anything he really wanted to know: the state of the country, the mood of the people or, most of all, how the Brigantians felt about their king. Vortebelos had a reputation as being a ferocious warrior, but less interested in the everyday needs of his kingdom. The winter had been hard and the northern spring late. There was talk of hunger in what was left of the towns, and clans fighting over the better land. Arthur knew that a hungry and factious kingdom would be only too happy to direct its spleen against outsiders, nominal allies or not.

By the time dusk began to gather they had been riding for the better part of twelve hours, and men, women and horses were thoroughly weary. They had crossed mile after mile of unforgiving moorland with barely a tree and only tussocky tough grass and peaty water for the horses on their infrequent breaks. For many of the men from the lowland kingdoms this was threatening country with no cover or sustenance. They would rather have risked the labyrinthine forest than these rugged horizons. For Arthur, though, there were memories of the high country of his boyhood. He would have been as happy to sleep out here as anywhere, knowing that, far from being barren, at this time of year the hills would be carpeted with berries and teeming with rabbits and ground-nesting birds. And there was plenty of old dry gorse to coax a good peat fire into life.

As the warm evening lingered late he was almost disappointed when the road began to dip down into a narrow valley with spindly woods of hazel, birch and rowan. Close to the sluggish summer river they came to a farmstead, deserted, much of its roof holed and its perimeter walls tumbled over. They had been good buildings once, rectangular in the Roman style rather than the round houses of native farmers. There were substantial barns and the protection of an inner courtyard. This had been the pension of an old legionary, Arthur thought, a man who had not wanted to go across the sea again, but who would not have been impressed by the homely comforts of Britannian farms, and who would have grown rich on the extra land he would have been able to bargain out of the administration because of its supposed loneliness. Yet it was still close to a good road, along which old comrades would pass occasionally, and travellers would welcome the prospect of a night's lodging even at well above the usual price.

CHAPTER XVI

The men made the camp ready, taking the horses to the meadow by the stream, finding brush for fires and clearing space in the old living quarters for Arthur and his staff, while the men at arms took up their posts in a circle around the buildings. Soon the smell of cooking wafted into the gloom, a domestic touch that the old farm felt all too rarely now. If all his journeys held moments as secure and secluded as this, Arthur thought, then the mission he had allowed himself to be given would have been a rewarding one indeed. The Overlord, his consort and his scribe settled around a fire, ate as soon as the food was brought, and slept in their cloaks while the clear night erupted in stars.

* * *

All the following day was spent high in the hills, with only one sharp descent into a dale, where the remains of old camps told of makeshift billets on winter nights when there had not been enough daylight to make Olicana. But Arthur's force had four hours of evening sun left, and so pushed on with only a brief rest for water. Olicana was a poor place, despite its position as the first crossroads east of the mountains. Once there had been thriving traffic passing from Ebvracum to the river port of Bremetennacum, close to the western sea. Now, though, Hibernian raids had all but killed off the trade, and with it Olicana's livelihood. But fast riders had been dispatched before they had set out from Mamucium to warn of the troops' arrival and prepare what shelter and victuals there were to be had.

Once he had arrived, two hours before dark, Arthur made sure everything was properly paid for. The people he found, like many outside the large towns, had given up the habit of using coins. Riding with thought for speed, not trade, Arthur carried little with him with which to barter. Instead he ordered Modlen to inscribe a sanction under his authority that could be exchanged for a generous supply of goods in Ebvracum. Word of his generosity, he knew, would travel faster along the outlying roads of Brigantia than any other news.

Most of his men camped on the outskirts of the town. Arthur, the two women and his personal guard of four men, however, found more comfortable lodging in the only building large enough to be a hall. He inspected his quarters, nodded his approval and left with two of his men to bid goodnight to his troops, leaving the other two guards to mind Gwenan and Modlen – less for their protection than to report to him if there were any signs of unpleasantness on Gwenan's part to her tongueless companion.

As he walked the two hundred or so paces along the town's main street he greeted the lines of curious locals for whom his night with them was a once-in-a-lifetime chance to see the greatest man in the land, a figure of mystery as much as power. He stopped to talk to a woman carrying a baby, the father grinning proudly beside her. He was just wondering how to stop her going into the more extreme details of the child's birth when one of his guards touched him on the shoulder.

'What is it, Evan?' he asked.

'Not sure, sir, but I don't like it,' he said, and nodded up the street. The crowd was beginning to spill across the road, closing off the way out to the camp. In their midst a detachment of Brigantian men at arms mingled, men Arthur did not recognise from the troop that had ridden with him from Mamucium.

Evan the guard nodded back from where they had come. The more familiar men seemed to be filling the street in the same fashion. Arthur frowned. Was this a threat or just a curious crowd? Either way he had let himself become vulnerable. Lulled by the success of his mission to the Catuvellauni and the Cornovians, he had temporally forgotten that the Overlord was always in hostile territory.

'Thank you, Evan. I want you both to leave me and return to the women.'

'But sir…'

'Do as I say. You can't protect me here against these numbers. I'm safer on my own. If there is harm to be done, they will want to be able to tell the story that I provoked a fight, not that I was cut down while listening to the people of Brigantia. But Gwenan may not be so fortunate.'

Evan bowed slightly. 'If that is your wish.'

'It is. Walk away slowly, as though you suspect nothing.'

Arthur smiled back at the woman with the baby as the two guards left him and patted the child's head. He moved along the line until he was level with a boy of about nine and squatted down on his heels, sword scabbard touching the ground, to talk to him.

'Do you know who I am?' he asked.

'Yes,' answered the boy, looking a little nervous, 'you're the king.'

'No, I'm not that important. Your king is Vortebelos. I'm Arthur. I work for all the kings.'

'Oh. My dad said you were like an emperor in the old days.'

Arthur smiled. 'Sometimes I wish I was, lad. Now, would you like to come and see my soldiers? You can show me the people you know as we go.'

The boy nodded. Arthur stood and took his hand. Together they turned and continued to walk slowly along the street, the boy pointing out smiling faces as they went. Ahead of them the way was blocked by troops, but the crowd of townspeople showed no disquiet, assuming they were part of Arthur's escort.

The Overlord ambled towards them, small boy in hand, as the Brigantian men adjusted their spears and planted their legs apart belligerently. Arthur carried on talking quietly as he came close.

'And these are your king's men,' he said. 'Why don't you ask them what they want?'

The boy shook his head and nestled up to Arthur.

'Quite right. I expect they'll tell me when they're ready.' He raised his voice so that all in the crowd could hear. 'What I would like them to do is to ride off to Isurium in the morning and tell King Vortebelos that Arthur son of Pendraeg, Overlord of Britannia Prima, Seconda and Caesariensis, by vote of the Council of Kings called Tygern Fawr, requires the wisdom of his counsel. We shall rest here a day and a night more before resuming our safe passage to his hall. We thank him for the generosity he has shown in sending so many of his trusted men to escort us, but that those who have ably brought us so far from Mamucium will suffice.'

Arthur looked up at the leader of the obstructing men and smiled. Then he looked around him at the townspeople. 'Do you think he heard?'

Laughter rippled through the crowd, and the troops shifted uneasily. They had lost the initiative, and now they looked merely foolish against one man who had proclaimed his authority and yet stood holding the hand of a small boy from their own clan.

'I think so,' whispered the boy.

'So do I,' said Arthur. 'Now, you will come and inspect my men with me, as every good general does at nightfall. Do you know why?' Arthur stepped forward, confident that the press of men would stand aside and let him pass. There was a rustle of arms which Arthur ignored, looking firmly at the boy, and the way cleared.

'No.'

'Because if a general cannot take the trouble to check on the well-being of his men, they will not take the trouble to fight properly for him. When you are a general, remember it and you will win.' Around him the Brigantians looked shamefaced as a murmur of approval ran through the onlookers. They stood aside. Arthur walked on as if there had never been a pause.

'Will I be a general?' the boy asked.

Once through the throng Arthur stopped and looked down at the boy.

'What's your name?'

'Meurig, sir.'

'Then, Meurig,' he said, reaching into the purse at his belt and pulling out a coin. It carried the head of the Emperor Gratian, he noted with a snort. It was not a heritage he wanted any great connection with. 'In ten years' time, come and meet me again. If I am still Tygern Fawr and you are ready, give this back to me and remind me about being a general.'

They strode on to the camp, Meurig clutching the coin with delight.

There was no more trouble that night, but as a precaution Arthur returned to his hall with a retinue of twenty men as guards. He found the band of Vortebelos's men had not waited for the morning, but had ridden off as soon as the incident was over. Arthur sensed that his arrival in Isurium three days later would give the King a problem: whether to greet him with all due pomp or make it clear that there was nothing he wished to confer with Arthur about.

The guards were told to be suspicious and watchful, but not to do anything to alienate the ordinary people of Olicana. There was no need to give Vortebelos any excuse for propaganda if he was looking for one.

In the mean time Arthur spent a day with Modlen writing dispatches. Riders were sent to Cunorix and Cunegnus reaffirming their treaties, to Myrddin, calling on him to meet Arthur as soon as possible in Ebvracum, and to the leaders of the Cantiaci, Atrebates, Trinovantes and Votadini, asking for early intelligence of Barbarian movements. All answers were to be sent to Ebvracum within three weeks. Arthur did not want to spend too much time in the north. Although Ebvracum was under his authority, not that of the Brigantian King or the Parisi, it was nonetheless an island in their territory, and Arthur knew his relations with both would not be best served if he was seen to be mustering his own strength independently.

XVII

OVERNIGHT THE CLOUDS had gathered and the rain scurried along the drains. Arthur stood at the door of his temporary house an hour after dawn and watched the water dispiritedly. If all the men started wet they would be tired and fractious by evening, and there was no hospitable township between Olicana and Isurium. They would have to camp in the hills: a pleasant enough prospect on a fine night, but less enticing with sodden clothes and fires of damp wood. The sky had the unbroken accent of determination, and there was precious little wind to blow the weather along. Arthur sighed and gave the orders to pack up and go. The men went about their business without enthusiasm. Modlen and Gwenan regarded him with more than usual morning sullenness. What, after all, was the hurry? Britannia could wait another morning for Tygern Fawr to carry out his grand diplomatic plan. Arthur wished his instinct told him things were that simple. It didn't.

An hour later, warmed as much as they were able by the generous breakfast supplied by Olicana's townswomen, the troop was assembled and on its way north-east again. For a time they followed the valley with its unrelenting rain. By mid morning, though, they were climbing into the cloud base as it sat a hundred feet below the summit of the moors. Arthur and his immediate retinue travelled in the middle of the thin column of men, but within minutes they might have been alone, as the van and rearguard were swallowed by the mist. Time became immeasurable without the sun. They seemed to be riding in a world without dimensions, bounded by the road itself and the back half of the horse in front. Only the sound of hooves on the stones of the old road told them they had companions, and even this was muffled by the mud to a rustle hardly distinguishable from the rain itself. Two days of this, thought Arthur, and Vortebelos will be able to present us as a vagabond rabble, not the Overlord in full pomp. He reached out to Gwenan, and felt her shiver in response. Turning his head to see Modlen, he saw her shrouded, her face spectrally beautiful in the uncertain light.

The weather was teasing him. Just when they had become so disorientated that Arthur was convinced they must have left the earth altogether, the road dipped just beneath the cloud line – or the watery blanket lifted a few feet; it was impossible to say which. Either way, they found themselves in clear air again, and the rain had stopped. A light breeze played about the horses' ears and blew shards of mist from the grey sheets above them.

The road fell away into a steep valley. There was a calculation to be made – whether to stop early and make camp in the woods or push on, relying on the cloud rising and the long evening to let them cross the moors. If they stayed in that valley they would have a full day's ride to Isurium in the morning. If they rode on the risk was that they would be caught in the open for the night. They dismounted by the river, its speed refreshed by the overnight rain, and filled themselves and the horses with its clear limestone waters. Above them the pale disc of the sun began to peer through the veil of grey. That was enough for Arthur. They would ride on. He was certain they could reach the end of the moors and the gentler forests beyond. They would be in Isurium within three hours in the morning, fresh enough to deal with anything Vortebelos had prepared for them.

The men from Arthur's troop and the Brigantian escort remounted, forded the river a little further downstream and picked up the road through the woods on the other side. Gwenan, as at home on a horse as any of them, sped on ahead of Arthur as he guided the less certain Modlen over the rocks and through the fast-running water. Soon there was a long gap between the first men over, with Gwenan at the back, and Arthur, Modlen and the rest. For a moment the trees hid them as Arthur and Modlen reached dry ground and found the hard surface of the road again. Just ahead there was a rustle in the undergrowth, and a deer bounded across the lane in front of them and stopped, looking back at the party crossing the river before darting into the bushes. Arthur glanced up, but Modlen grabbed his arm and pointed urgently. Arthur followed her finger, wondering why she should be so

CHAPTER XVII

interested in a deer. The woods were full of them. But he obeyed and gave the creature a second glance. It was a doe, quite young, but not in its first year. It seemed fit and healthy, but Modlen did not lower her arm when Arthur saw the creature. She continued to point until he too noticed the broken shaft of an arrow buried deep into its back, just behind the shoulder. A few inches either way and the deer would have been dead or crippled. As it was, the arrow was borne without concern, its pain now the dull ache of an old wound. Arthur squeezed Modlen's hand and smiled as the doe ran off in front of them. He smiled, but Modlen, he found, had eyes full of tears: another young creature carrying her man-inflicted wound with fortitude. Arthur nodded his understanding, then spurred his horse up the slope from the valley so that they could catch Gwenan and the vanguard before they emerged from the woods on to the open moor.

By late afternoon the sun had won the battle with the clouds – or they had passed beyond the reach of the rain – and the warmth raised steam from clothes and horses alike. Arthur gazed across the open country with the green ribbon of the road stretching straight before him, and for a moment allowed himself to think how splendid this land was and how absurd it was that he should have to keep the peace among the men (and as often the women) who lived on it.

* * *

The gates of Isurium were closed. The standard of Vortebelos was missing from its place on top of the watchtower. It was just before midday on the second morning after Arthur had ridden out from Olicana. The western road had joined the great north road a matter of minutes from the Brigantian stronghold which straddled the highway, controlling all traffic between Ebvracum and Hadrian's Wall. Arthur rode for the gates, expecting them to be thrown open at the appearance of his Brigantian escort. There was no such movement. Instead the captain of the escort rode up beside him and asked courteously but firmly for Arthur to wait short of the town while he went on ahead to (as he put it, with dubious diplomacy), 'ascertain what arrangements had been made for the reception of Tygern Fawr on his rare and illustrious visit.' Arthur fumed quietly, but had little choice but to agree. He could hardly storm Isurium with thirty men at arms and two girls.

He bowed his assent, called for his men to form up around him and requested the Brigantians to dismount between his troop and the gates. His trust in Vortebelos's hospitality was wearing thin even before they had arrived.

The Captain rode off towards the gates. For a time they remained resolutely shut, even for him. His horse stamped and strutted impatiently until eventually bolts were drawn and the right-hand gate swung open just wide enough for a man to pass. A solitary figure slipped out and beckoned the Captain over. They conferred. The message delivered, the Brigantian sentry returned inside the town, the gates were closed and bolted once again and the Captain trotted back to Arthur.

'Well?'

The Captain did his best to look apologetic. 'There will be a slight delay, I'm afraid, sir.'

'What do you mean, "a slight delay"?' Arthur demanded.

'It appears we have arrived earlier than had been expected. King Vortebelos is still out hunting. He had been scheduled to return by now, but it is not unusual for him to lose track of time on a fine morning such as this.'

'So what?' Arthur enquired irritably. 'Surely he left orders for me to be received? He had enough warning that I was on my way.'

The Captain shuffled uncomfortably in his saddle. 'He did indeed, sir.'

'And?' Arthur was losing his taste for the Captain's pointed politeness.

'King Vortebelos left specific orders that he must be with you when you enter Isurium. He feels strongly that it would not be right for his people to see the Overlord enter the capital of Brigantia without ceremony and without him at your side.'

'How very considerate.'

'Yes, sir.'

'Don't be facetious, young man, or I'll have you transferred to my staff in a position you will cease to enjoy.'

The Captain had the sense to keep quiet.

'And in the mean time I am to be barred from entry? I, my men, the horses, my companions,' he waved towards Gwenan and Modlen, 'are to sit around outside the gates in the hope that Vortebelos has had enough of hunting to return in time for us to eat before nightfall?'

'Those are my orders, sir.'

CHAPTER XVII

'Well, your orders are not good enough. Brigantia must learn manners, and Vortebelos must learn to put affairs of state before sport. You will have the gates opened, and I will enter, whether your king is ready or not.'

'Those are not my orders, sir.'

'I am the Overlord of all Britannia. You will take orders from me, even if they countermand those of Vortebelos.'

The Captain did not answer. But he did not move to open Isurium, either.

Eventually he suggested, 'Perhaps Tygern Fawr would like to dismount and rest? I am sure the King will not be more than a few minutes more, and then you will see how he honours you.'

'We already have the answer to that,' replied Arthur. He glanced up at the sun, calculating the hours before dark. There were nine, at least. 'We will not dismount. Neither will we wait for Vortebelos. We have better ways to spend to the day.'

The Captain looked concerned for the first time. 'I'm sure—' he began.

'Enough.' Arthur held up his hand to stop him. He raised his voice so that all the company could hear. 'I have no further need of you or your insolent compatriots. You will remain here, following your orders. You can tell Vortebelos when he eventually turns up that Arthur does not wait for kings. He will find me in Ebvracum. I shall expect him the day after tomorrow. His hospitality will be returned.'

'Sir, you are early. If he had known I'm sure he would be here now.'

'Then it is your fault for not sending one of your men ahead of us to give him the message. If the King is as eager to see me as you suggest, then I think you may be in for an unpleasant interview. But somehow I think your rank will be safe. You have done exactly as you were told.'

Arthur was not interested in anything the Captain might have to say in reply. He turned to his men.

'We will sleep tonight in Ebvracum, where our welcome is sure and our feasting finer than in the revolting hovels of the Brigantians.' Without waiting for a reaction he wheeled his horse and headed south at a gallop, leaving his men to follow as fast as they could. He knew the Brigantian garrison would be watching. He was not about to be seen cowering in the shadow of their defences and hoping for favours from Vortebelos.

Behind Arthur his men galloped in his wake, with Modlen and Gwenan showing that they were no strangers to horses at speed. The Captain of the Brigantian group thought about riding after them, even taking the women hostage to persuade Arthur to return, but by the time he had thought of it they were nearly out of sight.

The road from Isurium to Ebvracum was one of the best maintained in Britannia: flat, straight and much used. As they rode they passed wagons and carts, solitary riders and groups of travellers, merchants and itinerant hawkers, all plying their trade between the Brigantian capital and Ebvracum, the city that had never lost its imperial pretensions, its citizens never allowing visitors to forget that Constantine the Great had been proclaimed Emperor in its forum. The road was broad enough for a legion at full strength, with all its paraphernalia of transports and equipment, its battle machines and supplies. In his time as overlord Arthur had negotiated hard with the various kingdoms to make sure the great roads stayed open and mended. He argued that it was necessary when an army needed to move fast to deal with Barbarian raids. But he also knew that the trade in people and goods along the great highways was just as important, giving Britannians a fragile sense of unity and preventing the kingdoms becoming isolated. For it was isolation that led to petty ambition and the misunderstandings that brought war.

Once clear of the walls of Isurium and into more wooded country Arthur slowed his horse to a gentle canter, allowing the others to catch up and regroup around him. He was still angry, but his fury abated with his speed, and he began to assess the effect of the deliberate insult by the Brigantian King. Either Arthur could demand an immediate reassertion of fealty, or he could accept the excuses at face value and, having aired his displeasure, swallow his pride. The danger of this would be that Vortebelos would have shown that Arthur would go to any lengths to maintain the fiction of being the public servant of the Council, and that therefore any king powerful enough could treat him with disdain whenever it suited. The disadvantage of trying to humiliate Vortebelos in turn was that it could wreck any chance of achieving his inner Council, the Table, and risk having to mobilise an army not against the Barbarians but against the Brigantians, to bring them into line. Arthur wanted to avoid that, but did he want to do so at all costs?

At the speed he was riding, they would reach Ebvracum in little more than two hours. The sooner the better, Arthur decided. He had had enough of the open road. He hoped Gwain had arrived early enough to prepare the city. Since Arthur was expected to stay negotiating with Vortebelos for two days at least, there was a chance, a strong one, that his arrival would cause complete panic among his domestic household. The prospect was enough to put him back in a better temper. He slowed for a moment and grinned at Gwenan.

'You'll be safe in my bed again tonight. No more riding for a day or two.'

'Just as well,' she retorted, 'or my thighs will be so strong I'll crush you.'

'Tough talk.'

'You'll see,' said Gwenan, spurring her horse on to shoot past him.

'I will indeed,' he said, accelerating after her, making the mistake of catching Modlen's venomous glance as he did so.

When he judged they were more than halfway – an easy enough judgement, since they had just passed the junction with the road that led due south to Calcaria – Arthur called a halt to rest and water the horses. He settled himself down on the grass by the riverbank and called one of the men over.

'We will delay here for a while. When your horse is ready ride on as fast as you can and alert Ebvracum of my arrival. Find Gwain if you can. If not, my steward will need to know in any case. We should not take the city by surprise.'

Arthur lay back as his orders were carried out. Beside him Gwenan lay face down on the turf. Modlen leant against a tree at the water's edge, moodily snapping twigs and watching them float downstream. The Overlord only needed Modlen, the perfect secretary. Arthur needed them both. He sighed and absently stroked Gwenan's arm as he watched Modlen. They were both so young, so dependent on him, yet both wanted to be the only ones to be allowed with him all the time. They were frightened and jealous. And they were right to be. He could afford to gather lovers and servants from anywhere in the world. If he withdrew his protection from them they would at best sink back into serfdom, at worst be made to suffer more because of their former intimacy with him. Once in Ebvracum, he thought, there will have to be some way to reassure them.

He hoped his message had reached Myrddin. Although it was barely a month since they had met in the south, there was a lot of discussion to be had. He doubted whether the old man would have much time to listen to the dilemmas of his love life (which even Arthur admitted was becoming less than sensible), but he needed Myrddin's counsel on how to deal with the Brigantes if Vortebelos insisted on going his own obstreperous way.

Other travellers were fording the river in the opposite direction, and they gazed curiously at Arthur's entourage. He rode without displayed emblem or livery, so there was no way of saying whether his was a band of robbers or a troop on the way from Isurium. Life would have been easier if there had been.

* * *

Ebvracum was a far cry from the imperial city, with its bustling river port and flurry of legionary confidence, that Constantine I had known when he had marched out of the city gates to transform the Roman world two hundred years before. For half the intervening time Ebvracum had lived sumptuously and, it must be said, rather pompously on the glory of that moment, strutting its municipal state among the mere civitates – the Britannian royal capitals – as an imperial peculiarity. At one moment of intense self-importance its senate (the city still retained the name, even if with a Britannian accent and as a paltry example of the constitutional genre) had petitioned Constantine III to change its name to Constantium. Constantinople may have been the great city where his illustrious namesake had ended up, but Ebvracum had been where the legend had begun. The petition failed, largely because Constantine III was yet another imperial casualty by the time it arrived. But by then nature as much as political chaos had made the over-ambitious claim inept.

The warm weather that for decades had allowed the retired members of the garrison to plant vines and produce exportable wine had also caused the sea to rise and the rivers to flood with dispiriting regularity. This was not like the annual flooding of the Egyptian plain by the Nile, bringing fertility and plenty to the desert. This was a destructive surge every equinox, damaging the bridge, making the port unusable and soaking half the proud town houses to their knees. The mosaics of Ebvracum's floors were ruined by mud; the gardens were washed

CHAPTER XVII

away. Soon only the old fort itself, its official buildings and a few of the houses lucky (or originally vain enough) to have been given steps up to the public rooms were spared the watery squalor. Even in them, the cellars and hypocausts had become the homes of water rats and sticklebacks. With the receding waters had come disease and fear and too many people had left the city to make it more than a local joke in the days of Pendraeg.

History and residual constitutional status, however, had meant that Ebvracum was still useful, if not glorious. Arthur had worked hard over the last decade to repair the ravages of flood and dereliction. Wooden piles had been driven into the riverbed to provide new jetties, and drainage channels had been dug along the sides of the old streets. The worst damaged of the old houses, however grand in their heyday, had been dismantled, the dressed stone used to shore up the defences or patch up the buildings worth restoring. In the fort Arthur had given Myrddin a free hand in making the old governor's residence fit for the Overlord, a task he had relished, giving the rooms and the cloister-like courtyard the air of successful modern Brittanian kingship while gently drawing attention to the richness of Roman heritage that lingered in the frescoes and floors, the pediments and fountains.

Arthur moved the citizens away from the river into the further half of the old fort, using a few old buildings where they were serviceable, but mainly leaning modern wooden houses and shops against the solid brick walls.

He had no intention of making Ebvracum a fortress again – that would have alarmed the Parisi and Brigantes and sent a mixed message of insecurity and ambition to the other kingdoms. However, he wanted a measure of security he could rely on in a crisis, and so there were always sufficient men garrisoning the town, and quartered between the town houses and the port, to be able to guarantee the flow of supplies from the river. For his official duties he used the old basilica, a cold but monumental edifice with its network of offices and scriptoria largely intact from a century before.

All this Myrddin had overseen, through the years, with efficiency and just a hint of the town planner's pride, until he had been able to amble through the streets with his protégé and mutter that Ebvracum would never now be Constantinople, but it looked nearly as civilised as Moridunum – a remark fuelled not only by the fanciful pride of a

Demetian but by the comfortable knowledge that his own capital city sat so far above its river that only a flood of biblical proportions was ever likely to give more than a moment of damp irritation.

Myrddin had not yet arrived to Arthur's summons by the time Tygern Fawr, his entourage and their exhausted mounts rode in through the west gate of the old fortress from Isurium. The city was prepared for his arrival, though. The diminished population had been swelled by those from the surrounding country bringing their summer produce to the weekly market. While the women set up stalls or squatted by baskets around the square outside the old basilica, groups of wagons stood by just outside the walls to load stooks of fresh hay. Some still sold for coin in the market, especially those offering rough wine or mead by the cup, but most bartered with stores of new pots and jewellery, tools, nails, horseshoes and baskets, cloth and shoes. Either way, trade had been brisk, and Arthur rode in to cheers and caps waving, his toast drunk with whatever concoction was nearest to hand as he rode by. This was his city.

Still muddy and dishevelled from his journey across the moors, Arthur led his escort along the crowded street from the west gate to his palace. It was not a grand affair, and certainly would have made the Emperor Zeno in Constantinople roar with laughter at the presumption of Arthur's predecessors in comparing the Ebvracum palace with his. Nonetheless, it was a fine building towards the eastern wall, a short walk from the basilica, with its offices and administrators. Myrddin had had the fountain in its garden restored and its third-century mosaics and frescoes cleaned. Even he had failed to get the under-floor heating back to its former efficiency, but fireplaces and chimneys had been added where possible, and though it left some of the smaller rooms cold in winter, in the summer it was a palace indeed compared to the draughty timber halls of most of Britannia's kings.

Arthur dismounted and allowed his horse to be led down the street at the side of the palace to the stables. He ushered Gwenan and Modlen into the columned entrance, and grinned as he watched their amazement at the colours of the paintings, the glitter of the floors and elegance of the furniture. There were perhaps only two or three houses in Britannia where such antique finery was still in use, and neither girl would have seen anything like it before.

Arthur accepted the offer of a bowl of water and towel as greeting from his steward, dismissed his officers and issued orders for Modlen to be given new clothes and comfortable quarters overlooking the garden, waiting until she had been led away before explaining to the steward that while she could not speak, she could certainly hear and write, and any insolence on the part of the palace staff would be reported back to him personally in writing. Gwenan feigned disinterest, inspecting the head of Minerva (with a few additional Christian symbols around it) that dominated the centre of the floor. Arthur walked over and put an arm round her shoulders.

'And now I'll show you where we will sleep for the next few weeks,' he said. 'Come on, I'm sick of these clothes.'

* * *

Arthur waited. He waited for a response from Vortebelos. He waited for Myrddin to arrive. He waited for news of Barbarian raids or the flare-ups of border disputes or Caledonian incursions. None came. Britannia seemed to have stopped for the summer. Vortebelos ignored the instruction to appear at Ebvracum within two days, and Arthur was disinclined to fetch him.

He waited, but he was not idle, as clearly most of the city and its garrison had been for the three months since Arthur had last lodged there. Instructions had been left for roads to be mended, walls rebuilt, roofs repaired, drains covered over. Instead the rubble seemed to be lying in much the same places as before, by now enlivened with another year's crop of wild flowers. Arthur called for an explanation and received excuses from the bucolic Coritanian who had been left in charge – in theory a man with contacts among craftsmen and labourers and a knowledge of building that went beyond cutting down a few trees and knocking up a bit of lime wash. The reality, Arthur suspected, was more a tale of favours to indolent cronies and generous back-handers from suppliers. He was summarily dismissed and banished from Ebvracum, with the added instruction that if he was found within ten miles of the Overlord, wherever in the country that was, his ears would be cut off and his daughters taken as slaves. Gwain was dispatched to recruit a replacement with rather more energy and enthusiasm for the job.

In the mean time Arthur used his own troops to find workmen and oversee the moving and mending. Arthur had neither the resources nor the time to embark on any ambitious building of his own. But he was determined that Ebvracum, his only base outside the control of one or other of the kings, was not going to be inferior to any of their capitals. Given the ravages of the river's flooding and a hundred years of despairing neglect, even his programme of repairing the public buildings, the defences and creating a new riverfront by demolishing the inundated structures of the old Roman city was a major undertaking. The fortress itself on the north bank was not such a problem, because it was naturally higher than the city on the south bank. But there the river rested halfway across the old temple precincts when the tides were high and, when the rains were persistent at the same time, the water would lap across the original forum itself.

One excuse of the banished Coritanian foreman turned out to be true. There was a lack of workmen still living close enough to the city. Too much had been abandoned after the plague of twenty years before and the endless flooding for town life to hold many attractions, especially without anything to see in the old amphitheatre, and with most of the taverns closed. There were not the passing players or musicians who used to wander the empire, nor the supplies of oil and wine that used to come upriver. Ebvracum was a dull hole until Arthur appeared, and then the combination of his court and retainers attracted girls, hawkers and general opportunists to bring the place to life again, but he was not there enough to keep the buzz going all year round. Many people moved away – either to Isurium or out into the countryside, where there was a good chance of farming a few acres and building a more manageable house than from the damp stone remnants of an earlier and more prosperous age.

Ironically the answer to Ebvracum's plight came from the Barbarians. There were some who had settled nearby as long before as the chaos at the end of Vortigern's time, when he had needed allies and cared not from where they came. Over the years they themselves had found their farmsteads raided by successor bands, and had moved into the more defensible areas of abandoned Ebvracum. There had been little tension, though equally little conversation at first, but the dwindling citizenry had been pleased enough to have new neighbours of any kind. After all, most of the so-called legionaries had been Barbarian mercenaries in all but name. After fifty years the children and grandchildren of Vortigern's allies still spoke the languages of the sea's far-eastern shore, but they were as angered by shiploads of vicious incomers as any Britannian. Arthur found men glad of the work, anxious to prove that they belonged in Britannia, and happy to see some walls going up that would stop more than a passing cow.

Within two days of firing the Coritanian, Gwain had hired a Parisian stone mason just arrived from Petuaria, where he had been involved in much the same work — until it had all stopped in the spring in a panic over Barbarian raids up the estuary. Gwain liked the look of him (thoughtful but bloody-minded), and so did Arthur as he toured the bastions and walls and was given a stern lecture on the inadequacy of modern jointing and dressing, and complaints that you couldn't get anybody these days who knew how to fashion a column so that it looked like a column, not a sodding ('Sorry, my lord!') hexagon.

On the second day in the city the weather had forgotten its unseasonable cloud and turned blazingly hot. In the basilica's offices the scribes and tax men sweated in their woollen tunics and cursed their wives for not finding flax. In the garden of the palace the fountain flowed and peaches ripened. Gwenan marvelled at the musk of tansy and the evening rush of rosemary and the flowering lavender laid out in formal beds. She drifted, clean and dressed in white, with a golden brooch at her shoulder, along the paths and among the benches. No longer was she the prisoner, the plaything of kings to be passed on to the next visiting soldier in the next stinking hut. At last she dressed and felt like a Roman empress, the consort of the man who ordered those same kings. Here for the first time she tasted power.

When she had been called to Arthur's bed for the first time three months before, it had been as an apprehensive slave. As they had lain and loved in the little camp in the south she had felt content as a woman in a way that nothing had ever prepared her for, without fear or degradation. Then the journey north had brought all the terror back, though she had hidden it as best she could — the separation from Arthur, the appearance of Modlen, the danger at Olicana. Now, though, she felt safe and luxuriated in Arthur's attention, relished the sudden jealous silences as she passed other women, basked in the flattery of the men eager to gain favour with the Overlord. She bound her hair in elaborate plaits with purple thread. She would give him children and rule Ebvracum when he has away at war.

In the mornings Arthur would rise two hours after the sun, visit his troops and workmen, breakfast, then spend time with Modlen, dealing with dispatches and messengers. She had been allocated what had once been the deputy commander's office in the basilica complex, and she was inordinately proud of it, barely allowing Arthur to move so much as a scroll to sit down. She liked things right, she scribbled in a note to him, and one way and another she would rather attend him in his chambers rather than have him cluttering up hers. Arthur shrugged good-humouredly and removed himself to the far end of the main building, where he could receive Gwain, his officers and the usual queue of petitioners.

In the afternoons Arthur took to returning to Gwenan's bed while the heat made everybody indolent. Then he would wash, call for his horse and show himself around the town on the other side of the river. Sometimes he would call half a dozen of his men and ride out for a few miles along the old roads, winding through slim fields of ripening oats and barley to the farmsteads and hamlets dotting the rich land of the plain. It was harmless exercise, but it was also a way of assessing the mood of the people who were his only natural subjects. He needed them to owe their first loyalty to him, not to the kings of Brigantia and Parisia.

Arthur and his household had been in Ebvracum for nearly two weeks by the time Myrddin turned up. He was not in the best of tempers. The midsummer months were his time for study and relaxation in Moridunum, for the frescoes to be painted and the mosaics laid, the aqueduct repaired and his lover to be indulged. He did not appreciate being hauled across six kingdoms at Arthur's command with barely a day to order his estate and prepare for the journey. He strode into the basilica just as Arthur was about to leave it for the day.

Myrddin was not in the mood for affectionate greetings. 'Is this going to take long? Because if it is I'll have to send Bedr straight back to take charge at home.'

'Welcome, old friend,' said Arthur. 'It's good to see you here.'

'No it's not, it's a bloody nuisance. Are we at war, or am I here to untangle your love life again?'

Myrddin caught the glare aimed at him by Modlen as she collected the morning's parchments to carry back to her office.

'Who are you? You're new. One of Arthur's little problems?'

Modlen looked desperately across to Arthur, who seemed to be scrutinising a column at the far end of the building.

CHAPTER XVII

'Well?' barked Myrddin. 'Speak up, girl. Haven't you got a tongue in head? I asked you a question.'

Arthur leapt to his feet and came within an inch of the astonished Myrddin's face.

'Actually, old man, no, she hasn't.' He beckoned Modlen over to him and put an arm round her shoulder. Her eyes shone with tears of anger. 'And you can thank your friend Cunorix for that. It's his idea of how to keep his servants quiet.'

Myrddin stared at her, then dropped his head. 'He's no friend of mine. I'm sorry. My words could hardly have been worse chosen.'

'No, they couldn't have been, you're right,' Arthur said, looking down tenderly at Modlen and smiling. 'This is Modlen. She wrote the letter that summoned you here. So you see, Cunorix lost a tongueless servant and I have gained more than a secretary. I have done more business in the last three weeks with her than in all of last year.'

Myrddin made no attempt to hide his embarrassment. 'I was not pleased to read the contents, but the hand was fine – the script of a scholar. Your teacher must have been proud of you. The Overlord was lucky to find you. Please accept my apology.'

Modlen inclined her head in acknowledgement of the compliment, but her eyes still blazed.

'That's better,' said Arthur. 'Let's start again, shall we? Modlen, this is Myrddin. He is not always so rude, though it's getting worse with age. The country would not be what it is today without him. One day you and I will go back to his palace at Moridunum, and you can rummage through his library to your heart's content. He served my father Pendraeg and half of Armorica. They say he and Bishop Padrig in Hibernia were boys together among the Demetiae.' He asked innocently, 'do you ever hear from the good Padrig, these days, Myrddin? I've often meant to ask.'

Myrddin was beginning to regain his composure, but knew that for once Arthur was expecting him to show proper recognition of who held the real authority.

'Not for many years, Tygern Fawr. As you are aware, we do not see the world exactly the same way.'

'No indeed,' he turned to Modlen with a grin. 'Myrddin is not one of our churchmen. He takes a broader view of such matters – wouldn't that be right?'

'Very well put, my lord.'

Arthur continued to Modlen, 'Which reminds me. Is our bishop here today? Myrddin and I will need him tonight.'

She gestured that she would find out and walked away towards her office.

Myrddin still looked ashamed. 'I had no idea…'

'Of course you didn't. And I hadn't explained. But she is invaluable, Myrddin. She's barely a woman, but she knows Latin almost as well as you, and she is even able to use Roman letters to interpret Brythonic – a useful gift in our ill-educated times. I have records of my conversations with Cunorix and Cunegnus. She can listen quietly so that they forget she's there, and then writes it all out for me afterwards. If we manage to get this Council together this summer she will be my secret weapon.'

'And that's why you made me come here – to meet this secret weapon?'

'No, but it helps. I have a problem with Brigantia, Myrddin, and I now know it to be even bigger than when I sent for you. I think I'll need some of your diplomacy. And you need to know the results of my discussions so far.'

Myrddin sighed. 'I can see I won't be going home for a while.'

'Quite the contrary. A week – two at most. If it hasn't been solved by then we'll need to move on. Come on back to the palace. Gwenan will be pleased to see you.'

Myrddin snorted. 'I doubt it. You know I don't approve, and she knows it even better than you.'

Arthur led him out into the sunlight. 'You will. In time you will.'

XVIII

By the second day after Myrddin's arrival in Ebvracum, there had still been no message from Vortebelos, let alone his appearance with an explanation and apology. Despite the natural indolence of summer which might reasonably have excused procrastination by the Brigantian King for a few days, the delay was becoming a serious challenge to Arthur's authority. Even the patient Myrddin was prepared to admit that some sort of action would have

CHAPTER XVIII

to be taken. Sending a full-scale embassy demanding Vortebelos's compliance was likely to be met with defiant refusal. Nonetheless, the insolent silence couldn't be ignored, either. Arthur was in no position to force Vortebelos to come grovelling to him at once. On the other hand, he couldn't tolerate being treated as if he didn't exist. Myrddin decided that diplomacy must have its day, if possible. A messenger was dispatched to Isurium with an invitation to consult Myrddin, rather than Arthur, in Ebvracum on recent Barbarian movements in the Hibernian Sea. The old man's tiredness after the journey from Moridunum was offered as the excuse for not travelling to Isurium himself. It was a courteous message that provided Vortebelos a civilised opportunity if he wanted to take it.

The messenger returned in the early evening with a relatively polite but definite refusal. Vortebelos was not prepared to enter Ebvracum, even for the undeniable pleasure of seeing Myrddin again, since Arthur had not been prepared to wait even a few minutes so that he could be entertained appropriately in Isurium.

If that had been the end of the Brigantian message, Arthur would have had little option but to mount an armed expedition or meekly accept the snub. In fact, Vortebelos was prepared to suggest a compromise. Arthur and Myrddin were invited to meet him for a special consultation at the bridge across the river halfway between the two cities, when, as the messenger recounted, 'grave matters of state for the future protection of the Brigantian peoples could be discussed with benefit by the King, the Overlord and his most illustrious counsellor.'

'Pompous ass!' was Arthur's immediate reaction.

Myrddin smiled. 'Almost certainly. But it's a neat and peaceful solution.'

'So we just agree?'

'Yes, but we set the meeting for a week from now, and we arrive for the meeting with a full complement of men – a hundred and fifty, at least. And we send an advance team to prepare the site. You're not meeting Vortebelos round a campfire.'

'What do you have in mind?'

'Oh, I think a display of old imperial ceremony, don't you? Scarlet tents, trumpeters, a public dais with bunting.'

'One of your shows, in other words. Are you thinking of some of your fire tricks?'

Myrddin grinned. 'Perhaps not this time – unless it goes so well it drags into the evening.'

'A flock of rare geese as omens? A vision of a thousand virgins in chariots across the sky?'

'Don't mock what is divine, Arthur.'

'I'm sure they'd be divine. I'm just anxious about being upstaged by overenthusiastic magicians.'

'Very well, then, have it your way. We'll make it a dull little conference on the riverbank.'

'Good,' said Arthur, 'but you can have as many tents and pennants as you like. And after that you can go back to Moridunum. I'll need to be on the move again too if I'm to secure the first meeting of the Council for the autumn.'

'Very well. That allows you plenty more time to drift around the garden with your young lady. I'd appreciate some of your valuable attention for world affairs, though.'

'You can have as much of me as you want. I have all summer to "drift", as you put it, with Gwenan.'

'That's what worries me. You may have, but Britannia needs more urgency.'

'I know that. I'll not be neglectful.'

There they left the argument to rumble.

* * *

If Myrddin was master of the weather then there was no evidence of it on the morning Arthur rode out of Ebvracum a week later. Fog lay across the plain and an unseasonable chill came with it. Myrddin's calm assurance that 'it'll burn off by the time we get there' was greeted with morose and sceptical silence.

Arthur, Gwain, Gwenan, Modlen and Myrddin rode at the centre of the column, with two lines of troops on either side. Gwenan had been asked to stay in the palace and wait for their return, but had refused. This was her first chance to act as official consort, if not yet queen, and she was not going to let it slip. Arthur caved in. Myrddin shrugged.

It was a dismal procession, witnessed by incurious citizens as it passed – hardly the triumphant riding out of Britannian power that had been planned. There was just enough light to see the banners at either end of the line and half a field beside the road. Woodland would be dangerous if Brigantian agents felt like causing trouble. Arthur gave instructions to the outriders to watch for archers, but it was a futile warning. There would be no glints on arrowheads, and the tree trunks were barely visible. An archer would just seem like another stick. The only sensible course was to adopt Myrddin's air of blithe confidence and hope for the best.

For the best part of two hours the horses plodded along the main road, acknowledged only by a handful of peasants and traders, their carts forced to the edge of the lane by the vanguard. The meeting place lay another five miles further on when Myrddin touched Arthur on the arm and grinned.

'I was right.'

'Of course you were,' snorted Arthur, 'but what about this time?'

'The fog,' said Myrddin. 'It's thinning.' Thinning and retreating as though it wished to slink away embarrassed.

Arthur signalled to Gwain to move the troop along faster. With half an hour's ride to go before they would reach the conference field, they were trotting in bright sunlight and the last vestiges of the damp were rising in steam from their clothes and horses' backs. Arthur spurred the escort on. He had given noon as the time for the opening of ceremonies, but he wanted to be in place well before. Above all he wanted everyone at their posts and appearing to have been waiting nonchalantly for a good space of time before Vortebelos showed up.

They could see the encampment Myrddin had prepared from a mile away as they came over a slight rise before dropping into the river meadows. Pennants fluttered in the light summer breeze all round a dais, and an avenue of flags marked the line of the road ahead of them and on past the stage to the bridge that Vortebelos would have to cross.

The advance group formed an honour guard as Arthur rode up the avenue. He dismounted, inspected the arrangements and called for some ale to wash away the taste of dust and horse sweat. Gwain saw that Arthur was content, then peeled off to place the men around the field and ensure the majority were formed up on the far side of the bridge in case Vortebelos felt like attacking from the outset. This way he could not only be resisted, but the men would follow him back across the bridge, sealing off the retreat. Myrddin and Modlen fussed about on the dais arranging the seating. Cloth, dyed the old imperial purple and fringed with golden thread, hung down on three sides. The fourth was open, facing east and the side of the road. Myrddin had debated long and hard over whether Vortebelos should face Ebvracum or Isurium, and had decided that it would be too accommodating for Arthur to face Brigantian territory, too careless of an ambush to look south with no view of approaching forces, should Vortebelos have decided on a battle.

Gwenan felt spare. She had no official status or function, and for the first time she was fully aware of it. For a while she followed Arthur around but, though he never objected, she knew she was in the way. She looked back to the dais where Modlen was now sorting out her tablets and styluses. A soldier was bringing a small low table to set between the main seats; another was following with platters and bowls. Gwenan smiled. Here was a reason for her to be on hand. No serving girls had ridden with them, and there would be nothing demeaning about Arthur's lover making sure that the food was in order. She strode over, and with a winning smile relieved the soldier of his bag of food, setting out the dishes, and began to unpack. Glancing up, she was surprised to see Myrddin grinning at her in approval. He nodded. It was the first moment when she was not by Arthur's side that he had acknowledged her existence with any civility. Maybe she was making progress after all.

Gwain made sure the Brigantians would be confronted by a solid line of troops three deep on either side of the road. They did not have long to wait for business to begin. The men were barely formed up and Arthur was making his way back to the dais when there was a shout from the guards across the river. Arthur stopped and gazed at the horizon, where a cloud of dust on the road told him that the Brigantian party was approaching. He looked up at the sun.

'Are we late or are they early?'

Myrddin shrugged. 'Both. But it doesn't matter. We're ready enough.'

Gwain turned and rode across the bridge, but Arthur called him to stop and go back. 'Stay there on the bridge, so they have to stop before crossing. Give him the full greeting. Don't let him make a big show.'

Gwain raised his hand and turned his horse again, planting himself at the head of five others on the bridge blocking the road.

CHAPTER XVIII

'To our places, then,' said Arthur once he had watched Gwain and was satisfied. 'Myrddin, I want you between us to make sure there's some chance of me keeping my temper. Modlen, you sit behind Myrddin. Don't draw attention to yourself, but get down anything we say that can be used later. Gwenan,' Arthur paused and took her hand tenderly, 'you stay down here when they arrive. I want you to be the first to greet Vortebelos. Introduce yourself as my companion and his host for the day, chat a bit as though I was not here: about the journey, his wife, children, the price of bread – anything you like. It will confuse him completely. He won't be expecting to have to deal with a woman before he talks to me. Only show him up here once he starts to look as though he's trying desperately to get away without being rude.'

Arthur moved on to the stage and took his seat, the only chair with a back, beside Myrddin and winked at Modlen. 'Ready?' She nodded. 'Good. Just keep scratching away. If he asks what you're doing ignore him. Let Myrddin handle it.' He lounged as best he could and cradled the mug of ale.

'What does he look like?' Gwenan called up.

'Do you know, I can't remember. I've only met him once, and that was in his father's time. Myrddin? You saw him last year.'

'Nothing special. Lots of gold. He'll make sure we know who he is.'

The stocky little northerner who dismounted in front of them with a troop of nearly a hundred men at arms was indeed laden with gold. He looked (deliberately to contrast with Arthur, Myrddin suspected) like a Celtic warrior from the first years of Roman rule. He wore broad wristbands of bronze inlaid with spirals of gold. Anklets of gold held his breaches tight for riding. His black hair was worn long, and his moustache drooped down below the chin. Against his flax tunic above the breast a fine torque lay broad and flattened, its surface studded with gold animals in relief.

Gwenan caught Myrddin's discreet nod and stepped forward.

'Great Vortebelos, I am honoured to be first to greet you.'

The King, who had been about to stride up to the dais, looked at her with an unhappy mixture of confusion and contempt. 'So you might be, but who are you?'

'I am Gwenan, Consort of Tygern Fawr; she who has been instructed to inquire about your journey and whether you would care to refresh yourself before your discussions.'

'No, thank you, young lady, I'm quite ready.' He made to take a pace forward, but Gwenan skipped in front of him.

'And then I am to lead you into the presence of the most noble Myrddin, Counsellor to the Kings, and Arthur, Tygern Fawr of all Britannia, whose companion I have the honour to be called.'

'I'm in their presence,' Vortebelos began to look exasperated. 'They're barely a stride away.'

'Then I must show you to your seat and place your men under the protection of Gwain, High Steward and Master of all the Overlord's forces.'

'My men don't need anybody's protection, thank you – now will you get on with it and get out of my way?'

'Let me lead you,' smiled Gwenan beatifically, and turned slowly. She walked at the pace of a bride moving to the altar, with Vortebelos restraining himself from pushing her along. Fear of looking boorish in front of his men prevented him from shoving her aside, but it was a close call.

Only once the King was standing on the dais in front of him did Arthur break off from his conversation – pointedly conducted in Latin – with Myrddin and notice him.

He looked inquisitively at Gwenan. 'My dear, whom have you brought to us? Is this the famous King of Brigantia?'

'It is, my lord.'

'Then my thanks.' He rose, but made no move to embrace him. 'Vortebelos, I had hoped to have this pleasure some weeks ago, but I fear I was unable to catch you at home in Isurium. Such a pity.'

Vortebelos opened his mouth to protest, but Myrddin stepped forward. 'These things happen when our communication is perhaps not as efficient as it once was. And Tygern Fawr is being forgetful. He met you, of course, in the time of your father, and in Ebvracum, but the years pass. Come and sit after your journey. The Lady Gwenan,' he looked pointedly at her, and she smiled knowingly at his first and sudden use of a title, 'will find you something to drink. We have much to discuss. Your men may disperse and enjoy the sunshine as you wish. Come, come.'

Myrddin fussed about him, adjusting the stools and the table, fiddling with the cloth and cups, pointing out Modlen and indicating her role as secretary to the meeting and asking her to hand him a

CHAPTER XVIII

slate with a list of topics to be covered – clearly a novelty that left the Brigantian perplexed and angry that his own illiteracy should have been demonstrated so early. He waved the note away. Arthur had already sat down again and was gazing disinterestedly at the men milling about the road, some waiting warily, others dismounting and leading their horses back to the river to drink.

Only once a fresh beaker, more bread and slices of meat had been brought and laid in front of Vortebelos did Myrddin's chatter tail off and a welcoming wave of the hand make it clear that the young warrior was free to speak. Vortebelos cleared his throat, unsure of whether to show his irritation or play the game of false pleasantries that Arthur and his court had led him into. He did not want to seem an oaf. Neither, though, did he want to be seen by his men as part of their world of imperial subjection and grand schemes.

He began on safe ground: welcoming the Overlord to his kingdom of Brigantia, saying how proud he was to have Arthur's northern capital of Ebvracum within his territory and hoping that the Overlord would find more time than the occasional summer months to enjoy its ancient splendours, not (he admitted) that they were now in the state that they had once been before the memory of their fathers or their fathers' fathers. He was especially pleased to see that such splendid preparations had been made, properly reflecting the importance of such a meeting, one that would affect the nations of Britannia for generations to come.

It was, Arthur had to admit, probably all too true.

Myrddin returned the diplomacy, saving Arthur the task of seeming too grateful and allowing him to remain aloof from the discussions until he had a judgement to make. The Overlord listened, finding Vortebelos's strong Brigantian accent hard to follow at times. His vowels were flattened and sentences clipped, and he seemed to have stripped out all the words with Latin influence from Brythonic, leaving the language coarse and inelegant. Like the King's anachronistic dress, it seemed deliberately archaic. It was not just a matter of taste or northern fashion. It was, Arthur realised, deeply political – a statement that went beyond conservatism. Here was a man rejecting even the comfortable legacy of the empire, who barely acknowledged the need for Britannia to remain united, and who certainly put Brigantia's interests against the other nations to the south first. He would fight the Barbarians if they posed a threat, but Arthur guessed Vortebelos would welcome boatloads of them – and Hibernians – in if it meant strengthening his hand against Cunorix and Cunegnus. The Parisi, too, were going to have a hard time staying independent if he felt they were in the way.

Between the stage and the river the men of both forces mingled uneasily. Horses were watered and stiff riding limbs stretched. A few sat in the sunshine on the riverbank, chatting quietly, breaking bread, offering around each other's cheese and early onions. Old acquaintances were renewed and families asked after. A small knot of senior men and those ambitious enough to be interested remained close to the leaders and followed the exchanges. But on either side a good number remained in their saddles, alert for the first sign of treachery. There was discourse, but no trust. Peace was a much used but unconfident word. In the distance small cattle and adolescent lambs moved across the plain, unconcerned now that the noise of the riding had stopped.

Gwenan had retreated to the back of the dais, standing quietly behind Modlen as she scratched economically on her tablets. The notes were brief, but once transferred to vellum in Ebvracum they would be a record full enough for the historians in the monasteries to use – and more than enough for Arthur to show his Council when they met. For the moment the sentences had no bias. That would come once Modlen knew in which direction the talks would go.

Arthur caught his mind wandering. The effort needed to understand the Brigantian had made his concentration drift. He forced himself to listen more closely and looked across at Myrddin, conscious that he'd been slipping into the easy habit of letting his sage do all the negotiating while he shifted his thoughts from politics to Gwenan's body. The old man's face was grim. Vortebelos was complaining at length about holding off the Hibernians on one coast, the Barbarians on the other, while holding back the Votadini behind what remained of the wall. The Carvetii in the north-west he dismissed as 'no longer a problem' – a summary that Arthur found immediately worrying. If they were no longer a problem to the Brigantes then they must have been brought into line. They had been on fierce terms with Vortebelos's father, and there seemed no reason why things should have improved under his son. But the Brigantian King reserved his real venom for his neighbours to the south. The Parisi, he said, were incapable of providing protection against invaders (true enough, thought Arthur). They needed a strong hand from outside to govern and lick them into shape. Only he, Vortebelos, could provide that. Arthur and his rumoured Council of minor chieftains were only a short-term distraction.

'Are we, indeed?' intervened Arthur for the first time. 'And what would you regard as a long-term distraction?'

Vortebelos looked uncertainly at Myrddin. 'I meant,' he continued, 'the security of Brigantia cannot be tied to the convenience of southern nations. We must look to our own borders now.'

'You think we cannot be more effective together than separately?'

'If other nations had the courage of Brigantia—'

'But,' Arthur continued, 'you don't think they do? Or you do not trust them enough to display it in your defence?'

Vortebelos inclined his head. Myrddin moved to take back the initiative. 'Surely, my good Vortebelos, it would be absurd to suggest that any meaningful Council could be called without the full participation and support of Brigantia?'

The King grinned. 'Couldn't have put it better myself, old man. Therefore, since I have much better things to do with my time and my men, that is why the Council will be nothing more than talk. And if you think you can play the emperor,' he said, pointing to Arthur, 'forget it. I can handle you, Cunorix and Cunegnus as long as it suits me.'

There was an uncomfortable silence. Arthur gazed out across the countryside, as though thinking of more important things. Eventually he turned to Myrddin. 'Do you feel anything useful can be achieved here?' he asked quietly. 'I have heard the Brigantian view. It seems unlikely there will be much interest in the detail of mine.'

Within the time it took for the troops to separate and reform, the two men had embraced formally. Vortebelos had sworn loyalty and brotherhood. Arthur had reiterated his vows to protect all of Britannia, not just some of the kingdoms. The Brigantian had promised to send men to help any of his neighbours in the event of Barbarian invasion, and not to allow any alliance to the detriment of Britannia as a whole. Neither believed a word of it. There was an uneasy mounted stand-off as each waited for the other's forces to leave the parley field first.

Eventually Arthur ordered his men to come across the bridge, leaving the far side empty for the Brigantians to claim. He gathered Gwenan, Modlen and his household and, with a curt nod, spurred on his horse. In a few moments all that was left of the diplomatic scenery were a flew flapping banners and the sound of the carpenters knocking out the joints of the stage. Soon the road south turned slightly to the left, and a small knoll, more an undulation in the land than a hill, hid the remains of the pavilion.

Although the afternoon was well advanced there was still plenty of time under the sun to reach Ebvracum before dark. When the Romans had cared for this great northern road they had ensured that their legions marched through open country on either side. But in the last seventy years the forest had slowly crept back and reclaimed its ground – except for those few places where old families had retained and expanded their land or Barbarian settlers had pitched their huts. It was not yet wild country, but neither did it have the security that Arthur and Gwain would have liked.

The horses had hardly worked up a sweat when Arthur felt the unmistakable wind of an arrow soar past his ear. He looked to his left, the nearest tree cover. This time he spotted the arrow as it raced towards them. Instinctively he ducked, lying against the horse's neck, and raced on. From behind him he heard a whimper and a man's shout of rage. Turning to look back, a risk he had never taken since childhood, he saw a figure fall to the ground. No more arrows came. Around him his men formed a protective circle.

By now the party had split in two – the one with Arthur and Myrddin at the centre still riding forward, while the other larger one halted and grouped tightly in the road, from where outriders were already charging towards the edge of the forest. Arthur's group came to a bend in the road – the sharp bends that Romans made for exactly situations such as this. They rounded at speed, the horses barely keeping their feet on the turf-covered stones.

Once out of sight of the bend Arthur raised his hand and reined in his horse. The men halted and sat still, listening for movement in the trees or any sounds of battle behind them. For a moment there was nothing to hear; then came the muffled sound of a horse's hooves moving fast. Just one horse. A lone rider came galloping round the bend. Arthur relaxed. One of his own men.

'My lord,' the rider shouted.

'All over?' asked Myrddin.

'Yes, but...'

Arthur looked at the man's face as he drew up beside him. There were tears welling.

'What is it? Who was hit?' asked Arthur quietly.

The soldier bowed his head. 'Gwain says you should come back.'

'Is that wise?' demanded Myrddin. 'It was surely you the arrow was aimed at. We should ride on. Let Gwain deal with it.'

The soldier stood his ground, 'Gwain says you're to come back, my lord.'

'Well, I say—' began Myrddin.

'Be quiet, Myrddin. If Gwain tells me to return he has good reason.' Arthur nudged his horse back along the road. 'We'll all return.'

They rounded the bend slowly and approached the knot of men waiting silently in the road. Those who had left to search the woods could be heard crashing through the undergrowth to the right.

As Arthur approached, the protective circle of men parted and he could see Gwain crouched by a figure on the ground.

'Who is it?' Arthur dismounted and strode towards them. For a moment the horses blocked his view. Nobody spoke. Gwain's head was bent over a hand. For a second Arthur stopped, then ran forward. 'No!' he shouted.

Gwenan lay on her back, an arrow shaft rising from her chest. Modlen knelt by her, holding her hand. The arrow had been falling when it hit her, and had struck down to the left of her throat towards the heart and lungs. She was still alive when Arthur reached her, but blood seeped from the corner of her mouth and she could no longer speak. He knelt and kissed her, on the lips first, then the forehead, and called her name gently. He had seen enough arrow wounds to know that there was no hope. By now the arrow itself would be the only thing holding the body together. To pull it out, even if there was no barbed tip, would just kill her quicker and in more agony. In Gwenan's eyes shock and pain fought each other. There was no time left for tears or last words of love. Before Arthur could take her hand the light had faded and she had gone. Throughout the men had stood in silence, heads bowed, nobody wanting to invade the intimacy of her death, all wishing that one of them, whose job it was to guard the Overlord and his people, had been in the way of the arrow. Only in the minutes after Gwenan had died, while Arthur held her lifeless hand and let the tears flow, did a few wonder where the shot had come from, and why only three arrows had been loosed.

Eventually Gwain rounded up the men, interrogated the forest search parties – who predictably had turned up nothing – and came over to lay a hand on Arthur's shoulder.

Arthur sighed, bent forward and kissed Gwenan and stood up, still holding her fingers. The grief had given way to fury, quiet and unrelenting. For years afterwards men said that they had never, even in the thunder of battle, seen him as commanding and determined as at that moment.

'We don't know who did this,' he began, 'but we do know why. Myrddin...' All the while the old counsellor had remained mounted, outside the cluster, the shadow of a strange smile across his face. He returned to an expression of appropriate gravity as Arthur spoke to him. 'You will escort Gwenan's body to Ebvracum. You will take Modlen and ten of my men. There you will lay her with full honours in the basilica and wait for my return. My speeches and farewells to this woman will be made then. For now, the rest of you will come with me. We have a lesson to teach.'

Arthur strode back to his horse, remounted and rode off northwards at speed, leaving Gwain to urge on the men and catch him as best they could. It was a forlorn group that was left in the road. Myrddin was careful to make sure that Gwenan really was dead – he had known too many cases where unconsciousness had been mistaken for death; rough treatment then had killed them, not the initial wound. He examined her carefully, watched intently by Modlen, who still clung to the limp hand. He tore back Gwenan's clothes and probed the place where the arrow had entered, gauged its length in the body, listened to her heart and felt her neck for even the slightest hint of life. He was not certain, but there might have been a trace.

Myrddin drew his cloak across her face, whispered close to her ear, slipped his gold amulet over the arrow shaft until it circled the wound, laid his hands on her bare chest around it and breathed deeply. The amulet warmed and reddened gently. Leaving it in place, Myrddin drew the arrow, firmly but with great care. The shaft and head left Gwenan's flesh with a sigh, bringing with them only a few drops of blood. Myrddin kept his left hand on the chest, pressing lightly, using the other to reach across her temples. He altered his breathing, speeding it to the rhythm of a heartbeat, caressing her head and working the chest to the same measure. Without changing the pace, but increasing the vigour, he parted her lips, pushed his own firmly against them and shared his breath with her, drawing in air for two. He worked almost roughly now, kneading the heart but making sure the amulet still isolated the arrow wound.

After what seemed to Modlen an age, Myrddin withdrew his lips and spat out a mouthful of blood, then went to work again. The tongueless girl watched in a mixture of horror and hopeless fascination. All she could do was to keep stroking Gwenan's hand. Instinctively she felt the wrist and gasped. Myrddin heard her and turned his head.

'Anything?' he snapped.

She nodded.

'Then don't just sit there. Get some cloaks over her. Now. Water, one of you. And quick.'

Myrddin held the amulet to the wound and drew more blood from her mouth. Soon he too was certain she was alive again. He eased Gwenan's shoulders from the ground and gestured to one of the men to support her while others rolled their cloaks against her back. At first she seemed just as lifeless as before but then, as Modlen worried that she had only imagined life and that there had been nothing more than hope and tricks, Gwenan coughed. Myrddin grabbed a flagon of water and splashed it over her face and the wound. He moved the amulet to her forehead and began to sing quietly. Modlen could hear the words, but they were in no language she knew. Eventually Gwenan's fingers twitched, and moments later she opened her eyes.

'Welcome back,' said Myrddin. A cheer of astonishment went up from the soldiers. Modlen began to cry. Gwenan was her rival and her inferior in everything other than looks and speech, but she had no wish to see her dead.

'That was close,' confessed Myrddin. 'You had nearly caught the boat, I think.' He laid his hands once more on her chest, as though reading beneath the skin, then put on his amulet and covered Gwenan with a cloak to her neck. 'You can't talk, so don't try,' he told her. 'You are still gravely hurt, and you may still leave us. But I hope not yet.'

He looked at the sky and surveyed the woods. 'Modlen, keep holding her, and try to get a little water past her lips. Not much, and not too fast. She may not be able to swallow properly. The wound is closing, but it could open again if we're careless. Then my skills would be irrelevant. I can't do that twice.' He stroked Gwenan's cheek and smiled. 'You and I are probably going to regret this, but we've done it now.'

As he stood up he told the men, 'it's too late to get to Ebvracum tonight at a safe pace for the woman. Get a fire going, and build a shelter close to the trees and out of the wind. She must be kept warm and dry. I'll wait with her here until I'm sure it's safe to move her – or as safe as it's going to be this evening.'

Myrddin looked down at Modlen. 'If she lives she won't be the same as before, you know. We may all have to start again.'

Gwenan's eyes settled into focus, searched the sky and rested on the other girl's face. For the first time Modlen felt the squeeze of her fingers. The two of them, silent by force, stayed on the solid turf of the road while the men busied with gathering branches and bush, and Myrddin wandered back along the track in the direction Arthur had taken.

XIX

THE LAST PLANKS and coverings of the conference stage were being packed away, the carts turning towards Ebvracum, as the sound of galloping horses startled the carpenters. They watched in stunned surprise as Arthur and his men swept past, barely slowing to file across the bridge, and thunder on northwards. There were no imperial trappings now, just the intense horsemanship of warriors after their quarry. Arthur was not in calculating mood. He trusted that Vortebelos would be in no undue hurry to reach Isurium with all the summer evening's light ahead of him. Even so, the head start was enough for the Brigantian's troop to be within sight of his capital by the time Arthur bore down on them.

A slight rise in the ground had hidden the sound of the approaching attackers – for that is what Arthur was. He had no interest in negotiating. Nor did he pause to take up a battle position. Sword in hand, he spurred straight at Vortebelos, leaving his men to join the fight

CHAPTER XIX

with the Brigantians as they wished. Vortebelos was at the front of his procession, riding home unconcernedly. He was laughing, holding his reins with one hand, an ale flask with the other. Behind him his men shouted a warning as they wheeled to face Arthur's rampage.

It was too late. Before he or they could react Arthur was upon him. Caledfwlch, the same sword with which he had won the title of overlord so many years ago, flashed in the afternoon sun as he swung the stroke. His blow was fast and sure. Vortebelos never felt the cut as his head was severed, falling to the ground while his body slumped on to his horse's mane before tumbling from the saddle. By then Arthur had turned and was careering back towards the horizon, his men breaking from the skirmish before it had truly had time to begin and charging back after their master.

They disappeared as suddenly as they had arrived.

The slaughter of Vortebelos had been an act of savage revenge, taken with such efficient speed that only two other men had been injured in the ambush. His astonished soldiers stood in silence round the torso, its gold torque now marking the bleeding neckline like a memorial decoration.

* * *

The sun had disappeared and the gloom of evening made the forest dark and forbidding by the time Arthur had crossed the river once again and ridden back to the spot where Gwenan had fallen. He expected to find just a mark on the turf. Instead, on the fringe of the trees he saw a freshly built hut with a campfire outside and a pot bubbling in the embers. Myrddin stood peering into the flames. He didn't move as Arthur dismounted and strode up beside him.

'What are you doing here still?' demanded Arthur. 'I thought I told you to take Gwenan's body back to Ebvracum.'

Myrddin nodded. 'So you did – but I thought it better to keep her here and make sure she survives the night.'

'Survives?' Arthur repeated. 'What do you mean, survives? She was dead when I left.'

'Well, she's not now – though she was nearly beyond reach. She's sleeping. No, Arthur,' he said, as the younger man moved towards the hut. 'Leave her alone – at least till morning. Modlen will tend her better than you, however much you want to help.'

'She really is alive?'

'After a fashion – yes.'

'You brought her back?'

Myrddin smiled. 'I helped persuade her.'

'Is there a difference?'

'Oh yes, a very big difference.'

'And the archers – did you find them?'

Myrddin shook his head. 'No, these woods are too dense if somebody who knows them wants to hide. I wasn't going to risk another ambush, either. I wanted the men I had here to guard the women.'

Arthur slumped to the ground and glared at the trees. 'Then I have been a fool.'

'Why – by riding after Gwenan's assassin?'

'No – by finding and killing him. Vortebelos is dead. I hope he knew why, but I doubt it.'

Myrddin poked the fire with a stick. 'This could be interesting.'

Arthur snorted, 'Interesting? Is that the best you can say? It could be a bloody disaster.'

'We'll discuss it later.' He waved his stick towards the road. 'For the moment I suggest you give Gwain a hand sorting out your men. They look even more confused than you do.'

The men were still straggling back along the road. Few of them had been able or prepared to keep up with Arthur's ludicrous pace for nearly two hours. Most, sure that their general was unlikely to come to much more harm that evening, had let him gallop ahead with a skeleton bodyguard, and had paused at the river to let the horses drink and get the weight off their backs.

Gwain was already directing the operations for the night in what was left of the twilight. The carts carrying the supplies for the now-redundant conference earlier in the day had arrived. It had been the intention that they should try to reach clear ground on the other side of the forest before nightfall, but there was no point pushing on beyond the soldiers to somewhere less protected. Some of their baggage would make the night more comfortable, in any case.

Wood was gathered for fires and bracken cut for bedding. Men were detailed to fill water pouches and lead the horses to graze. Arthur joined Gwain to issue orders for the watch and distribute the camp so that Gwenan's makeshift haven would be protected on all sides.

CHAPTER XIX

Nobody discussed the strange events of the day. That would come later, once the stars were out. The troops were Arthur's most loyal guards, men who had ridden with him from nation to nation for years. However peculiar the events, they were certain that he and Myrddin had a purpose and a plan.

It was a warm night, though not sultry, and everybody would be glad enough of the fires before dawn. Hunger and tiredness began to fight for attention. A few rabbits were shot as they scurried towards the woods, and pigeons were felled from branches as they settled down for the night. Enough was gathered in and roasted for a sparse but adequate meal for all. They had camped in many more inhospitable spots than this during their years on the road with Tygern Fawr.

Once it was clear Gwain had everything under control Arthur rejoined Myrddin by the fire. For once in his life Arthur had no idea where to start the discussion. He badly needed Myrddin's explanation and advice, but asking for either was not going to be easy, and the old counsellor was not going to volunteer them until absolutely necessary. So they sat in silence, Myrddin idly playing with the embers and tending the pot, Arthur morosely gazing into the hut where Gwenan lay. Around them the men bustled and laughed as they prepared food and staked out spaces for themselves in well-rehearsed platoons.

Eventually Modlen appeared from inside the shelter and bowed to Arthur.

'How is she?' he asked, gesturing to the tongueless girl to join him by the fire.

Modlen sat down and looked Arthur in the eye. She smiled, then pursed her lips and inclined her head to the side.

'She'll live?' Arthur asked. Modlen nodded. He took her hand and squeezed it. 'Thank you,' he said quietly. 'It's been a hard day for you.'

'For all of us,' Gwain pointed out, joining the group and squatting down to warm his hands.

'So what did you do to Vortebelos?' Myrddin looked across to Arthur.

'Ask Gwain,' he said. 'He'll remember it more clearly than I will.'

Gwain shrugged. 'It was the attack of an avenging angel. He was completely heedless of danger, strategy, sense or anything except the sight of Vortebelos swigging ale on the way home to Isurium. He simply flew across the ground, swiped off the King's head and rode away again. The man never even had time to draw his weapon.'

'There was no denial that Gwenan's sniper was sent by him?' asked Myrddin.

Gwain chuckled. 'He was never asked. Executed where he sat.'

'And yet here Gwenan is — alive if not well,' said Myrddin.

'Not that I knew,' protested Arthur. 'When I left she had just died in my arms. I've seen death often enough to know the instant.'

Myrddin stared at the fire. 'Not always,' he said. 'There is a moment, sometimes brief, sometimes surprisingly long, if the damage to the body is not too severe, when the soul lingers. If the body can be given the chance to repair itself death can be forestalled.'

'Is that what happened?'

'Yes, I think so.'

'How did you do it?'

Myrddin sighed. 'I know what I did. I remembered what a Nubian healer told me once in Gaul about the way warmth, applied with great concentration, can stimulate the body to fight a wound, even a deep one like this. That's what I did. How I did it, I have no more idea than you.' He looked across the flames. 'Perhaps Modlen understands — she has as deep an insight as I do, I suspect.'

Modlen frowned across at Myrddin, surprised by this sudden admission of respect, then shook her head.

'So,' Arthur continued after thinking for a while, looking into the fire and stretching, 'the Overlord has finished a day of diplomatic negotiation by ambushing one of the most powerful kings of Britannia outside the fortifications of his own capital and cutting off his head. All in revenge for a murder that did not take place. That will look good. The summer's work will probably have been wasted now.'

Even among Arthur's intimate friends around the fire there was a feeling of silent embarrassment. Only Myrddin seemed cheerful.

'No, it's not going to be as bad as that. In fact, you may have turned the tide conclusively in your favour.' He picked up a stick, examined and twirled it before laying it with unnecessary care into the flames.

Gwain peered at him through the smoke. 'I don't see how, Counsellor.'

'With respect, sir, you are not a politician. Neither, for the moment, it seems, is your master, though I have done my best.'

'Well, that's something to be thankful for, at least,' muttered Arthur. 'So what's your thinking, Myrddin?'

CHAPTER XIX

'The way it will be seen, because I suspect the reports Modlen makes and those of the Brigantes will say much the same, is that Vortebelos rejected your invitation to join the Council. There was then an attempt on your life as you returned home – your life, not Gwenan's; why would anybody fire just three arrows and want to hit Gwenan? You're the only one worth sending a sniper for.'

'Or you?' suggested Arthur.

'You're too kind, but I doubt it. Not while I'm with you. No, you rightly surmised that Vortebelos had tried to assassinate you, and you took immediate and decisive action. An attack on you was an attack on the whole system of unified command by consent, and needed to be treated as such. And you did it yourself – you didn't order an assassination of your own. It was open combat. The fact that the man didn't even have time to piss on his saddle just adds to the glitter of the story.'

'Possibly,' said Arthur, not wholly convinced.

'The Counsellor has a point,' admitted Gwain. 'By the time the story has reached the south it will have been burnished nicely. The others will think again about resistance. Many of the kings have always... I don't know how to put this, My Lord...'

'Go on,' grinned Arthur. 'If you can't say it, only Myrddin can, and that will just make him feel even more important.'

'If you say so, then... they think of you as being a little too kindly, too cerebral,' said Gwain.

'Too soft.'

'Thank you, Myrddin, I'm quite capable of interpreting Gwain without your help,' Arthur said quietly.

'I think,' Gwain continued, 'this, coming so soon after the Battle of the Landings, will change their minds. They will know that you put what you see as the interest of Britannia above the need to keep any one of them happy.'

'Or alive,' Myrddin added, unabashed.

'You may be right,' said Arthur. 'Either way, I will have to move fast now, faster than I wanted. For the moment, though, my priority is to carry Gwenan back to Ebvracum as quickly and safely as possible. We'll debate anything else once we're there.'

Arthur curled his cloak closely around himself and lay down with his back to the fire. Myrddin did the same. Modlen touched her master's shoulder, then moved back to Gwenan's shelter. She was not sure how, but she knew that her own future was now intimately linked with her rival's survival. The thought shocked her. She had always been vaguely jealous of Gwenan. But it was the first time she had realised that her need to be close to Arthur made it more than that. If Gwenan had died, she might have been closer still. Now, though, she knew Arthur would be more grateful for Gwenan's recovery than in need of her comforting if Gwenan died. At least in the short term.

* * *

In the palace in Ebvracum Gwenan slept for three days. Once awake she was in great pain for many days more. Her left arm was almost immovable, and the wound in her chest, though surprisingly slight on the outside, was nonetheless home to a great deal of damage beneath the skin. Arthur spent as much time with her as he could but he, Gwain and Modlen were in almost constant session planning the imminent Council and dispatching messengers with the official version of the events of the previous few weeks. Myrddin had been keen to return home to his villa outside Moridunum even before the Brigantian conference. Once he was sure Gwenan would live he lost no time in setting out, promising Arthur that he would be prepared to interrupt his peace and quiet to attend the Council. As he pointed out, once the travelling was taken into account, there were barely more than six weeks left for him to enjoy the summer in the west, the sight of the tall wheat and warm evenings with a glass (he still had a few rescued from the old days) of fine Massilian wine. He maintained (at length) that wine — even the muck served up by Arthur when he could get it these days — didn't taste right out of a goblet, whether wooden or ceramic, and certainly not the base metal most kings passed off as silver.

Of Gwenan he took great care in the days before he set out. And he instructed Modlen intensively in how to tend the wound and coax her back to health. The girl was delighted at his confidence. She felt she was virtually his assistant, or at least apprentice. She delighted too in the ease with which he could read her script, even her shorthand on wax, and felt her own Latin improve as he answered her notes with a fluency that she had never heard. It was as if she was listening to the language as it was spoken in the far-off lands of its home, not passed through the filter of a Brythonic accent, as even Arthur's Latin was. With Myrddin she could almost have a conversation – as she hadn't since she had been so brutally silenced two years before.

Myrddin, for his part, began to realise that acquiring Modlen had not just been another of Arthur's sentimental whims. Quite apart from her obvious sweetness and her use as a witness with whom illiterate kings could not communicate unless she wanted them to, she had a sharp intelligence that made teaching her a genuine pleasure. Arthur was coming to depend on her to be his accurate memory and omnipresent secretary. Myrddin, for all the seriousness of his instruction, just enjoyed showing off his erudition to someone with the eagerness to understand. She also, he soon realised with a slight qualm, was quite capable of working out when he was passing off a trick as knowledge. Modlen could convey suspicion or derision with her eyes disconcertingly fast, and had the nerve to smile at his discomfort when he had been found out.

Her relationship with Gwain was less easy; not because he didn't trust her – if anything his awe at her learning made him trust her more than anyone in the Overlord's household – but because his own lack of Latin meant that they couldn't communicate. She understood him, of course, but written Brythonic was still an experimental language, and when she attempted to use Latin characters to approximate the sound, he couldn't really decipher them fast enough to answer her in anything but the most halting fashion. He knew it was his inadequacy, not hers, and that in turn made him embarrassed to be seen trying. On the other hand, while Gwain was Arthur's principal military deputy, Modlen had quickly become Arthur's political eyes and ears – and, increasingly, his adviser when Myrddin was not around to cast his paternal eye over policy. And, like Gwain, she was a professional deputy, not someone who had won Arthur's heart as Gwenan had – or so she thought. In truth Arthur would have admitted to himself that the distinction was not nearly so clear. But for the sake of the household and his own control, it was important that he keep any contradictory feelings to himself.

The Council was fixed for the third week of September, giving time to organise and travel but, as Gwain pointed out, giving each of the kings time to assess the harvest and turn up with a retinue of men unworried about leaving the fields.

The place to hold it was more difficult to decide. Arthur did not want to hold it in open country. Backed up by Myrddin, he was also disinclined to pick anywhere that one or other of the kings could regard as a national capital. That ruled out some of the towns that were both easy to travel to and still in a reasonable state of repair, like Corinium, Verulamium and Viroconium. Ebvracum was too far north to be convenient for the southern nations (who seemed to have a firm antipathy against venturing further than the territory of the Coritani). Equally, though, it would be too easy for Brigantian malcontents to disrupt.

There was no obvious place that was convenient politically and geographically. Quite early in their discussions Myrddin had suggested Londinium. Arthur had ruled it out as being too far south and too eastern to be reachable by the Dumnonians, let alone the Demetiae and Ordovices. Increasingly, though, he began to see the reasoning. It had always been an imperial city, not particularly identified with any nation, and therefore, like Ebvracum, he could argue it was part of the Overlord's territory. It certainly had some of the finest of the remaining imperial buildings, and its place as a trading port meant that it was in better shape, and larger, than most cities. It was accessible from the sea, too; not that any of the kings except the Dumnonian were likely to sail to the Council, but that fact would serve to concentrate minds on the Barbarian threat to the coast.

The independence of the Bishop of Londinium, Gwidellius, from any direct local authority might also be useful when it came to validating the Council conclusions. While he might be seen as owing his status to Arthur as much as the Church, he would not be obviously anybody else's man. Attendance by the kings themselves was always going to be the biggest problem, but Arthur felt that his journeys of persuasion that summer, and the object lesson he had taught Vortebelos, should have been enough to draw the rulers in – at least this once.

He was ready to move by the end of August, and he needed to be in Londinium as soon as possible if the Council arrangements were going to be as splendid as he wanted. The signs were good. Messengers were returning from the central and eastern kingdoms with the answer yes to his invitation. Myrddin would look after the west, and Gwain had been using messages to his family connections in the south-west to make sure there was reasonable representation from that end of the island. One or two kings were excusing themselves, usually on grounds of infirmity, and sending kinsmen as deputies. Brigantia was in shocked turmoil, of course, after the peremptory removal of its king's head, and seemed to be about to enter one of its periodic bouts of civil war. Since that was entirely Arthur's fault he could hardly complain about it. There was the advantage that if Brigantia was busy opening old wounds, the surrounding rulers would feel more confident of leaving their territory.

The one misgiving he had was in subjecting Gwenan to the journey. She insisted on going with him, and she was right – Ebvracum might not be the safest place to remain if the Brigantians decided she would be a useful hostage. Even if Arthur, not Gwenan, had been the real target of the original assassination bid, she would be too tempting a victim once Arthur's troops had ridden out. Her condition, though, left a problem for the future too. Arthur knew that he would have to be on the road almost continually before winter set in. That, he suspected, would be too much strain for her health, and too much distraction for him. At some stage soon after the Council he would have to decide where and in whose care to leave her. It was not a conversation with his lover to which he was looking forward.

The full entourage moved out of Ebvracum with some ceremony. It was Arthur's northern capital, after all, and he had spent almost more time there that year than in all the previous decade put together. He had every intention of returning, too. The thought was in his mind that, once the Council and his mission to rearrange the relationship between the Cornovii, Deceangeli and Ordovices had been complete, he might consolidate his watch on the Brigantian succession by basing himself there for the winter. It was not the warmest spot in Britannia, he admitted, but if the rebuilding carried on while he was away, he could make it snug enough.

As the Overlord and his retinue progressed – a procession of nearly three hundred including men at arms, domestic servants and their dependants – they passed through many miles of forest, interspersed with scattered farmsteads and villages of round houses that had not changed much in design for thousands of years. Occasionally they passed through or camped within the decayed fortifications of a Roman enclosure, often way stations built for the once-proud Ninth Hispana Legion, whose mutinous remnants had finally abandoned them seventy-five years before to support the ill-fated attempt by Constantine III to wrest the empire from Honorius. The camps were not much more than rotten stockades behind bramble-filled ditches, but the brambles were often a formidable defence in themselves, and the space behind them provided a ready-made clearing for the army of retainers and animals to spend the night.

Within eight days they had moved through the territory of the Parisi and taken the ferry successively (a full day was spent sending the boats back and forth) across the estuary at Petuaria, then rode into the heartland of the Coritani and the great old legionary fortress at Lindum, skirted the western fringes of the Iceni and were back where Arthur had begun his summer's riding three months earlier – in the borderlands of the Catuvellauni. He was careful to send word ahead to Cunorix, inviting him to join his progress, but making it clear that he was sure the King had more important things to do at this harvest season, and he looked forward to seeing him in Londinium before the end of the month. Arthur really did not want another encounter with one of his most powerful but least attractive electors before the other kings arrived for the Council.

A courteous (for Cunorix) reply came back welcoming Arthur to the kingdom and granting him safe passage, which was sheer cheek, of course, but not a provocation that Arthur was going to rise to for the moment. There was also a snide remark about hoping 'his little present' was 'keeping his feet warm'. Thankfully Modlen was riding a little behind and out of earshot when the message was delivered, otherwise, Arthur knew, the combination of fury and fear would make her miserable for the rest of the journey. It would be at least another week before they were clear of Cunorix's domain.

The patronising joke added to the diplomatic reasons for taking the eastern road to Londinium and avoiding Cunorix's capital at Verulamium. Whether he was there or not (the messenger had found him in the country sixty miles away), Arthur had no wish to sample his hospitality again so close to the Council. Quite apart from the politics, it would have been just like Cunorix to send a detachment of men to escort Arthur to Londinium, giving the clear impression that Arthur's security and that of the city were in the gift and goodwill of the King of the Catuvellauni. That would have destroyed the prospects for the Council before it began. Cunorix as a major part

CHAPTER XIX

of Arthur's alliance was one thing. Cunorix as the arbiter of the Overlord's movement was another.

As it was Cunorix made no obvious attempt to intercept them. When the main body of travellers was still several days short of their destination, Arthur sent Gwain on ahead to make sure Londinium was in some condition to receive him.

In theory preparations should have already been under way for many weeks. Orders, and enough payment to give a taste of the rewards to come, had been dispatched to Bishop Gwidellius as soon as the decision to meet there had been made. Much could have happened, or nothing at all, however. Until Gwain arrived he would not know whether their orders had arrived and been acted on or whether Arthur's agents had just been relieved of their treasure and ignored.

* * *

The sun was past its zenith when the Overlord's party emerged from the last of the woods and came out into the fields that lined the road before the walls of Londinium. The walls themselves had not been repaired much in Arthur's time in charge but, on the northern side, at least, they had not been seriously attacked or raided for stone, either. They had been built to last, and so they had.

Two fast riders had been dispatched in the morning to warn Gwain that Arthur was approaching. Word had spread, and Arthur was gratified to find quite a good throng gathered for the last mile into the city. There was plenty of cheering, much of it genuine. Londinium might be a shadow of its old glories, but it still saw itself as the most impressive (and most independent) place in Britannia. With Arthur in residence there was hope of proving the point and regaining some of its old influence. While in theory Bishop Gwidellius ruled the city as the foremost churchman in Britannia, there had never been an official (or universally accepted) confirmation of his status from any Pope, and each king was tempted to champion his own bishop's claims to supremacy. Arthur and Gwidellius were in very similar positions. It made sense to both of them to wrest the initiative back from the fractious and competitive kings.

Consequently Gwidellius made sure that Arthur was greeted with all the pomp at his disposal. Crowds lined the sides of the road, setting up a good noise from the moment the first riders appeared. Gwidellius himself was dressed in full vestments, and sat outside the city walls, mounted underneath an awning supported by poles held by four horsemen.

Gwain took up position just in front and rode forward to escort Arthur the last furlong to the Bishop. As he did so, two of Gwidellius's men stepped out and saluted with a pair of ancient silver trumpets rescued and polished for the occasion. The sound was more enthusiastic than expert, but it was a startling novelty for many in the crowd and Arthur's retinue who had never heard such ceremony.

Arthur emerged from his troops waving; he greeted Gwain, and was led to Gwidellius. As he did so he unsheathed Caledfwlch, which had so lately decapitated the King of the Brigantians, and held it high by the blade, so that the hilt matched the cross carried by the Bishop's herald. He stopped, allowing the great sword to be lowered, crosspiece first, into Gwidellius's hands. As he did so, the men carrying the awning moved forward so that it covered the Overlord more than the Bishop. Gwidellius blessed and returned the sword, and both men turned to face the crowd in a show of amicable unity as the trumpeters let rip again.

Gwain urged on the cheering. If only the Council would prove to be so simple to manage, he thought to himself as Arthur and Gwidellius turned and headed through the great stone gate into Londinium for the short ride to the old forum.

Inside the walls the street through the isolated houses and orchards was packed. Several of the horses, perfectly used to the terrors of the wild road and even of battle, baulked at the closeness of the bellowing people. Gwenan's bucked and would have bolted, had not the nearest man at arms grabbed the reins and tied them to his own steadier animal. Behind them the retainers leading the wagons wisely held back and let the crowd gather in behind the main attractions as they passed along the western wall of the old forum. There were gaps between the buildings, but the main entrance was on the southern side, closest to the river, and though many of those wanting a good view slipped into the forum from other openings, the main procession followed its solemn route round the perimeter and through the ceremonial arch.

Once in the huge open space, its grubby but proud colonnades sheltering stalls and ale houses, Arthur and Gwidellius were turned to the left and guided towards the western end of the forum. They stopped before an ancient building, not particularly high or large but with fine wooden doors set between carved columns that outshone their neighbours.

The Bishop dismounted and gestured for Arthur to do the same. When they had handed their horses over to grooms Gwidellius took Arthur's arm in a comradely fashion and led him towards the doors, now being swung open by monks on the inside.

'Welcome to my cathedral – or rather, St Peter's,' announced Gwidellius. 'It is not perhaps as grand as its namesake in Rome, though I'm told by those who have visited Constantine's church there that it's not much bigger. But this has the distinction of being far older.'

Arthur looked surprised. He could not conceive of a church more than 160 years old.

'Was it converted from the temple of Augustus?' he asked.

'No, apparently not,' Gwidellius said, guiding him inside. 'It's always been a church, although of course the building itself only took this form in the last century. But the tradition is that there were Christian rooms on this site on an upper floor as early as the reign of Nerva, less than thirty years after the death of Peter himself. They were semi-secret, of course, before our faith was tolerated – especially since they were so central – but nonetheless people have been meeting and praying here ever since. We will bless your mission – just a short service, I promise,' Gwidellius reassured him as Arthur glanced at him apprehensively, 'and then we will proceed to the quarters that have been prepared.'

Arthur nodded and, at Gwidellius's signal, an unseen choir in the further recesses of the church began to intone the Magnificat. The two leaders of Britannia, Church and Commonwealth, moved down the short aisle and knelt before the simple altar. Behind them Arthur's men formed a protective ring, but otherwise let the onlookers crowd into the nave, filling it and craning their necks to get a view. There was not much to see, if truth be told, a simple and private communion while the voices chanted. But it was an astute move by both men. The immediate visit to the church gave Arthur's mission the legitimacy it needed in the eyes of the faithful, and cemented his place in the affections of the few thousands who still scratched a living in the ruins of the old capital and the estates beyond the walls. Arthur's ready accession to Gwidellius's blessing likewise underpinned his authority over the gathering of kings and bishops that was to come.

Myrddin would have disapproved, thought Arthur, as he listened dutifully to the music. Increasingly the Counsellor mistrusted the religion that demanded a monopoly of spiritual expression and outlawed any opinions but those of its elite. It advocated peace, but only on its terms, which these days involved not only the abandonment of any belief other than Christianity, but also of any interpretation of its doctrine that did not accord with the view of those in power. Constantine had legislated for religious tolerance. His sons had begun the process of sidelining other beliefs until finally the bishops had turned the tables on Honorius and only allowed him to remain as emperor with their permission. Now, it seemed, the empire of Claudius had disappeared. Zeno ruled in name only from the edge of Europe, and Odoacer, a Barbarian soldier, ruled Rome from the other side of the country. In Rome itself, only its bishop, Felix, and the senate were left to carry on the pretence. And it was in Felix's gift that Gwidellius held his church in Londinium, not in Zeno's or Odoacer's, and certainly not in Arthur's.

After the ceremony the crowd parted, and they made their way back into the open air. Gwenan, Modlen and the main body of retainers had already been taken to their quarters a few minutes' ride towards the river. Arthur and Gwain were keen to follow, now that the diplomatic protocol had been observed.

'I think you'll like the rooms,' Gwidellius assured him. 'It's the only home in Londinium that still has its bath house working properly – apart from mine, of course.'

'I remember yours from your predecessor's time. It's nearly five years since I wintered here.'

'Ah, yes, I was in Gaul in those days.'

'And so whose place are you taking me to?' asked Arthur.

'It belongs to one of our most prominent men of trade – Flaminius of the Belgae. He owns half the granaries between here and Treverorum.'

'He'll be relieved and even richer after this harvest, I think.'

'I doubt it. Flaminius does well in the poor years. Prices are higher and everybody needs him more. He's not a man known for his Christian duty, sadly.'

'Is he there? I hope he will not be inconvenienced.'

'No, don't worry. If he's in the country at all at this time of year he'll be based at his villa on the road to Durobrivae so he can keep an eye on his stocks after the harvest – building warehouses out of reach of Barbarian raiders, if he's got any sense. But he keeps a good house, you'll see: just down to the left here.'

As they moved towards the river the houses became smaller and more closely bunched together, often with thatched shelters leaning out on to the street. The orchards and smallholdings that had surrounded the houses closer to the walls gave way to the open fronts of tradesmen – metalworkers and bakers, cloth merchants and weavers. Gwain even spotted a tavern with wine jars from Gaul, and promised himself the time to visit it as soon as his duties were over for the day. Londinium was one of the very few places in the country where you could still use coins minted under the emperors (or those who called themselves emperors) to pay for such things – especially the luxuries that were no longer made at home. There were enough visitors from across the sea to make the owners happy to carry on in the old ways. Unlike Arthur, they were unlikely themselves to venture much beyond the walls of Londinium. Why bother? They were safe, and rich in ways that nobody else in modern Britannia valued, so they were unlikely to be robbed of their eccentric wealth.

Soon Arthur and his escorts were turning left on to the road that led to the east, and the oldest gate of the city. A high wall bounded them on the right. In its centre sturdy gates were hanging open, and Gwidellius ushered Arthur through.

'Flaminius likes his privacy,' the Bishop smiled. 'I thought it might suit you too.'

'Indeed it will. Very thoughtful of you.'

'There will be petitioners, of course.'

'Of course, but I shall see none of them until tomorrow at the earliest, preferably the next day. For today I want to wash off the road and eat something that has not been cooked on a campfire. Gwidellius, I will ask you to come here again in the morning. We have a lot to attend to if this Council is to happen as I wish, and there's not much time, I'm afraid. I hope I can count on your support?'

'And that of the Lord,' the Bishop assured him.

'That will be welcome too, of course,' he said, and a smile twitched at the side of his mouth. 'I suspect I may need it.'

Gwidellius made the sign of the cross and wheeled his horse round in the wide courtyard. Only once he and his three monks had ridden through the gates and they were firmly shut behind them did Arthur dismount and hand the reins to his groom. Gwain and the others followed suit.

They walked through the portico of the house into a fine hall with a marble floor and in its centre a mosaic of a seascape – a great ship (perhaps the one Flaminius would have liked to own) surrounded by monsters and maidens in amiable confusion.

Arthur strode across it with barely a glance, dismissed Gwain and his officers to their duties and hurried to the smaller room beyond. There Gwenan, dressed in clean white linen sewn with red and gold flowers, stood in front of a rich green couch. Her light-brown hair had been braided. Arthur gathered her in his arms and hugged her gently – ever since her wound he had treated her as though she was made of thin glass, something she knew was kind, but which also made her worried that he thought she was too fragile to be his lover.

'You've found some perfume,' he whispered, kissing her hair.

She laughed. 'And you haven't. You smell of horse and dirty wool. I'll take you to your room and then I'm going to make you discover our host's wonderful bath. Modlen and I already have. It even has a hot pool, and the sweetest pair of Frankish slave girls, who are going to wash you – and only wash you,' she teased.

Arthur pretended to look disappointed and buried his face against Gwenan's neck. 'I thought you'd be doing that for me,' he said.

'No thanks. I'll be making sure the food is ready when you're clean, and then I'm going to explore this place before you start on business with Gwain again.'

'You've looked around?'

'Only a little – but enough to know I never want to leave.'

'That could be a problem.'

She stroked his beard, untrimmed since they had left Ebvracum. 'Not this month, it won't be.'

Gwenan took his hand and led him through a large living room and into an open courtyard. On the far side she kissed him and handed him into the care of two smart servants, who ushered the way into the disrobing room of the bath house. Soon he was stripped and washed. Once the worst of the dirt had been sluiced away he was ready for the warm luxury of the main bath where, as promised, two tall and blonde girls were ready with all the scents and ointments, combs, razors and scrapers of their trade. Arthur succumbed happily, feeling like a civilised man for the first time since he had ridden out of Ebvracum. No doubt his pleasure would have confirmed all the suspicions of his more radical and impatient kings – that the Overlord of Britannia, having been brought up in the care of Myrddin, was more Roman than Britannian – Roman in ways that they thought should have been stamped out sixty years before. As he slipped into the warm water and let the girls massage his tense limbs, Arthur couldn't have cared less.

And it was a feeling that lasted all through the long early autumn afternoon and evening, as he strolled on Gwenan's arm through the carefully tended terraced gardens that guided them between walls and fountains, rose hedges and fruit trees down to the river, and as they gazed across the water, watching the ferry ply back and forth just downstream of where the great bridge had once carried all the traffic to the road between the marshes on the Cantiacan shore.

XX

IN THE FAR NORTH-EAST CORNER of Londinium sat the great square enclosure that had held the barracks for the Imperial Governor of Britannia's Guards in the days before the province had been the breeding ground of a rebel once too often and been split into four, in theory less significant, portions. In the event, nothing had changed. Britannia had always bred rebels from among its legions – men who mistook their island fame for the right to rule the world. Only Constantine I had succeeded, but that had not stopped another century's worth of deluded or unwilling adventurers from making the attempt. Britannia had always believed itself to be more central to the future of the world than the world had ever been able to accept, or even take seriously.

Imperial pretenders and governors relied on their version of the Praetorian Guard just as much as the emperors themselves, and their lodgings in Londinium were sumptuous in comparison with any others that did not have the status of legionary headquarters. Of its fine facilities only a few rotting huts and the sorry walls of the commander's once-splendid house remained, its paint peeling and bubbling as the water trickled down from the all too obvious holes where the roof tiles had slipped away and smashed. The Bishop still needed troops of his own, of course, but not so many that those on duty could not be accommodated in his own small palace. The others simply went home to their families when not required, living in the city still but tilling the smallholdings that had crept across the spaces where once the town houses of the bustling metropolis had stood.

The old fort had not been properly used since a brief year or two in Vortigern's time nearly fifty years earlier. After that the army, just like many of the citizens, had fled the plague to smaller and safer villages outside the city and, though some had returned as the years went on, the fort itself had been left to the rabbits. Nonetheless, with six weeks' notice, and despite the demands of one of the best harvests for a decade or more, Gwidellius had been able to find enough idle hands and willing craftsmen to transform the grounds from dilapidated camp to places for six hundred men, their kings' pavilions and the hall that would hold the meetings of the Council itself. Each king had been asked to limit his retainers to twenty-five, but not even the ever-optimistic Arthur expected them to comply.

Gwain and Arthur had discussed long and hard while they were still in Ebvracum whether the kings should all be so close together in one place, rather than spread through houses in the city. Keeping them within walking distance of each other might be a recipe for strife – or worse, faction building. It would also make them easier to keep an eye on, however, without making the spying by Arthur's men too obvious beyond what would be expected. It would also negate a simmering cultural divide. There were a few kings, mainly from the south, who – like Arthur and Myrddin – preferred to maintain the standards and comforts of earlier times in houses with solid brick walls. But there were others – one of the most extreme had been Vortebelos – who rejected everything associated with the empire that had betrayed their grandfathers. Now, though they rejected the Barbarians' language and gods, they shared their fashion for halls of timber and thatch. They also shared a distrust of the fastidiousness appreciated by the New Romans, as they mockingly dubbed Arthur and his sort, considering it effeminate. Their hardier dwellings were more practical, it was acknowledged, in an age when tiles and dressed stone was only to be had by ripping down old buildings and only the kings themselves had enough slaves and servants to keep the fires in the old houses burning and the kitchens stocked with plates and sauces. In the interest of unity and intelligence, therefore, Arthur had decided that everybody (including himself, if only for the actual days of the Council) would live in pavilions of equal size and luxury, placed carefully in a wide circle around the meeting hall.

A circle was to be the symbol of the Council itself. Again they had argued fiercely to that conclusion. Myrddin, before he left for Moridunum, had been its proposer. At first, though, Arthur had talked about a long table, with himself at the centre, facing an audience of the elders and counsellors of the nations.

'Dangerous and impractical!' Myrddin had retorted, pointing out that the protocol of seniority would be impossible to decide without causing major resentment, quite apart from the idiotic idea of letting such a large and influential public eavesdrop on the workings of the Council. The invitation for each king to play the fool to his men and try to hijack the debate would be irresistible. Gwain had then advocated a square arrangement, with Arthur, Myrddin and the bishops of Ebvracum and Londinium each taking a side. Even if the majority of the retainers were excluded, it was pointed out, this would still allow the kings to fight over whose side of the table was the most senior.

The answer was obvious, but would require great carpentry, if nothing else, and would test the ingenuity and speed of any of the craftsmen in Britannia. Constructing a round table large enough to seat at least twenty in comfort (by which Arthur meant that no king should be knee to knee or within whispering distance of another) was an unprecedented task. As well as the table itself, chairs would have to be made, since the usual benches would be useless around the table. Chair-making was virtually a lost art, with few joiners attempting more than rough stools and benches. That, however, was what was commissioned, and Gwain had given orders that the craftsmen be found to finish it in time. Substantial rewards of land and animals were offered, but it was made clear by Gwain that the penalties for failure would be as painful as the terms were generous.

Two days after arriving in Londinium, and a week before the Council was due to begin, Arthur was taken by Gwain the short ride across the city to inspect the preparations. On the side a tall gateway had been erected. Inside, the ground was cleared of undergrowth and sheep had mown the grass efficiently as the construction crews moved in. The frames of the pavilions for the delegations were mostly ready, though without the finishing touches of cloth hangings inside or water for the cisterns. The meeting hall was more impressive than Arthur had expected, and was a fine achievement, given the time the men had had to procure the materials from scratch. Unusually for a modern building it was close to being square, with a set of timber pillars supporting the frame for a thatch roof. Two openings on each side allowed light in, but there was only one door visible from the main room, which Arthur would face. He wanted those entering to see him at the head of the table, round or not. The table itself was still a skeleton, but it was already clear that it would be an extraordinary sight, unlike anything seen before in Britannia.

'Oh, very good. Splendid. Splendid. This will shut the bastards up!'

Gwain and Arthur turned in surprise. Myrddin stood in the doorway, rubbing his hands. His clothes were stained with travel after the long ride from Moridunum, and behind him stood his young cousin, Vorteporix II, King of the Demetiae, staring around him in amazement.

'Well, Gwain,' Myrddin continued, 'I see you have everything under control. I'll go and find Gwidellius. I'll lodge with him, I think. I've had enough of tents.' And with that the old counsellor disappeared again.

The King of the Demetiae shrugged in embarrassment and stood peering around him. Arthur grinned, strode forward and gripped his hand. He had been a boy of seven when Arthur had taken the overlord's title, and though they had met fleetingly on one of his visits to Moridunum a few years before, Arthur hadn't seen him since he had succeeded to the kingdom.

'Typical Myrddin, of course,' said Arthur. 'Welcome. You're the first to arrive. But you've had almost the furthest to travel, so that shouldn't be surprising. Gwain will sort you and your men out, though we may have to find you somewhere temporary for a day or so. As you can see, this site is not ready to receive you as you deserve yet. How many men have you brought?'

'Only ten. Just my personal guards,' Vorteporix answered. 'It didn't seem right to take more away from the harvest, now that we have one worth reaping.'

'I can see that. I'm glad you're here, though. It will be useful to have at least one of our number who knows what Myrddin and I are hoping to achieve. Has he told you on the way?'

'Very little.'

'As usual. But that's a relief too. Myrddin's version is not always mine. We'll finish meeting the men working here, and then I hope you'll join me for the afternoon and meet my lady. Depending on your taste you might also like to sample my host's baths. They make Myrddin's place look almost Barbarian.'

The young king agreed readily enough. Arthur had hopes of him. Despite the mistrust that the eastern kingdoms had of the Demetiae – believing them to be half in league with the Hibernians (however many times those from the island to the west raided the coast) – Arthur knew that the Demetian leader was a shrewd diplomat. He had to be. His country would be easy prey for his neighbours otherwise. They might value demonstrable strength over compromise. Arthur knew which he would rather have on his side at a Council.

* * *

Over the following three days the members of the Council, the kings themselves or their deputies, trickled inside the walls of Londinium. Arthur was pleased by the accident that, of the first three to arrive, two, Vorteporix of Demetia and Candidianos of Dobunnia, were among his most reliable allies, though not, it had to be said, likely to be the biggest suppliers of men to any anti-invasion force. Theirs were small kingdoms, and so geographically placed that Barbarian assaults were virtually unheard of. Demetia's problem in the far west was, at it had always been, that Hibernian kings regarded raiding its coast as legitimate sport – an attitude that Vorteporix would admit was entirely mutual.

Arthur was less sure of Catacus of Atrebata, who had only succeeded Eldadus – the man who had given Arthur his Gwenan – in the summer, but he had heard nothing that indicated trouble. The Atrebates in the middle of the south of Britannia had seen off the occasional ship, but they were more troubled by pirates from Gaul and as far south as the coast of Iberia.

If the Dobunnians ever saw a Hibernian or a Barbarian in their comfortable mid-western waters, the chances were that they were thoroughly lost and half-starving by the time they had reached the tidal waters of the Sabrina. The Dobunni were far more concerned with the attitude of their powerful neighbours – in Siluria, Cornovia and Catuvellaunia, all of whom coveted the rich lands that lay along the riverbanks and around their ancient cities of Glevum and Corinium. Candidianos was disgusted, but not in the least surprised, when he met Modlen and heard about the brutality with which she had been treated by Cunorix.

Badoc of Siluria, the king who governed the territory between Vorteporix and Candidianos, was the next to arrive, and the first to disobey the injunction to bring as few men as possible. He arrived with virtually a minor garrison, and was nonplussed when he was shown to his incommodious pavilion, while the majority of his men were ordered by an unimpressed Gwidellius to pitch camp as best they could outside the walls. Candidianos remarked acidly there that must have been nobody left to pick the apples within thirty miles of Isca. The taverns and the women by the Londinium waterside would be doing good enough business over the coming week. Indeed, the population of the town had started to grow as soon as word of the Council spread. It would be a rare opportunity to take goods from bored troops. The last thing Gwidellius wanted was unemployed armies planting themselves within convenient staggering distance after dark and the city's gates closed with them inside.

Gwidellius was especially disconcerted that Badoc had brought with him Dubricius, the long-serving Bishop of Isca Siluria, perhaps in an attempt to assert the west's claims to ecclesiastical primacy. It was a discussion Gwidellius had every intention of avoiding, and he demonstrated the solidarity of the Church by immediately asking Dubricius to join him and Myrddin in his palace and to assist him at the ceremonial Mass with which he planned to open the Council.

Badoc's arrival stretched the hospitality of the remaining fine houses of Londinium beyond their capacity to treat the visiting kings equally, so, in the interests of diplomacy, the three who had turned up early were gently eased out of their comfortable lodgings and asked to take their places in the Council enclosure. Arthur reluctantly followed them, leaving Gwenan the facilities of the merchant's mansion to herself.

Gwain's cousin, Caldoros of Dumnonia, in the furthest and wildest south-west, trudged in soon afterwards, complaining loudly of the

CHAPTER XX

inconvenience of Londinium and wanting to know what was wrong with holding Councils in either the Atrebatan centre at Calleva or the Dobunni's at Corinium, both three days nearer home for him. The Dumnonian King was not only Gwain's first cousin, he was (if Myrddin's theory of Arthur's parentage was to be believed – and it had to be, otherwise his right to hold the overlordship was tenuous in the extreme) also Arthur's nephew, thanks to the illicit relationship between Uther Pendraeg and Caldoros's grandmother Ygraen – though even now the exact circumstances of Arthur's conception were secret. It was still conveniently assumed that she and Uther had first made love many weeks after Gorlois's death.

Caldoros's arrival gave Arthur the peculiar opportunity to hold what amounted to a regional summit before the Council began. For a day or so he had almost complete representation from the south-west of Britannia, but nobody from the rest of the island. He used it to the full. Although the four men he had with him had so far been only marginally affected by Barbarian raiding, many of whom were more lost than invasive, they also had come to enjoy the relative calm that their nations had felt during all of Arthur's period in office. Theirs were not the richest, or even the most populous, kingdoms, but they were Arthur, Gwain and Myrddin's homelands. Bishop Gwidellius complained that once they all started to talk fast together he could barely understand them, as their accents strengthened. By the time the next delegates arrived, Arthur had solid support for the positions he would take in the Council, and a useful promise from Caldoros to send a preparatory mission across the sea to their cousin Heol of Armorica. A treaty of mutual help that actually delivered, it could be make all the difference either against Barbarians, or against any of those in Britannia who decided that Arthur was an inconvenience.

From the furthest north before Hadrian's Wall the King of the Carvetii straggled in, almost incognito. He had travelled with justified nervousness through Brigantia, anxious not to draw attention to himself. He at least would not stretch Gwidellius's hospitality.

The Deceangelian King sent an envoy with his apologies, citing the danger to his coast from Hibernians, but, Arthur suspected, in reality taking the chance that his more powerful neighbours from Segontium and Viroconium would be attending, so giving himself some much-needed political breathing space. Arthur welcomed his envoy effusively

– he could afford to, since he knew that he would soon be negotiating the end of independence for the little kingdom.

The Parisi, similarly small and threatened on the other side of the country, nevertheless sent a full detachment. The garrison that Arthur had left in Ebvracum, on the edge of their lands, along with the demise of Vortebelos, gave them a certain degree of confidence. Perhaps of all the kingdoms, too, they stood most to gain from a successful Council, for their relative weakness in numbers, their long, flat coastline and the welcoming estuary of the Abus were as tempting as ever to Barbarian ships, despite Arthur's decisive victory on that shore only a few months earlier.

With two days before the Council's opening and with delegations arriving every few hours (the kings of the Trinovantes and the Cantiaci – the closest to Londinium – managed to turn up at the entrance at exactly the same time, leading to a mild diplomatic crisis), Arthur was now based firmly in his field pavilion. A few weeks earlier Gwenan would have expected to be at his side as each of the dignitaries rode in, but she had changed. She was still desperately tired, of course, from the effects of the wound and the long journey from Ebvracum. There was a deeper reason, though. She was somehow more self-contained and content not to be paraded as Arthur's consort, more concerned that her love for him not be mistaken as a desire for status and a place in the hierarchy of Britannia.

Coming from either Viroconium or Deva, Cunegnus would have had to pass Cunorix on the road somewhere. Myrddin and Gwain both laughed at the possibilities. Cunorix could just wave his Cornovian rival through or make an elaborate gesture of blocking the way so that he could arrive in Londinium first. Neither proved to be the case. Cunegnus turned up on the morning before the opening and swore that neither he nor his scouts had seen any sign of the Catuvellaunian King, even though he ridden straight through Verulamium.

Sure enough, Cunorix's sense of theatre prevailed. He waited pompously for an hour in the evening outside the north gate of the city until Gwidellius had come personally to meet him, as he had done Arthur. On the way Cunorix had swept up not Cunegnus but young Tegernacus of the Coritani, for whom this would be his first Council. Three days out from Ratae, the new king would have had little option but to accept his neighbour's company for the rest of the journey.

CHAPTER XX

The message was clear enough. The interests of the Coritani and the Catuvellauni, between them controlling most of the central lands of Britannia, were united, and Cunorix was very definitely the senior partner. With dusk setting in, their torch-lit entrance to the Council grounds was dramatic. As the last to appear, they were greeted outside the Table Hall by all the assembled kings, as if the whole assembly had been a poor show until Cunorix had completed it.

Arthur could hardly contain his irritation. Yet as he knew (and as Myrddin warned him firmly), that was precisely what the wily King Cunorix wanted. Any display of annoyance would make Arthur look as if he was setting himself above the kings, his electorate. However, to be seen waiting in a line for Cunorix to ride through the gates would just confirm the man's assumed status. Taking his counsellor's advice, Arthur crossed the city in the opposite direction and spent a few hours with Modlen, Gwenan and Myrddin – supposedly discussing tactics for the morning. In practice he spent barely an hour with Myrddin, another with Modlen – her role would be crucial, but it was important that she stayed clear of her old tormentor – and three with Gwenan and the expert assistants in the bath house. Cunorix could settle himself in without the pleasure of Arthur's welcome.

They would meet during the course of the evening anyway, but in circumstances that Cunorix would not be able to steal for his own purposes. Gwidellius was holding a pre-Council dinner in his palace for all the members – a chance to show off the hospitality of the Roman Church, emphasise the superiority of his claims through the grandeur of his apartments and bring the kings across town in a group as equals. There was the added justification that the evening promised rain and a chill wind, and the palace had a tile roof that was likely to provide more comfort than the thatch of the temporary pavilions, and kitchens that could produce a far better dinner. There might be growing resistance among the people to the old-fashioned ways and manners, but when it came to a formal banquet even the most radical king was prepared to exchange ideology for fine food. Vortebelos would have been the exception – but Vortebelos was dead, and his kingdom of Brigantia was too divided to have elected a successor or send a delegation.

So it was that Arthur stood with Gwidellius in the entrance of the Bishop's Palace, warmly embracing each of the kings in the party – two symbols, temporal and spiritual, of the unity of Britannia.

XXI

THE FIRST DAY of the Grand Council of Britannia, called by Arthur with a pomp that had not happened since his own election years earlier, opened in a Friday downpour – a late-September deluge testing the work of the thatchers to the full and seeping through the wicker walls of the temporary buildings. The pavilions, like the seats at the great table, were arranged in a circle around the main meeting hall, but even the couple of dozen paces from pavilion to hall was enough to leave hair and clothes sopping. The kings, some with serious hangovers, did their best to retain their dignity and not to be seen to scurry across the grass, which was fast turning to mud. They had been summoned by Gwidellius's trumpeters, adding injury to already sensitive heads.

Inside the hall three hearths had been set, diagonally placed so that nobody would be too close to the draught from the door. Each was tended by one of Arthur's most trusted men (he didn't want the sordid machinations of the Council to be reported to the outside world by casual servants), who fought a dogged but losing battle against the smoke, continually blown back in by the equally determined wind. The smoke was better than the chill and wet, though, and after being greeted formally by Arthur at the door, the kings were quick to gather by the fires and let the water steam out of their woollen tunics as they stared in amazement at the huge table that filled most of the space.

Gwain bustled about, showing each of them to their place. Even given its gigantic size, there was only room at the table for the kings themselves to sit in comfort. Their advisers, limited to one each (Myrddin had wanted to exclude even them, but Arthur pointed out that would mean Myrddin himself would have to stay outside, or at least out of sight), were perched on stools behind them. On the table were set jugs of hot mulled ale and wooden platters of honeyed cakes, and each king was assigned a specially commissioned goblet, made by Londinium's finest silversmith. This Council, Arthur determined, was not to be remembered as a routine affair.

The circle of the table was divided into four segments, so that no king was directly opposite Arthur. He was to sit with his back to the curtain that squared off the space. Patrolling the first quarter to his right was Myrddin. Directly across the table Bishop Dubricius officiated. The quarter to Arthur's left, closest to the door, was headed by Gwidellius. The kings were so arranged that none sat next to one whose domain was geographically adjacent (as Myrddin had rather pompously described it when drawing up the seating plan) – almost everybody had one territorial dispute or other, and those that didn't would have been equally keen not to be seen to be put in a supporting subsidiary position to a more vocal neighbour.

There were two seats vacant by the time everyone had found their places. Immediately to Dubricius's left (as far from Arthur as possible) a space was left for the new King of the Brigantes. Since there was yet no agreement on who that should be, nobody from the north had turned up. Myrddin had guessed the ruling houses would either all send someone or decide not to recognise Arthur's right to summon them after killing Vortebelos and ignore the event entirely. The latter seemed to be the decision.

The second seat was more mystifying. Corbalengus of the Ordovices, from the mountains in the far west, was usually to be relied upon to arrive early and loudly. Speculation ranged from concerns that he had been ambushed on the way (a suggestion refuted vehemently by the four leaders whose kingdoms he would have had to cross) to the more cynical suggestion that he intended to use the period of the Council to make an alliance with the Hibernians and carve himself another slice of Vorteporix's land. That was the more popular view, though Arthur suspected it reflected their general nervousness at being away from their courts for so long, rather than any real intelligence about Corbalengus's dubious intentions. Either way, Arthur would have much preferred the Ordovician leader to have been at the table. Since his mission immediately after the Council was to rearrange the political map of that region, Arthur wanted all the relevant players on hand to build up the spirit of unity that he knew was going to be sorely tested by his plans.

The trusted men came and went, refreshing the jugs with warmer ones and plates of food from behind the curtain at Arthur's back. On the other side sat Modlen with a stack of waxed wooden tablets and a collection of sharp styluses. She had no wish to be seen in the same room as Cunorix, and Arthur and Myrddin had a strong, though not equal, objection to the Council knowing that a written record was being kept. The objection was not to the record itself — it would be normal practice anywhere for the debate to be reported — but to the writing. There were several of the kings who distrusted such 'imperial' practices, partly for the reason that they were illiterate and had no Latin themselves, but mainly because they distrusted those whom they knew could write — churchmen, those who had been brought up in cities, or (far worse) those who had learnt their craft outside the island, like Myrddin. The Council would therefore be recorded privately for Arthur's close circle, rough notes on wax taken by Modlen on the day and written up as a summary on vellum afterwards and archived by Gwidellius, with copies for the library in the palace at Ebvracum and, unofficially, for Myrddin's own shelves in Moridunum.

For the kings and their public, proceedings were conducted rather differently. Next to Candidianos sat his official bard, designated by agreement as the composer of the record. He would listen and encapsulate each royal contribution in heroic verse, commit it to memory as it was spoken at the end of the day's session and, later that evening, recite it to his apprentices and colleagues, who would carry the words back to the courts of the individual nations.

The bishops disapproved of the bards and their practice, accusing it of relying on the traditions of the old religions and on the continuing skills of the reciters. What happened, they argued, if the bards were killed or simply grew old and forgot before they passed the record on?

The retort had equal validity. What happened to the record if Christianity waned, the Barbarians who had their own gods won and burned the libraries, and Latin was forgotten too? Nothing was certain, they pointed out, and they would rather put their trust in the stories of men and their skills for telling them than in the unread pages and unreadable writing of a dying civilisation.

So it was that the Council was called to order and its roll call of kings and bishops, its purposes and dignities, its significance and grandeur, were declaimed by the bard, moving round the table to stand behind

CHAPTER XXI

each as his achievements were recited. The memories and decisions of earlier Councils were recalled, going back beyond Arthur to Uther Pendraeg and his predecessor Aurelius Ambrosius. This Council was, however, to be among the greatest – to be remembered ever as the moment when all Britannia south of the Roman wall came together and showed that this land was not for taking by those beyond the seas, from whichever direction and homeland they sailed. An attack on one would be an attack on all. The great circular table itself became the symbol of their equality and unity, their brotherhood and common purpose. Just as a wheel turned, so whoever was speaking was at the head of the table.

For once, Arthur conceded, he couldn't have summed up the principal reasons for meeting, nor the mood he hoped would prevail, better himself. There was an appreciative silence as everybody came back from the flying rhythms and lofty syntax of the bard's elegant Brythonic and relaxed back into ordinary – or at least ordinary regal – talk.

Arthur added thanks to Gwidellius and his men for their hard work in a short time that had gone into preparing the Council grounds, and for the lavishness of his hospitality the night before. He could tell, by the expressions he saw around him, that everybody had enjoyed themselves and was now ready (he paused and smiled as he looked at the unusually pale faces, a few already resting heads on hands, as though to keep them from rolling off) to deal with the issues to which their excellent bard had so skilfully referred.

There was a grumble from across the room, close to Bishop Dubricius.

'If I may, Tygern Fawr?'

Arthur nodded and frowned. He was surprised to be interrupted so soon. The culprit was Cunegnus of Cornovia.

'Thank you. Such an opportunity to confer with each other – all together, so that there are no misunderstandings – is, of course, welcome. It gives us all a chance to know each other better. But Arthur, we've all come a long way, and a few of us wonder if it's all really necessary. After all, you – and I mean you and those members here who brought their own men to the cause – defeated the last incursion on the east coast only a few months ago, and that message will have reached back across the sea by now. And in the time since, many of us have had the pleasure of your company to discuss strategy with you face to face in our own halls. So why now – and why all the way to Londinium?'

Arthur frowned and fiddled with a piece of cake. 'It's a valid question,' he said, looking across at Myrddin, who was unhelpfully staring at the roof.

Cunegnus nodded. 'I'm glad you think so.'

'Londinium for two reasons,' Arthur began, after taking a moment to gauge the mood. Many of the kings were nodding in agreement with the Cornovian. 'And I hope nobody here will be insulted. The first is because it is under the authority of Bishop Gwidellius, and so is neutral for all of us. We can therefore leave any concerns about our relative status outside the walls. The second is that, thanks to his generosity, it means that no single nation has been put to the trouble and expense of preparing such an important gathering.'

'Very good of him, I'm sure,' muttered Cunorix, 'but one or two of us could have managed well enough, given a bit more notice.'

Arthur ignored him and addressed Cunegnus again. 'And I called the Council now because the matters we are to discuss cannot wait until after the winter – nor could they have been discussed properly by all of us until I was sure such discussions would be fruitful.'

'Good God, listen to the man,' Cunorix stage-whispered to the Carvetian King on his left. 'How can he call himself a warrior and talk like a tax collector?'

'There's a time and a place for both,' observed Arthur irritably.

'Ah, but how will we know which is which with you? It seems we must be careful – or, like Vortebelos,' he gestured to the empty chair, 'we might get it wrong.'

Arthur held Cunorix's gaze, and his own expression hardened. 'Precisely.'

The two stared at each other, neither wanting to be faced down. The silence around the table would have been uncomfortable, except that the kings were too interested in which of the two would compromise and try to move the discussion on. They knew that moment would shape the outcome of the next two days – and of the years to follow. If Cunorix could dominate Arthur then he would soon dominate the island, or have to be removed by force, like the Brigantian.

Cunegnus saw the danger. The last thing he wanted was Cunorix to win that particular tussle – or any other, for that matter. He stepped in adroitly.

CHAPTER XXI

'Well, I think that answers both my questions very fairly, Arthur. I think it is important that all of us have the same understanding of your reasons. I hope you will not take my intervention as criticism, and I can assure you that we have all been impressed by and grateful for the welcome we have received here in Londinium, difficult as the journey has been for some.'

'Of course,' smiled a relieved Arthur, 'and I cannot adequately tell you how much I appreciate the sacrifices you have all made to attend – or indeed how important I believe this Council will prove to be in years to come.'

'So,' Badoc of Siluria chipped in, 'perhaps the Overlord could give us an idea of what these vital matters are, and what he intends to do about them?'

'Thank you,' said Arthur. 'What I intend to do is, of course, irrelevant if you all tell me otherwise.'

'Naturally,' agreed Badoc, without sounding as if he believed Arthur for a minute.

Arthur continued. 'We have all seen what the Barbarians can do. We also all know that we are effectively surrounded. Beyond the wall our cousins and those to the north of them will not attack us alone, but they will take advantage of any lapse in our vigilance to keep us weak.'

The Carvetian King snorted. 'It's a bit more serious than that if you are between them – Brigantia and the Hibernians – every day.'

'We understand that,' continued Arthur. 'Hibernia also continues to be a threat to all on our western coasts, and their kingdoms' pleasure at allying with any forces that are against us, almost as though it was play, helps no one.'

Vorteporix stepped in. 'I've tried to make peace with them, especially since we have kinsmen in common…'

'And it shows,' taunted Badoc.

'But no treaty lasts for long. And if you ask for an explanation or threaten the hostages after an assault, there's always an apology and some nonsense about their kings not having the authority to control local clans. Load of bollocks, of course.'

'The Church there's no help, either,' Dubricius pointed out. 'Far too independent for any good to come of it – and this Bishop Padrig has the nerve to send letters to Rome complaining about us!'

'As I was saying,' said Arthur, regaining the initiative. 'We are surrounded by more than water. While our good cousin Heol does much to guard the ocean approaches, he is even more beset than us at times. Not all Barbarians come across the sea.'

'And some,' Gwidellius pointed out, 'have even agreed to become Christians.'

'As if that is enough to excuse invasion and plunder. Heol has been attacked from the east as though the old Gaul had disappeared.'

'Goths,' announced Myrddin, 'Goths and Franks. Half of them seem to be Caesars these days.'

'Quite,' Arthur continued. He was beginning to wonder whether everybody was going to interrupt him. 'And then there are the seaborne privateers, who not only make life difficult for Caldoros and Catacus, they've even been known to disturb Myrddin's wine merchant.'

'I suppose you think that's funny,' the old counsellor grumbled. He was answered by the first laughter of the morning. 'You like my wine well enough, Arthur – or at least you do when you can be bothered to turn up for some.'

'No, you're right. It's serious business. It's not only the flow of wine that's being interrupted. We are in danger of losing trade that has been the difference between prosperity and mere survival for hundreds of years. Which brings me back to our eastern coasts and the "settlers", as they like to call themselves. I have no objection to anybody settling in Britannia, if they respect us and do so with our permission. We have plenty of land and too many forests. But coming to live here is one thing. Doing it with hundreds of men at a time, using swords instead of silver, is another. And once they are here, very few of them can be bothered to learn Brythonic.'

'Or abandon their absurd gods for the one true Father,' invoked Gwidellius. Myrddin did his best not to even look as if he wanted to argue, but it was a struggle.

Arthur continued his catalogue of complaint against those who took land by force or infiltrated. He was careful not to allude to his own greatest reason for disliking them – their complete ignorance of and disregard for the fine parts of the old culture. He didn't mention it because he knew that it was the one point on which many of the men around the table would agree with the new immigrants.

Instead he ended his argument with an issue that he knew would be close to their hearts – or in their case an even more sensitive spot, their insecure vanity.

'All of this is mere irritation,' he said, 'in comparison with the real threat. They refuse – no, worse – they laugh when, after they have built their farms and cleared the land, set up their shrines and taken women, we require their cooperation and loyalty. They keep their own kings across the sea. They look down on you, on us, as conquered people, as though we have merely been keeping the land warm for them until they arrived. They are amazed that we do not bow down before the gods and their chieftains, that we do not welcome them as naturally superior, abandon our language and admit that they do everything better and more efficiently than us. Council, they treat you with disdain. That is why we have to fight them from our shores – before they land and infect the dignity of our politics which even every emperor from Vespasian onwards respected. This is our heritage over half a millennium. It is not to be mutilated by opportunists and adventurers, however difficult life may be for their people at home.

Arthur stopped and looked around the table. There was silence – a good sign – and outside the rain had eased. Gwain's men moved to pile more wood on the fires.

'We will continue these discussions as soon as we have brought life back to our legs,' he smiled. 'These chairs may be freshly built, but they are not stuffed with feathers.'

He stood up and moved round to where Dubricius was pushing back his chair and stretching. Arthur didn't want to be dragged into any conversation he did not control this early in the day. He put his hand on the Bishop's right shoulder.

'A word, Father, if I may.'

'Of course,' Dubricius assented, easing himself to his feet.

'Tell me about my own country. Is all well there? I only hear very distant reports or talk amongst kings. How is my brother?'

'Ah,' the Bishop cleared his throat, 'of course it is in my diocese, but not, shall we say, in a part I visit very often. Caradoc is pleasant enough when I meet him, though keen that I shouldn't mistake acknowledging me with any kind of fealty to Badoc. He is in an interesting place, you know – and he accepts the authority of none of those around this table. Perhaps he does so rather more noisily than your father – I mean, your guardian…'

Arthur reassured him, 'Idriseg has always been the only father I have known. How is he?'

Dubricius looked solemn. 'He's not well, Arthur. I've been told he can hardly walk. You should visit him.'

'Yes, you're right. I should. But—'

'I know, you are busy. He will not be with us long, though, I'm afraid. And Caradoc could do with your guidance.'

Arthur laughed. 'He might need it, but I very much doubt if he'd take it. Caradoc has never quite come to terms with what I have become.'

'Nevertheless, I think you should go. Elfael was your home, and it may need to be again one day. The people there will think better of you if you go to see them and Idriseg again, whatever views Caradoc has on your title.'

Arthur looked into the fire for a moment. 'What do you mean, "It may need to be again"?'

Dubricius shrugged and his eyes took in the kings gathered into little groups or conferring with their men.

'You're probably right,' Arthur admitted reluctantly. 'I'll do what I can.'

'Soon. Before winter.'

'Oh, you can be sure of that. I know those hills in winter too well to try to travel around them when I'm in a hurry. Thank you, Father – you give good advice.'

The churchman smiled. 'So I should. It's all I have to give.'

Arthur moved away now the kings were established in other conversations. He parted the curtains across the door and went out into the damp morning.

He turned left, waved at the guards and walked round the side of the hall as though he was going to the separate latrine area. Instead he cut into the small door used by the servants to bring food into the building. Modlen was standing behind the dividing curtain, stretching. She turned and raised her eyebrows in surprise. Arthur came over and gave her a comradely hug.

'How's it going?' he asked softly, almost a whisper.

She shrugged and moved her head from side to side.

'Cold?'

CHAPTER XXI

Modlen nodded.

'I'll ask Gwain to get you a cloak. You're too far from the fire.' He held her chilled hands. 'It doesn't make writing any easier. Do you have any notes I need to see now?'

Modlen shook her head and turned to her piles of tablets. There were two in one and a full stack in the other. She picked up the two that she had already used and handed them to Arthur.

'Not much on them. Did we really say so little of lasting importance?'

Modlen looked up at Arthur and smiled, though her eyes hardened. She pointed to a few lines of scrawled text.

'Yes, well, you're probably right – but I hope you took down some of what I said about the threats. It will be necessary to have the reasoning clearly set down somewhere before the bards get hold of it. Their version will sound better, but may drift some way from the truth.'

Modlen held her finger to her lips. Arthur gave back the tablets and stroked her face.

'You know what you're doing. I don't doubt you.' He kissed her head gently. 'Half of me would rather be in here with you and let Myrddin negotiate, but they'd never put up with it. Oh well – back to it, then.'

Modlen squeezed his hand and gave him a push towards the door as one of the serving men came through the curtain. For a moment he paused in surprise at the sight of Arthur there, but gathered himself together and followed the Overlord out of the door with only a slight surreptitious glance at Modlen, who was already sitting down again and finding a fresh tablet.

Arthur retraced his steps to the front of the hall and signalled to the herald to sound his trumpet. Without speaking to anybody, and ignoring Myrddin's inquisitory glare, but with an occasional friendly tap on shoulders as he passed, he strode to his chair and sat down, looking around him patiently as the members straggled in and took their places. For this second session of the Council he intended to let them have their head, get their complaints and suspicions out in the open. Apart from deflecting any divisive accusations, he would stay out of the discussion as much as possible. He had learnt well from Myrddin over the years. Influence on the outcome depended not on how much he said but when he chose to say it.

Finally everybody was seated. Their attention turned with expectation towards Arthur.

'I hope we've all had time to reflect and refresh,' he said, giving the impression that he was gathering his thoughts, but in fact making his pre-planned agenda seem spontaneous. 'I'd like us to spend a while giving each other an accurate picture of the difficulties we face – and I hope everyone will feel able to contribute.'

There was a murmur of approval and a few throats were cleared ready to butt in, but Arthur had no intention of letting them have a free-for-all with the most powerful and the loudest carrying the morning. He was also determined that he should start and finish with an ally who had been well briefed, rather than letting a doubtful supporter like Cunorix have the final say. That meant, he calculated, eyeing the assembly, starting and ending either side of Bishop Gwidellius. It was a good move, he decided. Since Londinium's bishop was sitting directly opposite, nobody could accuse Arthur of whispering a conclusion. And on the Bishop's right sat Caldoros of Dumnonia; to his left Candidianos of the Dobunni.

'The great advantage of a circular table,' Arthur continued, 'is that there is no order of merit for our discussions, and we can go round it in turn. Perhaps, Caldoros, you would like to set the scene that faces you each day.'

Caldoros looked surprised, but nodded and began confidently.

XXII

CANDIDIANOS FINISHED OFF the round of description with a calm summary of the problems of his country – which were, he suggested, more economic than military or political (he looked pointedly at some of those who had spoken before him). While this left the Dobunni in a secure position to mediate in any disputes – and, like Arthur, he put his talents at the Council's service – nonetheless it did limit his ability to match words with forces. For this he apologised.

It was not quite the ringing promise Arthur had hoped for – however, it was a great deal better than some of the fractious and occasionally downright abusive remarks that had gone before. Even with the hospitality, the circular table and the solemnity of the occasion, there were those whose frustration, ambition and insecurity made it hard to keep a civil tongue in their heads. Arthur had not realised that there was quite such a depth of feeling between the Iceni and the Coritani, for example. He would have thought that the wetlands that separated them would have prevented too much tension. Apparently, though, the Iceni — never the strongest nation — resented the relative strength of Coritania at a time when they felt they were bearing the brunt of Barbarian raids. The rant of the Deceangelian envoy against the Ordovices was more predictable, especially since he could speak freely in his neighbour's absence. It made the plan Arthur had discussed with Cunegnus even more urgent. It also looked as though he would have to travel in that direction as soon as the Council was over, since his intention to bring the three leaders together during it had been denied.

He was wondering how to bring the morning to a close. If he spoke at any length it would enable the more competitive kings to claim that he was abusing his position by ignoring their complaints and ploughing on with his own agenda. He thought of bringing in Myrddin, but if the likes of Cunorix had a problem with Arthur's attempts at manipulation, then their feelings about Myrddin's influence were explosive.

Across the table Bishop Gwidellius raised his fingers; it was hard to tell whether in benediction or the desire to speak. To Arthur's relief it turned out that they came to the same thing. Gwidellius set off on a long and idealistic homily on regal duty, its relation to the people, to the land of Britannia and the mistakes of recent history. If kings had a tendency to like the sound of their own voices, Arthur reflected to himself, they were nothing to churchmen. Neither were used to being told to bring their remarks to a close. Nevertheless, that was what Arthur did, waiting first until he could see serious shuffling and glazed expressions round the table.

All fire had gone out of the meeting, and the members were looking desperate to move and eat. From the Overlord's point of view things could not have gone better. He interrupted the Bishop in mid cadence and thanked him for the excellence of his advice and the timeliness of his reminders, and announced that food was waiting for them in their own quarters. They would reconvene, as usual, at the third trumpet call.

* * *

After the resumption Arthur steered the debate on to as dull ground as he could dream up, asking for reports from everyone on the state of the harvest and the roads – a subject on which Arthur claimed, to laughter, that he was more expert than any of them. He asked for reports of who of note had died, incidences of disease, whether farms were being abandoned or towns deserted. There had been nothing to match the wholesale plagues of forty years before, but it was clear there were still isolated pockets of sickness about, especially in those places where the recent wet summers had damaged crops and lowered even wealthy people's resistance during the winter. Myrddin nearly caused a full-scale row with the bishops when he observed that he would rather trust physicians with good pagan classical training, whether they came from Nubia, Manavia or east of Constantinople, than the multiplying schools of monks who relied on faith more than medicines. There was an embarrassed silence which suggested that the kings agreed more than they dared show.

It was into this hiatus that sounds of commotion outside the hall broke. Gwain left his place beside Arthur and went to investigate. A few moments later he returned and whispered into his general's ear. Arthur grinned. 'Oh well – better late than never.'

He looked up. 'Gentlemen – we are as complete as we can be. Corbalengus has arrived. I hope you will excuse me for a moment. Enjoy the fires while we pause.' He stood and, with Gwain and Myrddin following him, left the hall.

Across the table Vorteporix and Cunegnus glanced at each other. Neither looked thrilled at the news.

When Arthur returned it was with a short, dark man, soaked through from the final morning's journey through the rain. He glowered at his fellow kings, and Arthur summoned men to fuss round him, taking his sodden cloak and hanging it by the fire, finding a clean goblet and filling it with warm ale, showing him to the vacant seat reserved for him. Corbalengus barely nodded in acknowledgement, and declined to sit, moving instead to the fire, putting his feet close enough to the flames to watch as the steam rose from his woollen stockings.

'So,' he demanded without turning from the fire, 'what have you all decided without me?'

CHAPTER XXII

'Nothing,' assured Arthur. 'We have been spending the day informing each other of the true state of Britannia and…'

'Huh!' Corbalengus interrupted. 'I'll tell you the true state of bloody Britannia. Half the idiots round this table couldn't organise pigs in a farmyard, and the other half are screwing their slaves too hard to bother.'

'That is hardly the spirit—' began the Overlord.

'Oh, bugger off, Arthur. Do you know why it has taken so long to get here – apart from the fact that I've had to ride right across the whole fucking country? It's because nearly every fucking milestone between here and Deva points in the wrong direction – especially when there's two roads to choose between.'

'He should get out of the mountains more often,' muttered Cunorix to his neighbour. It was unfortunate that he was standing close enough for Corbalengus to hear him.

'Very funny,' the Ordovician growled. 'Arrogant savage.'

Cunorix stepped forward. 'What did you call me?'

'You heard.'

As Cunorix reached instinctively to his belt Arthur was glad he'd had the sense to make the kings leave their weapons in their own quarters. A fight was imminent.

Gwidellius stepped in. 'Not in my city, gentlemen. Here we keep civil manners. I'm sorry you had such an unpleasant journey, sir. Many of your colleagues have found similar obstacles on the road, and some have found it dangerous as well as inconvenient.'

Corbalengus transferred his icy glare from Cunorix to Gwidellius. 'So what? And who the hell are you?'

Gwidellius ignored the snub. 'I hope hell will not come into it. I'm the bishop of this city.'

'Lucky you. I admit I was curious to see Londinium,' Corbalengus said. 'I'm almost sorry to find it's a plague-infested ruin like all the others. Arthur, I thought you and your Gaulish magician here,' he waved towards Myrddin, 'were meant to be restoring these places to their imperial glory? I hope the rest of your plans work rather better.'

Arthur in turn was beginning to lose his temper, which, he realised, was precisely what Corbalengus intended to happen. He was not going to be given the satisfaction.

'If we could all take our places again,' he suggested softly. 'Corbalengus, we were taking a survey of the threats to our shores, from wherever they might come. Since your kingdom is exposed to the sea from the north and west, perhaps you would like to complete our picture. What Barbarian incursions have there been into Ordovicia?'

Corbalengus remained standing with his back to the fire as the others sat down. 'Nothing I can't handle,' he said.

'I'm glad to hear it. We all know the valour of your country. However, that wasn't what I asked.'

'I know. But it's the only answer you're going to get.'

'I see.' And Arthur could indeed see. Corbalengus was playing the same game as Cunorix and Vortebelos had done before him – attempting to make Arthur, and with him the entire concept of the Council and a united Britannia, seem irrelevant. It was not a game Arthur was prepared to play; however, he would need a compliant and cooperative Ordovician King later if his vision of a secure future for the kingdoms around Deva was to be put into practice. A little softening up was necessary.

He gestured Gwain to come over and whispered for a moment. Gwain listened and nodded, then moved towards the door.

Arthur turned back to Corbalengus. 'Since you do not feel you have anything to add to this phase of our meeting at present, perhaps I can arrange for your curiosity to be satisfied. And it will give you a chance to change from your travelling clothes. If you follow Gwain he will arrange for you to spend a little time out of the rain and cold. Your men will be suitably looked after as well, of course.'

The Ordovician King looked puzzled. He had been expecting a lecture or a conciliatory question.

Arthur encouraged him. 'I think you'll find that Londinium still has some interesting corners that have not yet fallen down.'

Corbalengus shrugged and followed Gwain out of the door. There was a strained silence. Arthur let them think for a moment or two while he summoned one of Gwain's deputies to take his place.

'Not, of course, in the spirit of the Council,' Arthur continued, as if the interruption was barely worth his notice, 'and I trust our colleague from Ordovicia will be feeling differently in time for our concluding session in the morning. Now, where were we?'

For the rest of the afternoon, while the rain fell steadily outside, the kings and bishops of Britannia calmly assessed the problems they confronted, from the unreliability of the harvests to the constant risks of flooding and disease that had made the remaining towns less attractive to their subjects than the old hilltop fortresses – which might have been useless hundreds of years ago against the Roman legions but were a lot more resilient against rebels and Barbarians. They talked about setting up inns at the junctions of old roads to ease travel, even though it was clear that they had neither the men nor the equipment to do more than keep the roads themselves clear of trees and brambles. They agreed to restore the network of royal tax grain houses – a way not only of guaranteeing supplies for Arthur's armies when he needed to deal with trouble, but also of making sure that they could reward their people for public work or issue rations in times of shortage. Corbalengus had succeeded in doing the opposite of his intention. He had made the men around the table realise that they had a common interest, even if they remained sceptical that it would last very long.

As evening approached Arthur called the discussions to an amicable halt and each leader returned to his men. Arthur went round the table explaining privately what he hoped to achieve the following day – a slightly different version to suit the particular vanities of the Council members. There were to be no more gatherings that night. The Council had seen enough of each other for one day and, though nobody said so out loud, they were finding the process of listening to the wide variations of dialect a strain. There were noticeable shifts even between the central kingdoms. Between the Dumnonians and the Carvetii it was sometimes difficult to believe they were speaking the same language at all.

As the sun began to dim, the rain eased. Arthur waited for Myrddin to collect Modlen and her bagfuls of precious tablets, and then rode out with his men across the city. Though he had intended to remain in a pavilion on the Council site with the kings, he decided that he needed the privacy of his lodgings more – and the attentions of Gwenan. He was also curious to find out how Gwain's instruction of Corbalengus was progressing.

Once back in the sumptuous surroundings of the merchant's house he fell first into his lover's arms and then into the hands of the bath-house attendants. After a day of talk among aggressive men it was hard to decide whose caresses were the most beguiling.

Gwain called in on Arthur before he retired for the night. They left Gwenan with the dinner guests – Gwidellius had rustled up some of the area's leading citizens (ship owners, metal brokers and chandlers in the main), who would be made firm allies for years to come by being brought into Arthur's inner circle on the night of the Great Council – and closeted themselves in the small room that their host was using as his private office.

'Did you make him behave?' asked Arthur, having been assured by his deputy that all was peaceful up at the Council site.

Gwain grinned. 'Oh yes, he behaved – eventually.'

'And how did you achieve that?'

'Do you want to know?'

'Yes and no – yes because I'd like to know how much it took to make him cooperate, and it will be useful for the others to think I ordered every twist of it. No because I don't want to have to lie when I deny it to him.'

'All right,' said Gwain. 'I'll keep it vague. We helped him out of his wet clothes, and there was an unfortunate delay finding new ones. Equally unfortunately the delay happened while he was outside in the rain. We found it hard to persuade some young ladies of the city not to play quite so roughly with his royal investments. Want to know more?'

Arthur guffawed. 'Dear, dear. I think I might blush.'

'Corbalengus did the opposite. He went a little pale. In fact, one delightful girl – who has clearly handled soldiers before, if you see what I mean – did something with her fingers that made him pass out. It required quite a lot of cold water to bring him round.'

'How do you know these girls, Gwain?'

'I don't,' admitted the chief of staff, 'but some of my men have come to know them very well in the last few days.'

'They sound as good as soldiers – maybe we should give them a permanent position.'

'Maybe we should.'

Arthur looked more serious. 'Make sure I'm called soon after daybreak. I want to be back at the table well before the others. Also, tell Myrddin and the bishops that I want to see them privately before the meeting begins. We'll talk behind Modlen's curtain – which means she need not be there, or at least not in her usual place. No – don't worry. I'll talk to her myself. It's easier, I know.'

Gwain looked grateful and followed his master back to the company.

* * *

Londinium's weather had changed for the better the next morning when Arthur and his retinue set out across the city an hour after dawn. The sun shone and steam rose from the horse dung. It was not the sort of autumn morning to be stuck inside around the table. At the entrance to the site Arthur, Modlen and Gwain dismounted and made their way quietly on foot to the main pavilion, while the guards skirted the outer ring to the stables. This time, though, it was Modlen who went into the main table room, and the men who slipped in the back door. Her instructions were clear enough. If and when any of the kings arrived early, and there was a chance they would hear voices through the curtain, she was to make as much noise as possible shifting chairs, banging jugs and goblets or dropping logs. To this end she set about moving all the chairs against the walls and sweeping and dusting for all she was worth. Arthur's men knew what she was about, but to the other retainers, standing around without offering to help, she was just an unnaturally keen servant girl doing her job – probably under threat, they joked, of a good spanking if she didn't. Modlen busied about, unconcerned. For once she could enjoy the role, knowing that the truth would have left her tormentors angry and baffled.

Behind the curtain Arthur found Myrddin already perched on Modlen's stool. He didn't bother to stand when the Overlord entered. Arthur found himself irritated, and then felt more so because of it – although had Myrddin leapt to his feet he would have been astonished.

'Got a plan?' asked the older man.

Arthur peeked round the edge of the curtain and grinned as he saw Modlen fussing and shooing her way round the great table. He dropped the cloth and turned back to Myrddin. 'Yes, of course. Have you?'

'Naturally.'

'Shall we see if they're the same before Their Reverences arrive?'

'It might be wise.' There was a conspiratorial glint in Myrddin's eye. Arthur realised his mentor was enjoying himself hugely, whatever his protestations about being dragged away from Moridunum. He was in his element, gently steering politics at the top, just as he had years earlier when he had engineered Arthur's election. 'What do you have in mind?' Myrddin asked.

'I need to bring Corbalengus back to our side, for one thing.'

'Was he ever on it? But yes, I know what you mean – though whether he's in any condition to speak after Gwain's entertainments remains to be seen.'

Gwain smiled. 'He should be just about functioning, though sitting for long may be a little painful.'

'Mind you,' said Myrddin, 'he's the least of our worries. I'd have thought the Brigantia situation and Cunorix's egotism, not to mention the likely duplicity of the Cantiaci, should be the main conundrums.'

'And the Barbarians?' suggested Gwain.

Myrddin snorted. 'If we fix the first three there won't be a Barbarian problem.'

'And if we don't, I won't be Tygern Fawr long enough to care about it,' muttered Arthur glumly.

'Don't be too sure. Cunorix will need someone to blame. But,' Myrddin looked at his pupil searchingly, 'let's get today's agenda fixed before we start worrying about that.'

'I think we should start quietly, continue quietly and end quietly, all guided and noted by the bishops,' suggested Arthur, with more hope than confidence.

'Hah!' exploded Myrddin. 'You know the Council better than that. They need stories to tell and ballads to sing. "Kings sort out the world by the fire" is not going to be the bard-inspiring line they have in mind.'

'Probably not.'

'No, no, no. We need high drama. A good row that we step in and bring to sudden solution – something neither you or I care a damn about, but which gets their dudgeon high and mighty. Then you can have your God Men calming things down, and we can have a little fun.'

Gwain was peering through the door. 'They're on their way.'

'Oh hell,' swore Myrddin. 'Very well – we haven't got time to debate this, Arthur. You're just going to have to trust me.'

'As usual,' observed the Overlord tartly.

'Quite. We'll have your alliances and your Overlord's Council by the end. And we will deal with Brigantia and Cunorix.'

'How?'

'By letting Cunorix think he has brilliantly outplayed you and put in his own puppet.'

'Oh good.'

'Don't be sarcastic, Arthur, it doesn't suit you.'

Arthur was disconcerted to see Gwain trying hard to suppress his amusement as Myrddin became nannyish.

'And the grand diversion?'

'Oh, I think I can count on our friends the bishops to provide that. No casus belli is quite as good as religion – especially theirs.'

'Not yours?' It was Arthur's turn to make his counsellor uncomfortable.

'Not entirely,' Myrddin conceded, 'though it has its points.'

Arthur and Gwain were saved from one of Myrddin's longer theological discourses by the arrival of the two bishops, Gwidellius of Londinium and Dubricius of Isca Siluria. Arthur greeted them both confidentially, and Myrddin rose from his stool, looking serious but careful not to catch the eye of either of the churchmen.

'Welcome, Fathers,' began Arthur. 'I felt it might be useful for the day's success if I let you know what I am hoping to achieve by the end of it.' The bishops nodded patiently. 'I need everybody to leave here in peace, of course…'

'God grant it,' Dubricius averred.

'Amen,' agreed Arthur, '…and united, so that any incoming threat, on whichever coast, will be met with the full force of Britannia's kings – of all nations. It is as a symbol of that unity that we all sit at a round table, where nobody can claim superiority, or, indeed, humiliation. But of course I cannot predict when and where the threat from the sea will occur – it might even come from the lands to the north, where the kings have never accepted my authority, just as they refused Rome's. They are quite likely to see our unity as a threat to their border lands and give encouragement to invaders when they can. So I need good intelligence and most of all the ability to mobilise quickly. That cannot happen if I have to wait for the authorisation of the full Council each time and – as you know – the kings will not allow me to maintain any significant forces of my own or give me the right to order one to be raised without their approval. Yet without that right any battle fought weeks after a landing will be, at best, much bloodier than necessary – at worst risking defeat. I tried to send the message back across the Mare Germanicus in the spring that invaders will not be tolerated. I was lucky. I had been warned by captives from a previous landing and had been able to raise regional armies on the strength of the information. That sort of luck rarely comes twice, however.'

Dubricius looked puzzled. 'What do you have in mind, then?'

'I need deputies,' said Arthur simply. 'A small group of kings or their representatives, agreed and appointed by the full Council of Britannia, who will be able to act on our joint decision. And to enforce the point I intend to name two consuls who can act on my behalf when I am at the other end of the country.'

'That has its dangers too,' observed Gwidellius.

'Less so than the alternative. It's for exactly that reason that I intend one of them to be Cunorix.'

Dubricius sucked in his breath. 'I do hope you won't live to regret this. And the other?'

Arthur smiled. 'Someone with a lot less vanity and a great deal more sense – who the others will support precisely because he is not Cunorix, and is no threat to them.'

'And who knows your mind,' offered Myrddin.

'Just so. Candidianos of Dobunnia.' Arthur looked pointedly at Dubricius as he said it. If there was going to any objection it was likely to come from the Silurians, who had an uneasy border across the Sabrina and Wye rivers with their neighbours in the rich lands to the east. In the event Dubricius looked him straight in the eye, understanding for the first time why this meeting with the ecclesiastics had been called.

'A good choice,' said the Bishop of Isca quietly. 'He is an able man. I understood, though, that he already enjoyed the title of Consul for Life?'

'In name, yes. Now I want the post to mean something. He will have the powers as well as the title.'

Dubricius thought for a moment, then said, 'I think it might help if my King Badoc nominated him.'

'It might indeed,' said Arthur, his spirits lifting. 'Thank you.'

From behind the curtain came a crash as Modlen employed her diversionary tactics. Arthur nodded to Gwain, who slipped out and round to the main entrance to take control as the Council members drifted in.

'Well, if that's all…' Gwidellius began to follow him.

'Not quite, I'm afraid,' Myrddin forestalled him. 'Tygern Fawr was not the only one who needed to speak to you alone. I had some news last night that I think may complicate matters. A messenger was sent to me by Heol of Armorica – a strange route, but there are many ties, of course – concerning Hibernia. He must just have missed me in Moridunum. One of my own men has brought it on.'

The others looked at him expectantly: the bishops with genuine interest, Arthur with curiosity about what earth-shaking information the old man had conjured up.

'It's a new allegation from Bishop Padrig. As you know, Dubricius, he and I were once briefly students together in the same school as you came to later.'

'Indeed. Côr Tewdws – a fine school.'

'But I'm afraid we never did see things the same way.'

'Even God?'

'Especially God – or more accurately, His Church. The gap has widened considerably since, as you can imagine. The message from Heol concerns the continuing feud Padrig has with our devious friends north of the wall in Alt Clut. You may remember that Padrig excommunicated King Cynwyd's father Ceretic for allegedly enslaving Hibernian converts to Padrig's Christianity after one of his forays across the sea.'

'An unpleasant business,' Dubricius agreed mildly.

'Well now he has extended the ban to Cynwyd and the whole kingdom. Apparently he was expecting an apology once the old man was dead, and he's tired of waiting.'

'Oh dear. Very inflammatory. I suppose that gives any Hibernian – or any other Christian king – the right to annex Cynwyd's lands as they see fit.'

'Precisely,' said Myrddin, 'but normally that would not be a big problem for us, and I suspect the Carvetians and the Votadini will be only too pleased to carve themselves a slice. The trouble is that Padrig has widened the issue – accusing Brigantia of aiding Cynwyd. He's authorised a Hibernian punishment raid across to our west coast, taking in Manavia on the way for good measure.'

Arthur looked astonished. 'But that could destabilise everything. And how could Brigantia do any such thing? It hasn't got a king at the moment to take anybody's side.'

'Thanks to you,' said Myrddin pointedly. 'I suspect Padrig is rather behind the times as usual and this was one of Vortebelos's little games. Out of date or not, though, the Hibernians are set to take full advantage.'

Gwain appeared back at the door. 'They're all in,' he said.

'Padrig has no right to take any such action without consulting us, through Rome,' announced Gwidellius crossly. 'It's simply unacceptable.'

'Oh quite!' Myrddin said, putting a hand to Gwidellius's back and guiding him out into the sunlight. 'And no doubt you will need to advise the Council on what action they should take.'

The two agitated bishops scuttled forward and into the main hall, followed by Gwain, while Arthur and Myrddin hung back.

'Is any of that true?' asked Arthur suspiciously.

'Not yet,' Myrddin answered solemnly before a smug smile started to creep across his face, 'but you never know.' He pulled Modlen's arm as she passed them on her way back to her tablets. 'Get ready for explosions, my dear. This could be good listening.'

XXIII

INSIDE THE MAIN ROOM none of the kings had taken their seats, as though reluctant to commit themselves to the meeting before the others. They grouped themselves in familiar alliances, murmuring the small talk of the powerful and the wary. Cunorix, his long black hair slicked back, moved from cluster to cluster blustering with false laughter and manly claps on the shoulder, for all the world as if he was greeting them in his own hall. Only Corbalengus stood alone, looking pale and fatigued as he studied the flames of the fire.

Arthur nodded distantly to those he passed on the way to his chair, sat, unscrolled the short parchment on which Modlen had written the brief Latin summary of the previous day and waited patiently while Myrddin ushered the Council members to their places. He lingered until there was general quiet, but not so long that Cunorix would see the opportunity to butt in with one of his supercilious asides. Arthur didn't look up from his parchment as he called out.

CHAPTER XXIII

'Good Morning. I trust we are all rested and refreshed?' There was not much point in waiting for an answer, and if any had come Arthur had no great wish to hear it. He glanced around the table, taking care not to catch Corbalengus's eye. 'Yesterday was useful, I believe,' he continued. 'We all now have a very clear idea of the state of Britannia and of each other's priorities. Today, however, we come to the heart of this meeting. If we succeed we can leave here tomorrow confident that we have the strategy and energy to improve our security and prosperity – all of us, not just a handful of fortunate kingdoms.' Still Arthur spoke with his eyes constantly moving, refusing to appear to land a significant word on any particular man. 'I'm sure none of you came all this way to participate in failure,' he paused and let his gaze rest on the fire, 'and just to be sure that we all know what we will be discussing I have asked the noble bard of the Silures, since Badoc was so kind as to include him in his delegation, to relate today's proposals to us in a form that we will find as pleasurable as memorable.'

He sat back in his chair and smiled innocently as Gwain brought in a stocky little man dressed in mud-stained white and carrying a small battered harp. Arthur nodded, a string was plucked for pitch and the elaborate sing-song recitation, first of each king and nation's titles and glories, began. This was tedious, but it was a tradition that Arthur knew he could not dispense with. The leaders would be listening out for any omission in their own descriptions and any nuances in others' that might implicate Arthur in an accusation of bias. The bard was a careful professional, however, and therefore adept at lavishing praise, especially on those who didn't deserve it.

The pleasantries over, the business of the day was outlined, with suitable embellishments of the expected brilliant contributions of the assembled kings. Arthur let them relax with their beakers of warm honeyed ale and spiced cakes, the latter a luxury that only a well-connected port like Londinium with ships bringing trade from Byzantium could readily provide. The agenda was simple enough. They would discuss and agree the supremacy of the Council, the evil of the threats from beyond the seas, and all the measures to be taken to maintain the dignity of each king and his people. What those measures would be, of course, it was the task of greater minds than the bard's to unveil.

The bard finished, bowed and was gently removed. There was a soporific silence and everyone looked to Arthur expectantly. He had no intention of taking the lead, though. That would be to invite reaction, little of it positive. He would bide his time. Besides, he could see Bishop Dubricius beginning to shift on his chair.

'You wish to speak, Bishop? By the way, it is a fine poet that King Badoc keeps at court. I'm sure we all appreciated and enjoyed his kind words. I hope you will convey our thanks to him.'

'Indeed, Tygern Fawr, indeed. Very fine.' Dubricius looked as though he was sitting on sore piles. 'However there is another urgent matter that we have had brought to our attention this morning that must surely take precedence over longer-term issues.'

Out of the corner of his eye Arthur could see Myrddin trying not to grin or purr too hard. Whether Dubricius knew it or not his timing was perfect.

'Really, Bishop?' asked Arthur, feigning impatience. 'The news I heard was certainly important, but do you think it should be taken now?'

'Certainly I do. It is of the utmost significance. It touches not only on the safety of Britannia, but on the honour of our Church.'

Just as Arthur had hoped, Cunorix could bear the suspense of not hearing important news no longer. 'And just what is it that My Lord Bishop is so anxious for us to hear? If the Overlord thinks we shouldn't be bothering our little heads with it, I know it really is serious.'

'Serious, of course, Cunorix,' said Arthur. 'I merely felt it could be taken later in the morning.' He knew he was goading the Catuvellaunian King to perfection.

'I think we should be the judge of that.'

Arthur sighed dramatically. 'Very well. If that is the will of the Council…'

'It is,' Cunorix bellowed.

'In that case, Dubricius, since you raised the matter, I will leave you to inform the meeting.'

Dubricius looked quizzical. Clearly he had expected Myrddin or Arthur himself to do the talking. Both had other ideas.

'As I understand it,' he began uncertainly, 'Bishop Padrig is encouraging – one might almost say ordering – the kings in Hibernia to send war bands against our northern nations.'

CHAPTER XXIII

Cunorix snorted. 'Nothing new in that!'

Corbalengus looked up, interested for the first time.

But it was his southern neighbour, Vorteporix of Demetia, who spoke first. 'What's irritated the old fool this time?' he asked. Padrig might have been revered in Hibernia, but in Demetia he was still thought of as one of their own who had become something of an embarrassment.

Gwidellius of Londinium, irksome as he found Padrig's diatribes, was less than happy to hear a fellow senior churchman described as an 'old fool'. 'Maybe I can explain,' he interrupted. 'It seems Bishop Padrig has been unsatisfied with the response he has received from Alt Clut to his offer to lift the excommunication of King Cynwyd's late father. He's therefore extended it to the whole of that kingdom and any he suspects of supporting it – which so far seems to include Manavia and Brigantia. It's highly irregular – highly! He has no right to do or say any such thing without the authority of Rome – or, for that matter, without consulting the Church on this side of the water. Disgraceful, really.'

'But he's done it anyway,' Cunorix pointed out with relish. He might not have been a supporter of Myrddin's old gods, but he enjoyed the chance to slap down the pomposity of the bishops, who looked to foreign powers for their authority. He had his own tiresome cleric in Verulamium.

The King of the Carvetii, whose domain bordered both Brigantia and Alt Clut, looked grim. 'No doubt the Hibernians will land on my shores – they'll say by mistake, of course – so I suppose I have no choice but to offer my neighbours support, treacherous though they are.'

'Well at least we won't have Vortebelos to put up with,' Cunegnus of Cornovia pointed out. 'The next lot in Brigantia may be easier to like – though I doubt it.'

Arthur shifted uncomfortably as several of the Council glanced in his direction at the mention of Vortebelos. It was a reference he had hoped to avoid. He glared at his friend Cunegnus.

Vorteporix saved his blushes by moving the discussion on. 'This means that we can't concentrate entirely on the Barbarian threat from the east. We'll need to watch our backs from the west as well. Do you think there's a chance of an alliance between the Barbarians and Hibernia?'

Myrddin stepped in for the first time that morning. 'If I may?' he began diplomatically. As an adviser to the Council he had no automatic right to speak. Arthur nodded his assent. 'I think that's unlikely,' Myrddin continued. 'I'm sure the Votadini would love to broker it if they have the chance – it would tie up all their neighbours at the same time and allow them to move beyond the wall into Brigantia – but there hasn't been time since Padrig's edict to pass such messages across two seas. I suspect we are forewarned.'

'Just as well,' said Vorteporix 'But it makes our decisions here today even more urgent. I propose we should have two related strategies – one for the defence of the west—'

'And south,' Caldoros of Dumnonia interjected. 'We share many miles of coast, Vorteporix.'

The Demetian King waved his agreement. 'Of course. And one for the defence of the eastern side – from Brigantia to Atrebata,' he added, before any further leaders could claim they were being left out.

Arthur could have cheered him, but he let the debate run. Far better that the Council thought it was inventing its own solutions.

He looked up to see Cunegnus watching him with a shadow of a smile. The Cornovian sipped his ale thoughtfully. 'That's going to overstretch you, Corbalengus, even with Demetia's help. Even though it's not represented here, there is a kingdom between us. If you're defending your shore and Manavia, and I'm plugging the northern river estuary at Deva and the south-west of Brigantia, we could be giving Deceangelia the chance of a generation to cause us trouble.' He glanced across the table. 'I hope you'll note, Cunorix, that I have no such worries about Catuvellaunia or Coritania in these circumstances.'

Cunorix bowed his head. 'I am grateful for my neighbour's trust.'

'I'm glad to hear it, but my guess is you'll have other things to worry about too before winter comes.'

Arthur steered the conversation away from that thorny issue of middle Britannia. 'Do you have something in mind, Cunegnus?'

'It seems a drastic step to take, and one that is hardly fair since their king is not here to defend themselves, but I can't see how this can be resolved without, shall we say, a new dispensation for the Deceangeli – and for Brigantia.'

Next to Badoc, the young Arcarix, son of King Megeterix of Deceangelia, who had been sent as his father's envoy, stiffened with alarm.

CHAPTER XXIII

'How new?' asked Corbalengus. For now his resentment at the indignities of the previous day had retreated to the back of his mind.

'Well firstly, we need Manavia as our fort,' Cunengus continued. 'While Vorteporix and you will still have to secure your coasts south of Ynys Mon, a really effective blockading force in Manavia can protect everything from Al Clut to Segontium, from Hibernians or anybody else who strays that way. It can't be done by a kingless Brigantia facing in two directions. We know that, because even Vortebelos was making sweet noises to the Hibernians before all this blew up. And for Manavia to be strong, it needs to be independent. And that is something that, with the best will in the world from you and me, Corbalengus, Deceangelia can never be.'

The Ordovician King nodded, but then looked at Arthur. 'He talks sense, Arthur, though naturally I can swear that Deceangelian fears about incursions from my side of the mountains have no basis in truth.'

'Naturally,' agreed Arthur, without any conviction but neutrally enough not to be seen as a challenge.

'Anyhow,' Cunegnus continued. 'I think the people of Deceangelia would be more secure and prosperous under our protection – don't you, Corbalengus?'

'Oh quite,' the King of Ordovicia announced firmly, though mildly baffled by the sudden turnaround in his popularity.

'Tygern Fawr...' Arcarix tried to interrupt.

'If we place our new border on flat ground in the middle of the current kingdom, along the line of the River Clwyd, so that neither of us has the advantage, that should make our intentions clear to our successors.'

'Very sensible.' By this time Corbalengus was all but eating out of his old enemy's hand. He could hardly believe his luck.

'But—' began Vorteporix, who was less than thrilled at the thought of a newly enriched Ordovicia to the north. He could almost hear Corbalengus's vanity expanding with his kingdom.

'But you will be thinking, my friends, this is no way to treat Megeterix of Deceangelia in his absence,' Cunegnus carried on. Vorteporix had been thinking no such thing, but he withdrew with good grace. 'I agree it would be unforgivable in normal circumstances. These, though, are far from normal times. Arcarix – I am not trying to cheat you or your father of your kingdom, I promise. I want to offer you a better one.'

'It doesn't sound like it,' Arcarix exploded. 'Tygern Fawr, you cannot allow this to continue.'

But Arthur could and did, letting Cunegnus carry on without comment.

'I suggest that we, the Council, cede Manavia from Brigantian control to Megeterix and make him one of the inner Council that—'

Arthur jumped in. 'Perhaps we should not rush ahead of ourselves.' He could see several of the kings who had been left out of his briefings over the previous weeks suddenly looking alert after listening with only polite interest to the leaders of the far west rearranging their territories. For a moment Arcarix too relaxed, but he tensed again when he heard Arthur's answer. 'In principle, Cunegnus, it is a sound idea in military and political terms. However, I think we can expect Megeterix to want a bit more than an island and the goodwill of the Commonwealth to give up his kingdom.'

'I don't see why. They're about the same size,' muttered Corbalengus, impatiently.

'Wouldn't you?'

'Possibly,' the King of Ordovicia admitted grudgingly.

'I think it would be better if there was some compensation involved.'

Cunorix, who was beginning to feel left out, guffawed. 'A sackful of useless old Roman coins, Arthur?'

'Not useless here,' bristled Gwidellius.

'So my men keep telling me,' Cunorix threw back at Londinium's bishop. 'No sex without a coin in the hole.' The Bishop reddened.

Arthur regained control, but only for a moment. 'Megeterix would find other currency more useful, I think.'

Arcarix was on his feet. His fist crashed down on the table. 'I must be allowed to speak. You have no right to take away my homeland or my father's kingdom. We have held Deceangelia for centuries—'

'Only because your ancestors let the Romans walk straight over you on the way to harder resistance in my country,' Corbalengus goaded, with old but deeply held national grievance.

Arthur intervened. 'I'm sorry, Arcarix, but you are wrong on both counts. I do not have to allow you speak because you are not yet a king or a member of this Council. You are here as an observer for your father. And we have every right to decide how the territory of Britannia is ruled. It is a sanction that every one of the Council

CHAPTER XXIII

submits to, though they would, no doubt, protest every bit as vociferously as you.'

'This is not just.'

'It will be – and I assure you, it will not happen without the agreement of your father, when I see him within a month of this Council. Now, sit down please. Hear the terms.'

Arcarix sat, his face red and his head shaking in fury.

'Megeterix will be given Manavia as his own,' Arthur continued. 'Cunegnus and Corbalengus, I'm asking you to allow any of the Deceangeli to go with him to Manavia and to make it worth their while by offering to double their holdings of cattle, sheep and goats. I also ask you to guarantee free access to your ports in Deva and Segontium indefinitely, and to each send him three ships of grain each per year.'

Cunegnus frowned. 'I can afford everything except the grain.'

'These are rich lands you are gaining, Cunegnus. Farm them properly and the grain yield will come easily.'

'Long time since you were a farmer.'

Arthur was having none of the grumbling. 'Arcarix and his cousins know how to if you don't. You will make him a prince of both your kingdoms, too – he will be the guarantee of good faith by both you and Corbalengus. He will have the first right of inheritance to the kingdoms, should either of your sons not be alive after your death. And he will report directly to the Council through me. If any unnatural harm comes to him I will impose the same sanction on you that Padrig has set on Brigantia. No doubt Cunorix and Vorteporix would be delighted to enforce it. It's a fair deal, and I ask the Council to vote on the offer. Myrddin, will you conduct it?'

Corbalengus cut in. 'That won't be necessary, Arthur. I'm sure Cornovia and Ordovicia can manage – at least for the next few years.'

Arthur looked to Cunegnus, who nodded glumly.

He turned to Arcarix. 'Will you agree to let me take this offer to your father? You don't have to accept anything else until then.'

Arcarix couldn't bring himself to make any move, but his silence was enough. The Overlord had won the day.

Gwidellius was looking concerned in his turn. 'My lord?'

'Yes?'

'I will need to protest to Rome on behalf of the Church in all Britannia. The Pope himself must hear of this. Bishop Padrig cannot be allowed to act in such a fashion. It's as if he's setting himself above the ecclesiastical authorities here. It is one thing to excommunicate Alt Clut – that's none of my concern – but Brigantia is.'

'Or rather, it's the concern of your colleague in Ebvracum, wouldn't you say?' Arthur pointed out quietly.

'Of course, but in this instance, the news has come to me first, and I'm sure swift action on his behalf—'

'I suggest a rider be sent to Ebvracum with a draft of the letter you and Dubricius wish to send to Rome. He can be back within the week,' said Arthur. 'I will not be leaving till then, so we can deal with it in plenty of time. And we'll see whether Padrig inspires any real action from Hibernia. However furious his edict, the kings may not wish to risk ships in the autumn gales.'

Arthur was perfectly happy for Gwidellius to stir up as much Papal indignation in Rome as he liked. He was also pleased to wrest initiative away from the rival bishops of the Cantiaci and Catuvellauni – both active in the game to speak on behalf of all Britannia's priests. But he couldn't allow Gwidellius to inflict resentment in the north. Ebvracum, like Londinium, was the Overlord's city, the city of Constantine himself, and its bishop had a right to expect equal respect. He had already found Myrddin's long stay during the weeks of Gwenan's recovery difficult (Myrddin, as usual, had failed dismally to hide his scepticism about the new religious order), and Arthur needed him to make sure the Brigantian nobles up the road in Isurium picked a compliant successor to Vortebelos. Part of the new strict fashion for extreme Christianity, they were more likely to listen to a bishop, even one of Arthur's, than anyone else.

Arthur looked over to the doorway and caught Gwain's eye. The steward nodded fractionally and disappeared out into the sunshine. 'I think, friends, that we have just seen perfectly the illustration of what can be achieved if we work together. Britannia is safer. Each of your kingdoms is safer and potentially richer. There are no arguments about borders that cannot be discussed and resolved when we choose to do so. Bishop Padrig thinks he is sending his Hibernian ships to punish us for supposed insults to his Church. He will find instead that we offer no hospitality to those who come to negotiate by force, by whichever sea they arrive. Let's stretch our legs in the sunshine while fresh ale is found. And then let us conclude round this table by doing

CHAPTER XXIII

as Badoc's bard asked us at the start this morning: making sure we can respond in kind to any of the dangers thrown at us.'

The door was thrown open and the sunshine streamed in. One by one the kings stood and ambled out on to the grass. Arthur stayed where he was, though, and called over his young cousin from Dumnonia, Caldoros. Myrddin strolled round to join them, but to his irritation Arthur waved him away to join the others outside. Myrddin always hated feeling dispensable, but Arthur knew what he was doing. If the others saw him go into a huddle with the old man they would assume that they were being manoeuvred into one of his schemes. If they saw him hanging around outside while Arthur chatted to his one direct relative on the Council, they would decide that Myrddin disapproved of whatever Arthur was going to propose, and therefore it must be, by default, something that was more in their interests. Few of them, especially Cunorix, believed Arthur was capable of thinking up a worthwhile political manoeuvre on his own. And Cunorix couldn't resist ambling over to Myrddin, grasping him by the shoulder and rubbing salt into the wound.

'You never could stand Padrig, could you?' he began.

Myrddin glared at him, or tried too. It was not easy standing sideways on with the brutish king thirty years his junior clinging to him. He was not going to be bated, though. 'We've had our differences. But he's achieved a lot in Hibernia – brought the kings together, stopped the squabbling.'

'So he says. We'll see if Arthur has the balls to do the same. After all, he has you as his secret weapon.'

'Hardly a weapon, Cunorix. Only a support, and sometimes an old head who can offer a wider view.'

'Of Britannia?'

'No, no. Arthur sees more of Britannia than I do these days. I've quite enough to do in Moridunum, and my back isn't made for long days in the saddle any more. The world, Cunorix. All those places from Byzantium to Nubia, and Armorica to the Barbarian forests of Germania that you have never visited.'

Cunorix relaxed his grip and shrugged. 'Since the Barbarians are so keen to come to us, I don't see why I should bother to go to them. I have a kingdom to manage.'

'So you have, Cunorix. So you have. But is that all – or enough?'

Myrddin extracted himself and looked for the more congenial company of Vorteporix. At least the accent would be free of the Catuvellaunian nasal whine. Behind him Caldoros emerged from his discussions, but Arthur stayed inside. He had no wish to mingle. Whoever he spoke to would either be wary or would become a focus of speculation for the others. He moved away from the table and through the curtain to where Modlen was arranging her writing tablets. She looked up and her face brightened. They were alone for once. Arthur stepped over, took her face in his hand and kissed her gently. She studied his face intently, then looked away, trying not to let a tear form in her eye.

'All well?' Arthur asked cheerfully.

Modlen nodded and waved at the neat stacks of writing tablets gathered around her stool.

'Good. I think we are winning, but it all depends on this last session. If it goes badly I'll have to extend the Council by another day until we can force agreement. I don't want to, but if necessary I'll hold any of the kings here until they all come into line.'

His scribe looked at him nervously. There was a hard determination in his voice that reminded her uncomfortably of Cunorix and the other men who had trashed her body and thrown it aside in the last five years.

But Arthur was oblivious to that, intent on the job in hand. He stroked her hair distractedly and spoke softly but with the same intensity. 'Whatever is said, this is what I want you to record. The rest is decoration. Understand?'

Modlen reached up and touched his face to show that she did. Arthur dictated for a moment, smiled then slipped back through the curtain, filled his cup from the ale jug and went to stand by the fire. After a few seconds Gwain looked through the door.

'Shall I bring them back in?'

'Yes, but let me out for a piss first. You can get them all settled while I'm gone. I'm not in the mood for regal small talk.'

Gwain grinned. 'Who is?'

* * *

The Overlord timed his return so that everybody had already sat down around the table and was beginning to look impatient. Even Myrddin, so used to being the instigator of any stratagem, was

CHAPTER XXIII

peering at Gwain, hoping for a sign that he could take as collusion. Since Gwain knew no more than Myrddin but didn't care either way, he stared impassively back.

In fact Arthur was hovering just out of sight, waiting for the moment when the chatter subsided but before one of the kings took it into his own hands to start on a theme of his own. Once there was reasonable quiet he bustled in and made for his place, but did not sit down. He gazed steadfastly at the centre of the table, as though drawing strength from the wood. The Council was now his audience, and he treated them as one. It was a natural talent, for among them only Myrddin had ever seen a play by Plautus in a working theatre. Within a few seconds there was complete silence, even Cunorix forgetting to shuffle or clear his throat.

'Kings of Britannia,' Arthur began, almost in a whisper. 'You are the Council, the custodians of our peace, the embodiment of our federation that has proved for over fifty years we need not fear Rome's capitulation in all matters except the Church's. Life has changed fast in that time, as Myrddin but few others among us can testify. But we are still together, and can talk to each other, even if sometimes the conversations are unhappy. For the most part we reach for the jug of ale before we reach for our swords. In the last sixteen years, since you and some of your fathers agreed (for whatever reason) to give me the title of Tygern Fawr, I have done my best to persuade you along this path and dissuade Barbarians and anybody else who thought that without Roman legions ours was land for the taking.'

He paused and looked around each of the kings in turn. Only the King of the Cantiaci refused to meet his eye. It was a gesture that told Arthur a great deal. The Cantiaci would be prepared to deal with Barbarians or anybody else from the continent who wanted a farmstead and a wife, it said.

'The Council does not meet often in full, and for good reason. To leave your kingdoms is dangerous and to travel is ever more difficult. I know that better than any of you. Perhaps if we carry through the decisions we took yesterday about milestones, inns and clearing the roads it will at least become tolerable, if never again a pleasure. So to ask you come so far, to Londinium, cannot be for the enjoyment of our company or the entertainment of our men – though both have been considerable. It cannot even just be to report on the condition of the island or to reconfigure without acrimony the political arrangements of those kingdoms facing Hibernia, though that too has been an achievement to be proud of. We must have a higher purpose. And we have.'

'You have given me a title, a task or two – to repel Barbarians and to maintain by consent good order among the kingdoms – and authority. But it is limited authority. You judge that I should not have my own troops beyond those I need for my immediate protection in uncertain times. I understand that. If I had the means I could become a tyrant like Vortigern or, I have been told, like Uther my father occasionally attempted to be. I have no such ambition, but you are right not to take my word for it. The temptation to impose my will by force could be too great to resist.'

'As in the case of Vortebelos?' mused Cunorix.

There was a tense silence. Then Arthur held his gaze. 'That was personal,' he said. 'Personal payment for a personal attack. No one else was hurt, and the kingdom was not threatened.'

'Though leaderless,' said Cunorix. 'I'm glad to know you have such a firm view of personal honour.' His sarcasm was quiet but sharp.

Cunegnus weighed in for Arthur. 'So perhaps now Brigantia can get a real leader, not just a thug in a gold neck torque.'

It was the sort of support Arthur could have done without at that moment. Candidianos saw the danger. 'Perhaps we shall eat earlier if we don't digress,' he suggested.

'Thank you,' Arthur continued. 'It is precisely because I cannot call this Council together quickly or often that I have called one now. You know the threat. Here is my request.' He paused to make sure that he had their attention. Corbalengus was yawning, Myrddin was staring through the doorway, as though there were endless inviting panoramas to enjoy instead of a wicker gate. It would have to do.

'Britannia needs a more flexible system for dealing with external threats. I cannot be everywhere at once, or march from one end of the island to the other in days to drive the ships away. If there is trouble beyond the resources of one kingdom, there has to be a way to muster men quickly under recognised command. I need to delegate, but who to and when, you are here to decide. Unless you agree, and believe it to be right, nothing I require of you will work.'

'You told us that yesterday,' Catacus of Atrebata pointed out irritably. 'What do have in mind? Or do you want us to spend all day doing the thinking for you?'

Gwidellius intervened. 'I expect you'll find Tygern Fawr has saved you that trouble, Catacus.' The first laughter of the morning lightened the atmosphere, but the King of the Atrebates was not sure he saw the joke as he reddened.

'I've had a few ideas,' conceded Arthur, 'and I've taken the liberty of exploring them with perhaps half of you this year as I've travelled. But half is not enough, and in any case some of the details have changed thanks to the advice you have given me. So this version may seem a little more developed.'

'Now he sounds just like Myrddin,' retorted Catacus, trying to recover his position.

'You mean it's too complicated for you already?' Cunorix jabbed, but it was the first sign that he intended to end up endorsing Arthur. Myrddin continued to stare into the middle distance, as though he'd heard nothing.

'The proposal is quite simple, I assure you,' Arthur promised. 'It is that we should create a smaller version of this Council, able to act immediately on your behalf. It would consist of two or three from among you who would be able to travel at short notice. But it would also have another group of men nominated by you who would be granted the authority, just as Arcarix is here for his father, to act and issue orders on your behalf between meetings of this full Council, which I suggest we set now for once every two years.'

'They would travel with you, I presume?' asked Badoc of Siluria.

'Yes. That's the whole point. They would advise me and inform you, each one being the representative of two kingdoms.'

'And are they all intended to have the same influence,' Badoc continued, 'or will some speak with greater seniority?'

'That is my whole aim, Badoc, to keep Britannia unified by giving each member of this smaller circle an equal position, just as you have here. We are meeting at a round table and at this table or a copy I and your representatives will always sit. It will be our symbol and the guarantee that none of you is treated as anything other than a king.'

'Words, Arthur. It will never work.' Catacus snorted.

'And you have a better idea, I'm sure?' Cunorix said.

'Yes,' Catacus continued. 'Get rid of this Council, get rid of this waste of time and best of all, get rid of the Overlord.'

There was a shocked and embarrassed silence. Now that the feeling that many of them had been keeping hidden was out in the open, none of the kings wanted to force a breakdown by joining Catacus. An hour earlier Corbalengus would have been enthusiastic, but he had the prospect of more land and power without dispute, thanks to Myrddin, and he had no intention of risking it before it was in his hands.

'And what about Barbarian invaders?' asked Cunorix.

'We can handle them. It will only be a few boatloads each summer.'

'Then you are a bigger fool than any of us thought,' Cunorix told him.

Vorteporix spoke before Catacus could answer the insult. 'It will work, and it will keep your kingdom a great deal safer than if the Council and Tygern Fawr was not here. He's our symbol too, you know? Our sign that we want Britannia, not chaos. Even if you are not frightened of Barbarians, without the Council what would there be to stop Candidianos or Cunorix or any of the rest of us deciding that we needed your lands?'

'Indeed!' said Cunegnus with feeling, glancing at his neighbours from the Dobunni and Catuvellauni.

Cunorix eyed Catacus like a dog playing with a rabbit. 'Atrebata – small country, good land, excellent rivers, access to the southern sea. I could use that. Besides, whether Catacus thinks he can deal with everything the Barbarians can throw at him or not, I can't take the risk that they'll use his rivers to come at me from the south while I'm fighting them in the east. I know the Council will not let me decide that young Catacus is unnecessary, but of course, if the Council is not here...'

Catacus had turned white. He looked around the table. Those that weren't watching the fire were looking at him and grinning. 'I didn't mean—'

'Good,' said Vorteporix. 'Then I think we can let Tygern Fawr continue. Who do you have in mind as your deputies, Arthur?'

'Communications are crucial,' he began obliquely. 'So is trust. I need two of you whose men can reach me in good time or who are regarded by their neighbours as worthy of command in the event that

CHAPTER XXIII

my attentions are divided. I hope that you will agree that I cannot achieve any serious security without Cunorix? Catuvellaunia can only be circumvented with difficulty – geographically and among you,' he avoided using the word 'politically'. It would have made him sound even more like Myrddin than was safe. 'If the Ordovices, Demetiae, western Brigantes and Cornovii are keeping the Hibernians busy, I shall need a strong Catuvellaunia at my side to deal with Barbarians from the east.'

'I agree, Arthur,' Cunegnus said, to Cunorix's considerable surprise. 'It's important that Cunorix has a role that we all confirm and understand. And nobody doubts his prowess.'

'Thank you,' said Cunorix.

'But I agree on one condition,' Cunegnus continued. 'The limits to your deputies' authority, and the methods that they can use to enforce it, are clearly set out by us before we leave here. With respect, Cunorix, you can be, shall we say, a little heavy-handed at times.'

'Then you have my apologies,' Cunorix said, and bowed with unaccustomed humility.

'Accepted,' said Cunegnus. 'And I hope the women and bards of our lands will soon be happy to sing your praises.'

Myrddin and Arthur looked at the King of Cornovia with growing respect. It was a subtle and impressive way of reminding Cunorix to behave. Both wondered, though, how Modlen would be feeling as she recorded what she had heard. Arthur suspected that her main fear was rising to the surface – that she would never be free of Cunorix.

Arthur was still standing. He would not sit until the Council was decided.

Myrddin felt it was time to say something, if for no other reason than that his silence throughout the morning would be more suspicious than his contribution. 'If I may speak?' he asked.

Arthur nodded.

'While Cunorix is indispensable I suggest it would be unwise, in such volatile times, to leave us in the hands of a partnership of two. I know that many of you don't like references to the old imperial days, but I think you will agree that they teach us a few things, and one of them is that the emperors were always better able to manage the state when they were aided by at least two Caesars, or when they themselves were not one of the two consuls.'

Arthur looked less than comfortable. 'However,' he said, 'I am not an emperor, and have no wish to be. Emperor of Britannia is, in any case, an absurd title. I hope the Council is prepared to accept that.'

'I'm sure we are,' said Cunegnus, 'and equally we have no wish for Cunorix to see succession to such a title as a possibility – I'm sorry to disappoint you, Cunorix.'

'Nothing could be further from my thoughts,' he said, without conveying much conviction.

'So Tygern Fawr is right on all counts to look for another of us who can balance matters – and before any of you think I'm putting myself forward, forget it. I'm too old, I have a kingdom than needs all my attention and now I have to keep the Hibernians out of Deva.'

'Well, if you are comfortable with Cunorix as Deputy Overlord—' began Badoc.

'Perhaps we should call him the Underlord,' muttered Corbalengus.

They laughed, though Cunorix had to force himself.

Badoc continued. 'I would ask you to appoint Candidianos. He has known Arthur's mind better than most of us, he has the honorary title, we know his wisdom. Would you accept?'

The Dobunnian King looked with astonishment at Badoc. He was the last source of compliments, let alone promotion, he expected. He wondered instantly, since he hadn't been party to the conversation earlier in the morning between Arthur, Myrddin and the bishops, whether it was a means of making him take his eye off his western border with Badoc's Siluria. 'Gladly – but only if my people are safe.'

'You'll have no trouble from my quarter. I swear this in the Council,' affirmed Caldoros, his neighbour to the south. The others around his kingdom, Cunegnus, Catacus and Cunorix, joined him.

Badoc smiled. 'Perhaps I should be harsher, Candidianos. If you join Arthur I can guarantee that our border will remain open and peaceful. If, of course, you just want to sit in Corinium and repair the drains then some of my men might call it a dereliction of duty and a provocation.'

'Well, then, I have no choice. Thank you.'

Arthur surveyed the table. 'Is everybody happy with that – Candidianos and Cunorix as my permanent consuls, to use Myrddin's term? Perhaps all those who agree could raise their ale cups.' Some hands were slower to do so than others, but no one held back completely.

'And now I ask you to do the same – yes, Corbalengus, you may drink out of it first – if you are content to send me your nominees to my Round Table, as I shall call it from now on. It can't be called a Council, because we are the Council, and the distinction must remain.'

Catacus was determined to retrieve something of his dignity. 'Perhaps you could just remind us of exactly what the duties and powers of these men will be?'

'Oh, for heaven's sake – we've been through all that!' exploded Cunorix.

Arthur was more patient. 'They will be your eyes and ears, Catacus. They will give me advice and command the men you send me if we need to engage Barbarian invaders. They will report the discussions at the Round Table to you and bring your views to us. Will that suffice?'

'We'll see,' grumbled the Atrebatan.

'Then,' said Vorteporix, 'let's raise our cups. To Arthur, Tygern Fawr and his Round Table.'

XXIV

THE INTENSE LIGHT of the morning sun on clouds in an October shower lit up the forest of the Sabrina's great western valley. Arthur, two hours out of Corinium, reined in his horse and gazed across to the hills beyond. If the roads were clear for the baggage wagons he would be climbing the slopes the next morning, in country that was the nearest to anything he could ever think of as home.

Myrddin and Modlen pulled up close behind him. In the last two months they had become almost inseparable – partly, Arthur suspected uncharitably, because the old adviser relished the company of a good-looking young woman who was intelligent enough to understand what he was talking about but couldn't interrupt him. Much of the time she was happy not to, gladly absorbing the knowledge tossed at her – either in Brythonic or, if the subject was sensitive for local ears, in Latin – especially when Myrddin talked of people and places beyond the seas. Modlen had her own way of stopping the flow if she had to. A gentle prod to her horse's flank would send her trotting forward to Arthur, or she would hang back among the guard until the words subsided. In the evening, after they had camped and eaten, she would spend a few minutes scratching a summary, a list and an opinion on to a tablet. It was often a salutary moment for Myrddin, as he realised the economy which her silence and scant writing materials forced on her thoughts. Modlen could write in ten words an idea that had taken him all morning to propound – and demolish it in ten more. She was, he was beginning to feel, the closest to an equal he had ever discovered, and he was disturbed to find he was starting to have great affection for her because of it. Another day or two and he would be leaving her on the borders of Elfael as Arthur turned north and he carried on to Moridunum. For the first time that he could remember the prospect of home seemed a little dull and empty.

Before that, though, they would leave Candidianos's kingdom and reunite Arthur with his foster-father, Idriseg. Myrddin anticipated that the visit was likely to be a difficult one, and that, as so often, homecoming would mean dealing with a pile of half-forgotten problems. He sensed that Arthur suspected it too, which explained why the Overlord had been uncharacteristically withdrawn and scratchy for the last few days. Leaving Gwenan in Gwidellius's care in Londinium might have provided an excuse, but Myrddin doubted it.

Idriseg had sent his apologies to the Council, citing his own frailty and his complete trust in Arthur to look after the interests of his old homeland. His was the smallest kingdom entitled to attend, and in reality he had few enemies against whom he had to defend his interests. Cunegnus of Cornovia, Vorteporix of Demetia and Candidianos of Dobunnia all regarded Elfael as a stable and insignificant neighbour that was nonetheless a useful sentry against the attentions of the Ordovices. Badoc of Siluria was deterred from tempting raids by the stern disapproval of Bishop Dubricius. That left Corbalengus. However, Elfael's borders were not with the Ordovician heartland, but with the tributary kingdom of Gwythernion, and Corbalengus had far bigger matters to keep him occupied to care much what was happening in the distant south.

In Idriseg's long reign nobody had ever seriously troubled him or even paid him more than absent-minded respect. It was one reason why Myrddin had felt so safe placing the infant Arthur in his care. Now, though, Idriseg was fading. Dubricius had doubted their old friend would outlive the year. Elfael was famous for its icy winters and

CHAPTER XXIV

wet springs. The seasons had been deterring its potential opponents for centuries before the Romans had come to the same conclusion. But now its deterrent climate was likely to prove its king's conqueror. That meant that Caradoc would almost certainly become Elfael's leader, and all the certainties of the kingdom since before Uther Pendraeg's time would be questioned.

Caradoc was no longer a young man, but he behaved like one. It was as if the quiet diplomacy of his father and the careful use of power by his foster-brother as overlord were provocation enough to drive him to fury. He despised one and was bitterly envious of the other. His greatest loathing, though, was reserved for Myrddin, whom he saw as the instigator of all his humiliations. If Myrddin had never appeared with the oh-so-special Arthur, Caradoc would not have spent his life feeling like a minor prince in his own kingdom. Only his sister Branwen had the influence to reason with him, and if it had not been for the solid loyalty of the men of Elfael to Idriseg, trouble would have been easy to foment. As it was, he'd made sure he had gathered around him a group of discontented men like himself who either resented the quiet lives of their farming fathers or just enjoyed the bravado and the drinking that went with Caradoc. There were plenty of girls happy to entertain the heir apparent and his band, too, despite his nominal marriage.

At nineteen Idriseg had insisted Caradoc be found a wife, partly in the belief that the responsibility of parenthood would calm him down, and partly to demonstrate that Idriseg expected the line of succession to continue and not be diverted to Arthur – Caradoc's greatest fear. The bride agreed was the thirteen-year-old Olwen, youngest daughter of the next-door King of Gwythernion. It was a useful cementing of the local royal houses, though Idriseg noted wryly that it was only the youngest daughter that his neighbour was prepared to risk with Caradoc. The young couple had no problem making children – five (two boys and three girls), though one of each had died in infancy and Olwen, at the age of twenty-two, had been left too damaged internally by the last to conceive again – but then Caradoc had been demonstrating his gift for fathering around the kingdom for a few years already.

If Olwen expected any care and attention outside the bedroom she was disappointed, especially after she was declared barren. For that she had to look to Idriseg, who loved her paternally from her first arrival, her sister-in-law Branwen and frequent tearful returns from Elfael's secret hills to the fertile valleys of her home. Now, at twenty-five, she was the central figure of loyalty for those in Elfael who felt outrage at the insensitivity of Caradoc's blatant accumulation of hard power as Idriseg's ability to control him weakened. Inevitably Caradoc's belief that everyone was against him and his disgust at the perceived glorification of Arthur grew, with a thread of justification.

Arthur had heard the stories, and knew that his return to Idriseg's court was likely to be turbulent. For one thing Caradoc was bound to have to show his followers that he was not afraid of his 'brother', whatever the fancy title. The Overlord would need a strategy as subtle as he had employed with the Council if he was to keep Caradoc in check in the next few days. And Arthur desperately wanted to spend what seemed likely to be his last ever few days with the man he still thought of as his father, his first for over five years, in peace.

So Arthur looked across the Sabrina's valley with apprehension, as much as longing. The longing was for a home that was there for him in wood and stone, but might never again be in spirit. His two confidants drew alongside and read his face, Myrddin's chatter dying away as he followed the direction of Arthur's gaze. Abruptly Arthur tugged at the horse's reins and steered him back on to the road, and the troop moved forward again before Candidianos and his guard had time to pause for the magnificent view.

The road between Corinium and Glevum was slippery as it dropped from the high plains into the valley below. Even the Roman engineers had not been able to find a route from the civil capital to the military town that did not involve the wagon drivers praying their horses' calf muscles would be strong enough to prevent the loads tipping them all down the hill. The scarp that the road tried to cut across often made Candidianos feel that he had two distinct kingdoms to rule, not one. Glevum still had its no-nonsense military hardiness: a port city of wharves and trade, crooks and dealers. Corinium kept its civilian gentility when the roads were dry and the old Roman buildings were swept and weeded; a place for the Dobunnian wealthy to bring their wives on a summer evening when groups of musicians, players and acrobats would draw a crowd as the well-to-do ambled among the half-fallen colonnades. There was little need for guards around the King in Corinium. In Glevum they would all need to keep eyes open and hands on their silver.

CHAPTER XXIV

Nonetheless in Glevum they rested the horses at midday and found plenty of tavern stalls happy to provide the troops and attendants ale, bread and fierce cheese, as Candidianos led the royal party into the old centurion's house, which still served as his deputy's headquarters. It was Arthur's last day for many in his new consul's kingdom, and Candidianos had sent word ahead ordering that the lunch be suitably lavish – not so heavy that they all wanted to sleep the afternoon away, but enough to impress the Glevum merchants that their king was one of the three most important people in Britannia, and that it was not every day that the Overlord passed through with him.

The plan was for the royal party to camp that night in the ruins of Magnis, close to the north bank of the river Wye, but it was already mid afternoon by the time the speeches and pleasantries were over, the procession reformed, and they were all out of Glevum's gate and across the Sabrina. There were still at least thirty miles to cover before the early autumn light faded completely. The wind was rising, making the horses skittish and promising a wet night to come. Candidianos had tried to persuade Arthur to delay and spend the evening in the relative comfort of Glevum, but without success. That would have meant arriving at Idriseg's hall in the hills half a day late, and Arthur wanted to be seen by Caradoc's watchers arriving on time and in good order by the end of the morning. He wanted plenty of daylight for the final climb into the low mountains, not for the scenery, but to assess the mood as he made his way to the heart of Elfael.

Sure enough, the rain began to hit their faces in a stern blast as they turned left on to the western road an hour or so after crossing the river. Candidianos rode side by side with Arthur in grim determined silence, but immediately behind them Modlen pulled up her hood and wrapped round her cloak as tightly as she could without dropping the reins. Myrddin grumbled to Gwain that he was getting too old to let politics get in the way of a dry night under a roof without holes.

Gwain, reasonably but unhelpfully, pointed to the leaden sky to the west. 'Tomorrow's likely to be just as bad. We might as well cut the hours of wet riding in half.'

Myrddin was unimpressed. 'It's all right for you. You'll be round Idriseg's hearth soon enough. I'm meant to be carrying on. I'll be riding into the teeth of it all day.'

The steward grinned. 'Your choice, Counsellor.'

***

The trees shouted and the rain drove into every opening all night. Magnis was splendidly but inaccurately named. It had been not much bigger than a village and border trading post, even a century before. Now it was little more than a few shacks taking cover in the lee of third-rate stone walls. They were enough, though, to keep most of the travellers dry most of the time, even if getting fires to do more than throw up smoke was slow and did nothing for anybody's temper. By the morning the horses had lost their enthusiasm for the journey and, though the wind had dropped, the slate sky released its rain without a pause. The river Wye was swollen, and had breached its banks in several places, a month earlier than usual. Now and then flood water lapped at the fringes of the muddy road instead of holding its place a meadow's width away.

Arthur knew the guard posts above the tree line on Elfael's hills as well as anyone, and he smiled as he saw that the clouds hung so low that the sentries would have seen next to nothing from their vantage points. He wondered whether a troop would have been sent along to greet him, or whether he would be left to stand around in the wet for a while until Caradoc felt like appearing in person.

The agreed border between Idriseg and Candidianos's kingdoms was a point on the road where the hills almost met the riverbank, so that the pathway was defended by a small cliff to the left and forested slopes rising sharply to the right. It was defensible for either kingdom, but with Elfael having the advantage of higher ground if need be. In Arthur's lifetime there had been no such need, but at least the border was clear, unlike that between Dobunnia and Siluria on the opposite bank.

They reached it by mid morning, and at last the drenching eased, though there was little sign that the sun would break through to lighten their sodden cloaks. From half a mile back Arthur and Candidianos could see that the road was blocked by horsemen. The only questions for the scouts were whose they were, and in what mood? Gwain folded his men in a protective curtain round the Overlord, the King and Myrddin, just in case the answer was less than welcoming.

The horsemen ahead stayed in a passive line across the road until Arthur's force were within calling distance. Then they parted and a lone figure emerged through the gap and rode forward a few paces. Gwain halted the troops and rode into the middle to consult Arthur, and was surprised to find him already riding forward alone.

CHAPTER XXIV

'I thought, sir...'

'Family, Gwain, all family.' Arthur was grinning hugely as he pushed on through his men. Then, when he was just out of the throng, he dismounted, handed the reins to the nearest soldier and walked purposefully forward, finally breaking into a run.

Gwain looked at Myrddin and shrugged. 'I hope he knows what he's doing.'

Myrddin was smiling too. 'Oh, he does, for once. That's not Caradoc out in front. That's Branwen.'

By then Arthur was grasping the hand that reached down to him, and the men on both sides raised their own arms and cheered. Candidianos and Myrddin rode forward too, and began to dismount, following Arthur's lead.

'Well, Branwen, I'd better keep going,' began Myrddin, as if he had been talking to her all morning. It was true that he had spent a night in Elfael on his way to the Council only a few weeks before, but it was also true that he liked to give the impression that he was liable to appear and disappear without warning. 'Good to see you, and even better to know that this young brother of yours will have someone to talk sense into him.'

'I have plenty of people who do that these days, Myrddin,' smiled Arthur, 'but you are right. Few have Branwen's gifts.'

Branwen gripped Arthur's hand tighter. 'I need his advice these days more than he mine. Elfael has been a happier country than it is now.'

'Princess Branwen,' Candidianos broke in, 'how is King Idriseg?'

She looked down to the ground, away from Arthur, for a moment, and her eyes were tearful when she looked up again. 'It's good that you've all come now,' she said. 'There may not be many more chances to see him.'

'Has he deteriorated that much in a month?' Myrddin asked. Branwen nodded. Myrddin paused, then said, 'In that case I'll delay a day, if I may. He's my oldest friend still living, and this island owes him far more than it knows. I can't ride past and miss him at the end. Will I be welcome?'

'With me and my father, of course. I can't speak for Caradoc.'

Arthur said, 'We'll deal with him later. For now we'll all come with you. Candidianos, will you join us?'

'Gladly, if you think it won't add to Branwen's problems.'

She smiled. 'We may need to build a larger hall, but I'm sure that can be managed by the evening. Of course you must come. My father will be delighted. It's been far too long since the King of the Dobunni was in Elfael.' She called forward two of her men and told them to ride to Idriseg's house as fast as they could so that the preparations could begin. 'We were expecting Arthur to bring his guards, so a few more will make little difference, and it will make my brother think twice before he starts anything.'

'Who, me?' Arthur asked with a childish smirk.

'Idiot!' Branwen said, and ruffled his hair. 'Come on.' A ripple of laughter spread through the troop as the Overlord of Britannia was treated like a small boy. Though Arthur did not realise it at the time, it was a scene that did more to prove to his men that he was worth following than all his political and battlefield skills. They had never thought of him before as a man who had a homeland and a family, only as a leader who seemed to come from nowhere to rule.

Hauling the baggage wagons up and down the hills of Elfael would be a slow business, and so Arthur and Branwen's party set off ahead, leaving the captain of Candidianos's troop and a small detachment of Elfael men to accompany the slower carts with the civilian staff.

Candidianos rode beside Myrddin on the narrow tracks, and Modlen found herself beside Gwain in their usual slightly strained silence. Gwain knew that it was his problem, but he could never think of anything to say to the girl, because she couldn't reply, and he was not a man of easy conversation at the best of times. Modlen was for once quite pleased to have some quiet after Myrddin's enjoyable but continuous monologue. Gwain might not have been fascinating, but he was as good protection for her as for Arthur, and she could relax into her own thoughts. Six months ago those would have been terrified and despairing. Now, though, they were calm and almost content. She was not like other young women, she knew, but then that was why she was one of the three most trusted people in Arthur's entourage. Things could be, and had been so recently, much worse for a girl who had known nothing but slavery and torture since she was nine.

They climbed steadily, and soon the valley and Dobunnia were blotted out by the lurking cloud. There was no rain, but the damp seeped into their clothes as they rose through the grey blanket, which also seemed to cancel all sound except the monotonous padding of the

CHAPTER XXIV

horses' hooves on soft muddy paths. Modlen lost all sense of time and direction. They might have travelled in that anonymous shroud all day. And still they climbed.

She was just beginning to feel that somehow they had all been spirited away into a lost and endless world from which they could never return, a form of hell where they would tramp the skies in wet clothes for ever, when they suddenly, in a few steps, broke through the top of the cloud cover. Modlen looked about her in astonishment. She felt like a creature riding out of the sea, the stray wisps of cloud flowing past her like wave crests. Up here, the sun was shining and blue sky above solid grey stretched out to the horizon as though they were riding on to an island and all other lands were a submarine dream. Elfael was showing her the best of its magic – how it could isolate itself from the cares of other kingdoms, how it could be overlooked by those riding west to the sea along the valley roads or those crossing eastwards to the richer, larger and (in their eyes) more significant lowland kingdoms. Yet, riding above the clouds in the warm sun, through orchards heavy with fruit, without the close enclosure of forest trees, as the larks rose and the red kites circled above her, Modlen knew that she had reached her own ultimate haven for the future. She looked across at Arthur, who was silent too, his hand in his sister's as they rode, and wondered whether it was a future she would ever reach and if it would be alone. Myrddin glanced back at her and smiled. Had he read her thoughts or planted them? They were thoughts more resonant of his years, however many those were, than hers.

The moment was broken as they dropped into the cloud once more, winding down into the woods until they turned westwards and crossed a brook that tumbled fiercely along the edge of a wide clearing. They followed the waterside back into the woods, and the Elfael horses lifted their heads and strode faster: the short path home. The ground was rising sharply again and soon, though the trees still surrounded them, the clouds slunk away and the light filtered through the red and golden leaves clinging to the branches.

Above them a hill towered to mountain height, higher than any Modlen had seen before, even on the journey over the peaks to Isurium. For a moment she thought they were going to have to find a path up its precipitous side, but instead they rounded a bend in the path, crossed the now-gentle stream and headed towards a secluded cleft in the face of the hill. The woods grew denser for a few paces then parted, as if they were just a final fence, and a little above them an ancient earth rampart topped by a high stockade projected out from the rock. Beneath a watchtower a gate swung open at the riders' approach and the roar of horns told all in Idriseg's hall that their Princess and Tygern Fawr were home.

Once inside the gate the troops fanned out on either side and formed a guard of honour for the royal party. Myrddin, Gwain and Modlen hung back as Arthur, Branwen and Candidianos rode forward and dismounted. In front of them stood Idriseg's hall, modest by the standards of the great buildings Modlen had seen in Londinium, or even Cunorix's palace in Verulamium, but it was princely enough. Just outside the doorway an old man lay propped on a bed in the sunshine, his arm raised in greeting.

Arthur walked up, dropped on to one knee and grasped the old man's hand. 'Father,' he said.

'Hello lad,' he said. 'You look well, but a bit wider, neither of which can be said of me. I'm sorry not to have come to meet you on the road. Even my legs don't obey me these days.'

'I thought you'd be inside.'

Branwen fussed at Idriseg's side. 'He was meant to be.'

'Oh don't be silly, girl. Of course I had to be out for this. And anyway, if I have only a few more weeks left I might as well enjoy the sun as long as I can. The smoke inside won't make me live any longer. Cheer up, Geraint – Arthur, whichever – you're meant to be pleased to see me.'

Arthur did his best to smile. 'I wish—'

'So do I,' Idriseg cut in. 'Is that Myrddin skulking over there?'

'Yes,' answered Branwen.

'And who's that with him? I think I know him.'

'You do, Idriseg. I'm Candidianos. I'm sorry I have waited so long for an excuse to visit you.'

'Heavens, man – you and Myrddin. I must be more ill than I thought. Oh well, better to see you now than not at all. Let's get you dry and find you something to drink. About the only thing Myrddin is useful for these days is that he sends me up some of his Gaulish wine from Moridunum. Time it was drunk by someone who appreciated it, rather than my crowd.'

Arthur rose to his feet, Idriseg's bed was lifted by four serving men and Branwen led the visitors inside.

Once cloaks had been divested and handed to servants to dry, the party gathered at Idriseg's bedside as cups of wine were brought forward and toasts to their safe arrival were drunk. Gwain stood behind Arthur, and Modlen hovered by Myrddin.

Idriseg peered at her. 'I know your man, Geraint, but not the girl.'

Briefly Arthur told her story, and Idriseg shook his head in disgust at Cunorix's viciousness. 'And this is the man they tell me you have appointed to run Britannia when you can't?'

'With Candidianos.'

'Well, good luck to both of you. I wouldn't trust him with a piece of cheese.'

Myrddin broke in. 'Better on the inside, as it were.'

'Not much, I'd say,' grunted Idriseg, 'but you may be right. And I mustn't judge your energy levels by mine.'

'And he has done us all a big favour, though he doesn't know it, by bringing us Modlen. She may be quiet, but she has more wisdom than all the kings around the new table.' Myrddin proudly put his hand on Modlen's shoulder, who blushed, much to her own fury.

Idriseg smiled. 'That might not be as hard as it seems, my dear, but I'm glad you have someone sensible with you all the time, Geraint. I have Branwen and Olwen. You will need her more as the years pass. Olwen will be back by this evening, by the way.'

Arthur looked around the hall. 'So Branwen tells me. And Caradoc?'

Idriseg looked down into his wine and muttered. 'Quite. And Caradoc. Who knows when, or in what state? I'm afraid he is no rush to join us, Geraint. I have tried, but—'

'I expected as much, Father. It doesn't worry me.'

'But it worries me, and it worries many of my people.'

'I have been thinking about that a lot on the way here,' said Arthur, 'and Branwen and I have been discussing it along the way, too.'

Idriseg sipped his wine and closed his eyes for a moment. 'That's a comfort, of sorts. Any solutions?'

'Of sorts, as you say.'

Branwen interrupted. 'Better than that, Father. Geraint – I mean Arthur—'

'Let's fix this, shall we?' grinned Arthur. 'To the rest of the world I am Arthur, Tygern Fawr. But in this house I'll be Geraint as long as you or Elfael want me to be.'

'What he is suggesting,' Branwen ploughed on, smiling, 'is risky, but it might work.'

'Then I'd better hear it,' said Idriseg.

'Caradoc's problem is—'

'Drink, women and bad temper – and stupidity,' Idriseg broke in.

'Yes, but not stupidity,' said Arthur. 'He's foolish, but that's because his jealousy drives him to it. His real problem is frustration, which goes all the way back to that morning Myrddin appeared and we found my sword. Suddenly he no longer really mattered, and he can't forgive us for it.'

'Nonsense. He's a prince. I'm an old and dying man. He should be running my kingdom.'

'With you, his sister and his wife critical of every move? It's a test he's bound to fail.'

'And you have something better for him?'

'Yes, but it will mean he will leave Elfael – possibly for ever, though he will succeed you in name.'

'Is another one of Myrddin's schemes?'

'No. He hasn't heard it yet, either. It's one of mine and Branwen's.'

Idriseg snorted. 'Then it has a chance of being sane. Go on.'

'I want to take Caradoc with me,' said Arthur, 'and leave Branwen here with you.'

'Will he go with you? Why should he, when he has the prospect, I'm afraid, of having my kingdom before the winter is over?'

'Because I can give him something bigger, if not better. As you know Brigantia has no king at the moment.'

'I hear you had a hand in that,' mused Idriseg.

'I'm not particularly proud of it, but yes, and it hasn't turned out too badly. I want Caradoc to take control of Brigantia west of the mountains and to give him the task of putting a new king in place in the east.'

'Is that wise?' asked Candidianos. 'I don't see Caradoc as a great negotiator.'

'He doesn't need to be – at least, not at first. The Brigantians understand a strong man. They need a bully who doesn't care whether they like him or not.'

Idriseg shook his head. 'Then you've read your brother wrong, Geraint. He cares very much what people think of him – especially you. The bravado is all pretence and anger.'

'It doesn't matter. I think he'll rise to the challenge and, though he wouldn't believe it now, I trust him. I need a man who has to prove himself and who wants the other kings to see him as an equal.'

'That will take time. And what happens to Elfael after me?'

'Caradoc remains King of Elfael in name, but Branwen will rule in his stead, and I will make sure he doesn't come back to interfere.'

Idriseg looked at his daughter and foster-son sadly. 'You're forgetting Olwen. She may not want to have Caradoc around much, but she will be queen, and will not see why Branwen should overrule her. Then your nephew, Idriseg ap Caradoc, is eleven already. It won't be many years before he starts to play the prince. He's a handsome boy, Geraint, you'll like him.'

'I'm sure, but you underestimate Branwen, Father.'

'No, I certainly do not. But neither do I underestimate the power of faction to undermine her, nor the ability of Gwythernion to look for division. It would suit them very well to have a queen under their thumb. Love her as I do, Olwen will be just as troublesome as her husband within a week of my death.'

'Do you have another idea?'

'No, not immediately,' admitted Idriseg, and lay back on his bed for a moment. 'Does it have to be decided today?'

'That depends on when Caradoc appears,' answered Arthur. 'I will want to speak to him as soon as I can once he's here, otherwise he'll just be so unpleasant it will make it difficult for me to give him anything without it looking as if I am weak myself.'

Idriseg was looking tired. He let his cup be topped up with wine, sipped it, then leant back on his cushions and closed his eyes. Branwen put a hand on Arthur's arm. He caught the meaning.

'But I'm sure we can leave it until this evening, at least. And we can discuss it later, once Branwen and I have talked through it again. For now we'll rest, then eat.'

Candidianos pulled Arthur aside as they moved away from Idriseg's bed. 'I have an idea too, but I want to discuss it with Branwen first, if you don't mind.'

'Of course,' agreed Arthur. 'It makes a pleasant change.'

'Does it? From what?'

'From Myrddin and I trying to shape the future.'

'We'll control our own kingdoms this afternoon, Tygern Fawr. Leave it to us, and enjoy being a boy at home for a few hours.'

'Thank you. I'll do my best.'

Myrddin hovered, with Gwain and Modlen just behind. 'What now?'

'Now,' said Arthur, 'I'm leaving the cares of Britannia to you three for the afternoon. There are others I haven't seen for too long.'

Gwain nodded and walked off to superintend the troops, both Arthur's and Candidianos's, since his captain hadn't arrived with the baggage wagons.

Myrddin looked pleased with himself. 'Good. Then I shall tell Modlen a few legends while you're gone. Are you ready for some hill climbing in the sun, young sprat?'

Modlen looked wary, but shrugged and followed her new mentor out of the hall, grabbing a water skin on the way.

Arthur drank the last of his wine and watched for a few seconds as Branwen had Idriseg carried through a curtained doorway to his private area of the hall. He frowned in thought, then gathered himself together and made his way outside, switching from his preoccupied private to his public demeanour as he did so. There were old friends to visit in their quarters, but plenty of others who he would need to flatter with confidential time if he was to leave Idriseg's house calm and in his favour for the turbulent winter to come.

* * *

A while later Arthur climbed the watchtower above the gate, greeted the sentries and then leant on the rail looking out across the wide bowl of northern Elfael to the matching hills of Malienydd beyond. All of them were bathed in late-afternoon sunshine, but the light had already dipped behind the mountain that protected the royal hall, leaving it in early shadow. There was a chill in the air, reminding him of the cold days to come and the morning's rain that still lashed the lowlands.

Although the round of goodwill visits, much of them spent admiring children and reassuring men that Elfael was important and he had not forgotten them, had taken more time that he wanted, there had still been enough left for him to wander out of the fortifications

CHAPTER XXIV

and far enough into the woods to find the neighbouring stream and sit silently chucking sticks at it as the wind tumbled down the valley and shook the trees around him. The intention had been to take his mind off the cares of all Britannia that had been obsessing him ever since he had set out on the road with Gwenan five months before and somehow pretend that he was twelve years old again. The trouble was that when he achieved it he also remembered that the pains he had felt then were, if anything, more intense: his feelings that he did not quite belong in Idriseg's family, without knowing why, his brother's constant jealous anger, his love for the village girls shyly but firmly rebuffed. As a result he was in an even more unsettled mood when he climbed the watchtower than he had been when he had set out into the woods.

Up the uneven road he could see the wagons of the rest of his entourage lumbering towards the first of the defences. He turned away from the landscape and looked into the cluttered yard between the fortifications and Idriseg's hall. Its normally quiet space was thronged, now that his and the Dobunnian men were added to the household. Word that Arthur was there had spread, and many of Elfael's great and ambitious had made their way to the court as quickly as they could, hoping either to enhance their standing or just to find a good feast and better gossip.

With the wagons, servant girls and the second wave of troops and horses to accommodate the fit would be tight – almost as full as at the times of major invasion for which the compound had been designed but, thankfully, never needed within living memory. Round the far side of the hall Candidianos strolled into view, his hand on Branwen's shoulder. They looked serious, but then she smiled and Candidianos's hand moved gently upwards to touch her hair.

Arthur watched from above, surprised and puzzled, wished the sentries well and scrambled down the watchtower ladder.

By the time he reached them Branwen and Candidianos were laughing, her arm resting lightly in his.

'Geraint, where have you been?' asked Branwen. 'We've been looking for you.'

'Just looking around,'

'For anything in particular? Everything's much the same, I think.'

'My past. Memories.'

Branwen looked into her foster-brother's eyes, and her face grew serious. 'Find any?'

'Too many.' Arthur pulled himself together. 'And you? What have you both been doing?'

'Branwen's been introducing me to your nieces, Arthur. You must spare some time for them. They'll take your mind off your worries – theirs are so much more pressing!' Candidianos chuckled.

'You're right. I should – and probably before their parents arrive to complicate matters.' Arthur started to move towards the door.

Branwen held him back. 'In a minute. But first we have to tell you about our other discussions.'

'Serious ones?'

'Oh yes,' said Candidianos. 'At least, I think so. I have asked Branwen to become my queen.'

Arthur looked at them both in stunned silence. Perhaps because he was six years younger than Candidianos and five younger than Branwen, it had somehow never occurred to him that their lives could be arranged any differently. And at thirty-five Branwen was almost beyond the limit of marriageability in his eyes.

She misinterpreted his look. 'Don't you approve, Geraint? I thought…'

Arthur shook himself into a smile and opened his arms to hug her. 'Yes, yes, of course I do. It's a wonderful idea. I'm just, you know, a little…' he stuttered.

'You'll get used to it,' Branwen grinned.

'Have you been planning this for long?' he asked.

Candidianos answered. 'Yes and no. I've been more than a little in love with your sister ever since I first met her twenty years ago, though I made sure nobody realised. But I only decided to ask her to marry me after she met us on the road this morning and I was watching her as we were riding here. I knew suddenly that none of my reasons for delaying made any sense any more.'

'Did they ever?' asked Branwen, searchingly.

'Probably not,' admitted Candidianos, blushing a little.

Over the shock and back in control, Arthur grasped his friend's arm. 'It makes perfect sense, and it will mean that I will never have to worry about either of you again, I hope. Have you asked Father yet?'

'No, he's still sleeping,' said Branwen. 'How do you think he'll react?'

'I think he'll sleep much easier tonight. But we mustn't tell anybody else until you've asked him – especially Myrddin. You know what he's like. He'll claim he's been planning it for years.'

CHAPTER XXIV

'I'm afraid he'd be justified,' said Branwen ruefully. 'He told me only a year after you were made Tygern Fawr in Corinium that he was certain Candidianos felt this way, and asked me what I intended to do about it.'

'And what did you say?'

'I'm afraid I told him not to be absurd.' She looked up at the rather crestfallen Candidianos. 'I'm sorry. It did seem absurd — you were so out of my reach, the great young king with the girls flocking around you.'

'I'm sorry too. I thought you thought I wasn't good enough.'

'And I think,' Arthur butted in, 'that you've both wasted an awful lot of each other's time — as well as a very useful alliance between our kingdoms which might even have made Caradoc behave. Come on, let's go and see if Father is awake before everybody out here gets too curious.'

He led the way inside and gently but firmly pushed away the line of petitioners. He was less successful, though, with the two small girls, a boisterous six-year-old who attached herself to Candidianos's leg and a rather solemn one of nine, who took Branwen's hand. The nieces, Arthur guessed, though he had been away too long to recognise them.

Idriseg's nurse barred the way as he nudged aside the wool curtain to the old man's room. Then she saw who it was, and stepped backward with a bow. The King's bed faced them, drawn up close to the fire. He opened his eyes slowly and looked wryly at the younger men.

'I don't want any state craft from you two for a while yet,' he said. 'Unless it's good news and easy to understand.'

The girls arranged themselves sitting by grandfather on the bed.

'I can promise that,' said Arthur, moving round to poke more life into the fire.

'King Idriseg,' began Candidianos.

'If you begin like that I know the promise is broken already,' he grunted.

'Not entirely, though what you say will effect both our kingdoms.'

Idriseg sighed. 'Well?'

'For many years we have been allies. Arthur could not have become overlord—'

'Candidianos, forgive me, but I don't have the energy to listen to speeches any more. There'll be enough of those from Myrddin later. If you have something to ask, do so.'

'Of course. King Idriseg—'

'Oh, for heaven's sake!'

Branwen broke in. 'Father, he's trying to ask you if I can marry him.'

There was a pause, then Idriseg reached over and lifted his wine cup from the table. 'Geraint, this man is even more indecisive than you. Are you sure he can be trusted to turn up when you need him?'

The five younger people stood baffled in silence. Eventually Idriseg spoke again. 'I'm glad you never found the courage to ask before, boy. I could not have managed without my daughter, and I cannot manage now. So there is a condition. I am very happy that she will be your queen, and you must marry her in Elfael, because I am too ill to travel anywhere else.'

'Naturally,' said Candidianos.

'Wait, that's not the condition. Branwen must stay with me till I die. I will not take long, don't worry. But I want my final days to be as the others have been: reasonably peaceful. And that cannot happen if,' he glanced at the two children sitting by his feet, 'well, you know.'

Branwen stepped forward and took her father's hand. 'I've waited this long for a husband. I can wait still.'

'No, girl. No more waiting. You'll marry tomorrow. We'll not hang around for a bishop. There are holy men enough in Elfael. But you'll stay for a week, Candidianos, and then you will leave her with me. Later you can have a ceremonial wedding in Corinium with as many bishops as you like.'

The Dobunnian King stared at the fire for a moment. 'It's hard,' he said at last, 'but I understand. May I visit?'

Idriseg laughed and reached out to him. 'As long as Geraint can spare you. In truth, lad, you will see as much of Branwen this way as if you left her at home in Corinium, Glevum or Aquae Sulis.'

Branwen looked up. Candidianos nodded. 'It's true. Thank you.'

Myrddin's only comment, when he ambled in with an exhausted-looking Modlen a few minutes later was, 'Thank the stars for that. Haste follows procrastination.'

Later still, after Olwen had returned and they had eaten, but before Caradoc crashed in drunk and raised the tension by yelling obscenities at all his family and their 'sycophants', Myrddin guided Arthur out into the cool autumn night and up on the top of the rampart between watch-posts. It was almost the only private spot left.

CHAPTER XXIV

'Are you pleased?' he asked.

'For Branwen? Yes, of course. Unexpected, though,' answered Arthur. 'The timing was a surprise.'

'I'd almost forgotten about their little attraction. I thought they had, too. But it should ease many burdens – for all of us.'

'I hope so.'

Myrddin turned towards him, away from the moonlit valley. 'It's time for you too, Arthur.'

'Time for what?'

'To find a wife – and I'm afraid I don't mean the lovely Gwenan.'

'Ah.' The lack of enthusiasm in Arthur's voice was palpable.

'It won't be a problem. I have just the girl in mind. And she won't split the Council, either.'

'Do I know her?'

'Certainly not. Much better that way.'

'You mean no preconceptions?'

'No conception of any kind,' Myrddin grinned at his own pun, 'but more importantly, no history. We'll keep it in the family, though.' He clapped him on the shoulder and strode back to the hall leaving Arthur glaring at the moon. Despondently he thought back through his lovers, beginning with Sioned and ending with Gwenan. He very much doubted whether his idea of a wife and Myrddin's would come anywhere near each other.

BOOK THREE

The Great Battle and After

Late Autumn AD *489–Summer 490*

XXV

THE CRISP MORNING LIGHT suggested it would be a fine November day as Arthur pushed aside the woollen blankets and stumbled over to relieve himself in a private corner. His joints creaked. Myrddin's joke that the Overlord was getting too long in the tooth for continual campaigning had some truth in it, though he liked to think that his early thirties were more the end of the beginning than the beginning of the end.

He sluiced his face in a bowl of chill water, let Modlen straighten his tunic and hair before stepping outside the tent. Around him the troops were already at their business, their mats and blankets rolled, their swords and shields wiped of the rime of light frost that had gathered in the clear night. The cooks had cauldrons steaming, and queues were forming for breakfast. Arthur strode to the edge of the camp and looked down from the hill, north towards Corinium some fifteen miles way, to which the road stretched without a bend. On either side well-kept fields and farmsteads, a few round houses grouped at their centre, spread for miles. In this rich part of Candidianos's territory the forest had been tamed for half a millennium, though the unsettled years of the last hundred had let patches of fresh woodland sprout where the farmers had failed or been driven away.

Candidianos appeared at his elbow and, optimistic in the sunshine, they both surveyed the calm beauty of the scene for a moment. 'I can almost see the smoke of my home this morning,' he said.

'And I can almost smell your excellent kitchen,' sighed Arthur.

'Are we staying in camp today? We could always take a fast horse and find a good reason why our discussions could only take place around my table at lunchtime?'

Arthur grinned. 'Tempting, but no. The messengers are coming here, and there may be no time for them to head out again. Besides, if we lunched in Corinium in the way you like to, we would only just be back in camp by dark at this time of year.'

'If we were lucky,' admitted Candidianos. 'There are moments when I wish you weren't always so sensible, Arthur,' the King complained.

'And Myrddin would say he wished there were more moments when I was. Come on, let's see if the army has left anything for their leaders to eat.'

They made their way through the lines of men, who quietened respectfully as the King and the Overlord passed. The effect was like a moment when the wind drops, then rustles the branches with a gentle breeze. There had been no fighting yet since they had mustered so that, apart from the normal minor ills of autumn, the men were fit and cheerful. None of the tension or forced heartiness that would be so plain the morning before a battle was in the air, either. This was an army and its civilian followers going about its business in its own country, well fed on a fine morning after one of the most peaceful years any could remember.

Arthur's steward hurried over and the Overlord clapped him on the shoulder. 'Good morning, Gwain. No ceremony this morning. We'll breakfast in the open and afterwards tell the men we will be happy to hear any questions or problems. But keep the priests away – I'm not in the mood for their advice.'

'Yes, sir.'

'Frankly there's not much more to do until the messengers come through. And we are not moving from here until they do.'

Gwain bowed. In the open and in view of the men he was careful to give the King of Dobunnia all the deference they never bothered with in private, or when only the immediate household were present. 'I'm sure the men will be grateful of the opportunity, sir.'

A table was set up in front of Arthur's tent, and they settled as the food was brought.

The site for the camp had been chosen carefully. Nobody could approach from the north or east without the army, small as yet, knowing about it many hours before the arrival. Yet they were beside one of the best-maintained thoroughfares in Britain, and the forces of the other kings of the south and west would have no trouble finding

CHAPTER XXV

them. The Barbarians would know where they were too, of course, but Arthur had every intention that they should. He was not there to avoid a battle. He was not at full strength yet, though. He had the western forces of his own men, a few from the Cornovii and Myrddin's kin in Demetia. The main body of the camp were all local Dobunni. There were others on their way. He was in no great hurry.

The Barbarian force had landed nearly three weeks before, and were moving slowly south-west towards rich pickings in unsuspecting territory, as they thought, and away from the men with fierce reputations: the Brigantes, Coritani and Catuvellauni. The Barbarians too had taken their time, using the waterways and wetlands in the east to penetrate deep inland, avoiding the Iceni altogether and not abandoning their ships until far into the kingdom of Cunorix. There, at Durobrivae, they had found a road to their liking: serviceable but little used, it seemed and – the scouts and spies told them – passing through lands full of cattle and the harvest but empty of the army of Coritania, which was busy fighting border disputes well to the north.

All of which turned out to be rubbish.

For the first ten miles there was food and forage in plenty, but the open land soon gave way to impenetrable woods, and the road, so promising at the start, petered out to little more than an overgrown track. On either side of the road, where there should have been at least a farm or a few sheep to plunder, there were only empty fields and the charred remains of huts. Now and again, about every two days, they had come to crossroads, but these all led either north-west, away from the heartlands they had come to seize, or south-east, where they were told Cunorix was marshalling a large army on high ground.

This too was rubbish. He was right behind them, and had prepared the way meticulously.

Arthur bided his time by the great road south of Corinium and supervised training sessions in his camp. 'News will come when it is ready,' he said. When he was young he had found that one of Myrddin's most irritating sayings, specially calculated to make him rage with impatience. Now, though, he had come to realise there was only so much you could do to force events – far better to prepare well, choose your ground and let others rush to you.

The first to do so was a messenger from Dumnonia. Caldoros had left Aquae Sulis the day before, and would expect to reach him before sunset tomorrow. Would Tygern Fawr still be in camp? Arthur reassured the herald and sent him back. One of Candidianos's men rode in to say that Badoc had been spotted just west of the Sabrina river, and was leading a force of at least a thousand men. The King muttered that he hoped Badoc would be on their side – not just of the river, but of the argument.

'He will,' Arthur smiled. 'Bishop Dubricius is full of evangelist fervour at the thought of a Christian victory.'

Only a month had passed since Arthur had left his home in the western hills and had said goodbye to his foster-father, Idriseg. They both suspected it was for the last time, but neither had shown it, parting as if Arthur was just a lad off around the little kingdom for a few days with friends. The tears had all been Branwen's, perhaps because they were not for her. The late betrothal to Candidianos had instead given her a new inner light of happiness that made her father feel both content and a little guilty that he had imposed on her more months of waiting.

That month, October, had been eventful and full of long-distance riding. Although Branwen had remained behind with the old man, Caradoc had left with Arthur. He had been surly and resentful at first, as he always was with any suggestion that he had not thought out for himself, but had come round a day or so later when, as they rode out of Viroconium with the Cornovii, side by side with the King as an equal, he realised that Arthur was serious about the real increase in his status the plan implied.

Much to everyone's surprise Caradoc's first official mission, accompanying Arthur to the King of Deceangelia, effectively swapping that kingdom's dwindling and insecure mainland territory for the slightly smaller but far more independent island of Manavia, had succeeded with only token argument. The King had accepted it when he was given solid guarantees of rights of entry to the port at Deva, marriage ties for his sons and daughters with the royal houses of Ordovicia and Cornovia and hostages to make sure the promises of grain supplies from Britannia were honoured. He also managed to double the number of cattle and sheep the Council in Londinium had thought adequate to offer his son.

Caradoc had been able to claim that it was his offer to provide men to bolster the defence of Manavia against Hibernian and Barbarian

CHAPTER XXV

raids, once he was in proper control of the western half of Brigantia, which had swung the old King's agreement. Despite the inevitable grumbles from the Ordovician and Cornovian kings having to pay to effectively add a third to the size of each of their own kingdoms, Arthur left Deva thoroughly pleased with himself. It was lucky Myrddin had stayed behind with Idriseg, otherwise he would have inevitably punctured the mood and warned his old student of the dangers of satisfaction.

Once into Brigantia, Arthur had left Caradoc in command of a combined Cornovian and Ordovician force of three hundred men to ride north and impose his authority. They were soon augmented by western Brigantians themselves, far more prepared to accept a brother of the Overlord than one of the thugs from east of the mountains fighting over the succession to Vortebelos – or anybody from east of the mountains, for that matter. The instructions Arthur left were clear. Impose but do not conquer. Persuade but not by torture. Impress but not by terrorising the women and destroying farms. He was fairly certain Cunegnus's Cornovians would do as he said. Whether Caradoc would be able to control either himself or the rest he was not so sure. As he pushed on through heavy October rain across the peaks to Ebvracum he profoundly hoped his optimism in his brother's ability to reform would not prove disastrous.

Ebvracum surprised Arthur. He fully expected precisely nothing to have been done since he had left in August. work on the palace had moved on, the walls at the river's edge were now high enough to keep the worst of the floods at bay, at least on the north bank, and the new confidence of being the Overlord's city once again, together with the absence of trouble-making raids from Isurium, had seen its markets and town houses bustle. Arthur's arrival, even for a few days, just after the harvest had the locals strutting in from the villages and the townspeople vying to be found in his company, however tangential the excuse. He was anyway in the mood to relax. He missed the old Gwenan, the Gwenan of lazy afternoons in the peach garden and bed, but the new Gwenan, severe and fragile, was less of a diversion and anyway was still convalescing in Londinium. Modlen occasionally crept into his bed at night, but it was always for comfort, and he never risked damaging her trust by taking full sex, though she herself began desperately to want him to. He knew well enough, though, that he needed her as his memory and ultimate confidante in the affairs of state and, if she was that, she could not be his mistress, especially now that Myrddin was intent on him finding a wife.

For two weeks he enjoyed himself as he had always wanted to since he had taken on his role over sixteen years before. He was truly, for once, commander of a united Britannia – not just in name but, since the Council and the pacification of the north, in reality, however temporary.

In Ebvracum Arthur saw no kings, greeted and dispatched messengers, kept Modlen working at writing up the records of proceedings, was entertained and feasted by the imperial city's finest, and for a couple of weeks supervised the completion of work as it was rushed to be finished before winter set in.

Then news arrived that the Barbarians had landed, with ships and an army that dwarfed anything that had come before. Arthur had expected some sort of response to the thrashing he had given them seven months earlier, but he had not expected it so late in the season. It must mean that the harvest had failed across the sea and supplies would not last through the icy months to come. Or it could mean that the Barbarians themselves were having their lands seized by new invaders from the uncharted lands and forests that stretched, it was said, almost to Byzantium. Had they sailed over in the spring to mark the anniversary of the previous defeat, he had planned to be ready to gather his army after a Round Table in Londinium and confront them head on in the Catuvellaunian heartlands.

For a night Arthur wondered how to respond. He could stay reasonably securely in Ebvracum and let Cunorix and his allies deal with the invasion, if they could, but that would have been politically disastrous, undoing all the progress towards a true Council under his leadership. He could just march south and hope to gather troops along the way. That was fraught with uncertainty, though. He might not find enough men to make much difference if he came to a beleaguered Cunorix too late – and defeat was unthinkable. For once some advice would have been welcome, but aside from Gwain and Modlen (one who never ventured an opinion and one who couldn't) he was without anybody whose advice he really trusted. There was no time to call either the kings or their envoys to the Round Table. The new system, by which he would always travel with representatives of the Council

CHAPTER XXV

and the table itself, was agreed but not started. The table was still sitting with the Bishop of Londinium, and it had been assumed that the representatives would be chosen and travel to join Arthur in Ebvracum after the winter.

The plan, when it came just before the light of morning, was simple enough, but it relied on everybody across Britannia playing their part, as they had promised only a few weeks before. Gwain and Modlen were startled to be summoned at dawn, the first to find as many fast messengers as knew their way, the second to make copies of the messages so that reserve couriers could follow on the next day in case of accidents.

The first instruction was to Cunorix. He was not to engage the Barbarians, however tempting. He was to steer them south-west, clearing the land in front of them along a known but unfrequented road and following half a day's march behind, gathering men as he went. He should make sure the Barbarian force was harried just enough to slow but not divert them, and spies should be sent to tell them of great riches ahead. Arthur himself would leave Ebvracum within three days and march in parallel, intending to arrive in Corinium well ahead of them, despite having to travel twice the distance. The Atrebates and their southern allies were told to muster on the hills by Cunetio and wait.

Now Arthur was about to find out if the strategy had worked.

By the middle of this day south-east of Corinium, he and Candidianos wanted to be certain that their western and southern forces were either in position or would be soon. From Cunorix, however, he had heard nothing official. He might have ignored the orders entirely. Arthur had his own observers, though, and from these, sent out from Londinium, he knew that the Barbarians were still on the move and had not fought more than a skirmish or two along the way – nothing that could be called a full battle – so the chances were that Cunorix was doing pretty much as he was told.

It was late in the afternoon before Arthur could be sure that all the pieces were falling into place. A herald from Cunorix rode in with the news that the Catuvellauni and the men of the east were on the same road as the Barbarians and catching them. The two armies were now only half a day's march apart and camped close to the upper streams of the Tamesis river.

Arthur took Candidianos to one side, out of earshot of the herald and his other counsellors. 'That gives us two days, possibly three. We should all be together by then. Can you supply the whole army when they arrive?'

'If you don't expect us to do it on our own for more than a week, we should manage. But don't drag this out with games, Tygern Fawr. My people will fight Barbarians, but not for the fun of it with winter on its way.'

'I won't, I promise. A week should be enough.'

* * *

Aelle docked at the wharves on the north bank of the river at Londinium, and invited the merchants and Bishop Gwidellius's customs men aboard to view his shipload of salted pork, leather and fine metalwork, although he unaccountably failed to show them the pile of exceptionally decorated shields on which his crew were sitting as the inspection progressed. Barbarian (how he resented the word) ships were always suspicious, but Aelle had been coming back and forth for years, sometimes with goods, sometimes with groups of people he swore were slaves from other Barbarian nations. Strangely he never seemed to reach a satisfactory price for them, and sailed away, usually in the late afternoon when there were only two or three hours of light left, swearing he could do better at Durobrivae. By the time he reached there, however, the story and the cargo had changed. There were no slaves. They had been dropped ashore and, while their captain was buying Britannian luxuries to take back across the sea, they were being escorted south to mingle with the settlers the Cantiaci had learnt to put up with in increasing numbers on the fringes of their great forests. They were forest people, and had a way with wood and charcoal that their Britannian neighbours, who preferred grazing the hills and heathlands, could never quite fathom. No one on the wharves of Londinium had a notion that this was the same Aelle who, twelve years before, had come with three ships and many warriors, including his three sons, to the coast and, ignoring the forts along the shore, had terrified the Cantiaci for two weeks. He had been disgusted by the speed of their flight into their hill forts then, but realised that much of the best land and all of the woods were virtually uninhabited. He had been making the journey

CHAPTER XXV

every few months ever since. Only once had there been any trouble. He had been lazy in his preparations three years before, and tried to drop his immigrant families too close to a riverside village. For the first time he had been met with force and, to protect the women and children in his party (he always maintained), had had to teach the Britannians a lesson.

This time he had once again come in more than one ship – five, in fact – all decked out with the same symbols of the earth goddess on their sails to show they were traders, but they had spread out. Only his ship truly carried trading goods. The rest, full of concealed men, were moving upriver deliberately slowly against the ebb tide.

Aelle had planned the journey carefully, ever since they had arrived in sight of the great estuary and its coasts two days earlier. Darkness would fall just as the tide began to turn. When he slipped the mooring ropes it seemed to the city's watchmen that he was heading back towards the sea. He did – just enough to pick up his little fleet as the water surged inland again. Sails lowered, rowing hard but softly, they swept upriver by the light of a cloudy moon.

The tide was at its height when they moored on an island in the stream several miles west of Londinium. Aelle, the men and their supplies were offloaded. By the time the moon was moving lower in the sky again and the tide was turning back to the ebb, the ships were gliding back downriver, though with only their helmsmen and a dozen oarsmen to crew them.

The river island, an 'eyot' in their language, was well wooded and screened by trees from either shore. There were no fires burning in the open. Aelle was greeted silently but warmly by his countrymen, and led quickly through the undergrowth. At the centre of the island a tight space, barely quarter of an acre, had been cleared and huts built, so close together that they were almost like an old Roman town. There was no hall. This was no ordinary village, and though it had taken several weeks of careful work to build, it was not intended to last more than another day. Aelle was led inside to warm himself against the chill of the autumn night. The fires inside would be smothered and smokeless at daybreak. As quietly as possible his men stowed their food and weapons, drank new ale and ate fresh bread and meat for the first time in weeks, then joined many others, perhaps three times their number, already laid out silently on the hut floors.

Had their leader allowed them, they would have talked all night, for there were years to catch up on. This was the fruit of all Aelle's voyages – an army perhaps five hundred strong, gathered from the families who had slipped ashore and become settlers in Britannia, where they were derided as Barbarians – not because they looked much different or had never been Roman, but because they kept their own gods and talked in a language so clipped and guttural that the Brythonic speakers joked that they could not tell the difference between their conversations and the dogs quarrelling beneath the table. The settlers knew who they were and from where they had left the continental shore. They called themselves Jutes.

In the pale early light of morning, under Aelle's orders, and not before signals had been given from the bank, the men slipped into small riverboats, ten at time, and were ferried to the northern bank.

There was a road less than a mile away – the road that led all the way from Londinium to Aquae Sulis – but Aelle's men were not interested in taking it. The Britannians liked their roads and feared the forests. And if surprise was the element Aelle wanted most, then knowing where the road was but keeping out of sight of it was essential. They would take woodland paths, follow the deer, push through the falling leaves and stiffening brambles, letting the river be ever present, except where the occasional port village clung to its sides. They were in no great hurry. Like Arthur and Cunorix they wanted to be in place when the main force from the north-east came close, but not too long before. And like the leaders of Britannia's kingdoms, Aelle had his scouts to tell him when that was.

* * *

The muster of the southern kingdoms in Arthur's main army was complete after a further two days of waiting. It was just as well because, had they not been, the Barbarian forces would have passed them a few miles to the east as they roamed towards the rich farmlands that were now all but undefended. The scouts were now coming and going in a steady stream, some monitoring the progress of the invaders, others keeping Cunorix and Arthur in as close touch as it was possible for horses to run across the twenty-five miles of unkempt road and open heath between them.

The news they brought was encouraging and concerning in equal measure. The invaders were almost exactly where they were meant to be, but the reports suggested that the numbers were a lot higher than they should have been if they just consisted of the men who had come off the ships. The scouts were speculating that many of the resident Barbarians of the eastern kingdoms (whom Arthur had thought likely to remain neutral) had been persuaded or tempted to rebel by the size and belligerence of the new forces. Added to this, Cunorix had driven his men hard, and they were more tired than Arthur would have liked before a crucial battle. However, he was cheered by the news that young Tegernacus and his Coritanian men had managed to hook up with Cunorix along the way without (surprisingly) coming to blows amongst themselves. It meant there was now a very substantial army able to provide one prong of the intended pincer on the invaders.

Early in the morning of the third day that all his southern and western men had been in the one camp, Arthur called the kings together: their 'host', Candidianos of Dobunnia, Badoc of Siluria, Caldoros of Dumnonia and Catacus of Atrebata. Between them they commanded a few over four thousand men. It was not everybody Britannia could muster, but Arthur believed it was enough to do the job without leaving the country exposed to opportunist raids just before the onset of winter, when attacks on granaries and hayricks would be far more damaging than the loss of face or territory that would come from defeat in an armed skirmish.

Arthur addressed his commanders. 'I want to be in position by nightfall, ready to engage the enemy at first light. If our information is right they should be moving along a road about five hours' march from here. That means striking camp here at least an hour before midday. Can you manage that?'

'Easily,' said Candidianos, 'as long as each man carries enough food for tonight and the main supplies are brought on in the morning. If we win, they should arrive just as we need them.'

'Fine. But leave the camp in place with fires tended tonight. I want anybody who is watching us from a distance to think we are still here. Even if the enemy are also told that we are on the move, it will mean their leaders are getting completely opposite information. And Gwain,' Arthur went on, looking particularly sombre, 'the men are to bring no beer or cider. And before you protest that custom says they should be allowed to drink before they die, I'm afraid that is my order. I want the men to be more alert than the enemy. If they

want to salute their God, they should do it before we set out today.'
The kings looked dubious, but did not protest. It was not going to be the most popular order, and there were those men who needed the valour that beer could give them. Who in their right minds would face a screaming Barbarian trying to cut you in half without the help of a few drinks? Arthur's answer — that you were less likely to get cut in half if your reactions were faster than the enemy's — was not going to be much consolation.

While Gwain and his staff went about the business of getting the men ready to march out, Arthur went through the plan for a final time, and made sure Modlen recorded it, in case there were arguments at the end of the day.

The scouts had identified an ancient crossroads that the Barbarian forces would hit inevitably on their way south. The road beyond them dipped sharply and all but disappeared into overgrown valleys and hills that seemed to lose their direction, as if crowding in after the open landscape bounded by high ridges through which they had been marching. Take the road to the left and the army would eventually reach the Atrebatan heartlands around Calleva. That, the locally planted informers would let it be known, was a minor prize, and would bring them no glory. If they turned right, though, they were on the main highway to one the greatest prizes in the land: the lands around Corinium. Control those, and they would control all of central Britannia.

They would be ushered along this most promising road because this was the road that Arthur's army was taking in the opposite direction. A few miles from their muster camp it climbed sharply and crossed a pathway that was older than the road by many centuries — the path that follows the spring line beneath the ridges that run diagonally across the country — and by which, miles away, Arthur himself had lounged with Gwenan in the May sun. The Barbarians had crossed it two days earlier, followed soon by Cunorix, and it was this path that the messengers had used to speed their intelligence. As the last of the Britannian men left it behind, Arthur's messengers peeled off to let Cunorix know the progress. They would be hidden by the long ridge from the invaders all the way, but would be able to see them clearly with just a glance over the crest.

The sun was just beginning to drop to the horizon behind them when Arthur reached the hilltop where he intended to wait. Below and in front the road dropped down slowly until it settled and ran straight in a wide valley a hundred feet below. There was no sign of movement along it yet. He was glad of that, because he had no intention of revealing his own position until he had to.

The late afternoon sun had lost all warmth, and he knew the clear night would be cold, close enough to freezing to leave a rime of frost on everything from cloaks to spear shafts and to make swords unpleasant to hold by dawn. Miserable as they would be, though, he could not promise his men warmth that night. Fires were not to show smoke until well after dark or lit within sight of the road, and even within the trees that cloaked the hill's flanks the flames were to be kept low: just enough to make the glowing embers take the edge off the chill.

Arthur himself had a fire set among the circle of homes that clustered on the summit, making a living off travellers. Any patrols of the enemy would expect to see signs of life there, though not more than enough for thirty people at most. The little village was known locally as Baydun – or Badonicus, as Myrddin would have insisted on calling it – and it had boasted a decent tavern since the road was built three hundred years before.

It was not going to be a good night to be a tavern-keeper, though. He had reacted with first awe, then horror, as the army had approached, and sheer fear when the four kings and Arthur himself had been ushered through the low doorway into the smoke. That was soon dispelled when Candidianos addressed him by name and complimented him on his reputation for serving the best roast pork in his kingdom this side of the Sabrina. Once the publican had been allowed to prove this to the intruding kings, though, and had been suitably praised and rewarded in silver by Arthur, he was asked to pack up and leave. The villagers were gathered together and evacuated under escort to the next settlement further back behind the lines. Arthur did not want accidental casualties among the local people if he could help it. Equally he did not want to give any of them the chance to hedge their bets on which side was likely to prove victorious in the coming battle and slip off with a warning to the Barbarian camp.

When the last of the civilians had been gathered up and were safely on their way, Gwain requisitioned the small round houses, built up the fires inside and allocated them to the commanders and their senior aides. Guards were stationed outside, but without fires of their own.

Gwain wanted them alert, and was prepared to change them often through the night rather than give them the temptation of gathering round a blazing log, oblivious to intruders. With all the arrangements in place, Gwain fetched Arthur and they made their rounds.

Making the rounds was not a routine process. Arthur and Gwain, sharing a mutton-fat torch, made their way slowly through the woods where the men were hidden, calling at each of the miserable fires in the dark. Arthur did not address the men in staged groups, gathered round by Gwain to be given the message about how to enhance their valour and glory. That speech would be left to the morning and to their own kings to deliver just before they engaged with the enemy. Instead Arthur spoke to the men as individuals, treating them not as equals but as fellow guardians of the freedoms and traditions of Britannia. He listened to their concerns, too – especially those of the eldest, who showed no fear but had none of the excited bravado of the young men on the eve of a first fight. To those who admitted that they did not really understand what the whole campaign was about, he explained a simple message – that unless they all won the next day, it would not just be a minor setback in some dispute between kings. Defeat would mean the loss of their language, their history, the stories of their families and peoples. It would mean that within their lifetimes Britannia would be a Barbarian land, with Barbarian gods and dominated by the clipped, ugly tongue that they already knew too well from the settlers from beyond the sea. Win, and there was a chance they could be free for at least a generation. They were not fighting for Arthur, or even their own kings. They were fighting for themselves.

He held a final conference with Candidianos and the others in the tavern, his temporary palace, just to go through the details for the morning yet again. The men were to be raised as soon as the first grey began to tinge the dark in the east. All fires must be smothered and covered with earth to stop the smoke rising. They were to assemble under their own king's symbol at the back of the hill. The night scouts were to report any movements on the road below in relays, riding with hooves muffled. While Gwain and Arthur had been out among the men one scout had returned with the news that the invaders were camped less than two miles away along the road, just as had been intended, on the westward branch of the crossroads. There was a slight rise between them and Badonicus Hill, so they would not be visible at daybreak, but the caution about smoking fires had been fully justified and they could soon expect to see the enemy's own scouts on the move. Catacus pointed out that if the Barbarian leaders had any sense they would already have spies lingering in the woods either side of the road, and urged that their own scouts keep in the lee of the hills above. Gwain went further, and ordered small foot patrols with orders to bring in any enemy watchman who spotted them but to leave in place any that didn't, so that the only returning intelligence would be that all was silent and deserted ahead. Arthur knew full well that news would have reached the invaders by now that his forces were mustering. He just hoped their movements that afternoon had been late enough to retain the surprise.

They were all tired by the time Arthur sent the kings and their close officers back to their sequestered huts, but he suspected that he would not be the only one finding it hard to sleep that night: all except Gwain, of course. Gwain could sleep anywhere at any time and yet be awake a moment before his general needed him. True to form, as soon as the conference had broken up, the sentries posted and the attendants dismissed, he had pulled a mat up to the far side of the hearth and settled down. Arthur was still hunched and peering into the flames when he heard the first light snores a few moments later.

Tygern Fawr shrugged, smiled and looked around the hospitable room of the inn, its sign of the Red Dragon painted fiercely on each of its ale jugs and benches. Was he the red or the white dragon of legend? he wondered. Only the morning would decide that.

There was a rustle behind him as Modlen finished stowing her tablets and moved towards the warmth. Arthur had tried to tell her to remain behind with the baggage wagons, but she had flatly refused. There was going to be a great battle, and whatever the outcome it had to be recorded immediately and accurately, and by her, not one of the passionate soldiers who would only see their own corner of the fight. She had shrugged off the danger. She would rather be killed with Arthur than be enslaved with the camp followers if he lost. And if he won, he would need her even more. Arthur had given in, muttering that it was only women who could tell him what to do and get away with it. Now she settled on the mat beside him. They watched the flames apart for a while, then Arthur reached out an arm and drew her to him, pulling the great cloak across them both. Neither slept, and occasionally Modlen rose and placed a log on the fire, but the retaining arm around her shoulders was enough to calm them both in the dragging hours.

* * *

Wermund had been expecting some sight of local resistance for days. It was unnatural that the land, with its straight if unrepaired roads, should have so little sign of life. His men were hungry, nervous and spoiling for a fight that had been denied them since they had left the ships behind weeks before. By now they had expected to be building new halls and clearing forests. Instead they were still marching on alien roads in an empty land. Wermund was no continental general. He was a man used to his battles in the narrow coastal country of Angeln, south of Aelle's Jutes in the corner where the great peninsula overlooked the cold waters of the sea. They were battles he had lost even there.

Much of Angeln was all but empty now, and the fleet he had commanded was built under the supervision of his conquerors. The men had been spared slaughter and allowed to take ship on condition that they never returned or that they conquered the fabled lands of Britannia in revenge for the humiliation of the fleet that spring. Their women and children were held hostage. They might be sent on if, after a year, news reached Slesvig that new lands were in Wermund's hands. If not, well, the girls would be kept if pretty enough, the rest and the boys killed or sent to the slave markets of Constantinople, and the women over twenty-five banished to the forests to survive as best they could.

As much as to keep up morale as because of any news from his spies, Wermund had turned right along the straightest road that led to where he had been told the men of Britannia had been camped for a week. He was battle-ready, if not battle-alert.

The first sign that he should have been came as the sun was just rising behind them, only moments after they had begun the new day's trudge through the autumn mud. One of his advance guard came shouting and tumbling down the hill to his right. He never reached his leader. He shrieked once, pitched forward and rolled until he was stopped by gorse bushes. When he was examined a few moments later the cause was simple to read. A short arrow lodged in his neck. That there was danger ahead was clear enough, but he hadn't had a chance to tell Wermund what he had seen: the full force of the kings moving steadily towards them on either side.

XXVI

From his vantage point, leaning against a beech tree at the edge of the little village of Badonicus, Arthur could see the vanguard of Wermund's forces drift into view half a mile away. He also saw the sudden rush as the scout was sent plunging back to the floor of the valley. 'Idiot!' he shouted. The orders had been explicit. Capture and contain. Somebody had either panicked or just been plain stupid. Contain did not mean 'send back to the enemy dead'. The fact didn't matter; the timing did. Arthur wanted the whole of the enemy army in view before he gave the order to attack.

Gwain read his thoughts. 'There's still time.'

'There'd better be,' Arthur grumbled back. He watched for a few minutes more as Wermund's men advanced a little further and then stopped. A small group broke off and carried on up the hill, clearly sent to reconnoitre the road ahead. Behind them the main body of men began to emerge into the growing sunshine. It was going to be a perfect day for a battle, a bad day for surprise moves. For that Arthur could have done with rain and low cloud: mists full of devils and enemies with cold hands and no breakfast.

'Gwain, I'm going back into the inn while this lot pass through. Have you got someone who can act the terrified local?'

'I expect I can find him.'

'Good – then I want the enemy told that everybody except him has run away and that there's talk that we have gone south to defend Venta. Be close, but don't intervene unless it looks as though they are going to start sacking the village. I don't think they will. I think they'll send a couple of men back to their leaders with the news and carry on. Let them – at least until the message has been sent. I want them confused. Then round them up and do whatever feels right.'

Gwain nodded and walked off briskly to make the arrangements. Arthur strode back to his hut and summoned four messengers, one for each of his kings' regiments. He wanted to know that everyone was in position: Candidianos on his left flank, Catacus on his right and Badoc and Caldoros ready to swing out from the trees on to the road in front of him, ready to confront the Barbarians head on. The only question he needed to know after that was how far away Cunorix was. With luck he'd have done as he was asked, and would be approaching the crossroads that the invaders had reached the day before and would be ready to turn in behind them, closing the trap on all sides. Arthur had a hunch Cunorix would make sure nothing was that simple.

Hanging around wondering about it was not going to help very much, Arthur realised, as he saw the enemy flooding over the rise along the road only a few hundred yards short of his vantage point. He watched as his stooge ran wailing to the Barbarian front line and told his story. He was pushed roughly out of the way and scampered up the hill to the left. Masterful performance, though Arthur. Ahead the invaders paused, so quickly that those behind began to crash into the backs of the vanguard. It was just the few minutes of disorder he had wanted. Arthur had no intention of letting them get organised.

The Silurians and Dumnonians needed to move out fast. Even as he thought it the village filled with troops and they surged past him out into the open. Below him the Barbarian army began to fan out hurriedly, filling the spaces on either side of the road before the trees crowded the low slope of the hills.

Badoc and Caldoros's men kept moving, breaking into a run as the road dipped, their swords swinging in front of them as if the air was enemy limbs, and they roared, invoking the spirits of gods the bishops thought they had banished a century before.

These were the tactics the Barbarians themselves like to use. The roles were reversed. They found themselves on the defensive, being forced into the static formations that they associated with the peoples who had inherited their fighting traditions from Rome and its last legions ninety years before. The invaders had no training, no coherence and, for the first time since they had left their home shores, they felt fear. In their midst, Wermund was screaming orders, hoping that he could be heard by enough of his close men to make a difference.

'Don't wait for them,' he yelled, 'drive on! Meet speed with speed.'

But the men of the west had the slope and the momentum. The best the Anglians could hope for was a sluggish trot fuelled by not much more than a few dried fish and cold morning air. It was unequal, and Arthur meant it to stay that way.

When the first swords had clashed and the first injured screamed Arthur sent a man off to Candidianos, telling him to appear and attack on the left flank as soon as possible. The size of the first force would be apparent quickly to Wermund and, while big enough to keep him busy, he would not expect to be overwhelmed.

The Dobunni had a harder task than their neighbours already in the fray. Once they appeared high on the ridge the land sloped away sharply, and they would have to make their assault through the trees. That would slow them down, but Arthur had calculated that it would also confuse the Anglians, who would be aware that they were about to be attacked from the north but unsure of the timing or the numbers, just as the fighting at the front reached its fiercest. From above there was nothing for Arthur and Gwain to do but watch the battle unfold. Catacus and his Atrebatan men were beyond the woods to the right, waiting for their call at the northern limit of their own lands. They were not in reserve, but Arthur wanted their contribution later in the day, and he wanted it swift and decisive. Before then he needed Cunorix.

The Anglians were fighting fiercely. Barbarians had a reputation for that, of course, but the vehemence of their counter charge was beginning to take the wind out of the first wave of Britannian men. Arthur had no idea that they were not just fighting for their pride as warriors, but for the freedom and survival of their hostage families. Even so, he had kept three hundred troops, commanded by one of Caldoros's brothers (therefore his own cousin too) back from the first attack, just so that there could be no stalemate. It was not a massive force, though, and he needed more than an extra charge – he needed a show. Bishop Gwidellius in Londinium had anticipated this. He had no troops to spare – the few that he had were needed to defend the city and its port – but he had sent the four trumpeters who had fanfared them into the forum before the great Council less than three months before. Now Arthur stationed them in pairs, a little in front of the action, just below the hill crests on either side. Only once their first peels of brazen silver had rung out across the battlefield did he unleash the new wave of Dumnonians.

The reinforcements leant new vigour to the front line and the fractional moment of stunned quiet that had come over the Barbarians, none of whom had ever heard the shrill bark of trumpets before, was enough to refresh Caldoros and his men. They burrowed deep into the ranks of the Anglians, just as Candidianos engaged them from the trees with his full force.

The combination of two new attacks and the trumpets lessened but did not stop the Barbarian resistance. Those towards the back paused but soon returned to the action as they saw their comrades beginning to fall back under the onslaught from two sides.

The sun was at its low height in the sky before Arthur could sense any new direction to the fighting. The invaders were proving as fierce as he had feared, if not fiercer. He had forced them back a few yards, enough for rescue teams to move in to help or begin to carry the wounded back towards the safety of the village, where they could be treated as best the battlefield physicians knew how. After three hours of fighting, though, the men of Britannia were not clearly winning yet.

A messenger rode in and dismounted for a word with Gwain before being led to Arthur. Modlen hovered close, ready to record the news.

Cunorix had arrived, it seemed, and would be in position to join the battle even before his herald would have time to return. For Arthur, this should have been the moment he could sense the day turning in his favour, but as usual Cunorix had made sure that nothing was certain. His orders had been to attack on the road from the east, boxing in the Barbarians and forcing them to confront fighters from three sides. After that, it would have been simple for the Atrebatans to emerge from the south and complete the trap.

Instead, the Catuvellaunian King wanted glory more than victory. Creeping up the rear of a battle along a Roman road was not his style. Before Arthur had time to lose his temper with the herald, Cunorix appeared on the hill to the left of the village and charged headlong down it, straight for the front of the fighting being held, but not much advanced by Badoc and Caldoros. It was bold, brave and spectacular, but it was not what Arthur had planned, and he just hoped that the Catuvellauni were bright enough to know the difference between Barbarians and the Silures. There was no guarantee.

Arthur turned first to Gwain. 'Get a messenger over to Catacus,' he ordered. 'I'll need him out of sight but ready to join in quickly. Exactly when will depend on what happens now that all the battle is in one place and the Barbarians can withdraw.'

CHAPTER XXVI

'Will they?' Gwain asked sceptically. 'It's not their way.' But he summoned the messenger and sent him off.

To Modlen Arthur instructed, 'Note this down: that Cunorix of the Catuvellauni joined the battle of his own accord as soon as he was in sight of the enemy, without formation or...' he paused, wondering whether it would be politic to commit to history what he felt about the clear insubordination of his consul, 'prior consultation with Tygern Fawr.'

There was not much for Arthur to do except watch the outcome.

* * *

To the south-east, the settlers from among the Cantiaci and Aelle's smuggled warriors were slashing their way through the woods less than two miles away. His own scouts had already warned him of the battle, and he had sent word back to Wermund that help was close. It was one reason why Wermund was fighting on and not retreating under the fresh onslaught from Cunorix.

The Jutes were not natural allies for Wermund. Aelle's people were northern neighbours of the Anglians, but neighbours are rarely friends, and they had not been quite sorry enough when Wermund had been defeated at home by those hungry for his land and rich fishing waters. When it came to fighting the Britannians, though, the divisions disappeared. Aelle knew that Wermund had to be able to report a victory, and he himself had been planning his subtle subjugation of the Cantiacan lands for years. Wermund might have the desperate men from more than thirty ships that had crossed the sea, nearing five thousand fighters, but Aelle had gathered more than half that again since leaving the eyot upriver from Londinium. And these were not strange lands to the Jutes. They had traded, mingled, farmed and travelled in them for years. There were some who could speak the dialects of the Cantiaci and the Atrebates almost like natives.

Before they reached the fighting more scouts returned, telling of how Wermund was now outnumbered and suffering hundreds dead, although there were terrible losses to the Britannians too. Aelle gathered his men in a forest clearing a short run from the action and told them they had a choice: run home to their farmsteads and pretend they had never left, lose and be killed or enslaved, or fight as true Jute men knew how: for their honour and the gods. Then he led them on to the battlefield.

* * *

Cunorix and his men were driving a wedge into the heart of the Anglian fighters, taking the pressure off Badoc and Caldoros and letting Candidianos concentrate on trying to swing his men round and hem the enemy in from the east. It was a bold move, and Arthur stifled his irritation and began to think that, after all, Cunorix's no-nonsense brand of violence had its merits. Get stuck in and go berserk. To hell with the strategy. It made Arthur wonder why he'd been bothering about it for the last two weeks.

The self-pity did not last long. A small group broke from the back of the Catuvellaunian troop and began to run up the hill towards Arthur's position. A few seconds later new voices were raised, and he could see the Dobunni being turned and attacked from two sides.

Aelle and his Jutes had arrived.

The breakaway group arrived exhausted at the hilltop and Gwain strode to meet them. He nodded after a moment and pointed the way back to the huts where they could find water and food before rejoining the battle. Quickly he came over to Arthur. 'Cunorix is down. Dead or near enough.'

Arthur nodded. 'I can't see any panic down there.'

'There won't be. They'll want revenge first, but it will give heart to the enemy. And who are their new friends?'

'I don't know,' admitted Arthur. 'Nothing has been reported to us about two landings.'

They were startled by the sound of harsh laughter behind them. Turning, they saw Modlen leaping and dancing, her tablets in a careless heap on the ground in front of her. She was laughing, but she was also cheering, her tongueless voice high and girlish as they had never heard her. There were tears, but they were tears of joy. For Modlen, the death of Cunorix was even more cause for celebration than it was for any Barbarian chieftain. It was revenge and freedom.

Arthur turned back to the business of battle. 'I have to be seen to avenge Cunorix,' he said to Gwain, 'though in truth Modlen is closer to how I really see his removal.'

'Shall I fetch your sword?'

'Yes, and I'll need my own troop with me. We'll go and join Catacus – see if we can turn the tide. Get a message to him quickly. Use a horseman. He's to move back to halfway between his present position and me. We need to attack in the open now, not appear from the woods as we intended him to do. I want the Barbarians to think that there are wave after wave of us ready, so that they cannot be sure that any moment of victory will last until nightfall. And get the trumpeters back. The enemy and our own men need to know that Tygern Fawr is joining battle in person. It's my last throw of the dice. I want you to remain here and direct messengers so that we can keep some sort of control, even if it's to retreat and regroup.'

'I hope that won't be necessary.'

'So do I. Whatever Modlen's account says, the stories of even a small reverse would take too much living down.'

A few minutes later, after he had kissed an instantly sobered and scared Modlen, Arthur was on his way with his own bodyguard of fifty men, leaving only a dozen to keep Gwain and Modlen company. They skirted the hillside, making for a point halfway to the southern side of the battle, but keeping out of sight. Once they were in position they waited for the Atrebatan regiment to join them. It was the smallest of the five forces brought by the kings, and Arthur's men did not do much to make it bigger.

Catacus was the youngest of the kings, barely nineteen years old, but he had the eagerness and the confidence of youth that Arthur had long lost. He had been desperate to join the battle for hours, and keenly felt the indignity of his men, and the insult to his kingdom, at being held in reserve, lurking in the woods, while the other nations slogged in the thick of the action. He was fuming by the time he reached Arthur, crouched with his men below the crest of the hill, and was about to launch into an angry rant at his overlord. Arthur was no fool, though, and could see the steam rising in his young commander as he went to meet him.

'Catacus, thank heavens. Just in time,' he said grimly, laying a hand on his shoulder. 'Cunorix is dead – and anyway, he ignored my battle plan. The Barbarians are far stronger than I expected. Candidianos is just about holding his ground, but not much more, and the Catuvellauni are close to being surrounded. We don't have long. Are your men ready?'

'They have been all day,' he replied gruffly. 'Perhaps we could have saved Cunorix if we had attacked earlier.'

Arthur shook his head sadly. 'No, he was struck because he wanted to fight his way to their leader, on his own if possible. And your men would have just been attacked from behind by the new Barbarians who arrived shortly after Cunorix. As it is I'm trusting that there are no more on their way.'

'Shall we go in now?'

'Yes, but only when I give the word. We don't have enough men to overwhelm them. The timing is everything – and a little spectacle. This is the Overlord of Britannia they are taking on, not some riverside warlord.'

The trumpeters were summoned and lined up on either side of Arthur's standard-bearer. The standard was the old Roman imperial rod, surmounted by the Overlord's personal symbol, the entwined dragons, moulded in silver so it caught the sun. It had rallied the men of Britannia all through Arthur's years in office, and it did so once again, giving new hope with every flash of reflected light.

Some eleven hundred Atrebatan men had answered their king's call. Arthur asked them to form up, not like the modern fighters of Britannia in an untidy but ferocious rabble, but as though they were legionaries of old, soldiers like their great-great-grandfathers had been in the service of the two Valentinians. Lines of twelve men, close together, shields in front, began to move on Catacus's word. At the top of the hill, in sight of the battle for the first time, the standard appeared, flanked by trumpeters.

They sounded fanfare after fanfare until the fighters in all but the front line looked up, and then Arthur stepped forward on horseback, seemingly alone. Behind him a cloud eased from the low path of the sun and its light blazed, so that he was a shadow against its orb. From his side he raised his right arm and in his hand he held high the sword that he had drawn from the rock altar in Corinium more than sixteen years before.

He called out, for the benefit of the men behind him, rather than those deafened by the noise of battle below. 'I am Arthur, Tygern Fawr, by the Council of Kings Overlord of all Britannia. And I have Caledfwlch, the sword left me by Constantine, Great Emperor, declared in Ebvracum. With Caledfwlch we have VICTORY!'

For those watching from below a man appeared out of the sun and in his hand he carried a short blade which caught the light as if his whole arm blazed. Then as he started down the hill, men appeared behind him, a narrow train also lit by the late sun. After the trumpets sounded again a flock of rooks appeared above them, swirling across the battlefield. To the men of Angeln it was a chill omen – a sign of the gods fleeing the forest and its defenders. The train of men moved slowly down the hill, deliberately, with their swords beating the shields rhythmically every two strides, and the train seemed endless.

At the far end of the battlefield Candidianos paused in the act of slitting a man's throat, smiled and dragged his victim up by the hair.

'See that?'

The Anglian gurgled in terror.

Candidianos called behind him. 'Any of you speak their heathen tongue?'

A young man from Cunorix's kingdom shouldered his way through.

'Good,' Candidianos held his sword against the Anglian's neck. 'Tell this creature that he can either die now or he can point out those birds and get the message back that the gods of Britannia have arrived.'

After the message was translated and the Barbarian had yelled it back in his bitter language a great roar erupted across the battlefield. Some of it was from the invaders as they disengaged and tried to fall back. Many of Aelle's men had suddenly lost the taste for being warriors and leached into the woods, putting as much distance between themselves and any others of their race as they could. Most of the noise came from the men of Britannia, their energy and confidence flowing back with the sight of Arthur and his celestial regiment.

Candidianos thought about finishing off the man he had grasped anyway, but then relented, clipped off his ear and passed him back through the ranks as his personal prisoner.

* * *

The light was beginning to edge into early evening grey by the time the last of the wounded on the winning side had been helped or carried to the makeshift shelters set up in and around the little hilltop village of Baydun. It was grandiose to call it a 'fort at the summit' by the time Arthur camped there, but for those seeking a warm fire and water to clean their wounds it was safety of sorts.

The carts carrying food, tents and dressings had arrived just after Arthur had left to launch his last attack and Gwain, and, watching the indecisive fighting, had worried that they might become Barbarian spoils. Instead they were welcome relief for weary and bloodied men.

The dead Britannians were buried in rows by their comrades beside the road. The bodies of the invaders and their Jutish allies were carried by the few prisoners allowed to live to a patch of ground on the edge of the woods and, stripped of anything but their tunics, thrown on to a great pyre laid out in the shape of a ship and sent to join their gods in flames. Their swords, jewels, armbands, leather and anything else of use or value was piled up in the camp to be distributed in the morning. The kings announced that each man was allowed to keep one memento of any Barbarian he had killed; the rest was to be divided under their officers' supervision between everyone who had taken part – after the kings had commandeered anything they thought especially fine, of course.

Wermund was among those captured and spared. He was an important symbol of the victory and Arthur would keep him close and parade him to the Council and anybody else who needed evidence of the victory. A message needed to be sent back across the sea, too, and this time it would be different from the provocation that had reached the Barbarian lands that spring. This time it would be sent with force.

Nobody on Arthur's side knew of Aelle's existence, and he had kept it that way, being among the first to slip away when he saw that the day was lost. He had every intention of returning, but not by that river, and not for a few more years. He was not going to jeopardise all his long plans because the men from Angeln proved as feeble abroad as they had been at home.

When night fell the battlefield itself was deserted, but at either end fire told its story. To the east the vast cremation pile burned steadily and fiercely, an immense monument to defeat. To the west a multitude of small fires lit the feasting and drinking of the victors, and the half-conscious moans of the injured who just wanted to see another day without pain. The kings, Arthur and Gwain feasted with their men and Arthur drank more – much more – ale than a great overlord should to retain his dignity. It was partly comradeship, but mostly it was relief. A huge weight had been lifted from his shoulders. It was hard at first to gauge what it would mean for the island, but for himself, that night, the defeat of the greatest invading force in half a century meant that no one could doubt that Britannia stood intact. He tried hard to show suitable grief for Cunorix as his men laid him out and stood vigil, ready to escort him back to Verulamium at first light, but inside he felt something of the elation that Modlen had let out. With both Vortebelos and Cunorix dead, the two great challengers to his authority were gone.

Carousing with the men gave Arthur a bond with them that they never forgot, but when he was leaning a little too heavily on Candidianos's shoulder for even that firm king to be able to stand straight, Gwain gently guided him to the inn that had become his quarters and, with a wink, handed him into Modlen's care.

While her master had been feasting and drinking she had been preparing a celebration of a different sort. From the innkeeper's belongings and Arthur's cloaks she had managed to find enough material to curtain off a portion of the hut from the prying eyes of the rest of his campaign household. She had assembled straw and the clothes of others to make passable bedding, too – nothing like the sumptuous comfort of the palaces in the cities, but better than many of their travelling bivouacs. She led Arthur to it and helped him lie down, covered him and waited, sitting close and stroking his head till he slept.

Later, when the camp was quiet at last and only the guards occasionally stoking the fire interrupted the snoring in the rest of the room, she slipped under the cover and made sure that Arthur gave her the one thing that he had always denied and that Cunorix had always demanded. For Arthur, drunk and never quite awake, a memory flitted at the edge of his mind: of a night in Myrddin's house many years before, and of Sioned's tears the next day.

XXVII

WHILE THE BODY of Cunorix was carried to Verulamium for the funeral, Arthur, Caldoros, Badoc and Catacus led the rest of the men back to Corinium with Candidianos. There the men were paid off with promises of land, cattle or, just occasionally, for those few who still lived in towns, silver. A great deal of bartering of the spoils kept the markets of Corinium busy until Christmas. By then Arthur and the nobility had long left: the three remaining kings for their own territories (much to the relief of Candidianos, who was beginning to feel the strain of keeping them entertained after less than a week) and Arthur for Londinium.

Bishop Gwidellius, thankful that his trumpets had been returned undamaged, made sure that Arthur's entry to the old forum was as triumphal as it had been before the Council a few months earlier. He still had Gwenan in his care, and it was to her that Arthur made his way as soon as the formalities were over. It filled Modlen with trepidation, though she was careful not to let it show. In the event she need not have worried. Gwenan, still lodging in the merchant's house that they had made their home during the Council, received Arthur with fondness, but without passion, and Arthur was far too gentle to force it on her. It was extraordinary, he thought, that only seven months before Gwenan had being lying with him for days at a time in the old deserted camp in the spring sunshine. She had been his eager mistress, his new freed slave, the girl who Myrddin saw as the threat to all his plans. But now, after her brush with death in the forest, for which Arthur had decapitated Vorteporix, she was more like his tolerant aunt, or his sister Branwen: concerned, kind, loving, but without any erotic charge at all. Myrddin, when he turned up unexpectedly three days later, and Modlen were delighted and relieved, but for entirely opposite reasons.

Myrddin was rejuvenated. The word 'hero' found its way into every second sentence. Even Modlen was tired of hearing about it after a few hours. Myrddin was, after all, basing his praise on the rumours he'd heard on the road and then on the notes Modlen had been transcribing from her tablets on to vellum as soon as she had been able to raid the supplies of the Bishop's secretary. It was accurate – Modlen prided herself on that – but she had embroidered by omission too. Only she and Gwain knew how hard it had been for Arthur to come to a decision as he had supervised the battle.

Soon, though, it became clear Myrddin had another agenda, and it was one which Modlen dreaded. Although she had not made love to Arthur since the night of the battle – and he still did not realise that she had done so even then, believing her reassurance that he had just had a drunken dream and fondled her a little in his sleep – she had begun to think that her place could always be in his bed, now that Gwenan had lost interest.

'Now, my boy,' Myrddin had said patronisingly, once he had taken stock of Arthur's mood, 'we need to discuss your forthcoming marriage.' They were not alone. Myrddin wanted allies, so he made

CHAPTER XXVII

sure that the Bishop and Gwain were there too, as well as a fifteen-year-old youth who had journeyed with him from Moridunum.

'Did you ever meet Medraut, Morganwy's son?' Myrddin asked, pushing the lad forward. Arthur admitted that he had not – at least, not knowingly – but he could see the resemblance to his mother and was pleased that her son was clearly growing into such a fine young man.

'He is, he is,' agreed Myrddin. 'He reminds me very much of you at the same age. Now, I have just the girl for you, Arthur, and one who will bring honour and, dare it be said, a touch of Gallic flair back to the House of Pendraeg.'

Arthur ignored the barb aimed at his choice of lovers and waited patiently for his mentor to let him know who he was to spend his life with.

'What you need is a consort, Arthur, who clearly rises above the local queens you come across as wives of the Council members. That makes it hard for me to choose somebody from Britannia itself, because there would immediately be cries of favouritism. Wherever your wife came from, the opposite end of the country would complain it was losing influence.'

'I'd thought of that, thank you,' said Arthur. 'Why do you think I've done nothing until now?'

'Oh, it was politics, was it?' chided Myrddin. 'I thought you were just interested in making sure your bed was kept warm. But credit where credit's due. I thought somebody from Hibernia might solve you a few problems, give you some insurance against attacks from that direction, but that would leave Caradoc with no one to fight, which would be counterproductive. And, of course, you spent too long with me in Demetia for the Hibernian influence to go down well on this side of the country. Going north of the wall had its attractions, but they are angling to get their hands on an alliance with Corbalengus in Ordovicia, so it would be no better, and all the eligible girls are on the young side. You might have to wait a few years before there's chance of an heir and I – I mean we – don't want that.'

'Difficult,' admitted Arthur, rather hoping that Myrddin had found objections to all the other possibilities too.

'Then there is Armorica, and I think I've struck gold.'

'That good?' Arthur muttered sarcastically.

'She's seventeen, a sort of cousin and you'll adore her.'

'Have you met her?'

'Actually yes, though not since she grew up. She was delightful at six.'

Arthur sighed, not encouraged by the smirks on the faces of the older men present. Medraut seemed to be studying his nails in extreme boredom.

'Go on, then. Who is she?'

'Her name is Gwynafir, and she's Budig of Armorica's niece – not his blood niece; that would be too much in the family, I think, but the daughter of his wife's sister.'

'Does she live up to it?'

'Live up to what?'

'Her name – "white and true".'

'What a ridiculous question! She's seventeen. Of course she does.'

'Of course,' Arthur answered, without great conviction.

Myrddin talked on, Gwidellius and Gwain smiling and nodding in approval. From the two teenagers there was less enthusiasm. That was hardly surprising, Arthur thought, but still he sensed an unease from both of them, which suggested more than boredom. Modlen's was understandable, but the boy Medraut he could not read.

'Budig's wife's niece? I thought she was from further south than Armorica?' observed Arthur.

'Yes, that's true, but Gwynafir has been at Budig's court many times.'

'So where does she actually come from? Will I have to speak Latin to her all the time, or learn something like Iberian?'

'Well, yes and no. Her parents come from Burdigala, but with all the recent troubles she has been spending more time with her aunt and Budig in Condate Riedonum than Aquitania.'

Next morning, as he relaxed in the old baths and allowed himself to be cleaned and preened the old Roman way, Arthur came to a decision. After he was dressed by Gwenan and her maids, overseen by Gwain as was proper, he joined Myrddin, Modlen (who had taken up her old position as Myrddin's perpetual student), Medraut and Gwidellius.

'I want to see her first, Myrddin – and that means going over the sea to visit Budig.'

'Excellent.'

'If I like her, I will bring her back and marry her here – or at least in Britannia.'

'Naturally.'

'The question is, where exactly?'

'Well, we can worry about all that before we leave, but I have Verulamium in mind.'

Arthur grimaced. 'Or Ebvracum, the city of Constantine, and my own now,' he suggested.

'And of course Londinium has its merits, as you found with the Council,' Gwidellius chipped in.

The debate was interrupted as Modlen's tablet dropped from her fingers and she fled from the room in tears. All the joy of being free from Cunorix, all the hope that emerged when she realised that Gwenan no longer wanted the role of lover, was now in danger from a foreign princess who was yet a cousin of her master, only a year and a little more older than she was herself. What could a slave expect? She knew she was useful, even necessary to Arthur – his eyes and ears when nobody else could be trusted, important precisely because none of the great men ever noticed her, just as they never noticed the stewards carrying jugs of ale – but she wanted, deserved, so much more. Fear was back, and this time it was fear that neither the death of a king nor the reassurance of a friend or master could dissolve, because with it was mixed with betrayal, even if the betrayer never guessed that he was the cause.

As the tears fell she was surprised and a little disturbed to find Medraut's arm around her shoulders. Somehow his attention brought her no comfort – it made her shudder.

* * *

There was an opportunity within a few weeks to test whether Myrddin's choice of Verulamium could work for the first wedding of an Overlord of Britannia for over thirty years – and the first ever that could be celebrated in a time of peace. At Christmas the Catuvellauni were due to announce who would succeed Cunorix. Arthur had not been to the funeral – even his sense of political duty would have been tested by giving an oration on the boundless great qualities of his former deputy – but the election of a new leader was a different matter entirely.

The swearing-in was due to take place on Christmas Eve, a double excuse for feasting. At Myrddin's prompting Arthur decided to call for a meeting of the Round Table on St Stephen's Day – just enough time for the kings and envoys to get to the city and over their coronation hangovers (as Myrddin put it). Gwain was instructed to arrange for the round table itself to be transported the short journey to Verulamium in good time. There was a chance that the added importance of hosting the meeting in the same week as the election would flatter the nobility of the Catuvellauni into choosing a leader that could bring some cooperative authority to the table, not just the thuggery combined with political posturing that had been Cunorix's stock in trade.

To achieve this would take some skill, it was realised, and the last thing that would work was either Myrddin's direct involvement or Arthur letting it be known whose candidacy he would prefer. Nonetheless, some influence would have to be brought to bear, and swiftly.

With grudging agreement Myrddin accepted that for once the Church might hold the key. He had a double motive. If Arthur was to be married in Verulamium then he would need the Bishop there to officiate, and so the sooner he was drawn into the Overlord's circle, the better – though that was not a consideration sold to Bishop Gwidellius when he was asked to call his colleague to Londinium for urgent consultations early in December. Only at the end of those negotiations was the Bishop of Verulamium taken to meet Arthur himself.

The churchman brought him two names: Mandubrac, who was a nephew of Cunorix and whose mother was sister to the old Trinovantian King, and Peredoc, who had the advantage of being no relation of Cunorix at all, but as his tribune had been responsible for enforcing the King's orders and summoning troops. He was a man who knew the secrets and the weak points of all the important men of his country, and those around. Myrddin immediately saw the danger. While Peredoc would need to be dealt with (whether that meant placated or, better still, removed), to elevate him to the kingship and the Council would bring as much threat as it would convenience – and the enmity of the many he had trodden on during his relentless career. Modlen, it turned out, could hardly bear to write his name. Peredoc had been the man who had personally carried out Cunorix's order to silence her.

Neither bishop complained too much, Arthur noted, when he instructed them to make sure that Mandubrac was gently but effectively supported. He was six years younger than Arthur himself, and as different from Cunorix as it was possible to be, though he had

CHAPTER XXVII

distinguished himself in the battle at Badonicus. He had been brought up in the shadow of the new church housing the relic of Alban, of which the Bishop was so proud, and was known for his scholarship and even temper, both of which had made him the object of Cunorix's sarcasm, but had equally made him be seen as reliable and honest (if a trifle dull) by those who would now be electors.

After a further two weeks Arthur readied himself to leave Londinium. He had no intention of returning for some time, and let it be known that straight after the Verulamium Christmas Council he would head north to Ebvracum, expecting to reach it by Epiphany. In the mean time Myrddin dispatched three emissaries to Budig at his Armorican capital in Condate Riedonum to instruct him to begin negotiations for the hand of his niece. They were equipped with more than words, taking with them as much old Roman treasure as could be gathered in Londinium without impoverishing Bishop Gwidellius. Gwain made it clear that if they failed to arrive with it safely, even if the excuse was robbery by marauding Franks, they would find their welcome home short and violent.

On Arthur's last night in the sumptuous riverside house Gwenan asked to come to bed with him, much to his surprise. She had been too ill during the autumn. Since his return from the battle, although she was less frail, she had shown no interest in returning to her old role as his voracious and ambitious lover. He had tried to provoke her, frustrated that his new glory as victor on the battlefield was not transferred to sexual conquest, by cavorting with the two Frankish slaves who were the bath attendants. They knew exactly what they were doing, of course, but Gwenan had just laughed and, while they were supremely efficient, the satisfaction lasted if anything less long than the vigour of the bathwater.

The last night in the sumptuous old rooms of the Londinium mansion could not have been a greater contrast. Gwenan had started by reassuring him that she was now fully recovered from her wound – in body, at least, even if her soul had changed. She loved him, she said, as she had done ever since he had taken her that spring, which seemed so long ago, yet they had never spent a Christmas together and now, she felt, perhaps they never would.

For all that, the night was as passionate and consuming as anything they had enjoyed in either their hilltop retreat or the summer heat of the palace in Ebvracum. Gwenan had demanded, taken and demanded again until neither could do more than lie and caress. They slept a little, but three hours before dawn they had woken and loved again.

'Thank you,' Gwenan said eventually.

Arthur frowned in the dark and held her more tightly. 'What for?'

'For this year. For this. For taking me from slave to nearly a princess.'

'You are my love. I don't need thanks,' he said.

She stroked his cheek. 'I have been your love, but when the light comes and you ride out I will never be again.'

'You are not coming with me?'

'Yes, but only as far as Verulamium, and not as the mistress of Tygern Fawr. This has been my last night of sex, Arthur. That is why I wanted it so much.'

'I don't understand.'

'You must marry Gwynafir. I cannot compete with that, but also I have changed too. That arrow has meant that I will never be completely well, and children would almost certainly kill me. Myrddin saved my life, but I do not have the strength I need to follow you round Britannia, even if you made your new wife accept it.'

'You will not even come to Ebvracum with me? I will not go to Armorica until the spring. There is no reason why you cannot be as you always were there, my lover before I am married, the mistress of my palace if not of me.'

'No. I would almost certainly get pregnant, and that I cannot allow.'

'What about tonight?'

'Tonight is safe. I know my body.'

'If you are not with me, what will you do? Will Gwidellius let you stay here?'

'Not in this house, and he does not have a safer one. The master here has his own interests, and I am not going to let him pursue them with me.'

'Has he...?' Arthur began.

'No, not while I am yours, but once that is not the case I would find it difficult to fight him off.'

'But you have a plan?'

'Yes,' Gwenan admitted. 'I will come with you to Verulamium. If the man they choose as king is the one you want, I will enter the convent there. I think I will be safe.'

'As safe as anywhere, I suppose.'

CHAPTER XXVII

'You are not convinced?'

They were silent for a while. Arthur tried to interest her in making love again, but she kissed his neck and pulled his hand away.

After a while he said, 'I think I have a better plan.'

'If it is "Come to Armorica with me",' the answer—' she began.

'Is no,' Arthur laughed, 'but it is better than putting you in a convent under a king who I don't yet know will succeed, let alone trust.'

'Will it be far away? I don't want to live in Brigantia under your brother.'

'Not that bad, either. Could you live with my sister, though?'

'Branwen? In Elfael?'

'Only until the spring in Elfael, I think. She will remain with King Idriseg while he lives, but I will be amazed if he survives the winter.'

'Will I, though? I have heard the winters there can be terrible.'

'Yes, but Father's hall is always warm. Branwen sees to that.'

Gwenan kissed him. 'All right, but how will I get there, and what happens in the spring?'

'You will leave the Council with Candidianos, and I will ask him to make sure you reach Elfael safely. He will. Then, later, after Father has died, he will have his public marriage to Branwen, and you will stay under his protection – either in Corinium or wherever he chooses. He loves Branwen as much as I love you. You will be as safe in her household as anywhere in the old empire, or even Constantinople itself.'

'No convent?'

'No convent!'

'But not as your mistress?'

Arthur sighed. 'Not if my sister has anything to do with it.'

'I suppose I cannot refuse?'

'You can – I just think it would be safer not to.'

'So do I.' Gwenan thought for a moment and then giggled, a sound Arthur had not heard from her since the early summer. 'Well, then, if I am not to be a nun and your sister is strict...' She rolled on top of him.

As they dressed in the winter dawn Gwenan was serious once again. 'You know Modlen loves you, don't you, Arthur?'

'Of course she's fond of me, and I protect her.'

'No, much more than that. She will be even more hurt than I am when you marry, and she is so vulnerable, because you and Myrddin are the only ones she can communicate with.'

'You think so?'

'I think more than that. I think if you ever let her think she cannot be at your side she will kill herself.'

Arthur was shocked. 'How do you know? She cannot tell you.'

'I can read her eyes. I know. You must keep her with you. Let her take my place until you marry.'

'And then?'

'Then she must only be your scribe, your recorder, I suppose – but that is for you to work out. You would not be the first prince to keep a mistress. I think that if you are travelling round the island Gwynafir will soon tire of it after the first season. And then, of course, you will need Modlen as usual.'

'Can I do that? I never thought of Modlen in that way.'

'Rubbish, Arthur. Of course you did. You just won't admit it.'

'Maybe.'

'Maybe is yes. You know it and I know it. The only person who doesn't know it is Modlen, poor kid. So if you want me and Branwen to make life easy for you, you will take care of her.'

Arthur kissed her. 'How can I refuse?'

'You can't.'

By the time the procession of Arthur and his household had left Londinium Myrddin noticed that he was in a better mood and less troubled than at any time in the previous half-year. Modlen noticed it too, and put it down morosely to the fact that Gwenan was going with them. She was right, of course, but she was stunned to tears when Gwenan insisted that she ride with her and, with Myrddin, Gwidellius, Gwain and Arthur safely segregated from them by a dozen soldiers, quietly explained what had been settled.

* * *

The bishops had lobbied quietly and effectively and, despite frantic threats and plotting by Peredoc – and even an attempted stabbing – Mandubrac was duly elected King of the Catuvellauni late on Christmas Eve, just in time for the Bishop of Verulamium to celebrate his Mass at midnight. Those on the Council who were members of the Round Table had gathered, together with a handful of nearby kings who were not, though the rigours of travelling so far in the dead of winter meant that most of the kings had opted to send princely envoys rather than attend in person. That suited Arthur fine, since he regarded the business of the year as settled, and he did not want a repeat of the egotistical histrionics that had made the September Council such hard work. It suited Candidianos too, since it meant there were no serious rivals on hand to question his official elevation as the sole deputy to Tygern Fawr. In reality he had always been that in Arthur's mind, but Cunorix had taken the expedient title.

The Christmas feasting became virtually continuous until Twelfth Night, for after the end of the two-day meeting after the election the snow descended heavily and steadily. By the following morning it was clear that only the most intrepid or idiotic riders would take their horses into the drifts that made the crumbling roads hard to find, let alone travel in the short hours of winter daylight. The citizens of Verulamium took full advantage of the opportunity. The season, the election of their new king, the presence of so many of the Council and the Overlord, and especially the news that was announced at the end of the formal proceedings, that he was to embark for Armorica in the spring to find a new bride, were all good reasons. In normal times the royal generosity would only have seen the stores open to the poor for the Christmas and St Stephen's feast days themselves, but these were not normal times. Verulamium was one of the few cities remaining in Britannia, eighty years after the legions left, that had the trade and the wealth to keep the ale flowing and the meat roasting for all.

On Twelfth Night itself Candidianos raised his cup to Arthur and announced formally the dead secret that he had married Branwen and would celebrate in Corinium as soon as the circumstances in Elfael allowed. Myrddin purred contentedly at the end of the table nearest the fire, despite the shortage of decent wine. Beside him Modlen scratched the news and the bard's oration on a tablet to be copied on to vellum and placed in the Bishop's library before she left. Next to her Medraut smiled without comment, his eyes moving from Arthur to Gwenan and back to Modlen, noting and storing his thoughts for the future.

The snow lingered for another week, frozen in temperatures that made it foolhardy to leave the fireside for anything but the most essential jobs. Even hunting was all but pointless, but the frozen land made ice houses for the kitchen stores, and the meat hung before the onslaught stayed fresh, though it was dwindling. Gwain observed gloomily to the steward of the new King Mandubrac's household that there would not be much to go round if the freeze continued through January. The decision would have to be taken to conserve the stores and lessen the handouts to the poor, who had gathered as news of the court's arrival had spread. In the paddocks the animals were kept in confinement, and the hayricks began to shrink. Duck eggs began to be bartered for long promises of work to be given in the spring.

After a few days more, though, and just as everybody's patience was beginning to wear thin with petty intrigues breaking out around the great table and whispered conspiracies starting to take shape, the weather relented. Clouds gathered, the temperature rose and the snow disappeared in a night and a morning. Verulamium was a stinking mess as the detritus of feasting, horse manure and humans without proper middens for a month began to thaw. Preparations to pack up and head out were as hurried as the stewards could make them. It was decided that the Great Table would be stored by King Mandubrac until the roads improved and it could be transported to Corinium for another meeting before Arthur left Britannia for Gaul.

With Gwenan due to travel west with Candidianos, Myrddin and Medraut, only Arthur was sorry to see the leaving, and he was morose as the morning approached. Since he had come to Londinium after the battle he and Gwenan had spent the best part of two months together, and the dismal weeks after her shooting in the north had become distant in their minds, even if the wound itself still showed as a livid scar on Gwenan's chest. Only the fact that his intention to seek a foreign princess to marry had been proclaimed so publicly prevented Arthur from reneging on all his commitments and asking her to stay with him. He brought up the subject obliquely once, commenting that if she could keep from becoming pregnant for all those weeks, surely she could manage to do it indefinitely. But Gwenan just smiled sadly, kissed his cheek and told him that all was for the best. If anything she looked a little relieved as the last embrace was taken in private. The western party was ready to leave a day before Arthur's, who was heading for Ebvracum, and Candidianos was tactful enough to promise his friend that Gwenan would be waiting for him when he passed through Corinium in the spring on the road to take the ship to Armorica. He showed even greater tact in not saying it in front of Myrddin.

CHAPTER XXVII

* * *

The winter proved to be vicious. Soon after Arthur arrived in Ebvracum the snow returned and sat across the land, cloaking it in misery. Nothing moved except the makeshift sledges pulling wood for the fires or fodder for the animals. The harvest had been good, and the places which had hosted armies or been in the path of the invaders had been resupplied well before the harsh weather set in. Even so, there were those without the land to have put enough by, or who had too many in the family to provide for them properly. Prices in the market in the sparse towns rose to punishing levels that only the richest or the desperate were prepared to pay. Fuel was plentiful, but gathering it was slow and chilling work, and many died of the ills that cold and lack of nutrition bring, especially the old and the very young. Arthur did his best in the Overlord's city of Ebvracum, opening the palace halls as a public place for warmth and hot bowls of stew, but as word spread into the country more and more forsook their meagre huts and trudged to camp in the forum, creating even more of a problem. Some fine old buildings were ransacked for wood or invaded for shelter. The old cities had been allowed to disintegrate for too long to now be able to cope with the reverse flow of people. Eventually even Arthur had to give orders that the forum be cleared and people helped to return home, even if this was under armed escort, though he made sure too that they went back with enough food to tide them over. For nearly a month his own troops dragged sleds across the countryside, laden with rations.

There was little surprise, then, when an exhausted rider from Elfael appeared at the doors of the palace late one afternoon at the end of February with the news that Idriseg had died over two weeks before. Although the messenger, a young cousin of Caradoc's called Glyn ap Erfil, had set out the following morning, the journey north-east had been unbearably slow and painful. Once the basic news had been passed on Arthur insisted that his kinsman sleep, be washed and given fresh clothes before he tell the full story.

'The evenings are as long here as anywhere, Glyn,' he said, 'and we have stories that need them.'

Later, after they had eaten, Arthur gathered his household to hear Glyn's full account and to made sure they were recorded — not just by Modlen, but memorised by two bards — one who travelled with Arthur and one who roamed the kingdoms around Ebvracum. It would be their task to compose elegies to be sung at the memorial feast that Arthur decreed for three days later, and to make sure that the songs were spread around Britannia when the snows were gone and the country was on the move once again.

In the mean time the Bishop insisted on saying Mass in Idriseg's memory in his freezing church, so freezing that Arthur half-joked to Gwain that it was clearly the Lord's intention that they all join his foster-father in the afterlife as swiftly as possible.

Sending Glyn home with instructions for Branwen on the disposition of the kingdom seemed unlikely to be welcome or to have much effect; nonetheless Arthur knew that some message carrying his authority would be expected, and he had, ever since the final meeting with Idriseg and the appointment of Caradoc to Brigantia, been thinking about the governance of his adopted homeland. With Branwen free to live with Candidianos, she would want to be as much with him in Corinium and Glevum as possible. The people of Elfael were fiercely independent, and would not welcome rule that made them subordinate to any of their neighbours – either Gwythernion to the west (where Caradoc's father-in-law was king) or Dobunnia to the east because of Branwen's marriage. For Caradoc, although he was heir, Elfael would always be too small a prize, because of Arthur's overlordship – and anyway, he was proving a highly effective general in Brigantia and a deterrent, if unsubtle, to the Hibernian raiders.

Arthur realised with a pang that what he really wanted was to give up all his own power and retreat to Elfael himself, as Branwen's regent in his own homeland: back to being Geraint of Elfael and no longer Arthur of Britannia. Cunorix, had he lived, would have loved that, and for all the reasons why it was unthinkable – the unravelling of the Council, the chopping-up of the Great Table, the vulnerability instantly of Candidianos and Cunegnus, the gloating of Caradoc as, unleashed, he imposed himself across the north and harassed Geraint of Elfael at home. All that he had achieved at Badonicus would quickly fall apart. Yet Arthur had a foreboding that this was his true moment of destiny. He had to choose between trying to hold Britannia together – as a power able to resist invasion from the east and raids from the west and north, while holding the balance between Budig in Armorica and the emerging Frankish territory being carved out of northern Gaul by Clovis – or following his heart, which urged him to retreat to Elfael with Gwenan as his consort and Modlen as his lover, where he could idle in Idriseg's old hall, secret in the hills, and venture out only to ride the kingdom's bounds delivering Branwen's judgements.

It was a dream none of the three women presently in his life would put up with, he soon realised, because their position and safety too depended on his. Arthur had no wish to stride the world, but it seemed, and had done ever since Myrddin had appeared out of the rain all those years ago, he could not avoid doing so.

In the end he left everything to Branwen, who knew the kingdom and those she could trust much better these days than he did. Glyn was sent back with news of the commemorations – the Mass, the poems and the solemn feast – and the call for Elfael to put its faith in their princess.

The death of Idriseg and the final severance of Arthur's sense of home and boyhood safety took its toll. He was left dispirited, in far deeper mourning than he had expected. It was, after all, not as though he had not been anticipating the news. In some ways he had been counting on it, because he needed Branwen's bond to Candidianos to be a certainty before he set sail for Armorica. His sleep was disturbed, his appetite shrunk and within days of Glyn ap Erfil's departure Arthur contracted a fever that at one moment seemed as though he could well succumb. Had Myrddin been on hand, there would have been more confidence in his recovery, but his wisdom was as far across the island as it was almost possible to be. Gwain was anxious to keep the true situation as secret as possible. If Arthur was in danger it might cause panic in Ebvracum, and news would soon spread, whatever the weather. Only Modlen was allowed to tend him. For her this was a kindness, and she would have fought to do it anyway, but Gwain's reasons were more brutal and pragmatic. The one person who could not reveal Arthur's true condition was Modlen – at least, not unless she wrote it down and smuggled it out to the Bishop's staff.

By the third night of fever it was sometimes difficult even for Modlen, who had shared his bed so much, to know if he was awake and delirious or asleep and dreaming aloud. At times he seemed to be directing battles or arguing with Myrddin. At others he would cry and whisper Gwenan's name, or Modlen's.

In the darkest hours, truly the middle of that third night, when Modlen, covered in a great cloak and leaning against his bed, had been dozing almost as fitfully as him, Arthur suddenly bolted upright, his eyes wide. 'I know that scent, I know your skin. Sioned. Not Sioned. Morganwy!' And then he collapsed on to his pillows once again and slept.

Modlen had heard, but she too was half-dreaming, and only years later, when so much was wrong, did the words come back to her and explain everything.

There was one more night before Gwain could be sure the crisis was over and that Arthur would live. Now, though, it was Modlen who slumped exhausted next to him and, while she had not caught the fever so badly, she was still ill enough for her and her master to lie together for a further week before they could rise for more than an hour or two. More days passed still until Gwain could hand back the full weight of government. By then the snow had all but disappeared, only remaining in heaps against old walls where the sun never reached, or where the drifts had been waist deep. It had been replaced with rain, though and, if the early spring flowers were starting to show their impatience and break into bloom, the wind was still raw and the roads sodden enough to make the thought of travel as impractical as it was uninviting.

There was no hurry, in truth. If Arthur in the civilised comforts of Ebvracum was taking time to recover his strength after the winter, then his less-fortunate people around Britannia would need even longer. Only in the far south-western parts of Dumnonia was it warm enough to feel confident in the coming spring, but there the rivers were so high after weeks of rain that, while there had not been the terrible frosts, floods were proving just as disruptive. There was relief in Ebvracum, too, that so much building had been completed in the previous summer, because the river rose to frightening levels, swamping much of the south bank and only being restrained on the northern side from washing to the palace and the forum by the new heightened walls along its edge.

Eventually Arthur was strong enough to ride out into the city once again with Gwain at his side as the markets started to bustle and workmen began sweeping clear the debris and repairing the streets. The first messengers rode in from distant kingdoms and rode back again with the Overlord's greetings and reassurance. For the first time

CHAPTER XXVII

in years no ships from Barbarian lands were reported along the east coast, though a dispatch from Caradoc told with glee that a clutch of Hibernian raiders had been sunk by March gales off Manavia well before they could reach the Brigantian shore.

Another month passed before word came from Myrddin that he had visited Armorica and that negotiations with Gwynafir's family had progressed to the point where Arthur could set out with confidence. So it was May, almost exactly a year to the day that Myrddin had burst in on Arthur and Gwenan in their modest hilltop camp, before Tygern Fawr set out from Ebvracum for the last time as an unmarried man.

For both him and Modlen the enthusiasm with which he accepted the good wishes of the city dignitaries was less than fulsome. Modlen had been careful not to overstep the bounds of his faithful scribe in public, but in private she was now openly his lover, and at sixteen was clearly a woman, not the waif of a year before – though Gwain had been quick to make it far plainer than Arthur exactly what 'in private' meant in her case: only in the confines of the innermost apartment in the palace, and never a gesture in the eyes of the world or the other servants, as Gwenan had been tolerated to do.

Modlen accepted it with resignation, but also realism. If she wanted to retain her place at Arthur's side once he was married then the act would have to be a good one. Her silence helped. There could be no intimacies overheard, no confidential chats betrayed. For Arthur himself the detail of her looks and gestures had become just as eloquent as words, and if something complicated needed to be said, she wrote it in Latin on wax: unintelligible to all but the priests, and impermanent, so that just a comb with a warm knife would wipe it away. With them secrets could stay secret.

She was becoming a good lover, too, and she knew it. Arthur had done his best to keep Gwenan in mind as his ideal, but he was beginning to see the previous year as an interlude – glorious but brief. Whatever Gwynafir's love might be, it was always likely to be tinged with business and official obligation. The marriage would mean permanence. He thought of Modlen as being the tenacious and equally permanent balance. He did not yet think of Gwynafir as real. Had he done so he would have been surprised and disconcerted to find that she thought of him in almost precisely the same terms for, though she was only a year older that Modlen, she had her intimates too (and one in particular), and they would travel with her to the new life on the island she thought of as an icy waste without a shred of charm.

Wild flowers were thrown joyously at Arthur and his party as they rode out of Ebvracum not long after daybreak on a gentle May morning, with a warm breeze promising summer from the south in their faces. Progress could hardly have been more different from the painstaking grind of the winter months. The horses moved fast, because this was not an overlord's tour. There were no baggage wagons, only half a dozen packhorses. Following the best of the roads, they could be assured of at least a modest hall for most of the four nights it would take them to reach Corinium. Lindum was the only town of note still in reasonable condition along the way. After that the lands of the Coritani and the Catuvellauni were crossed swiftly along the great road that would take them as straight to the coast as the Romans had known how.

In Corinium there was a pause. The entourage that would accompany Arthur to Armorica would not be particularly large, and anyway it would be drawn mostly from the court of Dumnonia, with its close ties in language and kinship to Armorica. There was a better reason for stopping than resting the horses and changing clothes, though. Branwen had ridden over from Elfael, and Candidianos had announced to the kingdom that they would celebrate their marriage properly three days after Arthur's arrival. Cunorix's successor Mandubrac would attend his first royal occasion in another king's land since his election before Christmas, transporting the Great Table of the Council with him. The neighbouring kings Badoc of Siluria and Catacus of Atrebata came too; even Cunegnus, sure now in the security of his borders, travelled down from Viroconium. Together with the well-wishing envoys from other regions, there was a quorum for a brief Council. That was necessary, because its approval had to be sought, on Myrddin's advice, both to agree to Arthur as overlord leaving Britannia and to appoint his deputy, Candidianos, with full authority to act while he was away.

Myrddin rumbled in two days after Arthur, just in time for the public wedding. He had thought about sailing straight to Armorica from Moridunum, but had decided that – though he loathed the overland journey, he disliked the extra days at sea more. Both his grumbles and his eventual arrival were expected. However, that he was accompanied by Seona, Morganwy and Medraut was not. Only Bedr, it seemed, was being left behind to mind the household.

There were drops in the air, but it was not quite raining as Candidianos, King of Dobunnia, led his neighbour Branwen, Princess of Elfael, through the few streets of Corinium from the forum to the chilly little church that had stood a short walk away for nearly two hundred years. Myrddin would have been happier to have had the grander and older temple to Juno next door swept and restored, but he knew that these days that would never have been acceptable. The King's people had turned out in their hundreds to watch the procession. Neither bride nor groom was in their first youth, and many citizens were unimpressed that their new queen seemed to be on the verge of being past childbearing, but the couple and their guests made up with dignity for what they lacked in glamour.

It had been decided that Myrddin would take the place of Branwen's father in handing her over to the priest, the Bishop of Glevum, who in turn gave her to Candidianos. During the service, short and rather dour in the new way that Christians seemed to think more spiritual than the great rituals of the Roman years, Arthur let the kings of Britannia take pride of place, flanking the couple. He stood back a little, and at one moment leant against the left-hand wall so that he could look at the congregation as well as forward to the action by the altar. So he saw the backs of men and, except for Branwen, the faces of the women that had shaped and accompanied his life. Sioned was missing, and his foster-mother had been dead so long that Branwen had taken her place in his mind, but otherwise they were all together in that small white space – those that had loved him and some he had loved. His eyes caught Morganwy's and, for no reason that his conscious mind could translate, he shivered when she smiled.

Outside there were pipes and whistles and drums playing as they came out to the crowd's cheers. Before they left the church, though, Myrddin enveloped Branwen in his arms: a fatherly gesture to many, but to him a chance to add his invocations to Ceres and Minerva to the Christian priest's blessing. She would need the fertile intervention of one and the strength of the other, together with the oversight of Constantine's god, if she and Candidianos were to reign as he hoped. Myrddin did see reasons for hope in the coincidence of the timing, which was lost on everyone except him. In the old calendar that day was the Ides of May, and its goddess Maia, the harbinger of goodness and growth.

A night and a day of feasting followed, though this second part was adopted with more vigour by the people than the court. For them Arthur's imminent departure and the brief Council meeting around the great table to approve it became the focus once the newly married royal pair had been toasted to their bed.

Corinium, Arthur thought back as he rode south afterwards, had been host to all the decisive moments of his life — at least, all those that were not claimed by Elfael. There he had pulled the sword from the stone, with or without Myrddin's help. From there he had set out only a few months before to the battle at Badonicus which had rid him of the worst of his enemies (whether Cunorix or Barbarian). There he had witnessed the wedding of the two people he trusted most in the presence of those who confused him most and yet who held him closest.

His immediate entourage for the last leg of the journey to the coast had shrunk to Gwain and Modlen, without whom he would not travel at all, and Myrddin. At the last minute Myrddin had decided that Seona should join them on the voyage, but that Morganwy and Medraut should return home to Moridunum. Gwenan, as promised, had remained with Branwen as the new queen's confidant and attendant. It was an arrangement that suited everybody, especially Modlen, but brought a pang of nostalgia along with relief to Arthur.

On the third day out of Corinium they rode through the last of the old cities at Isca and took the slender road west into the heart of Dumnonia. Its king, Caldoros, Arthur's true cousin, was waiting for them in the great port of Tamari Ostia, which they reached just under a week after leaving Corinium. It was the gateway to Armorica, but also the one place, Caldoros pointedly remarked to Myrddin, where a more plentiful supply of Gallic wine was still landed than in Moridunum.

They arrived later than they had hoped. They had ridden with less haste now that Branwen's wedding was over, and they were

CHAPTER XXVII

tired, partly because Modlen seemed to be sickening, though it was sporadic. Myrddin had seen the signs, though, and he told Seona to keep a woman's eye on her. She nodded and understood. Modlen would realise soon enough, but before they slept that night Seona and Myrddin decided to keep Arthur and Gwain in the dark until, if possible, they returned to Britannia. Realising he had a child in the making just as he proposed to Gwynafir would test even Arthur's formidable powers of diplomacy.

At the quayside in Tamari Ostia three ships waited for them as they rested and enjoyed Caldoros's welcome. They had fine sails and a Dumnonian crew who knew the waters of the west better than the paths to their own homes. Two dozen oarsmen, Barbarian prisoners who would rather be on the sea with the wind at their backs than languishing in land-bound captivity, gave each ship agility in calm water. One ship was assigned to Caldoros, one to Arthur and one to the troops who would escort them to Budig's court. Caldoros also held charge of the gifts, gold and fine cloth, that had been gathered from across Britannia as Arthur's wedding pledge to Gwynafir's father.

They were lucky. On the morning they had planned to set sail the wind shifted from a brisk westerly to a gentle and steady breeze from the north-east. Myrddin smiled and looked to the skies as they rounded the last headland, slipped the oars and let the sails fill. The ships leapt forward like horses let loose across the crest of the hills. Modlen, steered downwind by Seona, was instantly sick.

At the stern Myrddin stood with Arthur and put an arm round his shoulder. 'Well, my boy, you've taken a long time to leave Britannia and feel the sea beneath your feet.'

Arthur, Tygern Fawr, nodded. 'Behind me I am overlord, and at last that means something.'

'They are at peace, safer and more united than at any moment in my lifetime – or, for that matter, my father's and grandfather's times,' Myrddin said. 'That is your achievement, Arthur.'

'And yours.'

'An adviser does not achieve – he only creates the conditions for you to do so,' he said, tightening his grip on his ward. 'And are you at peace too?'

Arthur reached out to steady himself as the ship rolled with the waves, then peered ahead to the horizon. 'Behind me I am overlord,' he repeated. 'Out there I am nothing.'

'You are a prince of a great land, one day a father, soon to be husband to a young woman who will connect you to all the great houses of the new Gaul. Uther Pendraeg tried to steal that for himself; his son has earned that right.'

For a second the wind slackened and turned, and the sails lost the clean air.

Arthur watched as the helmsman caught the rudder and steered a new course that drew them forward once again.

'I prefer nothing,' he said.

FINIS

SIMON MUNDY studied drama at university, but soon veered towards writing poetry and reviews, and at twenty-three he found himself a music critic and arts journalist. A champion of the arts, he has served as Director of the National Campaign for the Arts and Vice-President of PEN International's Writers for Peace Committee, and he co-founded the European Forum for the Arts and Heritage; he remains an adviser to the European Festivals Association. His writing includes biographies, novels, non-fiction, playscripts and poetry. For the last forty years Simon has bounced between Mid Wales, the far north of Scotland, London and Brussels. He likes his indecision.

More novels by Simon Mundy:

Silent Movements

Flagey in Autumn

Non-fiction:

Making it Home: Europe and the Politics of Culture

Poetry:

Letter to Carolina

By Fax to Alice Springs

After the Games

More for Helen of Troy

Waiting for Music